the first feymora

Praise for Patricia Rae's *Curse of the Chosen One*:

What a lovely escape. It's a difficult book to put down once you've started. I look forward to curling up with the rest of the author's books.

—Author, MaryJane Butters

A fascinating narrative of "what if." This story took me in, and I cannot wait to see what develops. Patricia Rae has woven the Scottish Highlands' tradition into a story packed with human connection and undying affection. This series will have you captivated with the mysteries of the fey, and you will not wish to leave.

—Vikki J. Carter, *The Author's Librarian*
Author & Producer of the Podcast: *Authors of the Pacific Northwest.*

MARK OF THE FAERIE SERIES

THE FIRST FEYMORA

Book III of *Mark of the Faerie*

Patricia Rae

RaeDiance  Productions

Books may be ordered through booksellers or from the publisher's website:

www.MarkoftheFaerie.com

Hard Cover ISBN: 978-1-7345528-7-4
Paperback ISBN: 978-1-7345528-6-7
E-book ISBN: 978-1-7345528-8-1
Library of Congress Control Number: 2021905103

Cover and book design by Longfeather Book Design

I dedicate this book to my mother
for always believing in me,
even when I didn't.
Thanks Momma.

SCOTLAND

WESTERN

ISLES

(HEBRIDES)

ATLANTIC OCEAN

NORTH SEA

IRELAND

ENGLAND

Kirkwall •

Stromness •

ORKNEY
ISLANDS

Scrabster •

CAITHNESS

SUTHERLAND

ROSS
Faireshire •
Dornoch •

Torres • *Elgin*
×*Cawdir Castle*
NAIRN ELGIN
Inverness • BANFF

ABERDEEN

INVERNESS

KINCARDINE

FORFAR
Glamis •
Birnam • *Dundee*
Wood
PERTH *Dunsinane* •
Hill
Scone •

FIFE

ARGYLL

COLMEKILL
(IONA)

STIRLING *Macduff's Castle*
•INCHCOLM
Edinburgh • HADDINGTON
Glasgow •
RENFREW EDINBURGH
BERWICK
LANARK PEEBLES

AYR SELKIRK
ROXBURGH

DUMFRIES
NORTHUMBERLAND
KIRKCUDBRIGHT
WIGTOWN
CUMBERLAND

chapters

BONUS

&

summary of
mark of the faerie
books one and two

Isaboe McKinnon's incredible story begins on a late summer afternoon in 1746 in the Highlands of Scotland when she unwittingly passes through a portal in the forest behind her home and crosses over into the Realm of the Fey, changing her life forever.

After returning from a place of which she has no memory, the beautiful young wife and mother discovers she has lost her husband, her two children, and everything she knew as normal. Twenty years have mysteriously passed in the span of a summer's breeze, yet she hasn't aged a day.

Terrified and confused, Isaboe receives help from Margaret, a woman who as a young girl she had befriended prior to her mystifying disappearance. But Isaboe's fears soon become tangible when she realizes she has not returned from the other world alone. Having been abducted by Lorien, the powerful Fey Queen of Euphoria from the realm of the Underlings, Isaboe discovers she is with child, a gifted half-fey, half-mortal child known as a feymora, and the malicious queen intends to possess the child as her own.

Setting off on a journey to Edinburgh to seek information on Isaboe's now-grown children, the two women do not make it far before the raw and rugged Scottish Highlands prove too dangerous for them to travel alone. At a stop in the market-town of Inverness, a drunk and arrogant British officer, Jonathan Blackwood, seizes Isaboe, dragging her through the crowded streets. After an unknown drifter comes to her aid, she convinces her rescuer, Connor Grant, to travel with them for protection.

As they continue on toward Edinburgh, a romantic attraction starts to grow between Isaboe and Connor. The former Scottish rebel falls hard for his beautiful traveling companion, and in the days it takes the trio to make the journey, Isaboe grows even more confused.

After Margaret is injured in a savage wolf attack, Connor and Isaboe rush her into the city of Edinburgh at nightfall to seek medical attention. The following day, while their unconscious friend fights for her life, Isaboe and Connor finally confess their feelings for each other, just before Connor leaves the city to fulfill a sacred oath. Though he promises to return for Isaboe, and she promises to wait for him, once alone, Isaboe is rendered emotionally and mentally unstable by Lorien's twisted lies—so deceptive and convincing that she feels she has no choice but to abandon both her injured friend and the man who loves her.

Breaking her commitments to both, Isaboe travels north on horseback over the Highlands as autumn comes to a close, with only the manipulative Fey Queen as an occasional companion while the gifted child grows in her belly. Constantly fighting against the elements, and with faerie magic twisting her mind, Isaboe's erratic trek leads to the most northern point of the country towards Orkney Island. It is on this island that Isaboe believes one or both of her adopted sisters may still reside, and she is desperately hoping to find information on the whereabouts of her now adult children.

But Connor, the headstrong Scottish warrior, and Margaret, Isaboe's dearest friend, refuse to accept her abandonment. Using the magic-laden blue amulet that Isaboe had left behind—a gift of communication bestowed to her by her allies from the realm of the Underlings—Connor and Margaret are able to follow Isaboe's switchback trail, tracking her through the first months of winter.

Receiving mystical guidance from a mysterious old crone, Isaboe is finally able to draw on her strength to denounce the vile Fey Queen, freeing herself from Lorien's manipulative grasp. But before she can reconnect with her friends, Isaboe suffers an unfortunate encounter with the British officer, Jonathan Blackwood. Having found her alone and vulnerable, the vengeful officer takes her captive once again.

Crossing paths with Will Buchanan, a fellow Jacobite rebel who had been his trusted friend and comrade-in-arms twenty years earlier, Connor recruits him to assist in rescuing Isaboe from the soldier's camp. But in the process, Connor takes Blackwood's life. Finally reunited, they continue their journey on toward Orkney, now as fugitives for the murder of the British officer.

Heavy with child, Isaboe and her small band finally locate her now-aged sister, Saschel, who seems sincere about wanting to help Isaboe find her children. But when they discover that Lorien has not given up on taking possession of the feymora child, it is Rosalyn, a powerful sorceress and Isaboe's newly discovered birth mother, who arrives just in time to help Connor and Will save Isaboe's life. Assisted by Queen Brighid—an enlightened fey and the gifted child's fey guardian—the brave and determined group of fighting mortals is able to prevent the demented Fey Queen from taking Isaboe's baby.

Assisting as a midwife, Rosalyn helps Isaboe deliver a beautiful baby girl, Kaitlyn Margaret Grant, into her mortal world. Hoping that the worst is behind them, Connor and Isaboe say their goodbyes to Will and Margaret before setting off with Rosalyn, the first feymora, en route to Kirkwall, a seaside village on Orkney Island.

But knowing that Lorien and her forces are likely to reappear leaves a sense of dread hanging over the young family. Facing a future full of unknown challenges is just the start of a rocky road ahead.

New beginnings are often disguised as painful endings
—Lao Tzu

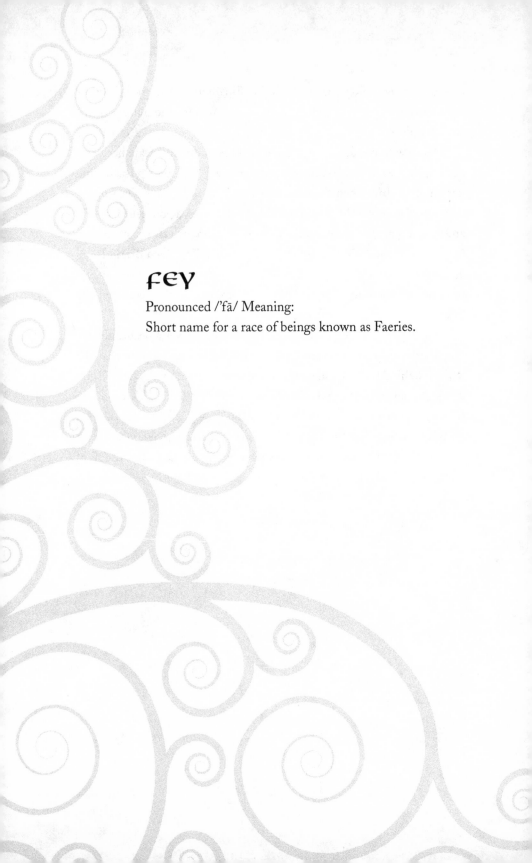

fey

Pronounced /ˈfā/ Meaning:
Short name for a race of beings known as Faeries.

chapter 1

a fresh start

Winter on Orkney Island meant the days were short, cold and windy, and the ocean winds that blew constantly across the open grassland bit at Connor's face, making his cheeks rosy as he pulled his horse up alongside the buckboard.

"I think we'll make camp here tonight," Connor said, peering into the covered shelter of the wagon. "We've only 'bout an hour left before sunset, and we could all use a wee fire to warm ourselves, aye?"

"Yes, that's a good idea," Isaboe replied. "I need to find a place to pee and get out of this wagon for a while."

Isaboe had been traveling for so long that she was road-weary and exhausted. During the past six months, she had traversed half the country—often alone, cold and hungry—and she would have loved to stay in the beautiful coastal village of Duncreag for a bit longer. She would've been totally content to lie on that comfortable bed, holding her newborn daughter while the man she loved held them both. Tucked inside that little cottage by the sea, she had finally felt safe for the first time in months, and she would have happily stayed there, burrowed up with her little family and enjoying every wonderful moment. Only two weeks earlier, this was a life that Isaboe dared not to think she would ever have again.

"Here, let me take Kaitlyn so Connor can help you down," Rosalyn offered, sitting above Isaboe on the driver's bench. She tied the reins to the railing before reaching down to take the soft bundle.

It had been most fortunate that Rosalyn had arrived on that unforgettable morning in a covered buckboard, providing traveling options on this trip. Isaboe had spent three months on horseback riding across the

Highlands of Scotland, and the further along in her pregnancy the more uncomfortable travel had become. But having just given birth only days before, she knew that nothing short of a feather bed and a plush, padded pillow would offer her any substantial comfort at the moment.

The traveling party had already been on the road for two days, and they wouldn't arrive in Kirkwall until the following morning. Under different circumstances, the trip would have taken less time, but the buckboard forced them to maintain a slow, almost leisurely pace.

Trying to get her newborn to eat was a struggle even under the best conditions, and the rough traveling didn't help. Isaboe had Connor stop for frequent breaks so she could attempt to feed their baby girl and to give herself a reprieve from the jostling. Even though she had told Connor she would be fine, Isaboe knew at the onset that it would be an uncomfortable journey. But since Kirkwall was only a few days' ride, even at their pace, she was resolved to tolerate it that long.

Staying in Duncreag was not an option. They were escaping from both the British army and an evil Fey Queen, for two completely different reasons.

Both Isaboe McKinnon and Connor Grant, her lover and the father of her child, were wanted for the murder of Lieutenant Jonathan Blackwood, the British officer who had assaulted Isaboe and threatened her unborn child before Connor's sword had sliced his throat.

Lorien, the powerful and manipulative Fey Queen, was determined to possess their daughter, Kaitlyn, whose birth had been foretold by mysterious forces, both seen and unseen. As a feymora, she was gifted with talents and abilities that were yet to be revealed.

However, to Connor, his daughter resembled a delicate, porcelain doll, and he had been reluctant to hold her. When he finally did, it wasn't for long. Born early, Kaitlyn Margaret Grant was so tiny and fragile that Isaboe had difficulty getting her to eat. She'd had two children before, but Anna and Benjamin had been eager eaters right from birth. She worked to convince herself, that with the right encouragement, her baby would eventually figure it out, though Isaboe's concerns for Kaitlyn's early birth were still very real. But with Rosalyn's help, the fourth member of their traveling party, Isaboe felt a little less frightened about what their future held.

After taking care of business, Isaboe made her way back to where Connor had started a makeshift camp. Slowly pacing in circles, Rosalyn was emitting soft, cooing sounds to the blanketed baby cradled in her arms. The tenderness she saw in Rosalyn's face as she held her newborn granddaughter touched Isaboe in a way she hadn't expected. She knew very little about this strange woman who had been instrumental in saving her life. Up until that eventful morning, Isaboe had known nothing of her biological parentage, but that too had changed when she learned that Rosalyn was her birth mother.

Adopted at birth by the wealthy Cameron family of Edinburgh, Isaboe had always felt unwanted by Marta Cameron, and the love of a mother was something she had never known. At the tender age of sixteen, when Isaboe had married Nathan McKinnon, Marta hadn't even bothered to attend her wedding. But that was now in the distant past, along with Isaboe's long-dead husband.

It was a time for new revelations, and Isaboe struggled to understand what they all meant. She was experiencing so many new emotions, each of which birthed new questions, leaving her feeling even more confused.

She also wasn't so naïve not to realize there was more to this story than what she had lived through during the last six months, but she wasn't sure she was ready to confront it all.

Seeing that her daughter and mother were content for the time being, Isaboe decided to look for Connor, who had gone off in search of firewood, though his options were limited.

"Can I help?" she asked when she found Connor carrying a large bundle of broken branches and dragging another bundle behind him tied loosely together with a rope.

"Aye, ye can take this. It's not heavy," he said, handing the rope to Isaboe. As they walked back toward camp together, he reached for her free hand. "How are ye feeling? I ken the ride has been a bit bumpy."

"For the most part I'm doing fine, though you're right about it being bumpy. I think I felt every rock and crevice we rode over. It feels so much better to be up and walking, even if it is windy and cold. At least *that* part of my body is grateful for the break."

"And we definitely want to keep *that* part of yer body happy, aye?" Connor said with a playful glint in his eye and a cocky grin.

"You do know it's going to be a while before we can be together again."

Connor furrowed his brow. "How long is a while?"

"Well, in the past, the healing took at least a month."

"A month!" he exclaimed, coming to an abrupt halt with a pained expression on his face. His earlier grin had been replaced by something that resembled immense disappointment.

Chuckling, Isaboe shuffled over to stand in front of him and looked up into the deep blue eyes that she so often got lost in. His shoulder length, sandy-colored hair had been pulled back and tied at the base of his neck, but a few loose strands had broken free, whipping about in the breeze. It had been days since he last shaved, and the stubble on his chin, combined with the scar that ran along his strong, defined jaw, made him look even more the warrior.

Connor had known struggle most of his life, and he wore the results of those conflicts like badges of a battle-worn soldier. Some were visible in the form of scars from years of fighting and from the end of a lash when he was a prisoner of war. Others lurked deep beneath his skin, and Isaboe suspected that the old wounds had been stuffed so deep he could almost forget they were there. But it was those hidden scars that defined who he really was, and there was still a lot that she didn't know about Connor Grant. While logic told her to tread lightly, her heart told her to hold on tight. For the moment, she was following her heart.

"It's not that long. I'm sure you'll survive," she replied. Lifting up on her tip-toes, she kissed him quickly before turning back toward camp, dragging the bundle of sticks behind her.

"Aye, I might survive, but I'll be none too happy about it," Connor grumbled as he followed in behind her. Isaboe didn't have to turn around to know that his eyes were on her, watching her every step. "My memories can keep me warm for only so long," he whispered sensually, leaning toward her ear.

"Well, then I hope for your sake you have a good memory." She cast him a sassy smile over her shoulder.

Shaking his head, Connor wrapped his free arm around her as they continued back to camp. "So, have ye and Rosalyn had the opportunity to talk much?"

"No. Not much," Isaboe mumbled toward the ground as she watched her footing. "I don't know what to ask her, or even where to start. It seems like she's not sure either." Glancing up at Connor, she shrugged. "Though, to be honest, we really haven't had a lot of opportunities. During those few days we spent in Duncreag, she went on frequent walks alone, or was off gathering supplies, for which I'm extremely grateful. It's been too uncomfortable for me to sit on the bench next to her on the buckboard, plus Kaitlyn's been fussy most of the time. On top of everything else, finding my birth mother has been just a bit too much to take in right now." Isaboe knew she had avoided asking the questions that only Rosalyn could answer, but she wasn't sure she was ready to know yet.

"Ye can ignore the elephant in the room for only so long. I ken what I'd be asking."

"I know, I know. Maybe tonight Kaitlyn won't be so fussy, and you could build us a nice, warm fire to sit around and talk."

"Not sure how nice or warm I can make it with this scrub, but I'll do my best. Maybe we can have Rosalyn do some of her *faerie magic* and make it a roaring fire, aye?" he jested.

But when Isaboe stopped short, Connor could see the pain and fear in her eyes and realized the repercussions of his words. She had given him only bits and pieces of what she had endured at the hand of Lorien, the malicious Fey Queen from the realm of the Underlings. The dark queen of Euphoria had told Isaboe twisted lies so convincing that she had agreed to abandon the two people she loved most in the world, and Lorien had been Isaboe's only companion during those three agonizing months.

"I've endured enough faerie magic to last me a lifetime. If you can't get a fire going under normal *mortal* means, then we just won't have a fire." Her expression and tone told Connor most unequivocally that this was a delicate subject, and he opted not to pursue it. Determined not to let those months of pain and separation define her, Isaboe had found the strength to take back her life, to make her own choices for her future, and her daughter's. But the wounds still lingered.

"If my lady wants a fire, then she shall have one," Connor said softly as he again wrapped his arm around her shoulder. "No faerie magic required."

chapter 2

truths told and mysteries revealed

After nursing well for the first time in days, baby Kaitlyn slept quietly as Isaboe sat next to the fire with a blanket wrapped around them both to keep out the cold winter wind.

Rosalyn took advantage of the fire and soon had a kettle of brewed tea hanging above the flames. The sorceress pulled together an easy stew of smoked lamb and vegetables that she had brought from her home in the Lochmund Hills. It was satisfying and warming, exactly what they all needed.

The wind that kept the clouds from lingering over the islands also offered a night sky filled with stars. The travelers made themselves as comfortable as possible as they prepared for yet another night sleeping on the ground. Sitting next to Connor in front of the fire, Isaboe was less concerned about her comfort and more anxious about what they would find when they arrived in Kirkwall the following day. "Do you know what became of the deed for the property?" she asked. "I haven't seen it since we left Duncreag."

"Aye, it's in my saddlebag. Why do ye ask?"

"No reason. I was just thinking about what we'll find tomorrow at the land office."

"Well, hopefully we'll find yer property and a new place to call home. That's what ye want, a home for Kaitlyn, aye?" Connor said, gently brushing a stray lock of hair from her face that had broken free in the wind.

"Yes, though it doesn't really feel like my property to claim."

"Isaboe, ye are a Cameron, Henry and Marta's daughter. Ye're entitled to that land, just as much as yer sisters were."

Isaboe quietly contemplated before responding. "Maybe, maybe not. I just wish I knew more. If I wasn't wanted, why did they adopt me in the first place?" As she asked the rhetorical question, Isaboe stared into the fire. It was a question she had asked herself many times, but still had no answer. She was the youngest of four girls, the only *adopted* child, and Marta Cameron had made no attempt to hide her feelings, or the lack of them. When Connor and Will had found the paperwork, it clearly stated that only three properties in Kirkwall had been purchased for the heirs of Henry and Marta Cameron, though they had four daughters.

"I don't know what I did to make Marta dislike me so much. I tried to be the daughter she wanted. I really tried, but nothing I did ever seemed to matter." Staring into the flames, she muttered to herself, "If she didn't want another daughter, then why adopt me? I will never understand that."

"Perhaps I can answer that for you." Rosalyn had been quietly sitting across the fire, just listening, but Isaboe's question offered her an opportunity to join the conversation.

Isaboe looked up at her mother with renewed interest. Staring into Rosalyn's eyes, she could see the residue of a challenging life, laced with wisdom and understanding. Streaked with silver, her long brown hair was pulled back and pinned, but a few strands gently tossed in the evening breeze. The fire light danced across her face, revealing fine lines earned from years of hard living, yet traces of her youthful beauty still remained.

"After Connor's visit, I left Lochmund Hills and rode into Edinburgh to see Sister Miriam. We spoke at length about you, Isaboe, and your adopted family. On the night you were born, I made Sister Miriam promise me that she would find you a good home. I made her promise that she would not place you into an orphanage. I couldn't bear the thought of that for you. I wanted you to have a mother and a father, parents who could give you everything I couldn't. Bless her heart, Sister Miriam did as promised and found you a good home.

"But as you already know, Marta wasn't completely on board with the idea. Sister Miriam told me that before the paperwork was signed for your adoption, Marta came to the church and questioned her about whose child you really were. She wondered why Henry felt so compelled to go along with the adoption when she was so against it. They already had three girls, so if they were going to adopt a child, why not a boy? Why not adopt a son to carry on the family name?" Rosalyn paused and looked across the fire. "For Marta, there was only one logical explanation—you had to be Henry's love child."

"So, he really *was* my father?" Henry Cameron was the only father Isaboe had known, and for the first twelve years of her life, she had been truly loved by that kind and gentle man.

"No. He was not your biological father. I never met Henry or Marta, and I wanted to keep it that way. I thought it would be best for you if I removed myself from your life. Sister Miriam told me the reason she approached the Camerons in the first place was because Henry was a very good man. Long-standing members of the church, they were also one of the wealthiest families in Edinburgh, so another child would not be a burden for them. Though he denied it, Marta was convinced that Henry had been unfaithful, even after Sister Miriam told her that this accusation was absurd. Apparently it didn't matter. She believed what she wanted to, and I'm sure that was why she treated you so poorly." Rosalyn paused, looking her daughter. "I'm sorry, Isaboe. I only wanted you to have what I couldn't give you—a family. But I hadn't counted on you having an unloving mother. I certainly didn't wish that for you." She spoke just above a whisper, and even in the dark, Isaboe saw the pain in the older woman's face.

What Rosalyn had just shared explained a lifetime of hurt and rejection from the only mother Isaboe had ever known. Despite Rosalyn's regret, it was difficult to forgive the pain and humiliation she had suffered growing up. Regardless of what Rosalyn's situation may have been at the time, Isaboe still didn't understand the abandonment of one's own child. She pondered the information for a few more moments before breaking the silence to ask the most pressing question. "Then who is my father?"

Rosalyn took a deep breath before responding. "I knew that would be one of the first questions you would ask, but before I can answer that, I need to start at the beginning, or at least as far back as I can recall. There are things you need to know, Isaboe. Things that I am just now starting to understand."

Connor rose to toss a handful of broken shrub branches onto the

fire, causing sparks to shoot up into the dark night sky. The sparks made
Isaboe flinch with memories of the vicious little fey and their stinging
bites. She felt a rush of anxiety as she watched the tiny flecks of light
rising with the heat, eventually flickering out into nothing.

Returning to his seat next to Isaboe, Connor wrapped his arm around
her waist and pulled her snugly against him. She instantly felt her anxiety
begin to wane. He was her protector, her rescuer, and of all the men who
could have been chosen for this task, none could have loved her more.
But even Connor could not protect her from the knowledge that there
was more to the nightmare than what she had lived through in the past
six months.

"Isaboe, you must know it was not a random chance of fate that it was
you who found your way to Euphoria twenty years ago. Just as Connor
was chosen by Demetrick, Lorien chose you." Rosalyn had a look in her
eyes that made Isaboe's heart beat faster.

"She told me I was chosen, but that it wasn't her doing. I didn't know
if that was just another one of her lies or if there really is something to
this destiny thing. The fact that I'm your daughter is the reason I was
taken, isn't it?"

"Yes, but it goes further back than just you and me. Your daughter and
I have abilities that make us different because we were both conceived in
the world of the fey, but faerie blood runs in your veins too, and we all
carry the mark of the faerie."

"What do you mean, *mark of the faerie?*" Isaboe demanded as she
pulled her child a little closer. Rosalyn stood and walked around the fire
to stand in front of Isaboe and Connor. Pulling up the right sleeve of
her shawl, she held her arm out toward the firelight as they both leaned
forward to get a closer look. Recognizing the dark starburst on Rosalyn's
arm, she glanced up into the sorceress's eyes with a dawning realization.

"I have that same mark, as did Anna. But I haven't noticed it on
Kaitlyn."

"She has it, but her mark is on the back of her neck, the same place
Connor marked you while you were in Euphoria together."

"I have a mark on the back of my neck?" Her hand instinctively went
to the place in question as she looked at Connor. "What does it look like?"

"It looks like this." Connor pulled a small pouch from inside his coat and dropped a ring into Isaboe's hand. Holding the smooth silver band in front of the firelight, she examined the three intertwined circles that were etched into its flat surface.

"This was Demetrick's ring. He said it had magic powers that kept the fey from knowing I was in their realm. He told me to mark ye with it so that I could find ye back in this world, though I canna say why I put the mark here." Connor said, gently touching the back of Isaboe's neck. "If I started lifting up every woman's hair to get a look at the back of her neck, I imagine I'd be slapped more than once, aye?"

"Oh, most likely a lot worse than just a slap," she replied with a smile. "You'd probably end up getting shot or stabbed."

"Well, then it's a good thing I didna have to. Ye just walked into my life like it was planned." As Connor hugged Isaboe a little tighter, she allowed herself to be lost in his eyes, just for a moment. Though she had told him it would be a while before they could lie together again, she could see the desire on his face. The heat that radiated from him, the look in his eyes, and his alluring mouth had not gone unnoticed, and she had to tear her gaze from his dancing blue eyes to refocus on the subject at hand.

"I didn't notice a mark on Kaitlyn. How could I miss such a detail on my own child?" she demanded, looking up at Rosalyn.

"The mark hasn't completely come in yet, so it's still very light. I had to look carefully for it, but it's there." Rosalyn returned to her seat across the fire before continuing. "Kaitlyn and I were both conceived in the realm of the Underlings, so we have abilities that go beyond our mortal limitations. You were conceived in this mortal world, but what is most noticeable, other than the birthmark, is your appearance. You are slender and petite, but what is most telling is your beauty. You've been told all your life that you're beautiful, and among your sisters and friends, you were the pretty one. You've always stood out in a crowd and have received unwanted attention. There have been times you felt that your beauty is a burden. Does this all sound familiar?"

Isaboe didn't respond. She didn't have to. Rosalyn had walked in her shoes.

"Well, she takes *my* breath away," Connor added, his voice rich with lust.

Isaboe's hair was tied back at the nape of her neck, but a few long auburn locks had come free and were dancing across her face in the evening breeze. Looking directly into her eyes, Connor gently brushed them back and then let his hand rest against the side of her face. Isaboe shuddered when she felt the tinge of electricity that shot through her at his touch. After staring at him for a moment, she clutched his hand tightly in hers before returning her attention back to Rosalyn.

"What other kind of abilities do you have, and what do you know about your parents?" Isaboe knew about her mother's magical gift. She had experienced it firsthand when Rosalyn pulled her spirit back from the darkness, *literally* bringing her back to life. But how her mother came to acquire this special talent was still a mystery. "Were your parents fey?"

"Demetrick confirmed that my father was, and that my mortal mother had been taken by the fey, much as you were. It explains my unique abilities, and why I can see, hear, and communicate with them. They have been part of my life since birth."

"So, how often do you see them, these fey people?"

"Occasionally they still appear, though not as much as when I was a child. For the most part, I can control when I want to engage and when I choose not to."

"And you think Kaitlyn will see them too?"

"Oh, yes, most definitely."

"As a child, were you frightened? I mean, when you first saw them, were you afraid?"

"No. They were always there, from my first memory. They were just part of who I was. They will be a part of Kaitlyn's family as well, even though you won't see them or even know about them, unless she tells you."

"That seems a hard concept to grasp," Connor said.

"Yes, but the good thing is, *we know*. Kaitlyn won't have to be confused or afraid to talk to us about what she sees, or what they tell her. We'll help her to understand that what she sees is unique, to her and her alone, and it's alright that she's different. The most important thing is that she be loved and accepted for who she is."

"Well, that won't be a problem. Between all of us, this will be the most loved child ever," Isaboe said with a smile, which Rosalyn returned. "You said that they were always there, from your first memory. Did you know they were faeries?"

"Not as a child. They were just the bright ones. I knew I was different when I realized that I saw and heard them but nobody else did. However, I didn't know what they were until Demetrick helped me to understand. He took me back to the beginning, to the day I was born, and explained everything to me—who I am and why I am different."

"What do ye mean he took you back to the day ye were born? I ken Demetrick was a great wizard, but unless he was there, how's that possible?" Connor asked.

"The ritual we did at my home, the one that helped you to remember it was Isaboe you were chosen to find, well it was a very similar *remembering* that Demetrick performed on me, and my first memory was from the day of my birth. I saw my mother, for the first and last time. She died shortly after I was born."

"You saw her? You *remember* seeing your mother on the day you were born?" Isaboe asked, amazed.

"Yes. I remember her face, how frightened she looked. I remember the face of each person in that room, and how horrifying it was for everyone. So much noise! The wailing was so intense, and the lights were so bright they hurt my eyes. Everything felt rough and cold." As Rosalyn paused and looked across the fire, Connor and Isaboe hung on her every word. "You know, there is a reason why we don't remember our birth. It's generally not a pleasant experience. We leave the warmth and comfort of a weightless, liquid cradle to be pushed down a tiny hole, only to be delivered into such a foreign, harsh environment. It can really be quite traumatic for an infant."

"I canna believe ye remember that!" Connor said, his voice laced with astonishment.

"What else do you remember? What was it that you were looking to find through this *remembering*?" Though Isaboe was unsure she really wanted to know, she needed to understand how her life was intertwined with this stranger. Rosalyn may be her birth mother, but she was a person Isaboe knew next to nothing about.

"I wanted to know who I was and why I was different, why I had to be isolated from the rest of the world, and why the voices never let me be. Demetrick helped put order into my life. He helped me to realize that there was nothing evil about me. It was the *bright ones*, the fey. It was always the fey." Rosalyn stared into the fire as if she were looking into her past, then suddenly turned her eyes up and locked gazes with her daughter.

"It's time you know the truth, Isaboe. All of it."

CHAPTER 3

AN INNOCENT CHILD

"I was born at night in a small room in the basement of a Catholic convent. At first I thought it was stormy. It sounded like a horrible wind, and great, beastly claps of thunder. I even believed I saw lightning. But when I later revisited the time of my own birth, I saw that it was the Underlings, the fey folk of Euphoria wailing like banshees, desperate to attain their prize. But the nuns were a fortress of protection against the fey that night. As the sisters held tight to their faith, and to one another, the Underlings could not penetrate their circle. They screamed their prayers to the heavens so they could be heard over the screeching of the Underlings. They prayed to their God that they all would be spared from the evil that threatened to devour the cursed woman—my mother—as she pushed forth my life from her body. In those initial moments, I heard the Lord's Prayer for the first time as the nuns fought against the astral beings who scratched and bit at their faces, tore at their robes, and screamed in their ears. I'm sure they thought Satan himself had risen from the bowels of the Earth, desperately trying to retrieve the woman who carried his unborn child. Looking back, I am amazed by their incomprehensible bravery.

"But it was my life that the Underlings desperately wanted, not my mother's. She was only the vessel, the woman who bore the feymora child, a child with unique abilities and strengths. Had they claimed me that night, I would've been raised by Lorien in Euphoria. But the nuns won the battle that night, though they had no idea who they were really fighting. As soon as I made my entrance into the world, at the moment of my birth, everything went still. The lights, the horrible sounds, it all suddenly came to an eerie, silent halt. The fey had lost."

"They wanted you, just like they wanted Kaitlyn," Isaboe murmured.

"Aye. Lorien is desperate to raise the feymora child as her own, to be trained in the ways of the faerie. She must be free of mortal influences so she can be used for Lorien's purpose—to completely open the portal between our two realms. If this can be accomplished, nothing will stop her from using her twisted ways to invade our world. All forms of Underlings, from faeries to trolls, would be able to cross over into our realm, and all of humanity would be at their mercy, exposed to whatever wicked and treacherous forms of play they would bring." As Rosalyn looked across the fire, she watched the glow of the flames dancing off her daughter's face. "But the demented games we mortals force upon our own kind are just as bad, if not worse. The greatest cruelty is unleashed upon the innocent, the children who have no idea what they did wrong, or why they are being punished.

"After my mother died, the nuns took charge over me. Because they feared that my mother had been raped by a demon, that made me the devil's offspring, and they contemplated doing what was best for humanity, though fortunately not one of them had what it took to snuff out the life of a baby. Instead, they decided to keep me alive, but isolated, so I didn't go to the orphanage like other abandoned children. Though they made sure I was fed, clothed, and my physical needs were met, no one ever got too close. I was only a toddler, but I have a vivid memory of two nuns holding me when an intense pain shot through my back. When I looked down, two small, lacy wings were lying on the floor covered with drops of blood. As a child, I was confused. What did a dead bird have to do with the pain in my back? It wasn't until I was older that I realized what the nuns had taken from me."

When Rosalyn paused, Isaboe watched a slew of emotions wash across her mother's face as she stared into the fire. But the twisted look of regret vanished as the sorceress continued. "As soon as I was old enough, I started my studies, but I always studied alone with one of the teachers. I often heard other children playing outside or preparing to go on outings with the nuns, and even though I begged to join them, I wasn't allowed around other children."

"Why weren't you allowed to engage with other children?" Isaboe asked.

"People fear what they do not understand. Underlings are not easy to explain, especially to those who cannot see or hear them. Most people only believe what they want to believe. When you're a young child, ignorant to the cruel ways of the world, it only takes a few beatings before you soon learn how you must behave in order to survive—even if that means pretending you don't hear the voices, or see the dancing lights, or the strange little creatures that taunt you while you are trying to study, or worse, in prayer." Once again, Rosalyn slipped away as she stared into the flames, recalling old wounds and bad memories. Only the sound of the crackling fire echoed in the heavy silence as Connor and Isaboe watched her quietly sifting through her past.

To break the moment, Connor got up and tossed another handful of broken branches on the fire, rekindling it back to life.

"Connor, would you please help me up? I need to change Kaitlyn's clout. There's a damp spot on the end of this blanket." Isaboe held out her free hand. "Here, you should take this. I'm afraid I might lose it."

After taking the ring and returning it to its place in his coat pocket, Connor helped Isaboe to her feet so she could slip into the buckboard with her squirming daughter.

Lifting the kettle from its resting place on a rock near the fire, Rosalyn poured hot, amber liquid into a mug. "Tea?" she asked, offering the cup to Connor.

"No, thanks," he replied. "Rosalyn, ye mentioned something about a feymora being able to keep the portal open between our realms. Can ye do that?"

"I've never tried. I believe that's a magic known only to the Underlings."

"But, ye do think it's possible?"

"Lorien obviously believes it is, and has gone to great lengths attempting to make that happen. So, yes, I think it's entirely possible."

With a blanket draped over her shoulder and the babe tucked underneath, Isaboe returned to the campfire. "What is entirely possible?" she asked, catching only the tail end of Rosalyn's reply. After making herself comfortable next to Connor as she nursed her child under the blanket, Isaboe looked up at Rosalyn, waiting for her answer.

"That a portal between our worlds can actually be kept open, and though I have no idea how to do that, I do believe it is possible. Obviously, mortals have crossed over, and the fey have as well. Demetrick told me that he had crossed over once. It's the time difference that baffles me."

"You think you're baffled by the time difference. How about me?" Isaboe murmured. "She—whose name I will not mention—told me that it took a great deal of magic to maintain her mortal form when she crossed over, so she never stayed for long. Do you think she kept a portal open when she appeared to me?"

"No. If she could do that, she wouldn't need a feymora child. Her ability to appear to you in our world is strong and powerful magic, but I believe that she can only transport herself, and only for limited periods of time. Did you ever see any other fey besides Lorien?"

"There were other creatures, the likes of which I'd never seen before. I wasn't sure if they were only illusions or if they were real, but I hope never to see them again. However, I never saw another fey, not like her." Then Isaboe shuddered. "Well, that's until the night I almost died. There was that amazingly strong fey woman who dragged me up the hill into the circle of stones, the same fey who killed my sister."

Talking about the event made Isaboe's stomach flutter with anxiety, as if just discussing the fey could somehow make them appear. "How long did you live at the convent?" she asked, needing to change the subject. Nothing good had ever come from her encounters with the fey, and Isaboe desperately wanted that dark experience to remain in her past.

"I stayed there until I was around the age of eight, and during that time there had been one too many bizarre accidents—a fire in the barn, a mysterious rockslide that killed a worker, and other strange incidents with no logical explanation. But when Sister Bernadine fell down the stairs, that was all the nuns could take. I tried to stop her from falling, but they didn't believe me. They all thought I pushed her, but I didn't. It was the bright ones, the fey who did it." Rosalyn's voice was laced with a child's long-forgotten innocence.

"I was angry at Sister Bernadine. One of the newer nuns had just given me a kitten, but it was time for my Latin studies. I hated Latin and was never good at it. After inspecting my work, Sister Bernadine informed me that it wasn't good enough. All I wanted to do was go play with my new kitten, but she made me do the lesson over again. I can still remember how much I hated her as she stalked away toward the stairwell, her black robe flowing behind her like the black plague, leaving her disease on everything she touched. At that moment, I said something I immediately regretted." Staring into the flames, Rosalyn mumbled, "*I wish you would just fall down the stairs.*"

When she looked up, Isaboe saw the regret in her mother's eyes before she continued. "It was an innocent grumble of an angry child, but the words were emotionally charged, and no sooner had those words crossed my lips when I saw the bright ones. Sister Bernadine stood at the top of the stairwell as they began to tug at her robe. I saw how frightened she was as she spun around, grasping at the air in an attempt to prevent her fall. I ran toward her, shouting at the fey to leave her be, but it was too late. I watched her tumble all the way down to the bottom landing, hitting every step until she came to an abrupt stop. I still remember the horrid thud I heard when her head hit the stone wall. As I stood looking down at the blood pooling next to her twisted, unconscious body, I knew I was in big trouble. I also learned that day how careful I had to be when speaking with emotion. Bad words and bad feelings tended to make bad things happen. Sister Bernadine died that day."

"Oh my God," Isaboe whispered.

"The next morning I was packed up and shipped off to live at The River Glenn Monastery. All the brothers at the monastery, with the exception of the Abbot, had taken a vow of silence. Other than him, I was not allowed to speak to anyone. I didn't even get to take my kitten with me."

"How long were you at the monastery? What did you do there?" Isaboe asked as she hung onto her mother's every word.

"I was the shepherd girl for almost seven years. My life consisted primarily of time spent with my sheep, either out in the fields or in the stables. Though I did continue my studies when one of the nuns came for a regular visit once a week. An idle mind is the devil's playground, you know. Plus it was rather an unorthodox arrangement to have a young girl living in an isolated sanctuary with a bunch of men, regardless of their religious inclinations. It was only appropriate that another woman check in on me regularly, though it was no secret that none of the sisters wanted the job. In their eyes, I was a nun-killer, the offspring of a demon. But they couldn't take my life. That would be a sin. It was their Christian duty to make sure that I was well treated and cared for. Just as long as I wasn't living under their roof, the sisters made sure that my needs were met."

"So, ye had no other outside contact? The brothers, the nuns, and yer sheep were yer entire life, for those seven years?" Connor asked.

"Well, there were the laborers who came each year during late summer to work in the fields and to help with the harvests. They were usually affluent young men who had been sent to the monastery for punishment, whose parents could afford to buy their spoiled brats' way out of trouble. There were also the young apprentices who hadn't yet taken their vows. As long as nothing unusual happened, I was allowed to talk to them, but never unsupervised.

"My greatest escape from my sheltered existence was the library. I spent many long hours hiding out there. I was only supposed to be in the library during study time and only with one of the sisters. But I discovered that if I went to the library during afternoon prayer, when everyone was in the sanctuary, I could hide out for hours, and no one would miss me. I read ferociously every chance I could, everything from Shakespeare to Socrates, and some wonderful tales of adventure by the great explorers. I read about other countries and the people who lived there. One day I found a book about Paris. It was a beautiful, leather-bound, hand-stitched work of art. I'm sure the brothers didn't know what was in that book. It must have been overlooked. Books with that type of drawings would never be allowed in the library. One day I snuck it back to my room and hid it under my little bed. Every night the drawings of handsome gentlemen and elegantly dressed ladies fascinated me. The streets of Paris, with its tall buildings, beautiful store fronts and fancy cafes seemed so hard to imagine, so opposite from my mundane life. I often daydreamed that someday I would go there. I would marry a tall, handsome Frenchman and wear those beautiful Paris fashions." Rosalyn stared into the fire, losing herself to another time.

"Did you ever make it to Paris?"

When Rosalyn glanced up at her daughter, for a second Isaboe saw something on her mother's face that resembled a mixture of pain and anger, but then it was gone, and Rosalyn's expression once again became stoic.

"No, I never did. Although, there was a moment in my life when I thought I might. Someone told me he would take me there. When you've been sheltered your entire life, and your experiences have been limited to what happens in a convent, or in a monastery, you can't *begin* to know what real life is like in the outside world. Or, for that matter, what people are really like. In my late adolescence, at a time when I was just entering the stage of becoming a young woman, I got a rude introduction to humanity and a brutal taste of reality," Rosalyn paused and took a deep breath before meeting Isaboe's wide-eyed stare once again. "I met your father."

"My father?" Isaboe's heart slammed in her chest at the acknowledgment of what she was about to learn. "Rosalyn, did he take you against your will?" She heard the anxious concern in her question.

"No." Offering nothing else, Rosalyn dropped her gaze to the campfire, and after a long pause, finally looked up at her daughter. "Isaboe, when I realized I had to tell you who I am, what I know about our family lineage, I knew that telling you the truth about your parentage would be the most difficult part for me to share. But I expected you would want to know; you have the right to know, so settle back and get comfortable. It's a long story."

ROSALYN'S STORY

※

A JOURNEY BACK IN TIME

CHAPTER 4

THE BARON'S SON

After pushing the wayward lamb up the bank while it baled pitifully, I began to climb back up the grassy incline. "Go on now, get back with your momma, wee one." I pulled myself up, brushing the dirt from the front of my smock as my young charge ran back to its anxious mother.

"Glad I could be of help. That's what I'm here for," I muttered, wiping the dust from my hands as I watched the lamb huddling into the protection of the herd. As the shepherd girl, I was completely in charge of watching over these careless sheep for the brothers at the River Glenn Monastery, and rescuing lambs was almost a daily occurrence.

It was late in the afternoon, and the sun was setting as I herded the flock back to the barn. But trying to keep the sheep headed in the right direction was often challenging. As stupid as sheep can be, they still had minds of their own and would go off in whatever direction they chose. Keeping them in line was often exhausting, but running across the heather in the afternoon breeze kept me cool.

The path taking the flock from the lower field up to the barn was a winding trail that provided a clear view of the front entrance to the monastery. On occasion, I would catch a glimpse of people coming and going, and on this particular afternoon, my timing was perfect. Clicking my tongue and tapping the sheep with a rod kept them moving toward the crest of the hill, and when we finally reached the summit, I saw an expensive-looking coach pull up to the front entrance, accompanied by two horsemen riding a few paces behind.

Thinking that my distance from the building was far enough that no one would notice, I stopped to watch as four men climbed out of the coach, two of whom were very well-dressed. The other two men, who wore modest clothing, appeared to be attendants, and it wasn't long before the portly Abbott wobbled down the marble steps to greet the newcomers. After pleasantries and handshakes, the Abbot escorted them into the building, but not before the younger of the two well-dressed men paused to take in his surroundings. He looked across the courtyard, and then up the hillside behind the cathedral. But his sweeping gaze stopped when it landed on the rise where I was standing, falsely believing that I was an invisible observer. Though I couldn't make out his face, I could feel his eyes on me and realized that I'd been spotted. Quickly, I turned my flock onto the path back to the barn and out of sight from the stranger's curious stare.

Avoiding attention was something I always tried to do. I dressed in simple, dark-colored smocks, wore hand-me-down shoes, and kept to myself. But as I grew out of my child's body and into a more-womanly form, more than once I caught a few of the Brothers watching me as they hid in the dark. At first, I had no idea why they were doing that, but it always made me feel uncomfortable. After it became clear why they were spying, I had no problem in calling them out, and they would scuttle away with heads hung low. But somehow, I was left feeling their shame, as if their indiscretion was my fault. After a while I found it humorous and sometimes even teased the perverted cowards when I knew they were hiding. I'd let the smock slip off my shoulder, or pretend I had an itch on my leg, requiring me to pull up the hem of my skirt and expose more skin than was proper. Occasionally I'd hear an audible gasp before the frustrated men would scramble away. I imagined the poor souls running into the sanctuary and dropping to their knees in front of the White Christ nailed to the cross, begging for forgiveness for their sinful thoughts. I may not have had much control over my own life, but if I could add a little discomfort to those who wished they could control me, it was a small, but satisfying victory, and it made me feel a little less like a victim.

By mid-morning the following day, I was busy cleaning out the stables, a task I performed weekly. The physical demands of raking and shoveling yards of manure-laden straw, and making numerous daily trips fetching fresh water from the well had been challenging at first, but I had grown into the task. Instead of the weak child who was thrust frightened and lonely upon the monastery seven years earlier, I was now a strong, fit young woman. My body had changed over the years, and I'd been told by a few farm workers that I had a lovely face, but being pretty was something I never really thought about. I'd been taught that vanity was a sin, and I had enough sins on my young soul already. There was no point in adding more.

As fall approached, the days were shortening; the leaves hinted at gold, and I could feel autumn in the air with its bone-chilling, northern winds. Straw laden with sheep dung made great fertilizer for the next year's crops, so each week the brothers working the fields came to gather the piles I made when cleaning out the pens.

As I wheeled the last pile out of the barn, I noticed the smell of rain in the air and clouds building on the horizon. *I hope someone comes to get this before the rains come in. It'll be a mess to clean up after...*

"Hey!" My train of thought was suddenly interrupted when a man seemingly came from nowhere and stepped out in front of me. In my attempt to dodge him, the barrow tipped over and all of its contents dumped out onto the ground. Frustrated, I tried to hide my anger as I glanced from the pile of dirty straw to the well-dressed young man standing only a few feet away, looking very out-of-place.

"What are you doing?" I shouted at him. "Why did you sneak up on me like that?"

"I am so sorry," he said, looking sincerely embarrassed. "I didn't mean to startle you." He gestured toward the pile that I would now have to reload back into the barrow. "Here, let me help you." Righting the barrow, he grabbed the pitchfork.

"Absolutely not!" I snapped, yanking the fork from his hands. "What do you want? Why are you here?"

"I...I was looking for the horse stables. I thought I'd take in a ride through the countryside this morning. My name is Marcus, Marcus

Vanderburgh," he said with a smile that was filled with perfect white teeth, a match for his handsome face.

Though he extended his ruffled-sleeved hand, I made no attempt to return the greeting. "You walked right by it. The stables are back there." I nodded over my shoulder in the direction he had just came from, wondering if he was touched in the head not to have seen it.

"Oh, so it is," he said, with a token glance toward the stables. "Silly me. I guess I was so distracted by your beauty that I didn't notice." He was so smooth as he walked casually around me, taking me in with his eyes. "I have to admit, I thought this week-long imprisonment would be nothing short of hell, until I saw you." Standing only a few feet away, he examined me in a way that made me feel uncomfortable, similar to the discomfort I'd felt from the spying brothers.

Marcus Vanderburgh was taller than me, with curly brown hair cut just above his ruffled shirt collar, and his garments were made of such fine cloth he could have just stepped out of my picture book. The clean, fresh smell of soap drifted from him when he strolled behind me. "What's your name, girl?"

I glared at him over my shoulder for a moment before answering, "Rosalyn."

"Rosalyn. That's a beautiful name for a beautiful girl. Rosalyn what?"

I didn't understand the question at first. It made no sense that a well-dressed guest should be in my dirty sheep barn attempting to strike up a conversation, and though I wondered what he was really up to, I finally gave him a curt reply. "It's just Rosalyn, the shepherd girl."

Laughing in a way that somehow made him seem grand and important, Marcus took a seat on a wooden crate that sat just outside the door of my private sanctuary. I was suddenly annoyed, wondering how long I would have to tolerate the man. "Alright, Rosalyn the shepherd girl," he said casually as he leaned back. Clasping his fingers around his drawn-up knee, just above his well-oiled, brown leather boots, he shot me a pompous smile. "What I want to know is why someone as lovely as you is dressed like...that." The expression on his face revealed his disapproval as he gestured toward my smock. "Why are you stuck out here in the middle of nowhere, shoveling sheep dung?"

Glancing down at my dirty smock I felt a stab of embarrassment, but it was quickly replaced with irritation. "Because it's my job, and if you don't mind, I'd like to get back to it." Jabbing the pitchfork into the dirty straw, I tossed a pile back into the barrow. "I thought you were on your way to the stables, going for a ride," I snarled over my shoulder. I didn't care for the way Marcus was staring at me and just wanted him to leave.

"I'll get around to it. I've certainly got plenty of time. I've got the whole bloody week to ride horses. I can't believe my father is making me stay in this Godly place. It's miles from the closest town, and there's nothing to do here. Up until yesterday when I saw you on the hill, I had resolved myself to a dreaded week filled with only silent monks for company. What in the world do you do here for fun?"

I examined Marcus carefully, as if he had spoken another language. Fun was a word I was unaccustomed to, and I wondered what mischief had caused him to be such an unwilling guest, forced into a retreat at the monastery. "Why did your father bring you here? Did you do something bad?"

Again he laughed, and this time it made his brown eyes sparkle. "You are a diamond in the rough, aren't you? No, not exactly. My father is the Baron of York. He owns all of this land, which will be mine someday, and he hopes that a dose of spiritual solitude will somehow tame my wild and unseemly ways. He says it will help me to connect with my higher calling, so I can finally become the man I was meant to be." Marcus spoke with a pompous accent, perhaps imitating his father, just before rolling his eyes. "I'll be twenty on my next birthday, and apparently that means I have to start acting like a nobleman, preparing to take over my father's post. I have no idea how being trapped here for a week is going to help me do that, unless of course, you could become involved with my spiritual growth," he said with leering smile.

"I'm not allowed to engage with the guests, and I shouldn't even be talking to you now. I mean no disrespect, my lord, but would you please leave? I have work to do," I said coldly before returning to my task. Though I wasn't sure what he meant about me being involved with his spiritual growth, I hoped that if I were rude enough, he would realize I wasn't worth his time and go away.

"Why are you not allowed to engage with the guests? No, don't tell me; let me guess. You did something bad. Hmm, what would a pretty little thing like you have done to be sent here, Rosalyn, the shepherd girl?"

Though his words may not have been meant maliciously, I felt my hackles rise. "Why are you still here? What do you want?" I snarled, feeling the heat rising on my face.

"I only want to talk. There's no harm in just having a conversation, is there?"

"Actually, there is. You do me no favors by staying here. I do not wish to be rude, sir, but would you please just leave now?" I quickly turned and left the wheelbarrow, the pitchfork, and the rest of the straw lying on the ground. Walking back toward the barn, I left the Baron's son sitting on the crate watching me stroll away.

"May I see you again?"

I heard him ask the question as I entered through the barn door, stopped just inside, and turned back around. "Why?"

He jumped off the crate and sauntered over to where I stood. "Because I'm here for a week, and even your sheep would be better company than the monks I'm destined to be stuck with. But I'm certainly willing to settle for you."

"Well, I'm not willing to settle for you, so if you don't mind..."

"You are a breath of fresh air!" The young Lord Vanderburgh smiled as he circled behind me. Turning toward him, I watched his eyes rake over my drab, dirty dress.

"Sir, I ask you one last time: Please, just leave! It would be inappropriate to be seen speaking with you. I'm not allowed...."

"To engage with the guests," Marcus finished. "And I certainly wouldn't want to cause you any distress. So I bid you farewell, for now. *Bonjour madame, jusqu'à ce que nous sommes retrouvés,*" he said the elegant words with a slight bow and a wave of his hand. Giving me one last, bright smile and a wink, he turned away.

I felt my heartbeat quicken for a moment as I watched him strut out of the barn and out of sight. Sprinting to the door, I stood inside the doorframe and watched him saunter back toward the horse stables, whistling and swinging his arms as he strolled arrogantly down the hill.

What did he just say?

chapter 5

french—the language of love

The rain came in suddenly the next morning, accompanied by a cold and vicious wind. The much needed late summer rains kept me in my cottage for most of the day, with only a brief journey out to herd the sheep back to the barn before dusk.

After eating a simple meal of porridge and hard bread, I turned up the oil lantern and took a seat on my bed. Shivering from the cold, I reached for my extra shawl and wrapped it around my shoulders. Bringing in the sheep had soaked my clothes and hair, and the dampness made it difficult to get warm. I considered starting a fire but decided otherwise after glancing at the few thin pieces of wood lying next to the soot-covered, stone fireplace. The laborers who came to help with autumn's harvest usually delivered a load of wood to my cottage before the rains came in, but that delivery hadn't happened yet. If I ran out, I'd have to haul it from the woodshed myself, a task I didn't look forward to doing in the rain.

Forgetting the fire, I briskly rubbed my hands together and was blowing into my cold fists when I noticed the Bible on the table with a ribbon between the pages marking the passage I had been assigned to study. For a moment, I considered doing so, knowing that one of the sisters would quiz me on the moral of the scripture when she next arrived. Instead, I reached under my bed and pulled out—The Book.

To me, this beautiful, cream-colored treasure was a piece of heaven, an escape from my mundane existence. Carefully, I turned the crisp parchment, transfixed on the images that jumped out from another world. It was such a fabulous city, with its foreign landscapes, beautiful churches and tall buildings. It was a city full of romance, of history and power, an environment completely different from what I knew. Nearly every night, the drawings and sketches of Paris came to life in my little cottage.

But it was the drawings of the people that most fascinated me. I would just sit and stare at the sketches of elegantly dressed women with their hair piled high on their heads, adorned with jewels and elaborate feathered hats. I remember thinking that if I focused hard enough, the high-born ladies flowing across the pages would come to life, sweep me up, and take me into their world. It was a place of ruffles, lace, and handsome gentlemen wearing tall hats and waistcoats with tails. It was a world of elegantly dressed couples, adorned in gowns, ruffles, and wigs as they strolled arm-in-arm down charming cobblestone streets. In my solitude, I brought them all to life, imagining that they were attending garden parties to honor the French nobility. They literally danced off the pages and took me on adventures in my own private fantasy.

The following morning the sun reemerged, so I took advantage of its warmth by taking the sheep to the upper pasture. I knew the warmer days were coming to an end, and I wanted to make the most of them before winter came in, bringing wet, cold days for long, grey months.

Sitting on a large boulder, I could easily watch over my herd, so I usually brought a book along to fill in the hours. Sometimes it was my Bible, and other days it was a textbook for a subject I was supposed to be learning. But some afternoons I would just sit and daydream, usually of traveling to faraway lands where everything was different and I had opportunities to do whatever I wanted. In my imaginary world, there were no black hoods telling me what I should do or, more importantly, what I wasn't *allowed* to do.

On some days I just sat on that rock in my silent defiance, wishing that the rest of mankind didn't exist, that it was just me and my sheep. However, there were days when I was grateful that other people were available to help ward off predators, as wolves were never too far away. On this day, the wolf was at the door.

When I saw the rider coming over the hill, I didn't give him much thought at first. But that changed after I realized he was on a direct path to my location. I will never forget how regal Marcus Vanderburgh looked on top of that black gelding as he crested the small mound. His riding crop, shiny boots, and embroidered waist coat seemed to amplify his arrogance. Sitting haughtily upon his horse as it trotted toward me, he stopped a few meters from where I sat, watching him. I couldn't help but notice his wide smile and rosy cheeks, flushed from the ride.

"Good morning, my lady. Lovely day, is it not?" Marcus called out as he sat atop a spirited gelding that continued to anxiously trot in a circle. Pulling hard on the reins, he finally brought it under control as I stared at him curiously for a moment before answering.

"Most of the guests take the riding trail that follows the river. It's a beautiful ride. You should go see it for yourself."

"If I didn't know better, I'd think you were trying to get rid of me," he said with a sly grin.

"Then apparently you *don't* know better." Now standing on the boulder, I jumped down and picked up my rod, and then walked as briskly as I could away from him and his snorting horse. I was wearing the same dirty smock as the last time I had seen him and was keenly aware of how I looked. I just wanted to put distance between myself and the young baron.

But I didn't get far before he trotted his horse up beside me. "This also seems a beautiful place to ride; it has fresh air, magnificent scenery, not to mention a lovely green-eyed girl. I believe the view right here is more than satisfactory."

I tried to ignore him. Keeping my gaze on my footing, I started walking faster, but his horse stayed right beside me as he kept talking. "That is unless you would like to show me the river trail and take a ride with me?"

Now I was annoyed. I stopped abruptly and looked up at him, "Why are you bothering me? I already told you, I'm not allowed to engage with the guests. Now, go away!"

I saw the determined look on the young man's face. Though he may have been slighted, I could tell he wasn't done. Shooting him a scowl, I turned my back to him and stomped off, but he spurred his horse and was quickly at my side again.

"Well, if we're being truthful, I'm not really a guest, now am I?" he said smugly. "My family owns this land. So, you could say that I own everything on it as well. And since you work here, that includes you."

I'd had enough of his prideful arrogance and spun around to face him. "I will have you know, my lord, that no one owns me, especially you. As far as I'm concerned, you're just a guest at the monastery, and I really don't care who you are or what you own. For the last time, sir, please leave me be!" I spat.

Watching the haughty expression melt off his face, I turned and continued walking, hoping he would do as I asked this time.

"Very well. I will honor your request. *Je vous souhaite une bonne journée.*"

I spun around to see him pulling on the reins to turn his horse back toward the river. "Wait!" I shouted, and took a couple of steps in his direction. "What did you say? Was that...French?"

Marcus stopped and turned his horse around. "*Oui madame. Connaissez vous le langage de l'amour?*"

"I don't know what you just said, but it sounds...beautiful." Part of me knew that asking him that was probably a mistake, but it just came out and it was too late now.

Immediately, his posture changed, and a smile grew on his face as Marcus Vanderburgh coaxed his horse back to where I stood. "I said French is the language of love. That is why it sounds so beautiful." When he smiled, his eyes were as dazzling as his teeth. Leaning forward, he rested his arms on the saddle's pommel.

"Have you been to France?" I asked. For some reason, I needed to know.

"Of course, I have," he said with another flash of arrogance.

"And Paris too?" Though I knew I shouldn't have been so interested, curiosity made me forget my place.

"*Oh, oui*, Paris! A grand *ville*, it is, a city full of life. Have you been there?"

"No, but I've heard it's beautiful. Do the ladies really look like..." but I stopped myself.

"Really look like what?" he asked as he dismounted. I watched closely as he walked over to stand in front of me, his gaze never leaving mine. "Look like what? It's alright. You can ask me anything. I've been there," he said with a smile that could almost have been called charming.

"Can you keep a secret?" I whispered.

"Of course, you can tell me anything," he said, taking a step closer. "I won't tell anyone."

I studied him for a moment, and though he was uncomfortably close, I held my ground. "I have a book in my cottage, under my bed. It's a picture book of Paris. I took it from the library, and nobody knows I have it."

"Oh, you little thief," he teased.

"I didn't steal it! I'm only borrowing it. You won't tell anyone, will you?"

"I already told you that your secret is safe with me, my dear. So, may I see this book? I could tell you if the drawings are accurate. I could even share with you some wonderful tales of the fabulous city. Maybe I could come by your cottage after supper, and you could show me."

I stared at him for a moment, knowing that what I was thinking of doing was ludicrous. "No. That would not be appropriate," I finally said.

"No, I suppose not."

"Maybe I could meet you in the barn," I suggested hastily. "But you must promise not to tell anyone where you're going, or that you're meeting with me." I knew I was taking a risk, but my curiosity made me brave, or foolish—most likely both.

"Oh, of course not. I won't mention it to anyone. It will be our little secret," he whispered. "The brothers go into the sanctuary after supper for evening prayer. When the clock strikes seven, I shall meet you in the barn. Is that agreeable?"

I knew I shouldn't, but to hear stories about the people and places in my book, that up until now I could only imagine, was an opportunity too good to pass up. "Yes, that'll be fine."

"Very well, then." Marcus shot me a pompous grin, then turned and remounted his horse. "I'm off to the river trail. I'll let you know if I find the scenery there more appealing than on this hill, though I have my doubts," he said with a debonair wave. *"Je compte les instants jusqu'à ce que je vous reverrai, au revoir."* Giving a jerk on the reins, he rode back in the direction he had come, and as I watched him ride away, I wondered how big a mistake I was preparing to make.

chapter 6

oui paris

As I went through the rest of my daily routines, my stomach churned with nerves, and I couldn't stop feeling anxious about my upcoming meeting with Marcus. Maybe it was foolish, and I was terribly afraid of what would happen if the brothers caught me with one of the guests. I had been whipped before when I should have held my tongue and kept my distance, and as a young girl, the thought of being punished was frightening.

Yet, at the same time, the feeling of rebellion in what I was about to do was thrilling. Yes, I had reasons to be concerned about meeting Marcus in the barn, but he was unlike anyone I had ever encountered before. He was confident and powerful, and it fascinated me. I knew his family owned the land and the monastery, but that wasn't what drew me to him. At the time, I didn't properly understand how hard I had fallen, all under a misguided attraction. But he was so different. He was handsome, charismatic, and *worldly*. He and his world were different from everything I knew, and I wanted to know more.

Dusk had fallen, and it was dark when I opened the barn door. Shivering, I made my way over to the wall and fumbled to strike a light. But when Marcus struck a match beside me, I jumped back. Seeing that I was frightened, he apologized as he lifted the chimney to light the wick. "I was beginning to wonder if you had changed your mind," he said, lowering the chimney into place. "It's already half past the hour."

As he met my wide-eye stare, he was hovering so close that I was sure he could hear my rapid heartbeat. I still remember how the lamp light reflected in his dark brown eyes, as well as the smell of him—clean and perfumed. In my world of wet sheep, I suddenly felt vulnerable and stepped back. "I...I was considering not coming. You didn't tell anyone, did you?"

"I already told you, Rosalyn, I would do nothing to cause you harm. You can trust me." Marcus was so smooth. Looking back now, I realize that he could easily read me, not much different than how I read my book, but at the time I didn't understand how he would use that to trap me. I can only imagine how often he had used the same lines and similar tricks on dozens of other women. Smiling at my silent reservation, he gave me the space I needed before finally breaking the uncomfortable silence. "Did you bring the book?"

Reaching under my cloak, I drew out my beautiful, pristine, leather-bound book.

"*Paris, France. Vie parmi les nobles:* Life among the nobles," he translated, glancing at the title. "May I?" He seemed to understand how important this book was to me, or perhaps he simply realized he would never get what he wanted if he didn't respect it as I did.

Handing it to him, I watched him slide his hand over it, caressing the stitched leather cover much the way I had. "Would you like to sit down?" I asked.

He smiled charmingly, "Only if you'll join me, ladies first." Marcus was all flattery and manners as he joined me on the hay bale we were using as a bench. He felt too close, but then opened the book and laid it across our laps before I could do anything about it.

As we flipped through the pages, every so often he would point out a drawing and explain what we were seeing. "Now, this is the Luxembourg Palace, and a very good sketch at that. I should know. I was there once for a wedding held here in this very garden. As I recall, my cousin Philippe and I had gotten ourselves into a bit of mischief. We were young and bored, and unattended during the celebration. That's never a good combination for a couple of boys who tend not to follow rules.

"Unfortunately for the bride and groom, the swarm of doves that were to fly over the ceremony was released prematurely. Instead of flying overhead, they flew straight into the crowd of wedding attendants, sending the people running! Some of the doves were caught in the ladies' hair, and the wedding decorations were strewn about the garden. The best part was that we didn't get caught. No one knew it was Philippe and me that let the birds out. *Oui,* that was a grand time!"

As Marcus shared his adventures in Paris, it was so easy to get lost in his words. Becoming absorbed in his stories had allowed me to leave behind my anxiety and my tedious life while I explored the Paris of his memory. His life was full of escapades, color, and excitement, and I soaked it all up. Sharing his adventures seemed to soften his arrogant edges, and he became someone I almost liked. Perhaps that was my downfall, that there was someone inside all that arrogance I was drawn to.

"Marcus! Master Marcus! Your lordship, where are you?" Suddenly interrupted by a disconnected voice outside the barn, I immediately felt my panic spike. Slamming the book closed, I clutched it in my arms and scurried over to the wall.

"Damn! It's Jeffery, my bloody valet. He must have discovered I wasn't in my room."

"He mustn't find you here with me," I whispered. Afraid of being discovered, I turned down the lantern and hid in the darkness.

"Why aren't you allowed to engage with the guests?" Marcus asked softly as he made his way over to where I stood against the barn wall. He seemed to realize my fear was real, even if he didn't completely understand it. "What have you done to be so isolated out here in this monastery, with only monks and sheep for company?"

I didn't want to answer, because I knew the truth would scare him off. He would leave me and take his wonderful stories with him, and I couldn't bear that. As much as I wanted him to stay, I knew he had to go. "You must leave now. Please, go." When I started to turn away, he caught me by the hand, and a spark of energy shot out from my fingertips at his touch, causing him to jump back.

"Did you see that?"

I couldn't respond. My mind was wrapped up in the energy that pulsated through my body from his touch, and he was too close. In the dark, my senses were flooded by his presence, with the energy that was *Marcus*. When he moved closer, I could feel his breath against my face, causing an overwhelming sensation to wash over me. I was on fire, not only with fey magic, but with an unfamiliar feeling that I didn't understand until later. It was called desire.

Slowly, he reached out and touched my arm again, but I managed to hold the magic back this time. "I have to see you again, Rosalyn," he whispered. "I only have a few days before my father returns to take me home. Tomorrow I'm committed to attend some sort of service with Bishop Randolph, but the day after…"

"Marcus! Your lordship, are you in the barn?" The valet was closer to the entrance now.

Afraid of being caught, I let out a muted cry, "You have to go, now!" I said, pushing him toward the door. But he grabbed me and pulled me into his arms, his lips dangerously close. "What are you doing? Let me go!" I shoved and fought against him, but he didn't budge.

"Not until you agree to meet with me again. The day after tomorrow I'll be taking one last ride. I want you to join me."

"I can't. You know that. Please, let me go!"

"Master Marcus! Damn, where did that boy go?" the valet muttered, now so close that the light from his lantern flooded in through the cracks in the barn wall. He was just outside the door and would be inside the barn in moments.

"Say you'll meet me. Say yes, my beautiful shepherd girl, or I fear my valet might find us in a precarious position, which I'm sure you don't want to explain. Just say yes, Rosalyn. Say it now."

"Yes," I whispered, finally conceding. Marcus had won.

"Splendid! I'll call on you after the midday meal, when the brothers are in the sanctuary. Until then, *Je vous laisse avec un baiser.*"

The kiss happened so quickly I didn't know how to react. He abruptly released me and then walked toward the door, meeting Jeffery just as it began to open.

"Lord Marcus! I've been looking all over for you. What are you doing out at this time of evening? Is someone in there with you?"

"No. Why are you out here, Jeffery?" I heard Marcus say as he pushed his valet backward before pulling the barn door closed behind him.

Logic told me that Jeffery wouldn't believe that Marcus was alone in the barn. I was sure he had expected to find something scandalous, but

I had already hidden myself deeper in the darkness, behind the hay bale with the lantern snuffed out.

Listening to them speak, I discovered that Marcus was an excellent liar, telling a boring story about horses being more interesting than old men. It was exactly what was expected of him, so Jeffery appeared to buy the lie without question.

Their voices began to fade as they walked back toward the monastery. After I was confident that they were far enough away, I made my way out into the night and ran back to my cottage. I vividly remember snapping the lock into place before leaning my back against the door with my eyes closed. In the silence of my abode, I could hear only my heart pounding as I tried to catch my breath. When I pulled my book from under my cloak, despite all the hours I had spent with it, now it was different and new. The pages had been brought to life by his lively stories and my fantasies would no longer satisfy me. Marcus Vanderburgh had awakened a taste and a desire for something more in my life than sheep and silent monks.

It was a desire for a different life, and a desire for him. I could still taste his lips on mine and felt the tingle where he had touched me. As I sat on the bed with my fingers on my lips, I could feel a smile slowly growing on my young and naïve face.

CHAPTER 7

LOSS OF INNOCENCE

Sister Nadine arrived the following morning for my weekly day of study, which I normally dreaded. Study time with the sisters was usually long and dreary. However, it fell on the same day as Marcus's spiritual retreat, and since he wasn't around, it was an opportunity to be in the library and have something else to focus on other than him. The encounter from the previous night kept replaying itself in my mind, as did the sensations I felt when he held me. I couldn't stop thinking about what tomorrow would bring.

Obviously, I couldn't really keep my promise to go riding with him. What if someone should see us? Yet, even knowing the risks, I desperately wanted to spend some time with Marcus, regardless of the chance I would be taking. After all, I had promised, even though it was under duress. If only there was some way I could slip away without…

"Rosalyn! Are you listening to me, child?" The nun's sharp voice snapped me out of my daydream. I cautiously looked up into her stern eyes, shadowed under a dark hood as she demanded an answer. "What was the name of the disciple who Saul met in Damascus? Do you know the name of the man who restored his sight in the name of our Lord Jesus Christ?"

"Uh…I, uh…" fumbling for an answer, I knew I was unprepared.

"Did you even read the scripture you were assigned?"

"I'm sorry, Sister, I'm afraid I haven't. However, I do know the story. From that day forth, Saul went by the name of Paul. He no longer tortured the Christian followers. He became a leader and one of Jesus' greatest disciples." I quickly recited the Biblical story, hoping that it would pacify the nun's righteous fury.

But Sister Nadine's stoic expression did not soften, and I watched her take a deep, frustrated sigh. "Child, I have done everything I can for you. I listened when you asked me to have Latin removed from your studies, but Mother Superior does have expectations. Now I must return and tell her you have been neglecting your assigned reading, a small task that should be easy enough for you to complete. After all you have suffered I would think you should understand the risks. Now drop to your knees and pray for Mary to forgive you, you foolish, lazy girl!"

I dropped to my knees, clasped my hands in front of my chest and bowed my head. *"Hail Mary full of Grace, the Lord is with thee. Blessed are thou among women and blessed is the fruit of thy womb, Jesus. Holy Mary, Mother of God, pray for us sinners now and at the hour of our death, Amen. Hail Mary full of Grace, the Lord is with thee…"* I continued reciting until all ten repetitions had been spoken. Still on my knees, I reached out and kissed the Sister's hand, asking for forgiveness before I rose to my feet.

"By next week you will be expected to have read the complete book of Acts, and be able to answer any question related to the scripture. You best have done so, because I'll not be here next week, and Sister Agnes isn't as forgiving." Sister Nadine spun around and walked to the end of the long, oak table, tapping her fingers on the surface as she went. Her black hood floated to the opposite end before she turned around.

"You must know, Rosalyn, you can't be a shepherd girl for the rest of your life. You're not a child anymore. It's time to make some decisions about your future, a future in service to our Lord. I've discussed it with Mother Superior, and she has softened her position regarding you. You will be allowed to return if you agree to take your vows. It would behoove you to consider doing so, and to come back into the fold of the Sisterhood. You have behaved yourself well these past seven years. There have been no reports of unexplained incidents or tragic accidents. It appears your years here have helped you to control the evil that lies within you. But you will have to prove yourself—prove that you are worthy. So, what do you say about taking your vows and returning to the convent? I could arrange it before winter sets in."

The thought of returning to the convent and the black hoods was bad enough, but to become one of them was an even darker fate than I deserved. I didn't want to be a nun. I wanted to run away to Paris with Marcus! But now it appeared that the decision was being made for me; I was to enter a never-ending life of servitude. My mind and body rebelled against the very idea, and I wanted to vomit. But the reality was that I would have no say in the matter. Sister Nadine had already cast my future in stone.

"Well, speak, girl! Or do you want to stay in that dreary little cottage through another cold winter?"

"No. I mean…I don't know if I'm ready to take my vows yet, Sister. May I please consider it awhile before I give you my answer?"

The nun stared at me with a cold, steely glare for a long, uncomfortable moment before she finally spoke. "I have no idea what you need to consider, but I'll grant you some time. It is a decision not to be made lightly, and perhaps you've at least grown enough to know the importance of entering the Sisterhood with pure intentions. In your position, to commit your life in service to God is a blessing, and a gift. And to be honest, my dear, I don't see any other paths that are open for you."

In Sister Nadine's eyes, I had no other options. I was, and always would be, a ward of their convent. As a child of the devil, I could not be let out into the world. That would be irresponsible and ungodly. They had no choice but to bring me back.

My world was caving in, and I was unable stop it.

"I have a meeting with the Abbot, so we are done for today. I will relay your response back to Mother Superior. Hopefully, she will see wisdom in your request for time, rather than regarding it as an insult. Sister Agnes will be expecting your answer by the end of next week. Good day."

I fought back my tears until the nun's black hood disappeared from view.

The following day, the sky was laden with dark clouds—appropriate for my frame of mind. I sat on a downed tree along the water's edge with my arms wrapped around my knees. My gaze was locked on a single leaf that was spinning in circles, caught in a tiny whirlpool. Pushed on by the rushing water, the rest of the fallen leaves had washed over the rocks and were now floating freely down the river, but this lone leaf was stuck in one place, unable to move, trapped by its own inertia and waiting to be pulled under. It was a trap that felt all too familiar.

After waking in a foul mood and with a heavy heart, I had spent most of the morning doing chores in an attempt to keep my mind occupied, but I couldn't shake the feeling of dread carried over from Sister Nadine's visit. The only thing I was thankful for on this gray afternoon was that Marcus seemed to be absent. I wasn't sure my fragile heart could survive seeing him, knowing he was leaving tomorrow and that I would never see him again.

Never again would I hear his wonderful tales that had opened a window into the world, a world where I saw a glimpse of what life could be like, but not for me. His stories fed my fantasies and teased me with a taste of what romance must be like, but I was convinced that it was far beyond my reach. As much as I longed to be a part of his world, I knew my fate had already been assigned, and as always, what I wanted mattered not. All was decided by the Black Hoods.

The sheep heard Marcus approaching before I did. Their small black noses lifted toward the hillside as their stubby tails twitched, and they bleated their warning even before he appeared on the riverbank.

A part of me had hoped that, due to the late hour and the rain clouds building on the horizon, Marcus had changed his mind about the ride, but apparently not. Looking over my shoulder, I felt the nerves bubbling in my stomach as he dismounted and made his way down to the river's edge. Thinking that if I just ignored him, Marcus might leave me alone, I turned my back to him, but that didn't change his course, nor did he seem thwarted by my lack of greeting.

"Here you are. I've been looking all over for you. Sorry for coming so late. Father will be here tonight, and I had to address a few issues with the Abbot before he arrives." Marcus walked along the log I was using for a bench before taking a seat next to me. "What's wrong, Rosalyn? Have you been crying?"

I quickly turned away so he couldn't see the tears I had been fighting all day, but he gently cupped my chin and turned my face back toward him.

"Talk to me, Rosalyn. Why do you look so sad today?"

The mere touch of his hand on my face sent a shock through me, but I pretended not to feel it. "It's nothing. I'm fine. I wish you hadn't come," I said honestly, brushing his hand away.

"Well, that's not exactly the reception I had hoped for." Marcus looked slighted, but the Baron's son wasn't the type to give up easily. "Tell me what troubles you, my little shepherd girl. I see something's amiss behind those beautiful green eyes." He was unbearably charming, and I took a moment to just look at him, to really examine his face. I wanted to etch his beautiful brown eyes and his charismatic smile permanently in my mind.

"What is it?" he asked again. This time, he seemed genuinely concerned.

Taking a deep breath, I turned to look out over the river. "Yesterday, Sister Nadine was here. She informed me that Mother Superior has decided it's time for me to take my vows and join the Sisterhood." Even I could hear the misery and resignation in my words.

"And become a nun?" he asked, looking surprised and even a bit shocked. "Is that what you want?"

"It doesn't matter what I want. It's how it will be." The acceptance in my voice was coated with sadness, and apparently wasn't lost on Marcus.

"That's not right! If you don't want to be a nun, Rosalyn, no one can make you. Just say no."

He made it sound so simple. I looked at him like he was from another world, because he was. "You don't understand. I don't have any choice in the matter. The decision has already been made for me. I can't say no."

"Of course you can! And if you can't, then I'll say it for you. I'll go to the Abbot myself and…"

"NO!" I cried out and quickly stood. "You mustn't get involved. If you say anything to anyone, it will only be worse for me. Please, just leave me be!" I turned and ran up the bank as the first drops of cool rain splashed against my heated face.

But Marcus was behind me before I could escape, and he grabbed my arms, stopping me as he spun me around.

"Rosalyn, why do you allow this? Are you telling me that you have no place to go, no place called home? Are there no other options for you, save living in fear and solitude for the rest of your life?"

I knew Marcus couldn't comprehend the fact that I had no say in my own life. It was a foreign concept to him, and there were no words to explain. We were from worlds so far apart there was no way to bridge the gap, let alone to properly understand how different our lives were.

Though I felt helpless and weak, I stood my ground and faced him, trying to make him understand. "You have no idea what it feels like to walk in my shoes. Your life is like the pages of my book–*a fantasy*. You live in a world where everything you want magically happens. Life for you is grand and enormous, full of splendor and color. Look around you, Marcus! This is my life. This is all I know. This and the convent are all I'll *ever* know!" No longer being able to hold them back, my tears finally broke free and blended in with the rain that was now streaming down my face.

When Marcus wiped the tears and the rain from my cheek with a brush of his thumb, I shivered at his touch before stepping back. "Why do you do this to me?" I shouted at him. "Why do you make me feel this way?"

Stepping closer, he cupped my face in his hands. Looking up through the rain drops on my lashes, I could see the intensity in his eyes, and for a moment, I saw something that resembled compassion. As I watched the rain dripping off his hair, I knew we were both getting soaked, but at that moment, I didn't care.

"What you feel is called desire, my beautiful Rosalyn. And if you give yourself over to the Sisterhood, you will never know the fulfillment of it. It will always be the forbidden fruit you were never able to taste. It would be such a shame if these beautiful lips went un-kissed, this beautiful body untouched." He whispered these words just before his mouth was on mine. I could feel his tongue on my lips, his body pressing against me as he wrapped his arms around my waist, pulling me into his embrace.

I was at war with myself. Part of me wanted to flee, but the other wanted to give into the urgency of his embrace and to the longing I was feeling. Whatever was happening both scared and thrilled me, and I remember thinking in that moment, that if I could only stay in his arms, everything would be alright. I wanted him to never let me go.

But when a bolt of lightning flashed across the sky, I slipped out of his embrace as the roll of thunder had the sheep on the run. Looking over my shoulder, I saw the last of my herd disappear over the rise. I retrieved my rod and ran up the hill, only to see the entire flock in a heated run back to the barn as another flash of lightening startled me, accompanied by another clap of thunder.

When Marcus caught up with me at the top of the bank, he quickly mounted his horse before reaching out to me, shouting over the downpour, "Even sheep have enough sense to get out of this bloody rain! Here, give me your hand!" I grabbed onto his arm, and he lifted me with one motion up into the saddle behind him.

Just as we caught up to the small herd, I noticed a lamb caught under a bush, bawling pitifully. When I pointed it out to Marcus, he brought the horse to an abrupt halt and jumped down, rescuing the lamb from its trap before handing it up to me. Back in the saddle with the lamb cradled in my arms, he kicked the horse into a fast run as the ride through the downpour soaked us all: horse, riders, and livestock.

Another flash of lightening chased us into the barn. After securing the animals in their pens, we took a moment to really look at one another, and to catch our breath. I was soaked and could feel the water running down my face, dripping from the ringlets of my hair onto my cold, wet, clinging dress.

"You look like you fell into the river," Marcus teased.

"Well, you look like a drowned rat in fancy clothes!" I snapped back.

He looked down at his embroidered waist coat, silk shirt and linen trousers, completely drenched from the downpour. "Oh my, Jeffery will not be pleased." When he looked back at me, a smile started to grow on his face, and within moments he was laughing. "*A drowned rat in fancy clothes?*" he kept repeating between chuckles. "I must tell you, my dear girl, I'm a man who prides myself on *always* being in control, and *always* looking my best in *any* situation." He chuckled again as he displayed the lapels of his drenched coat, now dripping onto the dirt floor. "I've been surrounded by yes-men and people-pleasers my whole life, but here, I have found a naïve shepherd girl who calls it as she sees it. I believe this is what humility must feel like."

He laughed again, and I remember a warm feeling growing deep in my chest at the sound of it. His laughter was contagious. It wasn't long before I felt a smile growing on my own face. Perhaps it was simply exhaustion from trying to keep my emotions in check, but I soon felt myself chuckle along with him. But since there hadn't been many opportunities for laughter in my life, it wasn't long before I felt uncomfortable, and the moment passed.

"We need to get out of these wet clothes," Marcus said pulling off his waist coat and tossing it aside. Next, he yanked the shift over his head. As it landed next to his coat, I remember shuddering at the sight of his bare chest.

I was suddenly feeling very vulnerable, but he grabbed an old blanket hanging on a hook and presented it to me. "Here, take off that wet smock and wrap up in this. I know it's not soft, but it's dry."

Somewhat shocked, I looked at him, wondering what he was expecting. "Here? You expect me to take off my dress, here in the barn? No, I'll just keep it on." Grabbing the blanket, I wrapped it over my wet clothes. Just then, another roll of thunder shook the barn, startling me.

"Rosalyn," Marcus gently slid the blanket off my shoulders and stood hovering behind me. "Your dress is soaked. The storm is not letting up. You can't go back to your cottage, and you can't stay in these wet clothes." When he stepped around to stand in front of me, I lifted my eyes to meet his. Standing next to his bare skin, now so close I could smell the soap he'd washed with that morning, I wasn't sure if I was shivering from being wet and cold or from his nearness. I could feel the heat radiating off of him. When he brushed a few wet stands of hair from my face, I felt the sensation from his touch shooting through my body.

"You are so beautiful. You have no idea just how captivating you are, do you?" he whispered, his mouth only inches from mine. "You're like a rare gem hiding in this oasis, just waiting for someone to find you."

As he unlaced my dress, there was a gnawing feeling that I shouldn't allow it, but I was held captive by his eyes and the soft shape of his lips, so close to mine. "What is it about you, Rosalyn that has captured me so? Why are you so different from every other girl I've ever met?"

Before I could reply, even though I had no answer to give, Marcus prevented it. Starting out soft and tender, his kiss soon grew demanding as his fingers danced across my skin while he continued to undress me. It was too close to intimacy, and suddenly it felt wrong.

Finally finding the strength to push him back, I took a moment to catch my breath. While still clinging to my clothes, I found my voice. "Why are you doing this to me? You're leaving tomorrow and I'll never see you again. You'll go back to your wonderful life with your fancy parties and beautiful girls, and you will soon forget all about me! And I'll go back to the convent to become *a nun!*" The weight of resignation hung in my voice, but the anguish was even heavier. "I hate you for telling me your stories! I hate you for making me feel this way. *I wish I had never met you!*" I shouted as the tears fell unashamedly down my face.

Though my vision was blurred, I began to feel the telltale signs of the fey as their formless figures sparked with energy from my unleashed emotions.

Marcus reached out for me, but I backed away. He held his ground and nodded, respecting my need for space, at least for the moment. "I will never forget you, my beautiful shepherd girl," he murmured quietly, as the same hint of compassion filled his eyes. "You have enticed me in a way no other has. I want to hold you and wipe away your tears, to show you how precious you really are."

When he reached for me again, this time I didn't fight. I went willingly into his arms. In his warmth, I felt myself unwind and surrendered completely to the ache in my heart. As I sobbed with my head against his bare chest, he held me and brushed back my hair. When I turned my face up, he kissed me gently before whispering, "Would you like to go to Paris, my precious flower?"

Shocked at his question, I wondered if it was a cruel joke. Staring at him with wide eyes, I pushed out of his arms. "What are you talking about?" But he didn't answer, instead he drew me back into his embrace, and this time kissed me hard. The kiss was long and so full of passion that I couldn't resist.

After finally pulling back, he picked me up and carried me to a soft pile of clean hay, then gently laid me down.

"What are you doing?" I asked, afraid of what I was feeling, and of what was about to happen.

"Close your eyes, *mademoiselle*, and let me take you to Paris," Marcus whispered as he finished undressing me. His kisses were passionate and demanding, and it didn't take long before I gave in to his touch.

What he offered was so tempting. It opposed the Sisters' offer in every way, and *oh*, how this rebellion, this human warmth, this opportunity to shed the shepherd girl's life tempted me.

Still, there was that nagging question, and I had to know. Pushing him back between his murmurs of love and sweet kisses, I looked up into his eyes. "Do you really love me, Marcus? Are you really going to take me to Paris?" I still remember how scared and thrilled I was as I stared into his beautiful, dark brown eyes.

"*Oui*, beautiful, Rosalyn." Marcus knew just what to say, and he obviously considered it his right, as well as his privilege, to take a maiden's innocence. The future Baron Marcus Vanderburgh used the luscious sound of the French tongue as he whispered empty promises into my ear.

Flashes of light sparked and danced in the steam that rose from our wet, heated bodies while Marcus kissed and caressed my tender, young flesh. Passion, love, and fear fed my emotions, causing the fey to explode all around me. But I chose to ignore them, and instead, gave myself to him.

CHAPTER 8

BROKEN

As morning began to shine through a split in the curtain of the only window in my little cottage, the sunlight made its way through to my closed eyes, pulling me fully awake. Snuggling under the warm blankets, still brushing away the cobwebs of sleep, I had the odd feeling that something about me was different this morning. As the event of the previous night flooded my thoughts, a smile slowly grew on my face. I wanted to remember every kiss, every touch, and all the words of love Marcus had whispered. Though the actual moment of unexpected penetration was painful, he had been gentle. Up until that night I hadn't known physical affection, or been touched sensually in any way, much less had sexual intercourse. I still wasn't sure how to feel about it. But at the time, Marcus had made me feel beautiful. He made me feel desirable, and in the passion of the moment, to feel wanted in that way, well, it was worth the temporary discomfort.

Rolling over onto my back, I ran my hand down the front of my body, much as he had, and tingled at the sensation. The area between my legs where he had pushed himself in felt tender, bruised, and invaded upon, but I touched it anyway. Closing my eyes, I relived his kisses and sweet murmurs in my ear, but along with his lingering touch, I felt a bubbling of uncertainty as I recalled his last words: *"There's something very unique about you, Rosalyn. You are too beautiful, too incredible to commit to a life of servitude. Go live your life, my little shepherd girl,"* he had whispered with one last kiss before slipping out of the barn and into the night.

Looking back, I should have known what he meant, but at the time, I thought he loved me. Didn't he say he was taking me to Paris?

Suddenly remembering that Marcus would be leaving early that morning, I jumped out of bed and tossed off my nightgown. Quickly washing up at the basin, I noticed the dried blood on the inside of my thighs. When I glanced down at the bed, thankfully it was free of blood stains, though my nightgown did not fare as well. I didn't have time to wash it. I had to prepare for traveling, so I left the blood-stained garment on the floor and put on a clean smock. As I brushed out my hair and pinned it back, my mind was flooded with all the tasks that needed to be done before I could leave.

The sheep, of course, would have to be fed. It wasn't their fault I was leaving so abruptly. I needed to pack a few belongings, though I realized that none of my clothing was worthy of Paris. I'd have to leave a note for Sister Agnes—no wait—Sister Nadine. I would let her know that, shockingly, I did have another option, and I would not be joining the Sisters of the Black Hoods. I remember smiling at the thought of what Sister Nadine's face would look like when she read my letter, and I wondered if it was cruel to find pleasure in that.

As I scurried about my cottage, trying to determine what to take and what to leave, I was startled by a knock at the door. When I opened it, a servant boy, not much younger than me, was standing on my stoop staring at me and holding a richly decorated box. I'd seen him a few times before from a distance, but we'd never spoken. Today was no different. After handing me the box, I watched him run quickly back toward the monastery before I closed the door and looked down at what I held in my hands.

The box itself was a work of art. It was round, small and white, and decorated with gold vines of ivy embossed on the lid and around all the sides. I ran my hand across the raised design and took a seat on the bed before lifting the lid.

The moment I lifted the silken fabric from the box, the smell of Marcus drifted out. Pressing the elegant blue scarf to my face, I closed my eyes and breathed in his scent before holding it at arm's length. It was gorgeous—silky and soft, the exact shade of a warm summer sky. I'd never held such a wonderful fabric, and as I slid the exquisite material across my arm and around my neck, I remember thinking, foolish as it was, that this was just the first of many fine gifts Marcus would give me.

But then I saw the card lying on the bottom of the box. When I picked it up and read the words, my world came crumbling down: "*Dearest Rosalyn, this scarf is from Paris, my gift to you. I hope you make it there someday, my little shepherd girl. Thank you for a night I will never forget. Au revoir, Marcus*"

"What? No! God, please, *NO!*" Ripping the scarf from around my neck, I threw the card and the box to the floor and ran out of the cottage. Feeling my heart in my stomach, I ran as fast as I could to the hilltop that overlooked the monastery. With each breath, I fought the fear that it was all a lie as I clung desperately to the hope that he'd be waiting for me.

But when I finally made it to the top of the hill and saw his carriage driving away from the monastery, it hit me like a punch in the gut. He was leaving without me.

"NO! MARCUS! DON'T LEAVE ME!" I cried out, but my screams went unheard. It ripped my young heart apart to see his face through the window of the coach, and even if he could see my anguish or hear the pain in my cries, he was too self-centered to care. Through eyes blurred with tears, I watched the carriage disappear from view as my knees buckled and I crumbled to the ground.

I spent the rest of the day in bed, crying. I didn't eat, nor did the sheep. They didn't even make it out of the barn. None of it mattered. I'd known the pain of isolation, the pain of a beating, but nothing had hurt worse than this. Life hadn't prepared me for the pain of a broken heart, or broken trust. This torture was far worse than any beating I'd ever received. Not even the sting from the willow branch could approach the agony that had wrapped itself around my heart.

I'd let him get too close; I had trusted him. My God, I *gave* myself to him! And he had used me. He played me like a harp and knew all the right strings to pluck. Now my young heart was in pieces, and my hopes shattered along with it. I remember lying on the bed thinking what a fool I was. How could I have possibly thought he loved *me?* I was nobody, just a simple shepherd girl, and he was the Baron's son.

If this was love, if someone could hurt another so intensely in the name of love, then I decided I would have nothing to do with it ever again.

In one day, everything had changed. As much as I dreaded the idea of having to live the rest of my life at the convent, from that day forward, I threw myself into my studies and prepared to take my vows. That was until a cold day in January.

chapter 9

a cruel reality

During the spring and fall rains, Mother Nature kept the water troughs full, making my job much easier. But water had to be fetched from the well during the dry weeks of summer, and I'd have to carry it by buckets up to the barn, insuring a constant supply of drinking water for the livestock. When winter came in and snow covered the ground, making a trip to the well and back was unrealistic, and large amounts of snow had to be melted into water. I'd spend hours shoveling it into a barrow before transferring it to a pot on the wood burning stove that cranked out heat in the center of the barn. It was pure drudgery.

It was early in the year, and the land had been covered with snow for weeks. I was completely soaked from the hours of laboring as I stood in front of the wood stove. After tossing a few more logs into the fire, I shoveled another scoop of snow into the large metal pot that hissed and steamed. My water-soaked cloak and gloves offered little protection as I held my hands over the rising heat.

After dumping the last pot of water into the sheep's trough, I stood up straight, stretching my back and feeling the effects of multiple trips with a wheelbarrow full of snow. Shoveling, lifting, and pouring heavy buckets of water had taken a toll on me, but I chose to ignore the pain. After wiping my runny nose with the back of my glove, I picked up the empty pot and turned toward the stove, startled to see another person standing in the barn. With a freshly shaved head and dressed in the traditional cap and robe of a young apprentice, he appeared to be a monk who had not yet taken his vow of silence. Standing just inside the barn door, he stared at me.

"What do you want?" I snapped, agitated at his sudden appearance. His wide eyes and shocked expression showed that I had apparently caused him to swallow his tongue. "Speak! Why are you here?" I asked, now even more frustrated.

The young monk finally found his voice. "I have a message from Sister Agnes. She...she waits for you in the library," he stuttered. He may have only been the messenger, but when I shot him a furrowed glare, he knew I didn't appreciate the message. As the nervous boy took a few steps back and waited, I could see how intimidated he was.

I had forgotten that Sister Agnes was coming that day for my weekly study lesson, and the nun had little patience for tardiness. "Fine. You relayed the message. Now leave," I spat.

"Wait!" I called out just as the boy turned to leave. "I'm soaking wet. I have to change my clothes first. Please let Sister Agnes know I'll be slightly delayed." I knew that showing up in Sister Agnes' presence looking the way I did would only bring an additional lecture. The young apprentice nodded at my request and hurried out of the barn.

Leaving the rest of my chores, I made my way back to my room in the monastery. Shortly after I had announced my intention to take my vows, and before winter set in, Sister Nadine had arranged for me to move out of my little cottage and into a room in the main quarters. My place at the convent wouldn't be ready until after the New Year, and though I was reluctant to leave the privacy of my own place, having a room in the monastery had its advantages. It was warmer, closer to the privy, but most of all, closer to the kitchen.

I would often find the cook working late, preparing for the next day's meal. A shy smile would usually get me an extra loaf of bread or a few slices of meat. Firewood was also delivered to my door every day, much better than the daily trip to the woodshed and hauling it back myself. However, moving into the monastery felt a little like the closing of a book, and I hadn't realized how much I enjoyed the freedom of living alone until I no longer had it. Yes, there were days when I may have felt lonely, but life with only sheep for company was uncomplicated. Sheep didn't expect anything from me except food and water. They didn't care if I knew all the books of the Bible or studied the sacraments. They didn't see the stains on my soul or make any demands of me. Life with sheep was simple, but it had been made very clear that my time as the shepherd girl at the River Glen Monastery was coming to an end.

When I entered my room, Sister Agnes was standing next to the fire as she waited for me. Her stern and stoic expression had me cowering as I closed the door behind me. It was not the first time I had shown up late for a lesson, and the nun was a stickler for punctuality.

"I'm so sorry, Sister. I forgot you were coming today." I scurried in and stood in front of the fireplace before removing my wet clothing. "I thought we were meeting in the library," I mumbled through cold lips. As I tried to unlace the front of my smock, my fingers were numb and clumsy, and I shivered while trying to complete the task. Glancing at the nun who had moved to a corner of the small room, I flinched at the look on her face under her black hood; it was rigid and icy.

"We were. We were to meet there over thirty minutes ago. The lesson time was eleven o'clock, Rosalyn, not eleven-thirty. Why have I been kept waiting?" Sister Agnes demanded.

"I...I was melting snow into water for the sheep and just lost track of time. I'm sorry Sister. It won't happen again," I said between sniffles. Cold, wet, and shivering, my fingers had turned into worthless, frozen stubs, and my nose was running non-stop. After I had wiped my nose with the back of my hand for the third time, apparently the nun couldn't take it any longer.

"Oh, Good Lord! Here, take this hanky. I'll do it for you." The nun shoved a white cloth into my hand and took over where my numb fingers had failed. "Why are you still tending to those sheep? You know you don't have to anymore. The Abbot tells me that you have refused to let anyone take over your duties." She stepped behind me and pulled the wet smock off my shivering body.

"I know I don't have to, but I want to. They're my sheep," I replied through quivering lips as I grabbed a rough, dry cloth, and began rubbing it over my damp hair. Though my clothes had been wet, they at least held in my body heat. Now, as I stood in the drafty room wearing only a thin, clinging shift and wet stockings, I couldn't seem to control the shivers. "I've been involved in the lambing of every one of my flock. They know me; they trust me."

"You can't be the shepherd girl forever, Rosalyn. It's time you let go and tend to more important matters." After hanging up my damp garments on a hook by the door, Sister Anges turned to look at me, and I watched as her expression melted into disbelief. In two steps, the nun was standing in front of me, and she abruptly placed her hand on my belly as confusion and anger grew on her face.

"What are you doing?" I exclaimed. Stepping back, I was shocked by the nun's sudden forwardness.

"*You are with child!*" the nun shouted. Staring at me with her mouth hanging open, her eyes were full of accusation.

"What? What are you saying?"

My ignorance turned the sister's look from befuddlement into rage. "Whose bastard child is it?" the nun shouted, appearing almost sinister as she stepped closer, her face only inches from mine, waiting for an answer.

"I don't know what you mean." Frightened by the nun's interrogating stare, I took another step back.

"Don't lie to me!" she growled, grabbing me by the arm as she yanked me forward. The nun began to shake me like a rag doll. "Who did you lie with? Who did this to you?"

"I don't know what you mean! I didn't do anything. Sister, you're hurting me!"

"Don't give me that. This is not Immaculate Conception. You've laid with a man who planted his seed in you, and I want to know who it was! Give me his name, Rosalyn. NOW!"

Fear, confusion, and the urgency of her demand had temporarily blocked out my memory, but the name the nun was looking for immediately became obvious. Had the encounter with Marcus in the barn left me with more than just a broken heart?

"*Whose child is in your belly?*" Sister Agnes shouted again before throwing me down on the bed. Looking up into the rage of the nun's face, I saw a black, flame-breathing dragon with fire streaming through her eyes.

"Marcus! I laid with Marcus!" I shouted, as Sister Agnes pulled back, preparing to take a swing at me.

"Marcus who?" the nun barked, halting her open palm in midair.

"Marcus Vanderburgh," I mumbled shamefully.

"The Baron's son?" Surprise crossed her face as Sister Agnes stood back. "I had heard that the Baron was here last summer, but I wasn't aware that his son had joined him. How did this happen? How did he even know about you? You pursued him, didn't you? You knew he was a man of nobility, a man of power and wealth, so you showed yourself, used your wicked little powers to tempt him into your bed, didn't you?" Hovering over me, Sister Agnes turned back into the sinister dragon while I cowered on the bed and listened to her vile accusations. "The Baron's son would not seek you out on his own accord."

"No, it wasn't like that. He pursued me! I tried to get him to leave me alone, but he wouldn't."

"You lying little whore!" The nun pulled back again, but this time she followed through. Her slap whipped my head to the side, and I could taste blood in my mouth. "A rich, handsome, young man smiles in your direction, and you spread your legs for him?"

"No, no! That's not what happened, I swear! I tried to tell him to leave me be, but he wouldn't take no for an answer." Hot tears ran down between my fingers as I held my hand against the sting Sister Agnes had left on my face.

"Are you telling me he *raped* you?"

"What?"

"Did he take you against your will? Did he physically hold you down, beat you, or force himself on you? Did he rape you?"

I wasn't sure what she meant, but I realized that having laid with Marcus was now causing me even more pain than I had originally experienced. Though he hadn't beaten me or physically held me against my will when he took me that night, he didn't have to. He had used the sweet sound of the French tongue to take his victim, and I had given myself willingly. Whether or not I knew what I was doing, to say otherwise would be a lie.

"Answer me, Rosalyn. Did he rape you?"

I looked up into the angry eyes of Sister Agnes and found my resolve. "No. He didn't rape me."

Before I could elaborate any further, the nun lifted me off the bed, and this time the slap came fast and hard, knocking me to the floor. The impact stung terribly, and I turned my face away, sobbing.

"You stupid girl!" the angry nun spat. "What were you thinking? Was he so dashing that you couldn't help yourself? You can't actually believe that the Baron's son was really interested in *you*? You just had to throw your virginity away to spite us all, didn't you? After all we have done for you, speaking in your favor to Mother Superior and preparing a place for you among us, *this* is how you repay our kindness?" The nun paused, but only long enough to take a breath. "Or maybe this was your plan all along?"

Sister Agnes continued to lean menacingly over me as I laid on the floor in a sobbing heap. "You thought if you proved yourself unworthy, we would leave you here with your sheep, leave you here until the next handsome face smiles in your direction. Your innocent little façade doesn't fool me, Rosalyn. I know what you're up to, and it won't work. You are, and always will be a thing of evil, born of the devil! It should be no surprise that you would end up being a whore as well!"

The nun's accusations cut deeply, but I could find no words to defend myself as I lay on the floor sobbing, wishing I could just disappear.

She grabbed me by the hair and jerked my head back, making me look up at her, but the tears running down my face did nothing to soften the nun's rage. "Give me one good reason why I shouldn't send you off to laundry labor camp for your sins of the flesh. Why, Rosalyn, why would you throw it all away for the temporary satisfaction of lust and desire? Answer me girl, or so help me God, it will only be worse for you!"

I saw the angry nun pulling her arm back and knew that another slap was on its way. "He said he loved me! He said he would take me to Paris!" I screamed with my arms over my head, preparing to deflect the oncoming blow.

But the blow didn't come. Sister Agnes stopped in mid swing and released her hand from my hair. I looked up at her, and for a moment, I thought I saw something in the sister's face that resembled remorse, but it was quickly gone. "Get up and put some clothes on. Make yourself look presentable. We need to go see the Abbot." The rage and anger may have vanished from her face, but she was brutally stoic. "You may as well pack up your belongings. You'll be returning with me to the convent this afternoon. When you are done here, meet me in the Abbot's office."

Even after I had changed into a dry shift and stockings, put on multiple petticoats, and donned a heavy woolen shawl, I couldn't stop shivering. The shock of what had just transpired had not worn off. I thought I was done hating Marcus, but now a new rage was raising my hatred to a new level. Not only had he lied to me, broken my heart, and shattered my dreams, he now had left me with a whole new problem; I was carrying his child!

Just as I was beginning to accept my future life as a nun, everything was now uncertain. If only I'd been stronger against him, more convincing when I told him to leave me alone. But I hadn't, because I was weak, and he used that weakness to get what he wanted. All of this was his fault.

Tears blinded my vision as I stuffed a few of my belongings into a basket. After emptying the small table beside my bed, the sideboard, and a small chest that held my personal items, I sat on the bed attempting to pull myself together. Walking into the Abbot's office like a blubbering child would earn me no favors. Though I had no idea what my future now held, I knew it would be decided by the Abbot and Mother Superior, and it was this unknown that caused me the most anxiety.

As I rose off the bed, I took one more look around and then remembered. Dropping to my knees, I reached under the bed. After pulling out a dark bundle, I sat down on the bed and folded back the flaps of burlap. It was still there, the ornately-decorated white box—just one of the gifts he had left me.

Holding the ivy-embossed box, my heart started beating faster, and I felt the rage boiling up inside me. All the feelings I'd had for Marcus were completely wiped out by a new loathing, and as each beat of my pulse pounded in my skull, I discovered new depths to my hatred that I had never felt before.

In one quick movement, I threw his token gift into the fireplace. Sparks lit up the fire pit as flames licked at the edges of the box. I stared at it, watching as the fire threatened to devour it, but something in me couldn't let it burn. Quickly reaching in, I pulled my farewell gift out of the flames and dropped it instantly to the floor. Though tendrils of smoke were drifting up and around the box, it wasn't burning.

After staring at it for a moment, I bent down and picked the thing up. It was still hot to the touch, and the bottom was covered in black soot, but I placed it onto the table and slowly lifted the lid. The scarf was still there, completely untouched by the flames. Lifting it out of its safe container, I couldn't help but notice his smell drifting out as well. He was still there, too. Even after nearly being sentenced to death by fire, his presence could not be erased.

Shoving the scarf back into the box, I wrapped it in the burlap and placed it at the bottom of my basket, underneath the belongings I was taking with me. At the time, I didn't know why I wanted to keep it or why I hadn't just let the fire destroy it, but something wouldn't let me. Even though I hated Marcus with every fiber of my being, he was still my first taste of love.

Although it symbolized a bitter and ill-fated love that had left my heart in shreds and my young life in ruins, I couldn't let it burn.

chapter 10

the abbot

When I arrived at the Abbot's office, the door was slightly ajar, and hearing the agitated voices on the other side made me reluctant to enter, so I stood outside and listened. "I think the best course of action, Your Grace," said Sister Agnes, "is that Rosalyn return with me back to the convent. We can let Mother Superior decide what to do with her."

"This does change the plans you had for her. I'm sure Mother Superior will be sorely disappointed to hear of this," the Abbot replied. "But if you want to know my recommendation, Sister, after the baby is born and placed in an orphanage, she can pay five years penitence in subservient labor for her sins."

I had to clamp a hand over my mouth to keep a gasp from escaping when I heard the Abbot's suggestion, and I felt the panic exploding inside my chest as he dictated my future. "After being cleansed of her indiscretion, and assuming you will still accept her, she can then join the Sisterhood."

Five years of subservient labor? I couldn't believe what I was hearing!

"Five years seems a bit extreme, Your Grace," said the sister.

"Hmm, possibly, but of course, Mother Superior will have the final say. That's just my suggestion. However, she did seduce a nobleman, the Laird's son at that, and begot herself with his child, looking for some material gain, no doubt. I'm sure had he been of lesser status, she wouldn't have been quite so eager to spread her legs."

I felt like I'd just been punched in the stomach. I couldn't believe the Abbot would say such a thing. He barely even knew me. He had no idea what had really happened with Marcus. What gave him the right to be my judge?

"Maybe if you had kept a closer watch on the young man, and not let him loose on the grounds alone, this wouldn't have happened in the first place, Your Grace." The sternness I heard in the Sister's voice gave me a wee bit of hope.

"It's not my position to tell the future Baron of York that he may not tour the grounds— grounds that his family *owns*— without an escort," the Abbot snapped back. "Besides, he had a valet here. It was not my responsibility to keep the boy's cock in his pants."

Silence fell in the room before the sister cleared her throat. "Regardless, Rosalyn will be the one punished, even though Marcus Vanderburgh is the real culprit here. But as you pointed out, he's the Laird's son. I'm sure he could care less about this son's bastard children, as long as they stay anonymous."

I could hear the sardonic tone laced in the sister's words before everything went silent again. After a moment, the quiet was broken by the sound of a chair being pushed, heavy and scrapping across the wood floor. "Where is that girl, anyway?" chided the Abbot. "I thought you said she was on her way here."

"Perhaps I should go check on her. She was quite upset when I left her."

Realizing that the sister was making her way to the door and not wanting to get caught listening, I slowly pushed it open. When I peeked in, I saw the Abbot standing across the room looking out the window as Sister Agnes met me at the entrance to his office.

"There you are. We've been waiting on you," said the nun.

As the Abbot turned toward me, his dark, purple robe flowed around his hefty torso in a sea of fabric before coming to a stop. A large, ornately-decorated gold cross hung from a thick chain that looped around his multiple layers of chin. Years of comfortable living showed in the man's girth, and on his pompous face.

"Come in, my dear," the Abbot said with a false smile.

I slunk into the room wearing multiple layers of petticoats, my cloak and traveling boots, but I still felt completely exposed. Carrying my entire worldly possessions in the basket I held at my side, I tried to be brave.

"Come now. Don't be afraid." When the Abbot waved me over, I timidly crossed the room, feeling as if I were facing a firing squad.

"Sister Agnes has just informed me of your…situation. We've been discussing what's to become of you. I must ask you a question, my dear. Do you want to be a nun? Has God touched your heart and called you into his service?" the Abbot asked with a strange smile on his portly face.

I glanced quickly at Sister Agnes, but her cold gaze gave nothing away. Was this a trick question? Was I supposed to say yes? I'd rarely been asked what I wanted before. I didn't know how to answer. To say that God had touched my heart and urged me to become a nun would be a lie. But honesty had won me no favors this day. Looking back at the Abbot, I stood as straight as I could, lifted my chin, and lied. "Yes, Your Grace. I do want to take my vows and join the Sisterhood."

The Abbot stared at me as if he were trying to determine whether my answer was sincere, and I wondered for a moment if being a man of God, he would see through my façade. But a grin soon pulled up the corners of his plump mouth. "Very well, then." He looked pleased as he waddled across the room to stand directly in front of me. The man's girth was almost matched by his height, and I felt a rush of panic when he reached out with a large hand and grabbed me by the chin, holding my face up toward the light.

Still feeling the sting from the sister's slaps, I knew that my cheek appeared red and swollen against my pale skin. I had tasted my own blood and felt the swollen split in my lip. If my face looked as bad as it felt, it couldn't have been a pretty sight.

The Abbot studied me for a moment before looking over his shoulder at the nun, who was standing like a guard in the corner of his office. "Is this your work, Sister?"

The nun didn't reply. She didn't even flinch.

"And you thought I was being extreme," he chuckled. Dropping his hand, he walked toward his desk and picked up a dirk. He turned and faced me, tapping the knife in his meaty hand.

Feeling a surge of panic, I watched as the Abbot stared at me, rapping the knife against his fat palm. I felt like a trapped rabbit. The trap hadn't been sprung yet, but there was still no way out.

"Since you still wish to take your vows, it is my recommendation that you perform five years of penitence to pay for your transgressions. After that time, if you still wish to follow the path of God, and you have kept your soul free from sin, you may continue your studies and prepare to take your vows."

"Please, Your Grace," I muttered, trying to find the strength not to cry. "Why should I have to serve such a long penitence? I didn't mean for this to happen. I didn't know what I was doing. Please, Your Grace, you must believe me." As much as I didn't want them to come, the first tears slipped out and down my cheeks.

"Of course, my dear. There, there, dry your tears." The Abbot placed the dirk back on the desk before stepping over to wipe my cheek with his fat finger. "But you are with child, and now you must pay for your reckless behavior. Five years will go fast, and I would think some sort of service labor should suffice. Nothing too terrible, but of course Mother Superior will have the final say." He smiled, as if that should make me feel better.

I didn't have any words to defend myself. There was nothing to be said. Once again, my life and my future were being decided for me, and the outcome was even bleaker than I had ever imagined it could be.

"If we're done here, I would like to be on our way." Sister Agnes broke the uncomfortable silence. "Daylight is short this time of the year, and I want to be back at the convent before nightfall."

"Of course. But you will want to eat something before you set out. The afternoon meal is just now being served in the dining hall."

I remember thinking that the Abbot probably didn't miss many meals. Just the mention of food set the man's round face aglow.

"No, but thank you, Your Grace; we really need to be on our way. I'll pick up a loaf of bread from the kitchen on our way out."

"Very well. Why don't you go take care of that while I talk with Rosalyn. Alone." The tone in his voice and the look in his eyes must have told Sister Agnes that it wasn't just a suggestion. She nodded and knelt before his extended hand to kiss the ring on his finger, then stood and floated out the door, leaving me alone with the Abbot.

When I glanced back at his smug face, I didn't care for the look in the Abbot's eyes. He said nothing at first, and the silence was thick, feeling like a guillotine waiting to drop. I lowered my gaze to the floor but was very aware of the Abbot's eyes on me.

"It's unfortunate that I hadn't taken the time to get to know you better, Rosalyn, and now you're leaving us. You've always been so reclusive and aloof out there with your sheep. Most days we hardly ever saw you. That's why I find it so hard to believe that the young baron had no problem in spotting you. Didn't act so elusive when he showed up, did you?"

The Abbot's insinuating remarks hurt, and I swallowed hard trying to keep my composure. He circled around me and then leaned in close. "You've enjoyed your time with the sheep, haven't you, my dear? You've been happy being the shepherd girl here, yes?"

The rolls on his face shook when he spoke, and all of his chins were uncomfortably close. I could smell his stale breath, felt it against my cheek, and I fought back the urge to shudder.

"Yes. I've been happy here, Your Grace," I said with as much control as I could muster, but he was hovering so close that I could feel myself beginning to shake.

"Good, very good," he said, now standing even closer, his disgustingly fat belly pushing up against my back. "My only regret is that I wish I'd been aware you were so easily persuaded to lift your shift."

Before I realized what was happening, the Abbot reached down between my legs and began to fondle me through my clothing. Reaching around with his other meaty hand, he slipped it into my cloak, squeezing and manipulating my breast. I heard the gasp slip past my lips, but I was paralyzed and panicked. When I heard him moan next to my ear, it was plainly obvious that he took pleasure in my discomfort.

Squirming, I struggled to free myself from his grip, but the Abbot was easily able to hold me in place with his weight alone. When he placed his tongue up against my cheek and then ran it up the side of my face, I felt as though I would burst into flames any second from the agony and the shame. Suddenly releasing me, he clasped his chubby hands in the front of his rounded belly and walked toward the window as if nothing had happened.

I had been violated twice in the same day, but at least when Sister Agnes had accosted me, it was merely for confirmation of her suspicion. The Abbot had just violated me with no good intentions, and it left me feeling repulsed and frightened. I wiped his saliva off my face and let the tears fall.

"You know, my dear, after you give up that bastard child, if you like being the shepherd girl, I could arrange for your penitence to be served here, back with your sheep. I could make life much more comfortable for you." When the Abbot turned away from the window and stood in front of me once again, I felt myself cringe, fearing another assault.

"We could get to know each other a little better," he said with a sly smile. "You'd like that, wouldn't you my dear?"

Closing my eyes and dropping my face to the floor, I couldn't look at him or hold back the tears any longer. When he lifted my chin, the tears were running down my cheeks, and I was shaking uncontrollably.

"Now, it can't be that bad. I know you've not had an easy life, Rosalyn, but in exchange for your company in my bed on those cold, dark winter nights, I could make your five years of penitence go much easier. But I can also make it much harder. It's really your call, my dear, because Mother Superior will not question my decision. I will get what I want. I always do." He dropped my chin and turned his back to me. "You probably shouldn't keep Sister Agnes waiting any longer. Best be on your way."

Quickly wiping my face, I turned toward the door.

"Rosalyn, aren't you forgetting something?"

His words made me stop. Turning around slowly, I saw him holding out a long purple sleeve with his hand extended. The proper protocol was to kiss the Abbot's ring upon leaving his audience. He was waiting.

Slowly, I slunk back toward him as he rolled his eyes with impatience. Making the last step forward, I leaned down to kiss his ring when he abruptly reached out and grabbed my face. Lifting me in one swift motion, he planted his fat lips on mine.

Struggling to push him off, I had no defense against his overpowering torso. I felt his tongue brush my lips and shuddered as I realized that it was as large and fat as the rest of him. The feeling of being completely under this man's control, helpless to stop his advances, was agony, and I beat against his chest to be free of his face against mine.

Finally he released me. "Just wanted to get a little taste of what's yet to come," he said as a wicked smile filled his disgusting face.

I turned and ran toward the door, but once again, he called out, stopping me in my tracks. "Rosalyn, let me remind you that no one would believe a *whore* over the word of a respected Abbot. It would be best for you to remember that."

Never looking back, I ran all the way to the front of the monastery where the carriage and Sister Agnes waited for me. Tears blurred my vision as I jumped onto the seat next to her, struggling to control my sobs. The thought of the Abbot touching me in the same way that Marcus had, brought on so much revulsion, that I felt the acidic bile rising to the back of my throat. But I had no choice. The Abbot had said so. I would be back, not as the shepherd girl, but as his secret little whore, to do with as he pleased. Marcus had tainted me, and the scar he had left on my soul would affect my life forever.

NOW YOU KNOW

chapter 11

bastard child

After finishing her spell-binding story, Rosalyn had gone quiet, and Isaboe watched the glow of firelight dancing off her mother's face as she stared into the flames. Though this story had taken place over forty years earlier, only months before her birth, Isaboe could see the hurt of a young, unprotected girl still lingering in her mother's face. If Rosalyn had thought she'd locked that part of her past away, it had certainly resurfaced tonight.

"Did you have to go back to the monastery?" Isaboe asked, afraid to hear the answer.

"No, I didn't. About a month before you were born, I received a message that the Abbot had requested I be sent back after your birth. There was no way in hell that was going to happen. For the first time in my young life, I decided to take control of my own situation, so I ran away. I ended up on the streets of Edinburgh—hungry, scared, and heavy with child."

"So, gimme a moment to catch up," Connor interrupted, turning to look at Isaboe. "Not only were ye adopted by one of the wealthiest families in Edinburgh, ye have faerie blood running through yer veins, and now, yer father's a *nobleman*? What else dinnae I ken about ye, *boireannach*?"

The look on Connor's face had to match her own as Isaboe stared back at him, but she had no response. This was all new to her as well. They were learning these things together.

"One must be acknowledged to be the child of a nobleman," Rosalyn said. "Isaboe's father may be from a long line of nobility, but there was nothing *noble* about him." She paused before turning her attention back to her daughter. "He never knew about you, Isaboe. I never even attempted to contact him. I was sure he had many bastard children throughout the land; why would he care about one more?"

A quick stab shot through Isaboe's chest at the word *bastard,* and it showed on her face.

"Isaboe, I'm so sorry. That was insensitive of me."

"It's alright. I've been passing myself off as a bastard child for the last six months. At least now I know it wasn't a lie." Starring at one another over the fire, Isaboe saw pain reflected on her mother's face, but there was also the burn of determination. As she watched their small fire dancing in her mother's somber eyes, she wondered if our eyes really are windows into the soul. For the most part, she had seen wisdom and patience in Rosalyn's, but with a guarded view, though Isaboe was sure that at one time innocence had resided there. Most importantly, Rosalyn had not let her time at the monastery define her. In some distant way, this woman's fight reminded Isaboe of her own.

"So, it was on the streets of Edinburgh that ye met Sister Miriam?" The uncomfortable moment was not lost on Connor, and this push in another direction helped lighten the tension.

"Aye. Fortunately, I fell in with a couple of homeless women who kindly watched over me, being that I was so young and in motherly way. They could tell that I knew nothing about surviving on the streets, living on other people's trash, or begging for my next meal." Her voice cracked as she looked at Isaboe, but her face remained stoic. "One day Sister Miriam was making rounds through the alleys, passing out bread and pieces of dried meat when the ladies brought me to her attention. I was showing signs of labor, and they didn't want to see me give birth in a filthy alley in Edinburgh.

"At first, I didn't want to go with the sister. I was afraid she would send me back to the convent, but she didn't. She kept me hidden in the basement of the kirk until you were born. She was different from the other nuns, and I trusted her, felt safe with her. I trusted her so much that I told her everything. I told her about the bright ones and how they never let me be. I told her about Sister Bernadine, about Marcus, and even about the Abbot. Oddly enough, she believed me, or at least she pretended to.

When you were born, I saw the opportunity through her to give you a better life." Rosalyn paused and sighed deeply. "So, now you know... all of it."

Isaboe locked gazes with her mother as silence fell over them like a heavy blanket. Learning her parentage and her mother's history was enlightening, but it wasn't comforting. On the contrary, it only made her feel worse. Rosalyn's story was not an easy one to hear. Life had not only been unkind to her, she had been robbed of her childhood, mistreated and misunderstood from the day she was born. Isaboe felt a tinge of regret for the times she had silently cursed her mother for abandoning her as an infant. The choice that Rosalyn had made all those years ago had provided a life of comfort and privilege for Isaboe, though void as it was of a mother's love.

"I think that's enough family history for one night," Connor gave Isaboe's hand a soft squeeze. "We all need some sleep before we ride into Kirkwall on the morrow."

After building up the fire with the remaining brush and checking on the horses, Connor returned to find that Rosalyn had already slipped into her bedroll, not far from the heat of the flames. He had just thrown down his own bedroll when a faint cry drew his attention to the buckboard.

The canopy over the wooden wagon provided some protection from the wind for Isaboe and their newborn, but when Connor peered in, he could see her struggling to find comfort. Although she had plenty of blankets to ward off the chill, the rough, wooded floor of the wagon was a far cry from a feather bed, and he heard her grimace each time she shifted, still holding Kaitlyn in her arms. A soft glow from the small lantern swaying slightly above Isaboe's head illuminated her face. As Connor stood quietly observing the scene, he felt his heart swell with deep intensity. In that moment, watching his child being cradled in the arms of the woman he loved, he couldn't imagine loving them more, or that Isaboe could be more beautiful.

"How are ye doing?" he asked, breaking the moment of silent observation.

Isaboe glanced up, offering him a half-hearted smile. "Alright, I guess. Though my body hurts all over, and I would give anything to be in a soft bed so I could sleep for about a year. Other than that, I'm fine," she said with a forced grin, but she looked drained and tired.

The movement of the buckboard caused Kaitlyn to whimper as Connor stepped in and sat next to Isaboe. Making soft, hushing sounds to calm her, Isaboe gently rocked her blanketed baby.

"So, how are ye handlin' everything that Rosalyn told us tonight? I ken that some of it was hard to hear," he said quietly.

"Aye, it was. Rosalyn's had a really difficult life. Though I'm glad she shared it with us, it's a lot to take in all at once. My father is the Baron of York? That's a hard one to grasp. But what bothers me more than anything else is what she told me about our bloodline, and that Kaitlyn wasn't the first child the Fey Queen tried to take. What if she tries again?"

Connor heard it in her voice, and even in the dim light, he could see the fear in her eyes. Brushing back a lock of her hair, he rested his hand on her shoulder. "There's no point in borrowin' trouble, *Breagha*. Regardless of what Rosalyn told us tonight, the best revenge against the queen is to live our lives. If she meddles with us again, she'll be in for another fight," Connor said firmly, before softening his voice. "Isaboe, I understand yer concerns, but we canna live our lives in fear. Tomorrow we'll make a new start in Kirkwall. As long as we're together, there's nothing she can do to us. I promise I'll take care of ye, and Kaitlyn, for as long as God gives me the breath to do so."

"Then I guess I have nothing to worry about," Isaboe said with a tired smile. As the anxiety gradually slipped off her face, she leaned into him, resting her head on his shoulder.

"Ye must be exhausted," he said, slipping his arm around her.

"I am. Kaitlyn hasn't been sleeping well, so neither have I."

"Aye, nobody has. For a wee thing, she certainly has a good set of lungs," he said, running a hand over his stubbled-face as he yawned.

"It looks like she might be out now," Isaboe whispered as she gently laid the baby down and moved to lie next to her. Connor got up to leave, but Isaboe touched his arm. As he looked down, the dim light of the lantern cast her face in shadow, but he could still see her wide pleading eyes. "Don't go. Please stay and lay with us."

Though they were all extremely road weary, she didn't have to ask twice. Quietly as he could, Connor kicked off his boots, removed his cloak, and snuffed out the lantern before taking his place next to his family.

chapter 12

kirkwall

The following morning, and after leaving Rosalyn and Kaitlyn at one of the only two hostels in Kirkwall, Connor and Isaboe located the land office and were now sitting across the desk from Mr. McEwen as he reviewed the documents. The mostly bald man, with only a line of hair that circled his head like a horse shoe, closely studied the property deed that Connor and Will had found in Saschel's home as his spectacles hung off the end of his nose, and Isaboe hoped there would be no question about her claim to her family's property. Standing, the man turned and pulled a scroll from the cubby behind him and rolled it out across his desk. After examining what looked like a map of Kirkwall, he ran a finger across the parchment until coming to a stop, and he tapped the location.

"I think we need to take a walk," Mr. McEwen said as he slipped on his cloak. Connor and Isaboe gave each other a wary glance before following the land clerk out of his office. "This property is prime kelp burning land," the man said. "And it's the stinking kelp that's pumping money into the local economy, bringing bankers, lawyers, and businessmen alike, all while lining the pockets of the lairds that own the land. Burning seaweed smells like the devil's rotting in hell, and they're all becoming *stinking* rich off of it." Mr. McEwen wasn't shy about expressing his views.

From under the hood of her cloak, Isaboe watched as raindrops splashed on the dirt road. Strategically stepping around the puddles, she managed to avoid getting mud on the hem of her dress as she tried to keep up with the men's longer strides. Leading the way, Mr. McEwen chatted on about how over the past forty years kelp production in Kirkwall had boomed. Isaboe didn't want to miss out on the details simply because she couldn't keep up.

"How's burnin' seaweed a successful business venture?" Connor asked.

"For years, we always used the seaweed to fertilize the fields before planting the spring crops. Smelled something awful, but it did the job. Then 'bout forty years ago, some educated fellow from the mainland comes up here and convinces the locals that there's money to be made in burning the shit. When seaweed is dried, burned, and cooled, it becomes a dark, oily muck called kelp. They use it in the making of glass, soap, and some other fancy stuff. This island used to be mostly farmland, but farming dinnae pay like kelp does."

"I'm sure the bankers and lairds aren't doing that work themselves," Connor scoffed.

"Hell no! The wealthy Brits are making a killing here in Kirkwall, but the laborers are all Scotsmen trying to feed their families. They're putting in long, hard hours harvesting seaweed, but dinnae get much reward. Most of them got more mouths than they can feed. I've seen whole families out working the kelp fields, even the wee little ones."

"And I'm sure their accommodations are a far cry from the grand townhouses we passed coming into the city," Connor offered.

"Oh, to be certain, there's a whole 'nother side to Kirkwall. Some of em' live in those cold, stone bothys ye see dotting the shoreline. Tis' a pity, but I guess if one is used to that, then 'tis good enough, aye?"

Isaboe bristled at the clerk's remark, and his tone. She silently wondered if in her previous life—growing up as one of the affluent—she had made someone feel unimportant for the contents of their purse, unintentionally or not. Shrugging off a quick stab of guilt, she focused on her footing when the men came to a stop. Tossing back her hood to glance around, she saw that the rain had let up to become a light mist, but the sky was still covered with thick clouds. The three of them now stood next to a plot of land that reached out to the green-blue waters of the North Sea, and foam lapped at the seaweed clinging to the rocks like a heavy, yellow webbing of dead foliage.

"So, ye can understand my confusion when I looked up this property on the township map." Mr. McEwen scratched his bald head as he looked up at Connor over spectacles dotted with rain and threatening to slide off his bulbous nose. "There's no record of it being sold, still owned by Henry Cameron, or his heirs, but as we can see here, it's not vacant."

Connor and Isaboe looked out over the strip of land along the rocky coastline. Long rows of strategically placed drying walls, along with multiple stone-lined pits, stained dark from years of burning seaweed, lay empty. A few small sheds, various tools, and scavenging sea birds were the only other things that interrupted the scenery.

"Can ye give us a point of reference here? That deed must tell ye where the property lines lie. How much land are we looking at?" Connor asked.

Mr. McEwen furrowed his brushy brow while working his lower jaw. He removed his glasses and wiped them off with the hem of his shirt as he looked out across the land, first left then right, as if he were attempting to locate landmarks. Isaboe watched him searching the shoreline that looked unchanged for as far as the eye could see. "From what I can figure, 'tis bout where that rocky crag spits out into the bay, then all the way over to where we can see the last stone wall, just east of that bothy there." Indicating the points of reference from west to east, the amount of land he outlined was substantial. "But that's just an estimate. We need to walk out the exact measurements as dictated on this deed to ken for sure. But it is a good chunk o' land."

"Aye, land that someone else is using," Connor said.

"That does seem to be the case," the clerk agreed, bobbing his round head. "Well, Mr. Grant, I think we should talk with the neighboring lairds to see what they ken about this," he said as he turned back toward town.

Up to this point, Isaboe had been silently standing next to Connor, listening carefully. When they had arrived in the city of Kirkwall that morning, the entrance was lined with lovely townhouses and stylish store fronts. She had immediately imagined herself living in such a home, hoping that her property might be just as grand. But now, standing at the muck-covered piece of shoreline dotted with black pits and stone walls, her hopes were quickly fading. "Connor, this is not the property I had imagined. I think we should sell it." She put her hand on his arm and looked up at him, hoping he felt the same.

"Let's go talk with the neighbors first. Someone has been trespassing on yer land and making quite a profit. Whoever it is, if he dinnae want to deal with a legal issue, maybe we can make another kind o' deal." Connor gave Isaboe a knowing smile. "How do ye feel about pressing charges against the trespasser?" he asked as they followed Mr. McEwen back to his office.

Isaboe wasn't sure how to answer. All she wanted was a quiet simple life in a comfortable little home to raise her child, and having to file a legal action to do so wasn't something she wanted to deal with. "Let's just see what this trespasser is willing to pay to prevent that."

"And I'll be reminding him that shoreline property is in high demand," Connor said, setting his jaw.

"Well, I think I'll let you handle that," Isaboe said as she slipped her hand into Connor's and fell into stride alongside him. "I'm going back to the hostel. Rosalyn said she was going to give Kaitlyn a bath and put her down for a nap. She must be hungry by now, and I know that's something Rosalyn can't do for her."

Connor was a buzz of information when he finally arrived back at the hostel, where Isaboe waited for him to fill her in on the details. With Rosalyn out purchasing supplies and Kaitlyn taking a nap, she encouraged Connor to quietly share what he had learned about her property.

"After McEwen and I left the land office, it didna take long to discover who'd been squatting and making huge profits off yer land," Connor said, his cheeks rosy from the brisk and wet walk through the cold streets of Kirkwall. "We made a visit to this Monty Breckenridge fella, and at first he acted like he didna ken what we were talking 'bout, but when I mentioned that I was hiring a lawyer, he started changing his story."

"Why, what did he say?" Isaboe asked.

"Breckenridge told us he had purchased the two other pieces of property years before from yer sister and her husband. Though he admitted knowing that the third parcel was owned by another sister, since no one ever showed up to claim it, Breckenridge assumed that all of Henry

Cameron's heirs were dead. In his mind, there seemed no point in letting good kelp-burning land go unused, and gradually he just encroached onto the other side of his property line. No one's ever questioned him, till now."

"So now what? Is he willing to buy the property and avoid a lawsuit?"

"Oh, aye! He offered me more than a decent proposal to purchase yer land, but I told him I'd havta let him know. I think we should let Breckenridge sweat it out a bit. After all, there might be other lairds who might want to throw their hats into the bidding. This could be both profitable and entertaining!"

Though Isaboe knew Connor wasn't a savvy businessman by trade, he had good, possibly vindictive instincts, and she agreed to hiring legal advice. It was important to her to handle the sale of her property as quietly and quickly as possible. There was still a wanted poster out there with her face on it, and the less attention they brought to themselves the better.

For the next two days, Connor and the attorney they had hired met with a number of parties interested in Isaboe's property, pitting them against each other until the highest bidder won. Monty Breckenridge paid well to prevent losing a large section of his current and future wealth. He also paid a little extra to stay out of jail when they agreed not to press charges for his illegal use of the land. With their pockets now lined with an unexpectedly large sum of money, Isaboe was able to have that beautiful townhouse in the city after all.

The following week was spent setting up a comfortable home in their rented, second-story abode. The sale of Isaboe's inheritance not only covered the rent for six months, some new household furnishings, and desperately needed clothing for everyone, it also provided a healthy cash reserve, making the future a little less uncertain for Isaboe and her family.

With the dark months of Lorien now behind her, the promise of a better tomorrow made each passing day a little brighter and less threatening. Isaboe could feel her health returning, both physically and mentally, and she was grateful every morning for waking up to another day surrounded by people she loved, and who loved her.

Outwardly, Isaboe did her best to appear as if everything were normal, but there were days when her mind would travel back to the months she spent alone with the Fey Queen. Lorien had been her only companion, constantly manipulating and twisting her mind while they traveled during the cold months of winter across the Northern Highlands. The experience still haunted Isaboe's thoughts and would send shivers down her spine, causing her to question what destiny and humanity were really all about. Focusing on caring for baby Kaitlyn kept her unsettling thoughts at bay, but that didn't allow Isaboe to completely relax.

After discovering the local bookstore, she created a small library in the corner of their home. Twenty years had passed while she was in Euphoria, and a great deal had happened during that time. After catching up on recent history and finishing a few novels, Isaboe found herself gravitating toward research—another new habit for her. Though she read books on demons and fey, on soul mates, and on metaphysical travel, she found no references to people who had experiences like hers and her mother's. But that didn't stop Isaboe from searching.

New neighbors soon became new friends. Isaboe and Rosalyn seemed to fit in well with the community, meeting other women who were happy to welcome them into the Orkney way of life. As they shared tea socials, needlepoint gatherings, and taking in the latest speakers at the theater, the relationship between mother and daughter slowly changed. Connor noticed a bond beginning to grow between them, and he saw that same connection between grandmother and grandchild each time Rosalyn held Kaitlyn. The simple act of being together as a family brought a fresh shine to both ladies' faces, and he was grateful to have played a part in reuniting them.

As a gradual sense of routine settled into their daily lives, it didn't take long before Connor needed to do more than move furniture around. Though financially they didn't need him to do so, he took a job at the blacksmith's forge. Isaboe may have made a nice profit on the sale of her land, but there was a limit to what Connor would let her pay for.

Having grown up in a wealthy family, Isaboe had never wanted for anything most of her young life. So after losing everything when she disappeared for twenty years to the realm of the fey, now that she had the means, she was determined to buy additional furnishings, artwork and novelties to decorate her home. However, Connor didn't see it the same way.

After a lengthy discussion on the matter, and Isaboe had finally agreed to stash away most of the proceeds from the sale, she still questioned Connor's reluctance to spend the money. "Why is it so hard for you to just relax and enjoy our newfound wealth?" she asked.

Connor felt his teeth clench. As sincere as she was, he knew that wasn't true. It was Isaboe's newfound wealth, and his pride had taken a hit knowing they were living off money he hadn't earned. "We dinnae ken how long we'll be here, or what may come up. We need to be prepared for what's next."

"Well, I'm not ready for what's next. I like it here and just want to stay put for a while." Isaboe paused, trying to calm the fussy baby in her arms. "Besides, what you make at the forge doesn't really amount to much."

Nathan had worked! Connor thought spitefully. Though the pittance he made at the forge might be a far cry from the earnings of a college-educated, bridge-builder like Nathan had been, Connor's pride felt stepped on. Did she think he couldn't provide for his own family? But one look at her teasing eyes proved that thought unfair. "It's enough to put food on the table," he said firmly, attempting to solidify his self-worth.

Isaboe softened and gave him half a smile. "Aye, it is. So, if spending your days in that dirty, hot forge makes you feel better because you're contributing, well then, don't let me stop you," she said, just before giving him a quick kiss and spinning away. Connor watched the swing of her hips as she walked toward the bedroom with Kaitlyn squirming in her arms and realized that there was more to his irritation than just his pride being stepped on.

As the days became longer, a sense of normalcy settled over the small family in their townhouse. Besides three small bedrooms, the home was complete with a kitchen, a dining room, a washroom, and a cozy sitting area. They were fortunate to acquire the rental before the spring seaweed harvest began and the town would be filled to capacity. The population of Kirkwall doubled at the onset of the kelp season, with businessmen and laborers alike, either looking to make a killing in the industry or just trying to feed their families.

The majority of Kirkwall's year round population consisted of the affluent and privileged, dusted with a taste of British culture. Attracted by the amount of money that could be made, the town's cosmetic appeal, and the long, pleasant summer days, the wealthy found the islands an attractive summer getaway. Residents of the coastal city took pride in their ornate townhouses, built one upon another with attractive architecture and well-dressed front doors. The industrial buildings, including such places as a hot, dirty forge, were tucked well away from public view. Those who dressed and lived well in Kirkwall had a city image to maintain, even as they conducted their own dirty business on the back-breaking labor of the poor.

Connor felt most at ease with his peers at the forge, though even at work he wasn't terribly friendly. In his core, he was a distant, guarded man. Years of watching his father toil on a small farm had taught him the value of a hard day's work and to be cautious of predators. But everything changed when the British army stole his family's land and burned their house to the ground with his father still inside. Overnight, Connor's life had become about the fight and the hatred, and he would never forget who the real predators were. The seeds of distrust and anger had been sown, and no longer did he take anyone at face value. In his experience, the wealthy and the powerful always had an ulterior motive behind their handshakes. Someone with too big a smile or too much enthusiasm always had something to hide.

For the sake of his relationship with Isaboe, he kept these opinions to himself and did his best to be neighborly. But as the weeks passed, Connor became more aloof and reserved, even with Isaboe, though he hoped she hadn't noticed. But when he suggested that they take the money from the sale of the land and leave the country, putting its dark memories and the British Occupation behind them to start anew in America, he hadn't anticipated her emotional reaction.

Isaboe had looked shocked, verifying that the idea offended her. "Absolutely not!" she snapped. "Anna and Benjamin are still out there somewhere, and I am not going anywhere until I know what became of my children."

"But we dinnae ken how long that may be, Isaboe. How long are ye planning on waiting before we move on? I realize ye like it here, but this city doesn't fit us."

"You mean it doesn't fit *you*! I'm completely happy here, Connor, and I have no intention of leaving until I learn the whereabouts of my children."

"And if that information never comes? Then what?"

Offering no response, only a hurt and angry glare, Isaboe refused to discuss the matter any further. It was one more thing they couldn't seem to agree upon.

I'm sure that Nathan would have been much better in high society, Connor thought, but how would he know? Isaboe never spoke of him. Whenever Nathan's name was mentioned, she would change the subject, and he couldn't help but wonder how often Isaboe compared him to her late husband. He began to suspect that in her mind, he always came up on the short end.

But that didn't stop Connor from trying to prove himself. If his timing was right, he would occasionally catch Isaboe without Kaitlyn in her arms or attached to her breast. Sneaking her off into his room, they would steal a few moments of passion in each other's arms, whispering words of apology for their last stupid fight.

Sucking gently on her lower lip and running his fingers over her hips, it was easy to remember why they were together, why he had fallen so quickly and so deeply in love with her. Those spontaneous, heated moments may have fed their love and desire for one another, but inevitably they would be interrupted by either Kaitlyn or Rosalyn—or worse, when Isaboe would gently, but firmly, push him away, insisting that it was still too soon. It seemed like they were never able to finish what they started, and Connor's sexual frustration only added to his surly withdrawal. As the days passed, he stopped pursuing Isaboe altogether. The time he spent at the forge increased, even after dinner, long after the sun had set. At the forge, no one questioned his relentless scowl or his foul mood.

Of course, he would've preferred to stay home if Rosalyn could find somewhere else to be, if the wee bairn would sleep through just one night, and if he could have Isaboe's beautiful, naked body beneath him. But such is the love life of many a new father—non-existent.

Settling into Kirkwall created a number of new acquaintances, and Isaboe's next-door neighbor, Abigail Graham, had become her closest friend. Fortunately, Abigail's husband, Foster, was one of the few neighbors to whom Connor was actually cordial. It was over a cup of tea at Abby's house that Isaboe discovered that not all was as quiet and peaceful as it appeared in their quaint, coastal town.

"I heard a bit of scuttlebutt today." Abby's eyes lit up as she placed her cup on the table. "Foster told me that they took Mr. McGuire in for questioning yesterday, you know, the man who owns the leather shop."

"Who are they and what are they questioning him about?" Isaboe asked, but without much interest. She didn't know Mr. McGuire, and it didn't really matter to her at the moment. Her daughter's contented face was her focus as she watched Kaitlyn sitting on her lap, happily playing with her stuffed doll.

"The British Army, of course. There's suspicion that he's involved with the rebellion."

That caught Isaboe's attention, and she lifted her gaze. "What rebellion?"

"You haven't heard? There's been a rumor going around for a while about a group of underground troublemakers who are trying to reignite the rebellion against the Crown."

Isaboe knew that after the Battle of Culloden twenty years earlier, Kirkwall had been one of the last strongholds for sympathizers of the Jacobite Rebellion, offering refuge for fugitives who were running for their lives. But when the British Army invaded the islands, they had snuffed out any surviving Jacobite cells and their defenders, or so it was believed.

Immediately Isaboe's thoughts went to Connor's late nights at the forge, working on the weapons contract. She hated the sudden stab of doubt, but couldn't help wonder if his distance had anything to do with this new rebellion. He worked with a group of laborers, men who may still hold loyalties to their motherland, and some of them may have fought for their country at one time. Rumblings of a Scottish rebellion must have been heard amongst Connor's co-workers, yet he had never mentioned it to her. Had he already been approached? Was he already involved?

"No, I hadn't heard," Isaboe muttered. "What else do you know about it?"

"Not much. And personally, we certainly don't know anyone who is involved with that sort of group."

"How would you? You already mentioned that they're underground, keeping their identities a secret. Your next-door neighbor could be part of their efforts and you wouldn't have any idea," Isaboe blurted before realizing how strange that sounded.

Abby looked at Isaboe for a long moment before responding. "Hmm, well, if you ask me, it's a wasted effort." She picked up her cup and took a sip before continuing. "The Brits have too strong a hold on the islands to let a cell of hot-headed rebels take seed here. If there is an underground movement taking place, it won't go far. That I'm sure of."

But Isaboe didn't have Abby's confidence. Though she had found a sense of welcome in their new community, Connor hadn't settled comfortably into Kirkwall. For him—being more a solider than a gentleman—the new environment seemed foreign and unnecessarily polite. For him, pleasantries with the neighbors were limited to the occasional head nod, and only when necessary. Isaboe watched him struggle to wear the image of a city-man, but it was like watching him try to wrestle into clothes that didn't fit.

Chapter 13

Frustrated
and Confused

"Look at him, struttin' round here like he owns the place, actin' like he's someone important," Rob McClaren spat under his breath. Being one of the more outspoken men in the forge, it was no secret he had little respect for the lead man, Phillip Duncan.

"It's the damn Brits. Faulkner's been usin' the profits he's makin' in textiles on the mainland to buy up property here in Orkney. Then he brings this arse-kissin' oaf to run his shop for im," piped up another disgruntled worker.

"I've 'bout had it with the goddamn Brits treatin' us like bloody slaves," hissed another.

From the safety of his workstation, Connor listened to the complaints of his co-workers, but it was hard to argue with them. He had stayed out of the workplace politics, but there had been plenty of opportunity to just listen, and he knew Duncan acted less like a lead man and more like an owner. Phil Duncan made sure that everyone knew their place, and he was very tight with the owner of the forge, John Faulkner, a wealthy business-man from London who owned a large section of shoreline property and many of the storefronts in town. Faulkner had given Duncan free reign over operations at the forge, but the bootlicker spent more time trying to impress his employer with profits than he did training his hired help.

Experience in the basics of tool making and weaponry was required for a man to be hired as a smith, but not everyone told the truth. Connor knew as well as anyone that when a man needs to feed his family, he'll lie to get the job. This was the case with the cowering and spineless Niles Ramsey. The scrawny man did his best to keep up with the stronger and more experienced blacksmiths, but his work always came up short, and today was no exception.

Strolling through the forge, Duncan examined the inventory as he went. When he came to Niles Ramsey's station, he had no mercy as he ridiculed and berated the sullen man in front of his peers, with threats of immediate firing, which was now a daily occurrence.

"Please, Mr. Duncan, just give me another chance!" Ramsey begged. "I need the job, at least until the kelp harvest starts. I promise my work will improve!"

It was a pathetic, yet familiar scene, and Connor heard a rumbling growl behind him.

"He gives us no breaks, treats his hired help like dogs, and then tells us we should be grateful to have a job at all." Rob spat on the ground. "'Tis bout time Faulkner ken what kind of vermin he's got runnin' this place," he hissed.

Up till then, Connor had quietly removed himself from the conversation and kept his focus on the shovel that was slowly taking shape on his anvil, but he couldn't stop the words from slipping past his lips. "That'd only be a waste of good breath," he murmured. "Faulkner couldna care less. Someone just needs to give Duncan a good arse-kicking, teach him a little respect," Connor said in between blows of his hammer.

"No argument there, friend, but we all need our jobs," Rob said quietly as he stepped up to Connor's workstation. "Any arse-kickin' hasta come from someone else. Ye interested?"

"Though it'd give me great pleasure, I'll pass," Connor said, shooting his co-worker a sideways glance while continuing his work.

"Ye're a man of few words, Grant, but I can see that there's more to ye than just the skill o' the hammer." Rob stepped closer and Connor felt he was being examined as the man spoke again. "I can tell ye ain't got no love for the Brits either. There's a group of us that meets once a week to talk about…politics. Ye might be interested. We could always use some new blood, new ideas."

Though he was pretty sure he knew what kind of group Rob was talking about, as well as what kind of politics were being discussed, Connor had put all that behind him. Looking up, he briefly met the man's waiting stare. "Not interested," he said bluntly before going back to his work. Feeling the steely gaze of his co-worker, Connor had the feeling that Rob wasn't going to take his rejection at face-value, but he also knew he couldn't get involved. There was too much history, too much rage. Though he had tried to keep that part of his life tucked away, he suspected that this wouldn't be the last time he would be approached. Connor knew he wore his anger like a badge, and it wasn't hard to miss.

"My favorite part was when the cranky old man finished his rant, took his seat, and then promptly fell over backwards!" As the family sat around the dinner table, Rosalyn enthusiastically recounted a scene from the play that she and Isaboe had taken in at the theater earlier that day.

Isaboe nodded at the memory. "Aye, that was funny. The whole play was quite delightful, from what I saw of it," she said looking down at the baby nursing at her breast. "Thanks to this little noisemaker, I had to stand out in the lobby and missed a good deal of it."

"You didn't miss that much. And little Kaitlyn wasn't nearly as bad as that rude man who coughed through the whole damn play. I kept praying that he would get up and leave. Honestly, I really wanted to stuff a stocking in his mouth."

Isaboe chuckled slightly and dropped her gaze down to her daughter still nursing, but when she looked back up, she caught Connor staring at her from across the table. It was the same heavy look he had been giving her for weeks, and it was beginning to weigh on her. She watched as he pushed his dinner around with his fork, but his eyes were not on his plate. They were locked onto the curve of her breasts, where the soft, pink flesh was exposed, and he was not nearly subtle enough for her to miss the desire she saw on his face. It wasn't until she gave him a slight smile that he realized he'd been staring. When his eyes lifted to meet hers, he held them for a moment before pushing back his chair. Standing, he walked over to her.

Even as he stood silently beside her, Connor was a hard man to read as he stroked her hair and looked down at the baby suckling at her breast.

She watched his face twitch slightly as if he wanted to speak but didn't know what to say. The touch of his hand felt lovely, but his continued silence not only curbed her pleasure, it was becoming frustrating, and once again he said nothing. He gave her a quick kiss before heading toward the front door.

"You're not going back to work now, are you?" she asked, already knowing the answer. "It's almost dark."

He paused with his hand on the doorknob before turning back. "I'll be home late. Don't wait up for me." The closing door punctuated his words.

Isaboe looked over at Rosalyn, but she only gave her daughter a sympathetic smile. The weight of Connor's distance was becoming more than Isaboe was willing to tolerate, but she wasn't sure how to address it. She only knew it couldn't go on much longer.

Having been married before, Isaboe knew that men could sometimes be difficult, but thinking back to her previous life with Nathan, Connor stood in such stark contrast it was like comparing a house cat to a caged lion. Nathan had been an educated man, an engineer of bridges, and he had confronted his challenges with calm, well-thought-out solutions. Life with Nathan was ordinary and simple, but at least she had known what to expect. With Connor, it was a completely different situation. What was behind his furrowed expressions, and why had he become so aloof? As Isaboe wondered, a quick thought flashed through her mind. It was a question she'd been afraid to ask, but a nagging voice kept repeating the same lines: *Maybe he doesn't want to be with me. Maybe he really wants to jump back into that damn rebellion, and he's only staying with me out of obligation.*

As she shook off her negative thoughts, Isaboe noticed that her baby had finally fallen asleep. Careful not to disturb her, Isaboe gently laid Kaitlyn in her cradle and then waited a moment to make sure she wouldn't wake up. Confident that the baby would stay asleep, Isaboe grabbed her cloak as she came out of the room, pulling it around her shoulders. "Kaitlyn should sleep for a while. I'm going to the forge," she said as she headed for the door.

"Are you sure that's wise? Connor may not want you there," Rosalyn said as she began taking the dinner dishes from the table.

"I can't take this distance anymore. If he won't talk to me here, then maybe I can get him to open up away from home." Isaboe gave her mother a long look before walking out the door, silently asking her to understand.

When Isaboe entered the forge, all work immediately ceased. Eyes looked up from their projects as whistles and comments rustled around her like the wind. She glanced around the forge, lit dimly by hanging lanterns and smoky fire pits. As her eyes finally landed on Connor, his back was turned to her, but just as she started in his direction, she jolted to a halt when he punched another man in the face, knocking him to the ground. When he then turned and briskly walked to where Isaboe stood, the look on Connor's face made her question her decision to come; perhaps her mother had been correct.

"Why did you hit that man?" she asked as he approached.

"He said somethin' he should've kept to himself," he snarled. Grabbing Isaboe by the arm, he quickly escorted her from the forge while the whistles and lewd comments followed them outside.

"What are ye doing here, Isaboe? This is no place for a woman!" Connor growled as they rounded the stone building.

"I came here to talk with you. Let go of me, Connor, you're hurting my arm!" she snapped, trying to keep up with his longer stride.

Finally releasing her when they were out of sight from the workers, Connor turned and addressed her. "Why are ye here? Is there somethin' wrong?"

"No," Isaboe said defensively, rubbing her arm.

"Then what's so important that couldn'ave waited till I got home?"

"And just when would that have been, Connor?" Isaboe stood tall and lifted her chin. "You never stay home for long, and when you are, you're distant. You leave first thing in the morning, come home for supper, and then you're back down here until after dark. What is so important here that it keeps you away from us? Why do you seem so angry and aloof all the time?"

Connor gave her a curious look, as if he didn't understand her question.

"Are ye seriously telling me that ye dinnae ken?" Though he looked stern and unsympathetic, Isaboe held her ground. Connor was her protector. She knew he wouldn't hurt her, but she couldn't let this nonsense continue; his anger be damned!

"No. I don't know. Tell me. Have I done something wrong?"

"It's what ye haven't done, Isaboe," he grumbled through gritted teeth.

"And what's that?"

Connor closed his eyes and took a deep breath, chewing on his bottom lip before he finally looked at her. His frustration was clearly etched across his face. "Ye've been married before. Are ye seriously telling me that *Nathan* never acted like this?"

"*What?* Don't bring Nathan into this! Just tell me what this is *really* about, and you can start by telling me the truth!" Isaboe paused and swallowed hard. "If you don't want to be with me, just say it!" Isaboe heard the fear in her voice, hoping desperately that she was wrong.

Connor softened his expression. "Seriously, Isaboe? Is that what ye think?"

"I don't know!" Isaboe almost shouted. "You won't talk to me. As far as I know, you're planning to run off to America, or, or trying to find a reason to fight someone – *anyone!*"

Connor ran his hands through his hair and took a deep breath, trying to gather a bit of calm before responding. "Ye really dinnae ken why I've been so frustrated?"

"No, I don't! Why don't you enlighten me?" She snapped, waiting for his reply.

"Ye've left me out in the cold, Isaboe. I get a few kisses here and there, but that's it. A man can only live on kisses for so long! It's been a month. How much longer do I have to wait?" With each word he spoke, the furrow between his brows deepened. She could see the veins above his temples pulsing, and the thin line of his mouth was rigid and tight. "I know we've not been gettin' along so well lately, but I am trying, Isaboe. I've been patient, and I ken ye have a baby to care for, but ye also have a man who needs ye. That's why I spend so much time here. I take out my frustrations by beatin' the hell out of a piece of iron!"

Listening to his words and seeing the honesty in his face, Isaboe felt her fear melt into joy. She attempted to hold back a smile, but without much success.

"So ye think my condition is amusing?" Connor's tone turned vicious.

"No, I'm not laughing at you. I'm just terribly relieved. I was thinking all sorts of things. Now I know you've been irritable and distant just because…"

But before she could finish, Conner grabbed her arm again and escorted her away from the view of the others on the street. She was startled when he shoved her up against a wall, harder than necessary, and it would have been humorous but for how dangerous she knew Connor could be. She wasn't afraid for herself, not with him; he was the man who fought against the fey and the Brits, and had done so just for her. In his beautiful anger, she was instantly flooded with visions of what his victims must have felt just before he snuffed out their lives. But at the same time, she felt a deep carnal stirring, and wondered what it was in his fierceness that triggered those feelings in her. Almost like waking up from a dream, she began to understand what had been causing his suffering.

"Aye, *just because* I want to take this body of yers *every* moment of *every* day, so much that I canna think straight," he growled. "And that makes it very hard to be around ye."

"Does it really?" Isaboe asked with a coy smile as she reached toward Connor's inner thigh.

But he grabbed her hand before she reached her intended target. "Dinnae start somethin' that ye canna finish, *boirreannach*. I'm just *fuckin'* horny enough to take ye right here in the street. Now go home, Isaboe!" Connor released her gently, but his look and tone were adamant.

Isaboe lifted up on her tip toes and kissed him. "I promise it will be worth the wait," she whispered with a smile before stepping away from the wall.

The hoots and whistles started the moment she kissed him, and Connor turned to see a handful of fellow blacksmiths standing outside the forge and making obscene gestures. Turning back toward Isaboe, he placed an arm around her shoulder. "On second thought, I'll walk ye home."

CHAPTER 14

FIRST CONTACT

After escorting her home, Connor returned to the forge, and Isaboe breezed in through the front door feeling less troubled after their talk. Looking up from her needlepoint, Rosalyn had obviously noticed her daughter's lighter mood and the slight smile that brushed her lips. "So, I take it things went well."

"Yes, I think things are much better, or, at least, they will be. Connor's just been a bit *frustrated*," Isaboe muttered.

"I'd say more than just a bit." Rosalyn dropped her work into her lap. "He's been stomping around here like a bull-elk in rut. So, what are you planning to do about that?"

Taken slightly aback by her mother's forwardness, Isaboe paused for a moment. "Well, I guess I'll take care of it when I feel I'm ready," she said, quietly chewing her bottom lip as she took a seat opposite her mother. It was flattering to be wanted in such a way, but there was more to her hesitation than waiting for full recovery.

Rosalyn watched quietly as her daughter struggled to say what was on her mind. "What is it?"

Hesitating, Isaboe finally met her mother's questioning eyes. "We live like a married couple, regardless of whether or not we're sharing a bed. But marriage hasn't even come up. Don't you think we should at least be discussing it? We have a daughter, and she's been given his name, but I haven't. Our neighbors all assume that we're married, and sometimes I feel we're living a lie. I know that Connor has needs, but what about my feelings? What about my needs? There is the issue of what's proper, and a matter of commitment on his part."

"Commitment?" Rosalyn said, shooting Isaboe a surprised scowl. "Connor is *completely* committed to you, and you know that. Whether or not he's made it official yet is secondary. And who gives a shit what our neighbors think? If you're holding out for a proposal because you think somehow your virtue is at stake, that ship has long since sailed, no?"

Feeling the sting of truth in Rosalyn's words, Isaboe dropped her gaze. They had all been through hell in the last six months and Connor had been her rock. He had been at her side through it all. She knew he was committed, but she still couldn't help wanting something more official. Even just a discussion of marriage would help to ease her doubts, but he had never brought it up on his own. When Isaboe had made a few vague statements about the subject, it seemed the conversation would always turn in a different direction, intentionally or not.

"I know, baby first and relationship second hasn't been easy for either of you," Rosalyn added. "But you know that he loves you. He's still trying to figure out where he fits into this new world. It's not been easy for him, Isaboe. You need to give him more time." She picked up her needlepoint before continuing. "And in Connor's defense, you've already given him a taste of the nectar, dear. He knows what he's missing." Rosalyn paused, shooting an upward glance to watch her daughter's reaction. "With all the time and attention that Kaitlyn has been demanding, you may not have noticed, but I have. Your man has been buzzing around here like a bee that can't get into the hive. He can smell the honey, but he can't dip his stinger into it."

Isaboe couldn't help but smile at her mother's analogy, nor stop the blush that rose to her cheeks. "So, here's the other thing. Obviously, Connor and I can conceive. I'm not ready for another child right now. Do you know if there's something I can do or take to prevent that from happening? I mean, other than abstinence?" Isaboe wasn't sure how, but if anyone knew, it would be her mother. Rosalyn's special gifts and years of study gave her powers, skills, and deep knowledge of the mysterious and the arcane.

"Aye, there is a mix of strong herbs that can be steeped into a tea. Drinking this daily has proven to be effective. It will most likely give you cramps for a while, but your body will eventually adjust."

"How long does it take to work?"

"You should be on it for at least a week. How much time do you have?"

"Well, by the look on his face this evening, I think I should get started as soon as possible."

Rosalyn gave Isaboe a smile and a nod. "I'll go by the apothecary in the morning to see if they…," suddenly she cut off in mid-sentence as an odd look fell across her face.

"What's wrong?" Isaboe asked, seeing her mother's transformation. But Rosalyn didn't answer. Dropping her needlepoint, she jumped up from her chair and ran to Isaboe's room, where Kaitlyn was sleeping. Isaboe was right on her heels, and when the two women rushed into the room, what they saw stopped them in their tracks.

The low-burning lantern offered only a soft, dim light, but it was bright enough to see that the baby was awake. Her eyes seemed to be following a swarm of iridescent blue balls of light that hovered above her cradle, floating on an invisible wave of energy. At least that's how they appeared to Isaboe—astral beings that were just too close to her daughter. Isaboe's protective motherly instincts reacted as she started toward her child, but Rosalyn reached out to stop her.

"It's alright, Isaboe. Look at Kaitlyn. She's not afraid; she's connecting."

Seeing that Rosalyn was right, Isaboe began to relax as she watched the expression on her daughter's face. There was no fear as Kaitlyn's eyes danced with the lights hovering above her. On the contrary, she seemed delighted. "Who are they? What do they want?" Isaboe asked, hearing the fear in her voice.

"I don't know why they are here, but they mean her no harm." Rosalyn's voice was calm and controlled.

"What do they want with my daughter?" It took every ounce of Isaboe's restraint not to rush over and snatch her baby out of danger, but she held her ground as every nerve was poised to strike.

"It appears they're just…observing. Maybe they're here to watch over her."

"She doesn't need the fey watching over her. I don't want them anywhere near her!" Isaboe started toward the cradle again but stepped back when the balls of light shot out across the room in a sweeping circle. Streaking by in a blur of blue energy, they barely missed the two ladies and then escaped, one-by-one, out the window that had been left slightly ajar. All except the very last; floating in the air directly in front of them, it suddenly transformed. What once had been merely a ball of light was now a tiny faerie fluttering on iridescent wings as it hovered in front of them, making eye contact. She was beautiful, minute, and exquisite in all her detail. With her sparkling eyes, pointed ears, and graceful wings, she was an incredibly attractive little being. A quick smile crossed the fey's delicate face when Rosalyn returned the unspoken greeting. Then she abruptly fluttered toward the window and disappeared before their eyes.

Isaboe quickly scooped up her baby before turning to Rosalyn. "What just happened?" she asked with an edge of panic in her voice, holding Kaitlyn to her breast much tighter than necessary.

"There was nothing to be afraid of. Kaitlyn was never in danger. I believe what we just saw were Queen Brighid's scouts. You remember her, yes?"

With eyes wide, Isaboe only nodded, recalling the brilliant blue aura of the beautiful Fey Queen who had made an appearance at her bedside on the night her daughter was born.

"When Brighid touched you with her wand, *before* Kaitlyn was even born, I knew then that your daughter was going to be someone very special." Offering a comforting smile, Rosalyn walked over to stand next to Isaboe. "I know this is hard for you to hear," she said, as she gently touched the soft down on the child's head, "but I believe that Kaitlyn will have powers that exceed my own. She has been twice endowed with the gift of faerie magic, once by Lorien in the realm of the Underlings, then again here in this world by Queen Brighid while she was still in your womb. Your daughter is more than just the wee bairn that you hold in your arms, my dear."

Isaboe didn't want to think about her daughter having anything to do with the fey, much less having fey powers. She looked down into the face of her infant babe, innocent, delicate, and apparently extremely gifted. "But what does that mean?" she asked, looking back at her mother as she heard the anxiety in her own voice.

"I don't know yet what her purpose in life will be, only that it will be of great importance. It's safe to say that her life will be far from ordinary." Rosalyn looked compassionately at her daughter. "I hope you can come to accept that, my dear, because I'm afraid you won't have much choice in the matter."

Isaboe swallowed hard, knowing that her mother was right, and quietly hating it.

After the incident with the tiny fey protectors, the tension between Isaboe and Connor seemed less urgent. Now that Kaitlyn was born, they all wanted to believe that Lorien and the Underlings were done with them. But the recent appearance of the fey brought on a flood of new worries. All Isaboe wanted was a normal life that dealt with only common, every day, *mortal* issues—things she could wrap her mind around. The reminder that her precious little girl would be anything but normal, and wondering how they would deal with Kaitlyn's abilities as she grew, gnawed at her insides. But it was obvious that their lives would never be simple or ordinary, and the sooner she accepted that, the easier it would be to face what their future would bring.

Rosalyn suggested that Kaitlyn sleep in her room from then on, just to be safe. If Brighid's scouts had found them, Lorien could too. There was no point in taking any chances. Kaitlyn was still young enough to be snatched away, raised, and manipulated by the evil Fey Queen for her own nefarious purposes.

Yet, as the days passed without more signs of the fey, their day-to-day concerns pushed the mysterious visit from the forefront of Isaboe's mind. It was now her turn to be in a foul mood brought on by cramps from the tea that Rosalyn prepared for her each morning. But, as promised, the uncomfortable adjustment subsided by the end of the week, allowing Isaboe to focus on other matters.

Asking her mother to watch Kaitlyn for a few hours, she set off to do just that. Knowing that it bothered Connor to spend her inheritance for trivial purchases, she waited until she was alone before sneaking off to the ladies' dress shop, which offered the latest fashions from London. She found exactly what she was looking for—a beautiful white nightgown. It was lacy and very expensive, but she didn't care. She'd promised Connor that it would be worth the wait.

Chapter 15

warrior, make me
a promise

The knives and swords that the crew had been working on day and night would fulfill an order placed by the British Army, scheduled for shipment to Fort Bradley by the end of the week. Rumor had made its way through the forge that Faulkner was going to make a killing on the order, but only if it was completed on time. Duncan had realized that the project was almost too large for his forge, but to accomplish it on time would greatly improve his standing with his employer, so he had pushed his men ruthlessly.

With checklist in hand, the overseer made his way through the forge, examining and documenting each weapon before it was placed into the box for shipping. For the most part, the making of a dirk was a simple task, but a sword took more skill and practice. Experienced smiths took to the challenge, heating the iron for hours to remove the impurities, folding the molten metal and striking the hardened steel until it became a perfect weapon—sleek, smooth, and lethal. But not every piece of work passed inspection, and subpar work was deducted from the laborer's pay. Iron ore wasn't free, and the Brits didn't pay for an inferior product.

"I'm tired of wasting good money on ye, Ramsey. Ye're finished here! And these worthless pieces of iron are coming outta' whatever ye might've earned, so dinnae bother asking me for this week's pay, cause there ain't none for you!" Even with help from his co-workers, Niles Ramsey was still an unskilled amateur, as his work reflected. Physically grabbing the man by the back of his shirt, Duncan dragged him to the front of the building and threw him out into the street, ignoring the man's pitiful pleas.

Connor and his co-workers watched as Ramsey tumbled to the ground, face-first and belittled. The men had stood by as Duncan terrorized their fellow worker, not willing to step out lest they be the next target. But they had taken the bumbling fool under their wing, helping him as best they could, and it was clear that the abuse was uncalled for. Ramsey may not have had much of a backbone, but he had a wife and two kids to feed.

Connor was standing nearby at the moment when Rob snapped; he watched with concern as his co-worker's fingers closed around a dirk, newly made and sharp as she would ever be. His weapon held low, the man stepped toward Duncan's turned back, and Connor had to make a choice. Murdering Duncan, satisfying as it would be, would be a costly mistake. "Not now. Not here," he said, grabbing Rob's arm.

When Duncan turned around, he saw that his crew was staring at him. "What're ye looking at?" he snarled as he stalked back into the forge, inspecting the weapons that were about to fill the boxes. "I'm not paying any of ye for even one blade over the order. If ye've met yer quota, get the hell out of here. Ye're done for the day!"

Taking off his blacksmith's apron, Rob tossed it onto his bench as he approached Connor, who was doing the same. "Ye shouldn't have stopped me, but thanks for keepin' a level head."

Connor only nodded.

"We've got a meeting tonight, Brother. You should come," Rob said quietly.

Connor knew it was a risk, but the incident with Duncan had stirred something inside him. Rob had thanked him for keeping a level head, but inside he was itching to give Duncan the arse-kicking he deserved, and knowing that he was making weapons for the Brits left a bitter taste in his mouth. "What the hell? It can't hurt to just show up and listen, aye?"

The cooked goose that had cost more than she cared to admit now sat on the dining table, cold and shriveled, looking less and less appetizing as the evening wore on. The once tall candlesticks, added for ambiance, now lay in a pool of melted wax, and the flames flickered only inches above the base.

Dressed in her new nightgown, Isaboe sat in the dark with arms folded across her chest, seething. She reviewed over and over again all the preparations she had gone through in the last two days to make this evening special. Knowing the weapons contract at the forge was almost complete, and that Connor wouldn't have to return to work after dinner, she had coerced Rosalyn to take Kaitlyn next-door to Abby's house for the evening so they could be alone. But he hadn't even bothered to come home.

She replayed in her mind what she had told him before he left that morning. *"Don't stay at the forge late tonight. I have a surprise for you."* What part of that had he not understood? She had given him the coy smile, a come-hither look, and rubbed up close to him before he left. When had he stopped paying attention? For weeks he had been hounding her, running his hands over her hips every time she walked by, yet somehow, he'd missed all of her signals. Infuriating, *foolish man!* After all she had prepared for him, he'd stood her up! Oh, yes, when he did finally walk in that door, she *would* have a surprise for him, but he wasn't going to like it.

The sound of men's voices in the street below drew her attention. Looking out the window, she saw Connor talking to another man, standing under the street lantern. Though she couldn't make out the conversation, the expression on both of their faces was serious. The other man did most of the talking while Connor listened, nodding in response.

A flash of recollection jolted her. A few days earlier Abby had mentioned hearing rumors that an underground rebellion was brewing. A lump grew in Isaboe's throat as she watched until the two men shook hands and the stranger disappeared back into the night. Quickly lighting a wall sconce to brighten up the room, she watched Connor enter the house with a dark expression on his face.

"Connor, who was that man you were talking to?" she asked as he closed the door.

"Nobody, just a fellow from the forge," he answered indifferently.

"What were you talking about?" She didn't like his aloofness, or the fact that he didn't offer up a name.

"It's not important. What's for dinner?" he muttered, brushing off her question while he removed his coat and walked toward his room without even looking at her.

He was ignoring *her?* Isaboe was already angry, and that only intensified her fury. Stopping him before he made it down the hallway, she let him know how she felt. "No, Connor. You don't get off that easy. I've heard the rumors, and I know what you were talking about, so don't lie to me!"

"This doesn't concern ye, Isaboe, and ye shouldn't listen to gossip." His reply was as cold as the hard look in his eyes.

"Don't talk to me like I don't understand what's going on. Everything you do concerns me, Connor, especially when it has anything to do with this foolish talk of rebellion! I know you. You can't stay out of trouble. It's your nature to get involved. Your rebellion already failed. Why are you doing this to us?"

"I'm not doing anything!" he barked. "Not yet. But if I do, it's about justice for all the lives the Brits have taken!"

"Justice? Don't you mean *revenge?*" she yelled back. "You promised me we were going to put the past behind us, but you're not even trying. You're still living in the past; you never let it go. This bloody cause almost killed you twenty years ago! Will you not be satisfied until it does?" Isaboe watched as Connor's rigid expression become more intense, but she didn't let his glare intimidate her. "Let me remind you, Connor; you killed a British Officer, and they are probably still looking for us. If you draw attention to yourself, you put this whole family at risk. You have another cause to fight for now, or have you forgotten what was hovering over our daughter's bed just a week ago?" Isaboe's fear that Connor would be pulled back into the rebellion was real. He was a warrior. Fighting for Scotland was in his blood.

At the mention of his daughter's name, Connor realized he hadn't yet heard her cries, even as her parents were screaming at each other. "Where's Kaitlyn? Where's Rosalyn?"

"Oh, aren't you the observant one," she said flippantly. "You're so involved in making a stand for *justice* that you can't see what's right in front of your face. Look around you, Connor. Look at me!" Isaboe waved her arms about the room before pointing out her lacy attire. "Did you forget that I had a *surprise* for you tonight?"

A sunken look melted over Connor's face when he realized what he had forgotten. As he took in his surroundings, defeat and failure began scrawling across his face, and Isaboe knew exactly how she looked—sensuous and livid.

She watched scornfully as Connor ran his hands through his hair, his mouth drawn into a thin, tight line. He knew it. He realized how bad his mistake had been and how much it was going to cost him. His frustration scrawled itself across his face.

"Well, I hope your cause can keep you warm tonight, because I want nothing to do with it!" she shouted, before spinning on her heels and retreating to her room.

After slamming the door behind her, she stood next to her bed seething. The next thing she heard was Connor's low, rumbling growl as he shouted his frustration. "*Fuck!* Goddamn bloody *fuck!*"

He's mad? What right does he have to be angry? I'm the one who was stood-up! Isaboe plopped down on the bed, infuriated and insulted. She had tried her best to make this relationship work, but Connor's hardened attitude was taking its toll on her patience. How were they to make a life together when they couldn't agree on anything—when they had nothing in common but mutual attraction?

"*Breagha...*" he said softly as the door creaked open. Isaboe stood up and threw a pillow at him. "Get out!" she shouted, holding another pillow in her hands.

Apparently deciding that if Isaboe really wanted to keep him out she would have thrown something more dangerous than a pillow, Connor moved forward cautiously. "I'm so sorry I forgot, my love. I'm a dunderhead and a jackass. Ye have every right to be mad at me. Ye look absolutely stunning. Is that a new gown?" Giving her his best, most charming smile he took small, cautious steps toward the bed and caught the next pillow she threw at him.

"No. You don't get to come in here, apologize, and then expect to crawl into my bed. That's not happening, Connor. Just get out!" she yelled before turning her back to him and sat down on the bed as she tried to control her rage.

Isaboe felt the bed move when he sat down behind her, but she didn't acknowledge him. She was angry, hurt, and damn sure he wasn't getting what he wanted tonight. When she felt his hand on her shoulder, she scooted down the bed, brushing him off, both literally and figuratively.

"This isn't going to happen. Just leave me alone."

"Isaboe, if ye only let me explain..."

"Explain what?" She turned to face him. "That the reason you stood me up is because you were with a bunch of hotheaded radicals planning to overthrow the Crown? Just how do you explain that, Connor, and expect me to be alright with it?"

She knew he had no defense, and he didn't offer one. Instead, he was affectionate, coy and sweet, trying to ply her into accepting his apology, and part of her hated knowing that eventually she'd give in. But Isaboe wasn't about to make it easy for him. Even though his stupid but persuasive charms, gorgeous blue eyes, and damned patience had slowly melted some of her earlier rage, she wasn't surrendering—not yet.

However, when Connor brushed his fingertips lightly over the ridged line of her shoulders, sending warm tingles down her spine, she could feel her defenses waning, leaving her vulnerable to his seduction. Her new gown was revealing, designed to create temptation, and soon his warm lips joined in concert with his fingers, murmuring little praises and seductions as he tasted her skin. Moving up from her shoulder to the dip of her neck, his lips finally approached hers, and she struggled to hold in the whimpers of pleasure he hoped to coax from her.

When he finally took a chance to go for a kiss, she shoved her hand into his chest, pushing him back. "No. Not until you make me a promise first."

"Whatever ye want, its yers, my love," he said, his voice husky as he ran a hand down her bare arm.

But she pulled away, putting space between them. "I want you to promise me that you are done with this ridiculous cause. Look at me, Connor. Tell me you won't get involved with this group of men. That tonight was it, and you're done with them." Isaboe searched his eyes, wanting desperately for him to say the right thing. "I need to know that protecting your family is more important than this rebellion."

"If ye feel that strongly against it, then I promise. I won't get involved," he said easily as he again reached for her.

Mark of the Faerie

"No," she said, pushing his hand aside. "That's not good enough."

"I gave ye my promise. What more do ye want from me?"

"I want to hear from the man inside." Isaboe slid closer to him, looking deep into his soul. "What say you, Braden MacPherson? Can you make me the same promise?"

That seemed to properly catch his attention, and a piercing look hardened his face. Darkness filled his eyes as his expression became stoic and threatening.

Isaboe thought she had seen all the features of his multi-faceted personality, including the hidden side that he tried to keep in check. But this was a new look she hadn't seen before. His furrowed brows deepened, his eyes appeared black beneath half-closed lids, and his mouth drew into a tight, thin line as he worked his jaw. He looked mysterious—dangerous even. A shiver ran down Isaboe's back, and she questioned if calling on Braden had been as brilliant a move as she'd thought.

He then sat up straight and locked gazes with her before placing a fist against his chest. "I give you my word, as a Scotsman and a warrior. May the wolves tear out my heart and the buzzards spread my innards to the far corners of the Earth if I break my promise to ye."

Isaboe finally let out the breath she hadn't realized she'd been holding. "Well, that was a wee bit extreme, but it will do."

Braden instantly melted back into the man she knew, who had only one thing on his mind. Giving her a coy smile and slithering closer, Connor gently kissed her exposed shoulder. The eyes that looked lethal only seconds before now smiled playfully. "So, am I forgiven?"

"For now. Though I know it's just a matter of time before you say or do something stupid again." She was still a bit angry, but as he smiled with his damn, smoldering blue eyes, what was left of her defenses melted away like vapor.

When she leaned in closer, he took that as the invitation it was. Running his fingers gently up her arm, he slid the strap of her lacy new nightgown off her shoulder and kissed where it had lain. Isaboe shivered as he gently nipped at her skin, and the musty smell of Connor that she found so comforting, so enticing, eased away the last of her anger. He was here with her now, and there was no doubt that both he *and* Braden loved her enough to choose her and their little family over some doomed cause. Damn, she loved this stupid, ignorant, hotheaded fool!

Coaxing her to lay back, he kissed the line of her neck up to her mouth, and when he finally reached her lips, she moaned against him. The kiss was hard and wet, and Isaboe felt the hunger of it as he pulled her closer into him.

"Wait." Pushing him back, she took a good look at his face, focusing on his features. A moment ago she was looking at a battle-hardened solider, a man she didn't really know. Now, it was Connor hovering above her, the man she loved. Yet, she wondered if there were more sides of him still hidden, just waiting to make an appearance.

"Yes, my love?" he asked softly as he brushed a thumb over her cheekbone.

Isaboe let her eyes dance with his before answering. "I was only trying to be sure of who it is I'll be making love to."

He gave her a cocky grin. "Who would you prefer?" His voice was husky and deep as he sensually ran a hand through her hair.

"Well, to be honest, Braden kind of frightened me."

Connor chuckled. "Dinnae worry, *Breagha*. I hear he's crazy about ye." Pausing, he kissed her softly before leaning back. "And I dinnae think ye need to worry about him showing up again tonight."

Staring up into his eyes, Isaboe tried to catch another glimpse of the mysterious soldier in Connor's face. She was somewhat surprised when a part of her was a little disappointed that Braden wouldn't be back tonight, but she kept that thought to herself, and instead wrapped her arms around her lover's neck and kissed him deeply. Maybe, with a little coaxing, the warrior in Connor might make an appearance after all.

CHAPTER 16

THE HOODED MAN

"I've been goin' over the numbers, and I believe we'll see a damn decent profit on the Brits' contract," Phillip Duncan said to his companion as they walked briskly through the dark alley. "With the final package shipped ahead of schedule, Faulkner should be more than pleased."

"Gardy Loo!" shouted a disconnected female voice from overhead, and both men stepped quickly to avoid the foul-smelling liquid being dumped from a second-story window.

"Why do ye care if Faulkner's pleased?" Duncan's companion asked, stepping around the muck. "It's not yer pockets that are being filled."

"By keepin' the cost down and fillin' Faulkner's pockets, he'll ensure me a more proper position," Duncan replied with a self-satisfied smile. "I'll be done with that disgusting, dirty forge, and the low-class assholes I have to tolerate. Faulkner promised that if I showed a bigger profit this year, I'd be seeing a management position in my future, working for him in London." He stood a little taller when he mentioned the big city.

"Sounds like Faulkner's dangling one hell of a carrot. That'd be a taste of the good life, Phillip, something that ye ain't used to. So, what's yer plan to make the forge more profitable, and who are ye gonna have to rob to make it happen?"

Duncan snickered. "Does it matter? All I care about is getting out of this stinking place before the kelp harvest begins and getting out of that dingy little rental; t'ain't fit for rats. I deserve to live in the big city, in a grand home more suited to my status, and I dinnae care if I have to step on a few bastards to get there."

"Well, good luck with that, and watch yer back," the other man said as he turned and walked down another alley, leaving Phillip Duncan alone with his delusions of grandeur.

But his wishful thinking was abruptly interrupted when a large hand reached out from the dark, pulling him into a tight space between the buildings. Duncan squirmed, attempting to free himself, but his attacker threw him up against the cold, wet wall.

"What the...?!"

"Shut up and listen," growled the assailant as he held Duncan pinned against the building. "Yer days of being a tyrant are over." He was a hooded man with a voice that was low and muffled, his face covered by the darkness. "The next time ye treat a fellow Scotsman like a dog, ye won't be coming back out of the shadows. This is yer only warning."

In the next moment Duncan was forcibly shoved, landing face-first in the mud. When he looked back at the alcove, there was no one, only darkness. With his heart thumping in his ears, the frightened man quickly rose to his feet and ran the rest of the way home.

With the weapons contract fulfilled, business at the forge returned to its usual pace, which kept only the six best blacksmiths working. The making of tools, household items, pots, pans, and candlestick holders once again took precedence as the men worked on restocking the inventory for one of Faulkner's many storefronts.

"There's another meetin' tonight," Rob McClaren said as he wiped his brow with a dirty rag. "Ye coming?" he whispered, tucking the rag back into his pocket as he stepped toward Connor's workstation.

"Nay. I promised the little lady I'd stay out of it," he said between blows of his hammer.

"Ye're lettin' a woman tell ye what to do?"

Connor continued his rhythmic swinging without flinching. "If I hang out with yer ugly mugs, I get kicked out of her bed. It wasn't a hard choice to make."

Rob could only nod. "Well, if I had a woman at home that looked like yers, I'd probably make the same choice. If ye ever get tired of her, let me know."

This time Connor stopped his hammer in mid swing and shot his co-worker a warning glare from under his furrowed brow.

"Hey, yer misses is a hard one not to notice," Rob said defensively. "And her mother ain't bad either."

With that comment, Connor stood up straight, turned and faced him. Rob was dangerously close to crossing the line.

Raising both hands, Rob stepped back. "Dinnae mean any offense, Brother, just saying. Ye can't fault a man fer lookin' at a beautiful woman."

Connor didn't say a word; he didn't have to. His eyes said it all. He regarded his co-worker for a moment, debating whether leading the man into a fight would reinforce his reputation. It would send a warning that Connor Grant and his family weren't to be fucked with. Or would he be just acting like another hotheaded asshole? Finally, he shrugged and returned to his work.

Rob started back to his own station, but then stopped and turned toward Connor. "What I want to ken is how a lug like you got a woman like that?"

Never looking up from his work, a slow smile crossed Connor's face. "Blessed by a wizard," he said just quietly enough that his companion would assume he'd heard wrong.

But before Rob McClaren could ask for a clarification, a sudden burst of energy at the front of the building pulled everyone's attention from their work. Rob and Connor both looked up to see a pitiful-looking Niles Ramsey standing in front of his former lead-man, twisting the hat he held in his hands and pleading for his job back.

"I'll not waste any more of my time or Faulkner's money on you, so go beggin' elsewhere!" Duncan snarled and turned back toward the forge but stopped abruptly when he saw that all the smiths had ceased their work to watch how he would handle the situation. A quick flash of terror crossed his face, and he refused to meet the gaze of any of the men standing in his forge. Turning away from their judging eyes, he called out, "Wait."

Ramsey spun around with a hint of hope in his eyes. "Aye, Mr. Duncan?"

"Go see McCoy at Faulkner's stables. Tell him I sent you. Maybe you can shovel horseshit better than you can bend iron. I'm giving you another chance, Ramsey, but dinnae make me sorry. If I hear you're slacking, you'll not work in this town again."

Ramsey mumbled a few quick words of gratitude and promised he would work like the devil before running off in the direction of the stables.

"What'd ye make of that?" Rob asked after the rest of the men had returned to work now that the entertainment was over.

"Looks like Duncan has had a change of heart," Connor said as he removed his apron.

"Duncan ain't got no heart." Rob shot his co-worker a wary glance as he stepped up next to Connor. "So, is this yer way of stayin' out of it?"

"I dinnae ken what ye're talking about, Rob, and I'm out of here, done listening to ye flap yer geggie." After walking up to Duncan to collect his few coins for the day, Connor left the forge, but he could feel Rob's eyes burning in the back of his head.

Foster and Abby Graham owned and operated the local theater, and it was Abby's job to prepare the stage for upcoming performances, such as this week's speaker. It was an early summer morning when Isaboe took Kaitlyn to the theater to help Abby hang a new curtain. She brought a blanket for her daughter and placed it on the stage floor, giving her a few toys and hoping to keep the child occupied while she worked.

"Thank you so much for giving me a hand today, Isaboe," Abby said as she carried a large pile of dark, red fabric in her arms, piled so high it almost covered her face.

"Here, let me help." Isaboe took one end of the heavy curtain and helped Abby lay it out across the floor against the back wall. "This is beautiful fabric."

"Isn't it wonderful! It came from London. Foster placed the order last time he was there, and it just arrived yesterday. This is really going to class up the stage, don't you think?"

"Oh, absolutely. So, where do we start?" Isaboe was eager to help and was glad that Kaitlyn seemed content, sitting on her blanket and shaking her rattle.

"We'll start right here." Abby pointed to a rod hanging from the ceiling several inches above their heads. "Let me go get the hooks," she said as she walked to the other side of the stage.

Noticing a stool only a few feet away, Isaboe retrieved it. Stepping up, she saw that she would be tall enough for the task. Just as Abby handed her a curtain-hook, Kaitlyn caught her attention. Still sitting on the blanket, the baby was feverously shaking the small, cloth-wrapped metal rattle.

"Your daughter seems to really enjoy her toy," Abby said as she lifted the curtain and handed one corner to Isaboe.

Stabbing the hook into the corner of the thick fabric, Isaboe hung it before looking over her shoulder at Kaitlyn. "Oh, yes, that's the rattle Connor made for her. He even made the wooden beads. The little harness bells he picked up at the stable make a pleasant sound, don't you think? It's one of her favorite toys." As Isaboe watched Abby staring wistfully at Kaitlyn, she didn't miss the longing in her friend's eyes. "Do you and Foster want to have children?" she asked, reaching for another hook.

"Well, we'd both love to have a family, but so far..." Abby paused and dropped her face, "the Lord hasn't blessed us."

Isaboe saw the pain in her friend's eyes. "I'm sure a child will come," she said, offering a smile and moving the stool over before taking another hook from Abby.

"We've been married for over five years now. If it was going to happen, it would've happened by now. I don't think I can conceive." The defeat and disappointment were clear on Abby's face, and Isaboe felt a stab of sadness for her. "His mother wants him to leave me." Abby's words were as cold and hard as her expression. "If I can't give him children, I'm not sure he'll stay."

"Oh, Abby, Foster loves you regardless. So what if you don't have children? He would never leave you."

Abby's stare was rimmed with doubt as she placed a hand over her heart. "Won't he? I don't know for sure. A lot of people come and go out of this theater; some of the women are very beautiful and appealing—women who I'm sure could bear his children."

"Don't talk like that. You're still young, and anything is possible," Isaboe said softly as she placed a hand over her friend's. "You need to appreciate what you have today, right now. You and Foster have a great relationship. I know that. I've seen you two together. His mother must be blind if she's telling him to leave you, either that, or she's just a stupid cow!"

"I know you're right," Abby replied with a forced smile. "I just feel so inadequate. It's my job to give him children."

"That's nonsense. You're a fine woman and a wonderful wife. Don't underestimate how important you are to him," Isaboe said as she pulled the stool over and stepped up again.

Abby didn't respond, just forced a smile and nodded before she handed Isaboe another hook. At the same time, a *clinking* sound drew Isaboe's attention, followed by a baby's pitiful sob. She looked over her shoulder to see that Kaitlyn had thrown her rattle a good six feet away from where she sat on her blanket. Not yet able to crawl, the baby was leaning toward the rattle with a pained look on her face and holding out a little hand.

"Oh, sweetie, you've lost your rattle. Hold on. Mommy will get it for you," Isaboe said as she reached up to secure the last hook in place.

But Kaitlyn wasn't patient, and she wailed again.

"I'll get it for her," Abby said. Lowering the fabric, she stepped over to the table and laid down the handful of hooks.

Glancing back at Kaitlyn, Isaboe saw the expression on her daughter's face change. In the next moment, the rattle zipped across the floor and jumped back into her pudgy, waiting hands. She immediately clasped the rattle and shook it with a satisfied little smile. Isaboe's eyes widened as her mouth opened, but she shut it quickly, stifling the gasp from escaping as she glanced over at Abby, who was just turning around.

Stopping short with a puzzled look on her face, Abby mumbled, "Uh, Isaboe, Kaitlyn has her rattle." She turned and glanced at the startled mother, who was still standing on the stool and holding the curtain as she stared at her baby over her shoulder.

Hoping that shock wasn't written too unmistakably across her face, Isaboe stuttered for something to say. "Uh…oh, I see that now. I… I guess I must have been mistaken."

"But I heard it hit the floor, and I thought I saw it lying over there." Abby pointed to the spot where it had indeed been laying.

"I guess it wasn't as far from her as we thought it was," Isaboe said with a forced smile.

Shooting a confused look at her friend, Abby glanced back down at Kaitlyn, now contently sucking on the little rattle. "I suppose that's right. How else could she have retrieved it so quickly, otherwise?"

Isaboe watched Abby muddle over what she thought she had seen and what Isaboe was trying to make her believe. "Is this hanging far enough from the floor?" she asked pulling on the curtain and trying to turn the attention away from her daughter.

Abby continued staring at Kaitlyn with confusion before she finally tore herself away and came to stand next to Isaboe, who was still standing on the stool.

"Yes, I think it's a fine length. Here, let me grab the rest of the hooks."

Isaboe did her best to pretend that nothing had happened, but worry kept her from relaxing, and the conversation with Abby felt forced, clouded with anxiety. After putting up a few more hooks, while constantly glancing over her shoulder at her precocious daughter, Isaboe grew more concerned that Kaitlyn might do something again. "Oh, I just remembered," she said suddenly, "I promised Rosalyn that I would make rolls for dinner tonight. I haven't even started that yet, and you know how long it takes for bread to rise." Stepping down from the stool with a forced smile, she began to gather her belongings. "I'm sorry, Abby, but I need to go." She picked up Kaitlyn and her blanket before looking back at her friend, who seemed a bit taken aback by Isaboe's sudden announcement.

"Oh, alright. That's fine. Well, thanks for helping."

Flashing Abby a smile, Isaboe quickly walked out of the building. Once out on the street and holding her daughter on her hip, she glanced down at Kaitlyn. "Don't you ever do that to me again, young lady!" she scolded, but Kaitlyn only smiled innocently. "What am I going to do with you?" Wondering what else she would have to deal with as her daughter grew, Isaboe's thoughts were laced with uncertainty as she made her way home.

The following day, Isaboe pushed Kaitlyn in the stroller as Rosalyn walked alongside them, and she carried some of their purchases they had just bought on a trip to the market. The baby was forced to share her stroller space with the other fresh goods they had purchased, and anyone passing would have to look closely to see the sleeping baby tucked between a week's worth of groceries.

Rounding the corner, Isaboe noticed that a crowd had gathered and formed a circle in the street. Spectators were shouting at what appeared to be two men in the center, squaring off and throwing punches.

"Rosalyn, have I ever told you how I met Connor?" Isaboe said as the scene triggered a memory.

"No, I don't think you have. Though Connor did mention when I first met him that a couple of women had coerced him into traveling with them for protection, but that's all he told me."

Isaboe paused for a moment before she recalled the event. "Margaret and I had only been traveling a few days on our way to Edinburgh to start my search for Benjamin and Anna when we arrived late one afternoon in Inverness. We were tired, hungry, and looking forward to sleeping on a bed after two nights on the ground. But we quickly discovered that we had arrived during the summer games, and the city was full of people. There were no available rooms at any of the hotels. Margaret and I had just left yet one more hotel that had turned us away when we came across a bout in the street, very much like this one." Isaboe gestured across the road to where a crowd was growing. Waving their money in the air, the spectators rooted on their chosen fighter.

"Margaret got pulled into the excitement of the match, and she placed a bet on the man she thought would win, as did a particular British Officer: Jonathan Blackwood." Isaboe heard the hint of vile in her voice when the name crossed her lips.

"Blackwood? Isn't that the British officer who Connor killed?"

"Yes, the same monster." Isaboe answered, and for a brief moment, an uncomfortable silence hung in the air between them.

"I didn't realize you'd encountered the officer in Inverness," Rosalyn finally said.

"Unfortunately, that was the first time our paths had crossed. He had been eavesdropping at the hotel we had just left and knew we needed a room. He also put money on the fight, but he was looking for more than just a payout on a good bet. He was drunk and arrogant, feeling rather cocky about himself, so much so that he offered up his room to Margaret and me should his chosen fighter win the match."

"He was going to give up his room to you?"

"Only if I agreed to have dinner with him first. Of course, Margaret immediately jumped on that and pushed me into saying yes. I'm sure in his mind he assumed dinner with me meant *dessert* would follow. To an arrogant drunk, it must have seemed like a good wager."

"Foolish man," Rosalyn scoffed.

"Yes. Not only was he full of himself, he was a cheat. I saw him slip something into the hand of the man he placed his bet on, and that fighter won. Just before Blackwood started to collect his winnings, the man dropped the piece of metal that the officer had given him, and I called him out for the cheater that he was. That was when all hell broke loose!"

"Why? What happened?"

"The crowd turned on him for rigging the fight, and that's when Blackwood grabbed my arm and pulled me away from Margaret. He made horrible threats as he dragged me through the crowded streets. It was awful! All the while, dozens of angry gamblers were chasing after us, and they eventually cornered him after he had pulled me down a dead-end alley. Holding out his sword as he challenged the group that surrounded us, the bloody coward tried to use me as a shield. But in all the eyes that stared back at us, I didn't see anyone who was willing to take on an officer." Isaboe shivered, recalling the moment. "But then, a hooded-man stepped forward to take his challenge, and because Blackwood was so inebriated, all Connor had to do was land one good punch to his jaw and it was over. The others were immediately on him and had him in cuffs before he could recover, leading him off to jail. And of course, he blamed me for his arrest, and for being demoted in rank."

"Were you injured?" Rosalyn asked, concern showing on her face. "Being dragged through the streets must have been horribly frightening for you."

Isaboe held back a shudder as she recalled the last encounter with the officer. Only weeks before Kaitlyn was born, Blackwood had discovered her traveling alone and held her against her will in a cold tent in the middle of winter. Isaboe had truly feared for more than just her life that night, and the outcome would have been much different had it not been for Connor showing up when he did. But Connor's sword and their escape had made them both fugitives, wanted for the murder of the British officer.

"It was frightening, but other than a few scratches, some bruising on my arm and a few rips in my dress, I was fine. I was extremely rattled from the whole event, and it was painfully obvious that it wasn't safe for Margaret and me to travel alone. So, when Connor mentioned to the constable that he was on his way to Edinburgh, well, yes, I guess I did coerce him into traveling with us. And, as they say, the rest is history."

Rosalyn chuckled. "Yes, so it is. And what about Margaret? How did you first meet?"

Isaboe went silent as she thought about her friend. "She was only a twelve-year-old girl when we first met. That was before I was taken to Euphoria. She lived near us and was extremely fond of Benjamin and Anna. On the day I went into the forest, Margaret warned me about the danger of going there on mid-summer's eve, but I thought those worries were ridiculous. After I disappeared, she joined the searchers for weeks, always suspecting that I had been taken by the fey. When the bridge project was abandoned, her family moved away, but fortunately for me, New Faireshire was rebuilding many years later, and that brought her back. I know I've already said this many times, but if it weren't for Margaret, Connor and I would never have met. I most likely would be dead, or insane, by now."

"When we were all together, it was easy to see how close you and Margaret are."

"Yes, she will always have a special place in my heart, even though I don't know when or if I'll ever see her again." Isaboe sighed. "But the bond Margaret and I share is pretty incredible."

"Hmm, maybe you were sisters in another lifetime," Rosalyn said with a smile without breaking her stride.

Isaboe shot Rosalyn a sideways glance, and pushed the stroller a little faster to keep up with her mother's pace. "Do you believe in past lives, Rosalyn?"

"That was just a speculation, my love. But I do think it's rather narrow-minded to believe that our souls only experience one lifetime. If, as the deeper teachings of the church say, our souls are infinite, why should we believe that we are limited to one body that has only a very short lifespan, and that we will have no further experiences after its death?"

"If people have had previous lives, do you think we can recall them?"

"I believe it's possible. With the right guidance, we can tap into the sacred place in our souls where those memories reside." Rosalyn paused and looked at her daughter. "Why do you ask?"

"Oh, no reason. It's just that some of the books I've been reading lately have got me thinking, that's all."

"Yes, I've seen you burying yourself in them." Rosalyn studied her daughter for a moment. "You do know you won't find what you're looking for in books."

"I don't even know what I'm looking for, Rosalyn. I guess I'm just looking for answers."

"Answers to what?"

"Don't you ever wonder *why us?*" Isaboe stopped, as did Rosalyn when she saw the look on her daughter's face. "Why was I taken to Euphoria? Why did I have to lose twenty years and everything that was important in my life? Why was your mother taken? Obviously, you are part fey, as is my daughter. I've been trying to find any mention of someone else having experienced what you and I have gone through. What is it about our bloodline that is so entwined with the fey?"

"I don't know, my dear, but it's a question I've often thought about, especially since you've shown up in my life again." Rosalyn let out a long sigh before stepping closer to Isaboe. "I know that whatever fey magic I have not only gives me special abilities, but it also maintains my youth. If you put me alongside a hundred other women my age, I'd look close to twenty years younger than *any* of them, but I can't explain why. I don't seem to be aging the same, nor do I have the aliments other women my age suffer from. You and Kaitlyn will probably be much the same. Though most women might say it's hardly a problem, I really don't know what our futures will look like." Rosalyn paused and placed her hand on her daughter's. "Isaboe, if I never find out the answer to *why us*, I think I'll be alright with that. Because the truth is, my dear, I'm not sure I want to know. I may not like what I discover."

Isaboe could see the apprehension in her mother's eyes and felt it match her own. The books she had been reading were very limited on the subject of the fey or people who'd had direct contact with them. Speculation about past lives and soul mates only created more confusion, and it seemed that the more she read the more uncertain she became. After what her mother had just shared, she now had even more questions, and that only added to her anxiety.

chapter 17

cleansing of the soul

Summer brought longer, warmer days, wildflowers in bloom, and the pungent smell of seaweed. It was the beginning of kelp season, and Connor watched with morbid fascination as miles of coastline were covered with harvested seaweed, laid out to dry before being burned into kelp. Nor did he fail to notice the temporary shanties that sprung up on the shoreline to house the laborers from surrounding islands. He watched as Kirkwall's upper class swelled with bankers and businessmen travelling into the city to see what fortunes could be made.

The old-timers told tales of how the stench of burning seaweed could make a woman's womb barren, drive fish from the coastline, and poison sea life beyond the rocks. But now that the lairds could realize bigger profits, Connor thought scornfully, farming had become a thing of the past, and the unpleasant odor had become synonymous with the smell of money. Not even the old myth of a sea monster that so hated the smell of burning seaweed that it cast disease on all forms of livestock could prevent the landowners from lining their pockets.

Outdoor summer gatherings were becoming more commonplace as the weather warmed and the days grew longer, and life in Kirkwall had become a buzz of activity. Lectures were a popular draw at Abby and Foster's theater, along with art fairs, traveling musicians, and carnival acts that provided entertainment for the residents.

Even though these events created more opportunities to socialize, Connor encouraged Isaboe not to attend, reminding her that her face was still on a wanted poster for murder. Only when she promised to keep her head covered and stay discrete did Connor agree to an occasional outing, but he usually found a reason not to attend.

Since arriving in Kirkwall, he had learned a great deal about kelp, and the abuses the industry had brought. He was one of the few who moved between the social ranks—from the dirt and drudgery of the forge to a pleasant stroll through town with Isaboe on his arm—and Connor bitterly saw the contrast between afternoons spent in art galleries and the rancid pulse of the kelp business. It didn't sit right with him. The ingenuity and greed of the lairds had created an abundant lifestyle, and a respectable society didn't question the ethics of how the game was played, fair or not, as long as the needs of the community were being met.

But the polite and proper activities of the wealthy were a far cry from the games that took place on the back streets of Kirkwall. Among the poor laborers, service people, and lower-class citizens, entertainment was a luxury few could afford. When not working the kelp beds from dawn to dusk, spontaneous bouts of music lit the streets, played by anyone with a fiddle, and would bring the dancer out in the old, the young, and everyone in-between. Occasional tests of strength, boxing bouts, and tossing of the stones were common as well.

It was along the back alleys and in hidden rooms that Connor discovered there were other games being conducted discreetly. It wasn't uncommon for him to notice a well-dressed fellow on the wrong side of town, looking for a back-street whore or an illegal dice game, and the dark, dingy dwellings were perfect hiding places from the judging eyes of their neighbors. Connor knew that gambling and prostitution were illegal under British rule, but as long as everyone kept quiet about it and no one got hurt, why would anyone object to a perfectly lucrative industry, illegal or not?

With summer's onset, Isaboe noticed a change in Connor's attitude. Though it seemed that the worst of their battles were behind them, they still bickered, most often about their future. She knew how much Connor wanted to go to America to make a new start, but she'd come too far. She was determined to stay in Scotland and continue her search for information on the whereabouts of her children. It was a debate that always led to an argument. But the fine line between loving and fighting was easily muddled, particularly when sexual attraction was their primary common denominator, so Isaboe and Connor often settled their differences in the bedroom.

But late at night, it was not uncommon for Isaboe to be awakened by Connor fighting someone else, an invisible enemy. She had learned to step away when he was like this. More than once when she had attempted to wake him from such a nightmare, she had to move quickly or get struck by a swinging fist. For the most part, Braden McPherson was only a ghost, but she knew he was available for Connor to call on if he was needed. Some days, Isaboe would meet Connor's eyes only to see Braden staring back at her. It seemed he was always there, pacing in the background, ready to kill if necessary. While Connor wore Braden like a badge of honor, that didn't put their neighbors at ease.

When it all became too much, Isaboe desperately wished for Margaret to be there, supporting her and sympathizing with her. Fortunately, she had found the next best thing in the sweet and ever-empathetic Abby Graham, who was the only person in Kirkwall that knew she and Connor were not yet married. It was over a cup of tea one afternoon, and feeling confident that Abby wouldn't admonish her, that Isaboe had shared her secret.

"I don't mean to be rude or pass judgment on Connor," Abby finally said after a long, uncomfortable moment, "but you must know that if he's not willing to make you his wife, there are plenty of other eligible men who would jump in line to do so." She silently studied Isaboe for a moment before continuing. "You have a daughter together. What is he waiting for?"

"I understand your point, Abby, I do. But I'm sure he believes he's doing the right thing, and he has his reasons for waiting. That man would pull the stars down for me if I asked him to." Isaboe paused and thought about their last argument. Taking the chance that her friend would not pass judgment, she opened up, "Abby, I…I've been married before. I have two children that were taken from me and placed in an orphanage. Since Connor and I arrived here, I've sent out a number of letters hoping to find them, but so far…" Isaboe dropped her gaze and took a deep breath before looking up at her friend again. "...nothing. Though I won't to go into the details, I need to wait here in Kirkwall for information on their whereabouts, so we can finally be reunited. But Connor is tired of waiting. He wants to go to America, sooner than later. And it doesn't help that we come from completely different social backgrounds. I'm afraid he feels that we're just too far apart to find common ground." Isaboe paused as a mischievous grin crossed her face. "So, I've come up with an idea to help him see things differently,"

"Isaboe, what are you up to?"

Pulling a scrap of blue, red, and green tartan from her bag; the plaid of the MacPherson clan, Isaboe showed it to Abby.

"And what are you going to do with that?"

"I want to purchase the whole outfit; kilt, plaid, purse, and stockings."

"Tell me how getting your hands on very *illegal* Scottish accoutrements will get you a marriage proposal?" Abby asked doubtfully.

"These are his family colors. When he sees that I went so far as to track them down, he'll know that I have no doubt he's the right man for me." Isaboe saw the uncertainty in her friend's eyes. "Abby, I love Connor, and I know he loves me too. I also know that he only wants what's best for me and Kaitlyn." She looked down at the piece of fabric in her hands, "He'd walk away if he thought that would be best for me," Isaboe murmured, fearing the truth in her words. "I need to make him understand that I know what I want, and it's him." She glanced up, hoping to make her friend understand. "He'd lay down his life for me, without question, Abby. What woman wouldn't want someone who loves her like that?"

It was only a few days later, on an afternoon outing, that Isaboe realized her fear may have been based on more than empty anxiety. She had managed to convince Connor to join her at an outdoor art fair in town, and though the crowd it drew wasn't his first choice of company, he had agreed and at first had done his best to be polite. But the event was like trying to mix oil and water, and it wasn't long before Connor had heard and seen more than he could tolerate. When one man said something he should have kept to himself, the pleasant stroll through the art fair became laced with silent tension.

Connor's temper inevitably burned whenever the subject of the British occupation was raised, and to see a fellow Scotsman lauding the Brits was the ultimate sin. It may have been twenty years since the British had defeated the last rebellion, but Connor hadn't been given the luxury of time to adjust to the fact that his country was now run by the enemy. It was a bitter pill to swallow, and unfortunately, so was his tongue.

"So, ye think the English Crown has yer best interest at heart, aye?" Connor nudged his way through the crowd to address the Scottish traitor. The well-dressed businessman wearing a white wig had drawn the attention of more than just his peers.

"Connor, don't do this," Isaboe muttered as she reached out to grab his arm, but he brushed her aside.

"I didn't say that," the man replied smugly. "But we cannot deny that since the Crown has taken over Governorship of Kirkwall, business has been good. I just happened to be in a fortuitous position to capitalize on the English invasion of Orkney, so if the Brits wish to spend their summers on the islands, I certainly don't feel taken advantage of. They at least have my pocketbook's best interests," he chuckled, as did the men around him—a homogenous line of white-ruffled shirts, knee-length jackets and matching knickers, all nice and tidy above the white socks and shiny buckled shoes.

"And where do ye think that money they're linin' yer pockets with came from?" Connor asked, jutting his chin as he stopped in front of the man.

The well-dressed man glared at Connor coldly. "Does it matter?"

"It does to the farmers whose land the British stole." Connor paused as he eyed the crowd, now focused on him. "And it should matter to every one of ye!" he said a little louder. "The way ye've all embraced the British Monarchy is a disgrace, linin' yer pockets with their blood-money. Those people out there workin' the kelp beds, so all ye fancy businessmen can live the good life, they used to be farmers, tenants of clan leaders who sold out to the Brits. They're fellow Scotsmen who got thrown off their land!" Connor paused, seeing the angry stares burning in his direction, but that didn't shut his mouth. "When the Brits took yer kilts, did they take yer balls too?"

"You are out of line, sir!" the other man snapped, aghast.

"Aye, I may be, but at least I'm not a traitor, turnin' my back on my own countrymen."

"Connor, please, let's just leave," Isaboe pleaded, horrified by his out-spokenness. This unpleasant scene was something she had desperately wanted to avoid.

"Watch your tongue, man." The businessman stepped forward, regarding Connor as if he were measuring his character. "The likes of you cannot appreciate the intricacies of financial politics," he said smugly. "So, I advise you to keep your opinions to yourself on matters you know nothing about." With a pompous grin, the man started to turn. "And go back to your own side of town," he said, just loud enough for his comrades to hear.

Isaboe shuddered as she watched Connor's face shift, and instantly it was Braden glaring at the man under an angry, furrowed brow. Reaching out, he grabbed the businessman's jacket lapel, stopping him in mid-stride and spinning him around, startling the man and everyone watching as he pulled him closer—nose to nose.

"Connor, no!" Isaboe shouted as she tugged at the arm that was clutching the shocked businessman in an iron grip. As Connor's free hand balled into a fist, she knew if he let it fly, the outcome would not be good. "Let him go! He's not worth it."

Isaboe watched everyone freeze, waiting to see what the crazy Scot would do. "Please Connor, let's just leave," she said again, pulling on his arm.

Finally releasing his grip, he gave the man a slight shove, causing the traitor to stumble back a few steps before catching his balance, but Connor never took his steel-focused gaze from the British bootlicker as he slowly gave into Isaboe's tugs.

"Yeah, you better listen to the little lady," the businessman shouted as he readjusted his jacket, attempting false bravery in front of his peers now that the threat of being plummeted had passed. "And you better hope our paths don't cross again, peasant!" he spat.

"Is that right?" Connor growled as he turned around. "And what are ye goin' to do? Slap me with yer little white glove?"

Again, Isaboe pushed against Connor, knowing that if he really wanted to engage with the man, she wouldn't be able to stop him. When he finally turned and walked away from the crowd, she was at least grateful that he'd been able to hold himself back.

But that was where her gratitude ended. Once on the road back toward home, their walk was laced with tension. Isaboe kept a steady and furious pace in front of Connor, heat radiating off her face. She didn't understand why he felt it necessary to speak his mind when it wasn't asked for. He never held his tongue, never considered the consequences of his actions. Now, she'd been embarrassed in front of their neighbors and would possibly be ostracized. Why did he have to be so rude? Had Connor never lived in civilized society before? Common courtesy dictated that politics weren't worth making enemies of your neighbors, but apparently Connor hadn't learned that lesson. She knew how he felt about the Occupation, but they still had to survive in this world, and drawing attention to themselves as rebels was foolish.

Since Rosalyn had taken Kaitlyn on a separate outing, the house was empty when they arrived home. Isaboe stormed in through the front door and forcibly slammed it shut, with Connor only steps behind her.

"This is no longer my country, Isaboe!" Connor shouted as he slammed the door for a second time. "I've tried to accept that the goddamn Brits run Scotland now, but it's not *my Scotland* anymore! While these bloody fools are sucking the English cock and praising 'em for all the new business they've brought, how can ye expect me to keep my geggie shut? The goddamn bloody Brits shouldn't even *be here!*" His eyes flared with rage, matching the tone of his voice.

Affecting a false calm, Isaboe hung her shawl on a hook before turning to look at him. "Well, they are, and you're just going to have to get used to it. You're right; this isn't your Scotland anymore, but we still have to live here. These are our neighbors, some of them my friends. You can't keep insulting them or threatening physical harm just because you don't agree with their politics." She did her best to maintain control, but he was testing her limits.

"That's where ye're wrong. These people are not my neighbors, nor my friends, and we dinnae have to live here. We can go to America, to Carolina. There's room to breathe there with plenty of land for the takin'." He crossed the room to stand in front of her, paused and searched her eyes. "We could make a new start there, *Breagha*. We could start a new life in a new land."

"Until I hear back from the fostering families, you know we can't go anywhere," she responded. Did he not understand how important finding Benjamin and Anna was to her? She did not want to hear about *America* again!

As Connor turned away, she watched him running his hands through his hair in frustration. It was a familiar topic of late, and it always ended the same. Connor wanted to leave Kirkwall, but she refused to even discuss it until she received information on where her children might be. However, it had been more than twenty years since Isaboe had last held them, and the trail was growing cold. She knew that Connor had done his best to remain patient and understanding, but as the months passed without any leads, he had grown increasingly surly. From across the room, she watched him struggle to control his smoldering rage, with her and with the British Empire. Their future was already uncertain, and the distance between them was growing. They were at a stalemate.

Standing at the opposite side of the dining room with his arms folded across his chest, his chin dropped, and his brows furrowed, he looked exactly like the warrior he was. As he stood like that for a long while, just looking at her, Isaboe felt the weight of his stare as she looked back at him. It was obvious he had something he wanted to say but was struggling to find the words.

"I watched ye at the fair today," he finally said, breaking the silence. "You ken a good deal about expensive paintings, exotic vases, fine and fancy things. Ye were in yer element. When ye told that fellow yer parents had a painting by the same artist, he seemed quite impressed. But it dinnae mean anything to me; none of it does." He paused, dropping his gaze to the floor before looking back at her. "In the last few months, I've watched ye come back to life here, and it's been a radiant thing to see. Ye've made friends here. This town suits ye, and ye deserve to have the best that life can offer."

Isaboe stepped forward cautiously as he spoke, but she didn't like what he was implying and felt anxiety bubbling up in her stomach. "What are you trying to tell me, Connor?" she asked, now standing directly in front of him and looked into his face for an answer.

His nervous gaze went everywhere around the room, except to meet hers. The beads of sweat on his brow, the uncomfortable shifting from one foot to the other, all told Isaboe that whatever he was trying to say caused him a great deal of angst. When he finally found his resolve and confronted her, his sky-blue eyes were filled with uncertainty and fear—a rarity.

"I ken ye've always had the best things in life, fine clothes, fine homes, and expensive art, but I canna give ye the life that Nathan did. I'm a farmer and a fighter, and thanks to Demetrick, I can bend iron, but there be no fancy university in my past, no degree to hang on the wall." Taking a few steps away, Connor snarled to himself and began running his hands through his hair again before he turned back to look at Isaboe. "If this is the life ye want, this town is full of young, aggressive businessmen, bankers, and lawyers. If I walked away tomorrow, they'd be lined up and knockin' at your door by evening." Connor swallowed hard before continuing. "Ye dinnae owe me anything, Isaboe. Ye're not obligated to me."

Had he been on the battlefield, he might have been prepared for it, but when Isaboe's hand hit hard across his face, it was obvious that he hadn't seen it coming.

"You bloody coward!" she shouted. "You call yourself a warrior, but you don't even have the balls to look me in the eye and tell me to my face! Your lame excuse that I can do better is pathetic. Don't you think I already know that?" As Isaboe yelled in his face, Connor leaned back from the sting in her words. "I'm not stupid, Connor, and I'm not blind. I know what's out there. Men have been making passes at me *all my life*, and this town is no different!"

Jealousy flashed through Connor's eyes. "Who? Who's been making passes at ye?"

"You're impossible!" Isaboe snarled. Turning her back on him, she took a few steps, but then stopped, turned, and started in again; cutting Connor off before he could say anything.

"If you *don't* want to marry me, if you *don't* want to be a father to our daughter, then there's the door. *GET THE HELL OUT!*" Isaboe's hand shook as she pointed to the front door. "You're right, Connor; I'm not obligated to you, and obviously you feel no obligation *to me!*" she screamed as tears burned her nose and welled in her eyes. Turning her back to him again, she fought to keep control.

Letting out a long, heavy sigh, Connor took a couple of tentative steps and stood behind her, gently placing his hands on her shoulders. "That's not what I was trying to say, Isaboe." His words were soft and apologetic.

She spun around to face him. "Then just what were you trying to convey? Because it sure sounded like you don't want me. Do you or don't you want to marry me, Connor?" As she searched his eyes, the tears finally broke free. "Please, just tell me the truth."

Connor cupped her face in his hands and met her gaze. "Oh, *Breagha*, I want nothing more." He brushed a tear from her cheek with his thumb. "The thought of wakin' up beside ye every day for the rest of my life is more than I deserve."

"Then why, why don't we ever talk about marriage?" Isaboe saw the hesitation in his eyes and felt the fear growing in her chest.

"I'll answer that question if ye answer one for me first. Why dinnae we ever talk about Nathan?"

Instantly Isaboe felt her defenses rise as she pulled away from his hands. "Why should we talk about Nathan? This has nothing to do with him," she snapped before turning away from Connor's stare.

"And that's why we dinnae talk about marriage! I will not have another man in my bed, Isaboe, even if it is only his ghost!" As Connor raised his voice, Isaboe turned to walk away, but he reached out and grabbed her arm, making her stop and look at him. "It's been a year since ye last saw him, Isaboe, and more than twenty years for most people. He's gone. I'm here!" He slapped his chest in emphasis. "I ken that he was yer husband and the father of yer children. I ken that ye loved him, but how long are ye gonna pine for him? I'm not Nathan! I'll never fill his shoes, nor give ye the life he did. So tell me what is it that ye want, Isaboe? Do ye love me enough to let him go?"

Isaboe saw fear in Connor's eyes as she stared at him in disbelief. "Is that what you've thought, all this time?" It had never occurred to her that she could hurt Connor by staying quiet about her late husband.

He dropped his hand from her arm. "What else would I think? Every time his name is mentioned, ye look so sad. It makes me feel like I've been punched in the gut. I won't take second place to a dead man." Isaboe reached up and stroked his face as she looked into his eyes. "I am so sorry if I led you to think that. That's not why I've chosen not to talk about Nathan. That's not it at all. It's just that..." Turning away, she walked over to the dining table and took a seat. She sat staring down at her hands that were folded in her lap, before finally lifting her face. "I have something to tell you."

Connor tentatively walked over to the table and took a seat next to her. "What?"

It took another few seconds before she found her voice, though she struggled to speak the words. "Do you remember the morning Kaitlyn was born, the morning I woke up after that horrible ordeal?" The memory made a shiver run down her spine.

"How could I forget?"

"Do you remember what I said to you when I first woke up? I told you that I knew it was you in Euphoria, that I knew you were Kaitlyn's father. I said: *it's always been you.* Do you remember that?"

"Aye. Where are ye going with this?"

"When I was in that dark place, in that void between realms, I saw things there, in the darkness," she whispered, as if someone might be listening.

"What kind of things?" Connor asked cautiously, his furrowed brow deepening.

Isaboe studied his face for a moment before continuing. "I saw images, flashes of past lives. But it was more like I *felt* them, *experienced* them, in no time at all. It's hard to explain, but, Connor, in every one of those lives, *you were there.* You may not have looked like you do now, but I know. I felt it in my soul. It was you." Isaboe looked into his eyes, hoping she could explain what she felt, what she believed.

"Are ye tryin' to tell me that we've been together before in some other life? Like soul mates?" His expression told Isaboe that he wasn't sure he believed her.

"Yes, that's what I'm trying to tell you. We were meant to be together. It wasn't just by chance that Demetrick chose you. Up until last year, I didn't really believe in anything like destiny, but now..." Isaboe stood up and walked over to the wall. Leaning back against it, she dropped her face and let the tears fall.

Connor walked over and stood in front of her, lifting her face to look at him. "I dinnae understand, *Breagha*. I'm not sure I believe in destiny either, but none of this explains why ye won't talk about Nathan."

"Don't you get it? Maybe what the Queen of Euphoria told me was right, and that our paths have already been chosen for us. Maybe we really don't have any control over what happens to us, because it's already been decided." The tears ran unabated down Isaboe's face now, all her fears on display. "Nathan was a good man, Connor. He didn't deserve what happened to him. He took care of me; he loved me." She paused to catch her breath. "But I was meant to be with you, and *he was in the way*. Don't you see? I'm as guilty of his death as if I pushed him into that river myself!"

There it was. She had finally said it; self-loathing in every word.

Connor hugged her tightly, letting her sob into his chest. "No, no, Isaboe, it's not yer fault. Ye had nothing to do with what Lorien did to ye. Ye can't blame yerself."

She drew back, her vision blurred with tears, but she could still see the compassion in his eyes. "I'm not sure I believe that. Margaret told me not to go into the forest that day, and I ignored her. It was my actions that caused all of this to happen. Nathan's death, the loss of my children, my sister's death—all of it is my fault!"

"And what if ye could take it all back and make another choice? Where does that leave us? I'm not sure how I feel about past lives and such, but I ken that ye had no control over what happened. We can't change the past. We can only move forward from here. If Nathan loved ye even half as much as I do, he wouldn't want ye doin' this to yerself. He'd want ye to be happy. He'd want ye to find love again, *Breagha*."

Isaboe slid down to the floor and dropped her face into her hands. Connor followed suit and sat on the floor beside her, wrapping an arm around her shoulders and holding her while she cried into his chest.

When she felt she could continue without breaking down again, Isaboe looked up at him. "Nathan was my husband. We shared a marriage bed, and I know that he loved me. But Connor, I don't miss him. There's no room in my heart for him anymore. You've taken it all. And though I know I should feel badly about that, I don't. Does that make me a bad person?" Isaboe searched his eyes as they sat on the floor, propped up against the wall.

Connor chuckled quietly and smiled. "No, that doesn't make ye a bad person. And I'd be lyin' if I said I was sorry to hear ye say that."

Wiping the remaining tears from her cheeks, Isaboe stared long into his soft gaze. She noticed how the blue of his eyes looked like fractured glass in a perfect orb, a pool of desire she often lost herself in. Taking a deep breath, she hoped she could put into words what she felt in her rapidly beating heart.

"You awoke something in me that I didn't know existed. All you have to do is touch me, and I feel it stir. When you make love to me, our connection is so much more intimate, yet, at the same time, raw and hungry. Nathan was my husband for six years, but I never felt like this with him." Placing her hand on his chest, she checked her words before continuing. "Do you feel it? Does it burn so much it's frightening, but addicting?" Searching for confirmation, her eyes danced with his. "Do you feel it, too?" Her breathy words came just above a whisper.

Clutching her hand in his own, Connor pressed it against his heart, and Isaboe could see the love in his eyes. "Not a day goes by that I dinnae question how I ended up being the lucky man that Demetrick chose. When I look at yer beautiful face, everything else pales in comparison. I ken I dinnae deserve ye, but I'm more grateful than I can put into words for every moment that I get to hold ye, kiss ye, touch you." Caressing her cheek, Connor stared into her eyes. "I'd give up everythin' I believe in just to keep ye in my arms." He lifted her hands and kissed the back of them, holding her eyes with his own.

A smile slowly grew on Isaboe's face as she touched his, the same face she had slapped hard only moments before. She so badly wanted to kiss him. "I love you so much, it hurts," she whispered, their lips so close they nearly brushed.

"Aye, it hurts me too," he replied with a sly smile as he rubbed his offended cheek, but apparently it didn't hurt enough to distract him.

The kiss started out soft and passionate, but soon turned greedy. With the house to themselves, the urgency of their desire soon had their clothes flying and their bodies entwined. Connor and Isaboe made love that afternoon on the dining room floor, on the table, up against the wall, and then they retired to the bedroom to complete a blissful evening of sexual healing.

CHAPTER 18

AN UNEXPECTED VISIT

The following morning the house awoke to its usual routine. After being bathed, fed, and changed for the second time, little Kaitlyn's needs had finally been attended to, and she was content for the moment. Finding a warm spot of sunshine beaming through the window onto the floor of the front room, Isaboe laid the gifted child on a blanket. The sun's morning rays cast the baby in a golden halo as Isaboe softly brushed the child's cheek with one hand, while offering up a stuffed doll with the other. One of the doll's feet immediately found its way into Kaitlyn's mouth as she squeezed it in her pudgy little fingers. Occasionally, she would pull the doll out of her mouth, holding it above her head, wet, matted, and covered with baby drool. But the excitement showed in her unusually large green eyes, and before long the gooey treasure would find its way back into her mouth. Standing, Isaboe hovered over her child and felt the joy of experiencing her baby's excitement.

"How does that taste?" Connor spoke softly when he stepped up beside Isaboe, slipping his arm around her waist as he looked down at their daughter. "Ye're workin' on chewing the wee doll's foot off, aye?"

When her father appeared, Kaitlyn instantly threw the doll aside and looked up at him. Connor must have looked like a giant, but the smile that broke out on her radiant little face, and the cooing sounds she made, showed no fear, only excitement. She kicked her legs and began waving her arms, demanding to be picked up.

"I think she wants you to hold her," Isaboe said, noticing Connor's hesitation.

He didn't hold or interact with his daughter very often. She was a baby, after all. As a warrior, there was little that could intimidate him, but babies were a foreign concept. The few times Connor had attempted to calm his distraught daughter had only brought on bouts of panic, similar to feelings he'd experienced just before going into battle. But at least on the battlefield he had knowledge of what to do. Here, his fear had no outlet.

But recently, it had become obvious that Kaitlyn adored him, and any opportunity to be held by her father created a flurry of excitement. Seeing that beautiful, toothless smile and the anticipation in her eyes, he couldn't just walk away. He had to pick her up. At least she wasn't crying.

As soon the infant was in her father's arms, she began gently patting his face with a childlike innocence, enjoying the prickle of his morning beard and his soft smile. But when she pulled a lock of Connor's hair, he gave her a furrowed look and a low growl. The girl's tiny gasp told Isaboe that the moment of peace had passed, and she waited for what would come next.

But the baby's reaction surprised them both. Instead of crying at her father's look and the grumbling sound of his disapproval, she pulled his hair again. When she received the exact same reaction, this time Kaitlyn giggled right out loud. The more she pulled, the more he growled. The more he growled, the more she laughed. Dad, it seemed, had become her new favorite toy.

A knock at the door drew Isaboe's attention from the merriment in her living room and brought Rosalyn out of the kitchen. When she opened the door, Isaboe took a couple of steps back, shocked at what she saw. Standing right in front of her on the porch of their home was her dearest friend: Margaret MacDougal. Standing next to her with a broad smile on his large face was William Buchanan.

"Margaret! Will!" Isaboe exclaimed, as she threw her arms around her dear friend, pulling her into a fierce embrace.

Before Isaboe had released Margaret, Connor was at the door with Kaitlyn still in his arms. "What, life on the mainland too boring for ye now? Comin' back for a little more excitement, aye?" Connor passed the baby off to Rosalyn and turned to greet his friends.

After more than a few hugs, greetings, and hearty handshakes, Connor asked the obvious question. "What brings ye here? Shouldn't ye be running yer establishments back home? Not that we're unhappy to see ye, but why are ye here?"

"And why are you still… together?" Isaboe asked the other curious question.

"Well, before they answer any of your questions, at least invite them in, for goodness sakes," Rosalyn reprimanded the young couple, still standing behind them and holding their daughter. "Good to see you again Margaret, William."

As Rosalyn greeted their friends, Kaitlyn silently clung to her grandmother. With wide eyes she observed the new visitors.

"And you too." Margaret returned Rosalyn's greeting with a hug before smiling at the baby in her arms. "Well, look at how you have grown, wee one. How's my namesake doing?"

Burying her face in her grandmother's shoulder, Kaitlyn shied away.

"Oh, she's forgotten me already." Margaret sounded disappointed.

"Well, she was only two days old the last time she saw you," Isaboe replied before pulling Margaret back into her arms. "It's so good to see you!"

"And you too," Margaret replied, giving Isaboe a long embrace before releasing her. Holding her at arm's length, she took a moment to observe her dearest friend. "I have to say, you're looking much better than the last time I saw you. The color's returned to your face, and you've even put on a little weight."

"Have I?" Isaboe asked, looking down at her middle and wondering about Margaret's comment.

"Oh, you look great, beautiful as always," she replied with a supportive smile.

"Here, let me take your wraps, and please, make yerselves at home," Connor said, escorting his guests into the front room.

After everyone was comfortably seated, and tea and biscuits were served, Margaret then began to fill them in on the events that had taken place in the months since they'd last been together.

"Well, we got back to William's hostel and spent a few days with Ian before continuing our trip south to New Faireshire. After the second day there, this guy comes in and sits down at my bar," Margaret said, nodding toward Will, "and I think he's coming in to say good-bye, aye? But instead he makes me an offer. 'Maggie,' he says, 'why don't ye sell this place to Dunivan, come back, and run the hostel with me? It could use a woman's touch.' And I say to him; "Is that a business proposition or a marriage proposal?" And he says 'Both.'"

"You got *married?*" Isaboe asked, shocked. "I didn't even think you liked Will."

"Well, he kinda grew on me after a while." Margaret patted Will's beefy leg, giving him a sideways grin. "After a couple of days of courting me, using all his immense powers of persuasion, he listed all the reasons that this union made sense. And since I couldn't think of any reason not to, I said yes. We got married two days later."

"Ye didna waste any time, ye old dog," With a cocky smile, Connor threw the jab at his old friend and comrade in arms.

"Well, when a man finds an amazing woman like Margaret, why wait? I ain't getting any younger, and Maggie seemed like a perfect fit for me. She definitely keeps me in line," he said with a crooked grin through his full beard. Looking at his wife with undeniable admiration, he gently squeezed her hand. "I didna see any point in waitin'."

Will's comment was only a statement of fact, but the look Connor and Isaboe shot each other was not missed by anyone in the room.

"Well, congratulations," Isaboe said, breaking the uncomfortable silence. She stood and opened her arms, and Margaret rose to return her hug.

"So ye came all the way back here just to tell us ye got hitched?" Connor asked.

This time it was Will and Margaret who shot each other a look. "That's one reason, but not the main reason," Margaret replied. Isaboe watched the expression on her friend's face become serious as she reached out with a comforting hand. "Isaboe, you might want to sit down first."

Isaboe tentatively took her seat as she stared up at Margaret with wide eyes. "Why? What do you have to tell us?"

Margaret took a deep breath before sitting back down as well, and she silently held Isaboe's gaze for a moment before speaking. "We found Anna."

Instantly, Isaboe felt the blood rush from her face and was thankful that Margaret had suggested she sit. "How? When? Where?" She suddenly felt her heart racing.

"After we were married, we stayed in Faireshire for another month until Dunivan could get his finances together. Late one night I woke up hearing faint voices in our room, but no one was there. I got up to investigate and realized that the sound was coming from the chest at the end of my bed, where I kept this." Margaret reached into her bag and pulled out the blue amulet, still hanging from its original green cord. When they were saying goodbye all those months ago, Isaboe had given it to her in hopes of staying in touch through its mysterious powers.

"I woke up William and had him open the chest. When we found it…" Margaret paused, looking intensely at Isaboe, "*it was glowing.*"

"Glowing? I'd never seen it glow before."

"Nor had I."

"I told her not to touch it," Will interjected. "The damn thing scares the hell out o' me. But she wouldn't listen to me and grabbed it anyway."

"I had to pick it up. I just had to."

"And then what happened?" Isaboe sat on the edge of her seat, hanging on every word.

"I had a vision. It was a flash and then gone, only a couple of seconds at best. But in those moments, I saw Anna. I saw her as a grown woman, in her home, in the city where she lives, even the name of the street, right down to the house number. I knew how to find her."

Baffled at what this new magical madness meant, silence fell over the group as everyone absorbed the enormity of Margaret's story. Finally, Isaboe's anxiety became too much, and she could no longer remain silent. "And you met with her?"

"Yes, we did. And Isaboe, she's a beautiful woman, looks just like you, except her hair is darker. You could be sisters. She's married, has a baby boy, and seems very happy. I thought you might like to know that," Margaret said with a comforting smile.

This was it. This was the reason they had traveled all the way back to the island—to deliver this message. It was the news Isaboe had waited for almost a year to hear, though it had felt like a lifetime. As hard as she tried, she could not hold back her tears of joy.

Connor moved closer and put his arm around Isaboe's shoulders, giving her support while she did her best to pull herself back together. "So, ye spoke with her?" Connor asked.

"Yes. We went to their home, met her husband, Jared, and their beautiful baby Gabriel, only a month old. After introducing ourselves, I explained how I had known her as a child. Though she had no memory of me, the name Margaret did mean something to her. I made up a reasonable story of how I'd found her which, fortunately, she accepted."

"Where does she live?" Isaboe wanted to know everything.

Margaret hesitated before answering. "Edinburgh."

"Edinburgh!" The look of surprise on Isaboe's face quickly changed to a look of anger. "I *left* Edinburgh, traveled clear across the country looking for any information on how to find her, and she was right under my nose the whole time?" As Isaboe sat back, fury crossed her face. "Of course, she was."

Though Isaboe wouldn't say the words out loud, they were all thinking the same thing; Lorien had known. The Fey Queen had done everything she could to get Isaboe out of Edinburgh as soon as possible, for more than one reason, they now realized. She couldn't risk Isaboe meeting Anna accidently on the street. If that had happened, all of Lorien's nefarious plans would have been ruined.

"Did you ask her about Benjamin?"

When Isaboe had discovered that her legal mother, Marta, had fostered out her children, it was clear on the paperwork that they did not stay together. At the time, Benjamin was five-years-old and Anna only two.

"Aye. A few years back Benjamin sought her out, and they've now been reunited. They stay in touch. He lives in Glasgow. He's an engineer, married, and has two children. Following in his father's footsteps, I'd say."

Margaret leaned forward and took Isaboe's hands, compassion showing in her eyes. "Marta may not have kept your children together, but she made sure they went to good homes. They've both had good lives, my love. You can have peace now."

Isaboe knew that she could never have those moments back with her children, that for twenty years she had been cheated out of experiencing their childhoods. She couldn't be there for those special moments—first loves, weddings, and babies being born. Those were all stolen from her by an afternoon nap. Since awakening from her twenty-year dream, she had been fighting to accept what had happened, but the brutal unfairness of it still left a hole in her heart. This was as close to closure as she could hope for, and at least now she could move on.

Turning away from Margaret, Isaboe buried her face into Connor's chest as she cried. Lifting her chin, he wiped the tears away as he smiled down at her. "This is the news we've been waiting to hear, *Breagha*. No more tears, aye?"

He was right. This last year, she had shed more tears than she thought was humanly possible. Looking back into his sparkling eyes, she nodded and wiped her face before standing once more to embrace Margaret. "Thank you, thank you, thank you, my dear friend. I have no words, but you already know what's in my heart," she whispered in Margaret's ear while still holding her in a tight hug and struggling to contain her emotions.

Up until this point, Rosalyn and Kaitlyn had been quiet observers. But the babe seemed to have sensed her mother's distress, and it wasn't long before her pitiful whimpering drew Isaboe's attention. Taking the little girl back into her arms, she looked at her own mother, whose eyes were also rimmed with emotion. Instinctively, Isaboe reached out and hugged her tightly. If anyone in the room understood what she was feeling, it was Rosalyn.

"Well, this calls for a celebration!" Connor said, standing with a full grin on his face. "Good friends and good news deserve good mead, I'd say."

CHAPTER 19

A MISSED OPPORTUNITY

After Rosalyn had taken Kaitlyn to her room for the night, the four friends continued talking for hours—eating, drinking, and sharing news. Any further talk of marital status was avoided, and made louder by its careful avoidance, but for the most part, the conversation stayed light.

That was until Connor ended the ease by asking a heavy question. "And what have ye heard about Blackwood?" Connor's sword may have dealt the killing blow, but it was Isaboe's face that had found its way onto the wanted poster—WANTED FOR THE MURDER OF A BRITISH OFFICER.

"Well, glad ye mentioned that." Will's face lit up. "Did a wee bit of my own investigation, and come to find out, it doesna seem that the Brits are all that eager to solve this case. There's no active investigation. Apparently, Isaboe wasn't the first woman he'd held in his quarters against her will. Rumor has it that his soldiers ratted him out, sayin' Blackwood got what he had comin', messed with the wrong man's woman."

"They bloody sure got that right," Connor said viciously.

"So, it's probably safe to come back to the mainland now, if that's what you want," Margaret added. "That is, unless you're happy here in Kirkwall. It seems to be a lovely city."

They fell into a brief, awkward silence, and Connor welcomed being drawn away by a knock at the door. "Rob. Aren't ye on the wrong side of town?" Connor jested when he saw his co-worker standing on his stoop.

"It canna be that great. They let ye live here," Rob said.

With a slight grin and a nod of acknowledgment, Connor motioned for his friend to enter, but Rob declined. "I dinnae want to intrude. Just want to talk privately, if ye have a minute."

Connor was acutely aware that Isaboe had been cautiously watching the exchange taking place at her front door, and when he started to go outside, she approached him with Kaitlyn on her hip and questions in her eyes.

"Connor, who is that?"

"It's just Rob McClaren from the forge."

"What does he want to talk to you about?"

"That's what I'm going to find out. Ye dinnae need to worry, *Bregaha*. I gave ye an oath." Holding his hand against her cheek, their eyes met, and he just wished it wasn't anxiety that colored her pretty face when she looked back at him. Knowing that Isaboe and Kaitlyn were counting on him, Connor wasn't about to do anything foolish. "Do ye trust me?"

Staring into her eyes, he watched her pause, and she studied him for a moment before finally softening. "Yes, of course I trust you."

"Good. Then go be with Margaret and Will. I'll be right back," he said with a smile and a pat to her backside.

Stepping outside, Connor walked over to the railing where his co-worker waited for him.

"Sorry to interrupt. I see ye have guests, so I won't take much of yer time." Rob McClaren's expression was serious.

Connor dismissed his apology. "What can I do for ye Rob?"

"I've discovered a Redcoat spy in the ranks. If he takes what he knows back to London, there'll be trouble for everyone." For all his quiet urgency, Rob's face gave nothing away.

"So, ye have a rodent that ye need to dispose of. That still doesna explain why ye're here."

"Because, this rat has money and connections. He doesn't ken that we're onto him, and I wanna keep it that way. I have it on good authority that he's booked passage on a ship to Scrabster tomorrow. I also heard that General Harrington just happens to be in Scrabster. More than just a coincidence, I'd say. Our rodent has valuable information that could prove harmful if it landed in the wrong hands."

"Who is this powerful rat?"

"Tobias Whitmore, the newspaper mogul."

Connor's eyebrows shot up when he heard the name of the prominent businessman. He wouldn't have suspected him for a sympathizer, or a traitor. "Whitmore? Are ye sure about this?"

"He's been part of the cause for six months now, though a couple of us had reason to question his loyalties. We laid a trap, and his arse got stuck in it. Aye, I'm sure."

"That still doesn't explain why ye're standing on my doorstep, Rob. What'd ye want from me?"

"To make sure he dinnae board that ship on the morrow."

"I'm not yer man, McClaren."

"Look, Grant, ye might *say* yer not involved, and I understand why, but I see that same spark o' rebellion in your eyes, Brother. I wouldn't ask if it wasn't necessary. It has to be someone he doesn't know. If any of us shows up at the dock, he'll be suspicious." Seeing the wavering doubt on Connor's face, he pushed forward. "We just need ye to keep Whitmore off that ship, that's all. I'll take it from there."

Standing with his arms folded against his chest, Connor stared at Rob and contemplated his request. He hadn't shared much with his co-worker or let on who had inspired their lead man at the forge into a sudden change of heart regarding the treatment of his workers, but Rob had guessed correctly, and Connor felt a spark of excitement at the thought of vengeance. It was hard to imagine letting a goddamn British spy just sail away with valuable information that would certainly cost honorable Scotsmen their lives. However, only moments before he had looked into Isaboe's eyes, and in them he'd seen the trust he had asked for. Helping Rob McClaren now would be a clear violation of that trust, and Connor was torn down the middle. He stared hard at Rob, knowing that his stoic face gave nothing away, but inside he felt complete uncertainty. "I have guests, so if ye dinnae mind."

Rob studied him for a moment before he nodded. He then turned and slunk down the steps of the second story townhouse and onto the cobblestone street.

"What time does the ship depart tomorrow?" Connor asked without turning away from his door.

"Ten o'clock," Rob spoke over his shoulder.

Without looking back, Connor disappeared into his home and closed the door behind him.

Before retiring, Isaboe went to Rosalyn's room to nurse her daughter and put her to sleep for the night. Her mother, who sat in the rocking chair reading, looked up as she entered. "It must be bedtime," she said, rising from the rocker.

"No, don't get up. I can sit on the bed to feed her."

"Here, sit. Babies are happier when they are rocked while being nursed. It's beneficial for both mother and child," Rosalyn said with a comforting smile before heading for the door.

"Wait. Rosalyn, please stay. Could we just talk for a moment?" With Kaitlyn contently nursing, Isaboe waited until her mother returned to the bed and took a seat. "You've been rather quiet today. You haven't said much about Margaret's news."

"I've just been staying out of the way to let you have some time with your friends."

Isaboe quietly nodded as she looked at Rosalyn for a long moment before finally breaking the silence. "Don't you think it's a bit odd that Margaret received the vision of how to find Anna and not you? Obviously, someone from the realm of the Underlings knows where Anna is. Should we be concerned?"

"Possibly, and though I didn't want to share any of this with you tonight, I've asked myself that same question, and more. I agree it's a bit concerning that the message came to Margaret. However, she had the amulet, and it was a gift from Queen Brighid, so I'm certain that the vision came from her as well. I will investigate to see what I can find out. Until then, let's not borrow trouble, alright, my dear? You've finally gotten the news that you waited so long to hear, so let's celebrate that for now and be grateful for the gift."

Rosalyn smiled with as much confidence as she felt she could show, hoping to put her daughter's worries at ease. But the truth was that she too was concerned. Why hadn't the message come to her? And who else knew about the vision? But the most looming concern was that someone from the Underlings knew where Anna was. She had faerie blood running in her veins as well. Was she safe?

The following morning, Connor stood at Isaboe's bedroom door as he watched her getting ready for the day. Her auburn hair fell over her pale shoulders as she sat at the vanity. She was staring at her reflection, but by the look on her face, her gaze went beyond what was before her. Lost in her own thoughts as she ran the brush mindlessly through her hair, Isaboe hadn't even noticed him.

In his silent observation, Connor felt his longing for her, his need to keep her close. Their months of domesticity had given their relationship time to grow beyond the physical, and she had burrowed deeply into his heart and taken up permanent residence. It wasn't only her mysterious eyes and beautiful face he loved to watch, or her porcelain skin he found so much pleasure in touching. Isaboe was his connection to everything important in life. On many days, he would wake up and just watch her lying beside him, silently reminding him why he needed to keep putting one foot in front of the other and moving forward. She was so many things all rolled together, and it was his goal in life to not just love her, but to watch over her and Kaitlyn and keep them safe.

When she finally saw Connor's image in the mirror, Isaboe gave him a coy smile. Taking that as an invitation, he stepped up behind her. Softly sweeping the hair from her neck, he began planting small kisses on her exposed skin. Closing her eyes, she tilted her head to the side as she emitted soft sounds of contentment. "You woke up in a good mood this morning," she whispered behind sleepy eyes.

"How could I not? I wake to see this radiant face every morning."

Looking up at him, Isaboe stood and wrapped her arms around his waist. "Well, I'm glad one of us had a good night's sleep."

"Did Kaitlyn keep ye awake last night?"

"No, I had a night of bad dreams. I can't remember what they were about, but, I woke up feeling unsettled and a bit frightened this morning."

"Hmm, well maybe I can help change that," he whispered as he again began planting kisses down the side of her neck. "Maybe ye need to lie down, and I can tuck ye back in bed."

"Did you forget we have guests in the house?"

"No," he said before leaning back. "I just want to make sure ye're getting enough rest."

That is what he whispered in her ear, but that wasn't what he was really thinking. He wanted to throw her down on the bed and nibble her entire body, starting from her delicious lips all the way down to her silken thighs, but he kept that thought to himself. Instead, he simply kissed her softly on the lips.

Taking the opportunity to be lost in each other was short lived as the sound of a crying baby interrupted their brief moment of intimacy. Isaboe threw a robe over her nightgown and started to turn toward the door, but then stopped to regard his attire. "You look rather dapper for going to the forge."

"Not going to the forge today. I'll be taking Buchanan for a walk around the city this morning."

"You didn't go the forge yesterday. Can you take two days off and still have a job?"

"I'm the best bloody smith Duncan has, and he kens that. If I dinnae show up, I dinnae get paid. I think we can handle that for a day or two."

"Well, don't make a habit of it. I plan on taking Margaret for an outing myself and spending a little money," she said with a sassy smile before easing back into his embrace.

With his arms wrapped around her, Connor looked down into Isaboe's eyes and gave her a sensual smile as he stroked her hair. "The night before Will and Margaret showed up, we started a conversation that we didna finish—ended up in the bedroom instead."

"I remember it being more of an argument than a conversation" she said, returning his playful smile.

"Well, I was trying to avoid mentioning that," he said, rubbing the side of his face where Isaboe had slapped him.

"Oh, does it still sting?" she asked with mock sympathy.

"Aye, maybe not physically, but I've got one hell of a memory."

Isaboe planted a kiss on his offended cheek. "Does that help?"

"It'll do for now," he whispered, giving her a crooked smile. "But I was thinking that maybe we should try and finish that discussion."

As Isaboe stared at him solemnly for a long moment, her eyes lost their sparkle, and he now saw something that looked like fear flash across them. But before she could express herself, Rosalyn entered the room with a screaming child in her arms.

"Sorry to interrupt Isaboe, but your daughter is very hungry."

Seeing that the opportunity was over, she turned from Connor to take the crying babe from her mother's arms as he stepped toward the door. "Connor, please don't go yet. We haven't finished our talk."

He heard the concern in Isaboe's voice and didn't miss the anxiety he saw on her face. "We'll talk later," he said, giving her a quick kiss before walking out of the room.

CHAPTER 20

A COVERT OPERATION

"I thought ye were taking me on a tour through the fair city of Kirkwall. Lovely as these grimy back alleys are, they're all we've seen," Will grumbled as he accompanied Connor through another seedy section of the city. "And what's that smell?"

"This is where life happens, Will, where the real people live, and that stench in the air?" Connor took a long, full sniff. "'Tis the smell of money and humanity, and in this city, there's too much of both. But we're done here. Let's go see what's happenin' down at the docks."

"Mac, what are ye up to?"

"Just showin' ye around the city, Brother," Connor said with a grin and a slap on his friend's back before turning around to make his way to the harbor.

"Alright, Mac," Will said as he fell into step next to Connor, "I've seen that look o' hunt in yer eyes and I've fought alongside ye long enough to ken when somethin's up. I thought ye were *retired.*"

Connor shot his friend a sideways glance but offered no reply.

"I've always supported yer decisions, Mac, even when I didna agree, and I realize I'm on a need-to-know basis, but I do have one question."

"What's that?"

"If ye're not gonna tell me what we're doin' this morning, maybe ye can tell me why ye haven't put a ring on Isaboe's finger yet."

"It's none of yer business. I've got my reasons."

"And what's that? Cause ye're a bloody idiot?"

"Up yer kilt. I dinnae owe ye an explanation," Connor snapped.

"Aye, ye dinnae owe me, but ye owe Maggie. She was sure that the two of ye would be hitched by now. What are ye waiting for man? Isaboe's a gift. You could never get a woman like that on yer own."

Connor stopped in mid-stride and turned to his friend. He felt his anxiety bubbling and couldn't stop it from showing on his face. "Ye dinnae think I ken that? I think that every time I look at her, and I constantly wonder why she stays!"

"Maybe cause she loves yer arse, ye fool. What's really going on, Mac?"

Running his hands through his hair, Connor paced in a circle before coming to a stop. He looked at his friend and took a deep sigh before answering. "Look Will, I love her more than life itself; ye ken that. But when Demetrick chose me to protect her, maybe it wasn't just an evil Fey Queen or a demented British officer she needed protection from. Maybe she needs protection from…me," he said, spitting the words out as he tapped his chest before dropping his gaze to the dirt. "There are days I think the best thing I could do for her is walk away." Connor knew the anguish that came out with his words, but it was freeing to finally say the thought that had been haunting him since the beginning of his relationship with Isaboe.

Will only shook his head as he listened. "We left here six months ago, and I thought ye would've grown up some by now. But I see ye're still the same hot-headed young rebel lookin' for a way to sabotage anything good in your life. Ye have a family, Mac, a woman and a child to care for. It's time to grow up and start taking care of what's really important," Will said with a fatherly scowl.

Connor gave his old friend for a long, uncomfortable glare before responding. "Let me ask ye a question, Will. How many years did it take before ye tucked yer balls between yer legs and started sucking off the British tit?"

"Fuck you, MacPherson."

"No, fuck you, Buchanan! Ye've had twenty years to adjust to this *fucking* British rule and their *goddamn*, bloody laws! I've seen clan leaders—that at one time I held the greatest respect for—bend over like bitches in heat and take it in the arse!" Connor spat in the dirt. "I can't tell ye how many times I've tasted my own blood from biting my tongue. I dinnae ken how long I can keep my geggie shut before I get in real trouble. The scars on my back may have healed, but that's all. The fuck-ing Brits have taken everything from me, Will—my father, my home, and my country."

"All that rage is gonna keep Isaboe from ye too!" Will growled as he jabbed Connor in the chest with his finger. "Damn it, Mac, ye've been given a second chance. Dinnae throw it away over a cause that's been dead for decades. Have ye not killed enough Redcoats to avenge yer father's death? It's over. Let it go."

"And just how do I do that? Tell me, Will, cause I dinnae ken how." Connor returned to pacing in circles as he continued. "Isaboe thrives here. She's come back to life in this city. It suits her. She's happy here, but inside I'm dying! I've tried to get her open to the idea of leavin' for America, but she won't hear of it." Connor paused, frowning at Will before he started in again. "Isaboe's the only thing that keeps me focused and walkin' the path I know I must, but I dinnae ken how much longer I can do it. How do I put out the fire and not kill the next bloody fool who goes off about how great it is that the Brits are dumpin' their blood money into our country—*a country that is no longer ours!*" Connor growled through gritted teeth. "This is not my Scotland anymore, Buchanan, and ye can't expect me to just let it go!"

As Connor watched Will study him closely for a moment, he saw something resembling empathy in his friend's face. "Aye, that's exactly what I expect ye to do, and so does Isaboe. Ye have a family now, Mac. I ken that ye've had a lot shoved down yer throat in a short amount of time, but be a fuckin' adult, goddamn it! Take care of yer responsibilities, whether ye chose 'em or not!" Apparently done with his lecture, Will turned and continued in the direction of the docks.

Letting out a heavy sigh, Connor watched his friend walking away. Annoyed by the sting of truth in Will's words, he shook his head and silently followed Will to the harbor.

The two men leaned against the railing as they watched the multitude of people mingling on the harbor shore, most of whom carried luggage and were waiting to board the next outgoing ship. After a long stretch of silent observation, Will apparently could keep quiet no longer. "Who are we looking for, Mac?"

Just as he asked the question, the answer came into view and Connor stood straight up, locking onto his target. "Follow my lead," he said, taking a few steps before stopping to look back at Will. "When I give ye the signal, this is what I want ye to say."

"Oh bugger, Mac. What are ye getting us into?" Will grumbled.

After relaying his instructions, Connor pulled up his hood and blended into the crowd of travelers, with Will in tow still shaking his head.

Dressed in his top-hat and overcoat, Tobias Whitmore looked much like the other businessmen on the marina, but his darting glances marked him as a target. Only a few hundred yards from the boarding plank, he began to make his way toward the ship, but his traveling plans were interrupted when he felt the tip of a knife jab into his side.

"Aye, that's a dirk in yer ribs. Just keep walkin' or it's in yer lungs." Connor whispered in a dark, husky voice as he held the knife to Whitmore's back, persuading him in a new direction away from the ship.

"What the...?"

"Shut up and act natural. Keep walking or ye'll be drownin' in yer own blood."

Maneuvering quickly through crowds, it was a short walk back into the city and to the dirty alleys they had just come from. Turning off the dirt road, Connor pushed Whitmore through a narrow corridor, then into a small dark room. With Will still in tow, he followed in behind and then shut the door, throwing them all into darkness.

"What do you want with me?" Whitmore's voice revealed his fear, but before he could ask another question, Connor threw a burlap sack over his head and wrapped it against his neck. Slamming the frightened man up against a cold, wet wall, Connor shoved his forearm hard into his back, expelling the breath from his lungs. The tip of Connor's knife found its way to the underside of his chin, poking the tender skin ever so lightly.

"If ye want to live, shut up and dinnae ask any questions," Connor hissed in his ear before stepping back to light a candle on a small table, the lone piece of furniture in the dank, nasty-smelling room. Grabbing

Whitmore's coat lapel, he dragged his captive to the front of the table. "Now start emptying yer pockets."

Tobias Whitmore shook as he pulled out a bag of coins, a pocket watch, a boarding pass, a set of keys, and a newspaper from the pockets of his overcoat, dropping them onto the table in front of him.

"Everything!"

"That's it. That's all the money I have on me!" the man sniveled through the bag still over his head.

As Connor forcibly shook the man, he let out a slight whimper. "Inside pockets, keep going."

"I...I don't have anything else!" But before he could protest further, Connor threw open Whitmore's coat and started patting him down. Reaching into a breast pocket, he pulled out a leather-bound ledger and two wax-sealed letters. The ledger had a strap stitched to the back that attached to a lock on the front, requiring a key to open.

In the next moment, Tobias found himself lying on the floor face down with a knee in his back and his hands being bound behind him. With the hood still over his head, Connor could hear the panic in his voice.

"Wait! I gave you everything. What do you want from me? Who sent you?"

But Connor halted his questioning. Pulling the hood just high enough, he crammed a gag into the struggling traitor's mouth, leaving the man squirming on the floor as he tore open and read the notes. Dropping the ledger on the floor, he broke the lock with one well-aimed stomp from the heel of his boot. Holding the open book before the dim flame, he flipped through the pages. Satisfied he had found what he was looking for, he pulled another sack from inside his cloak and stuffed everything from Whitmore's coat pockets into it.

"Let's get outa here," Connor said as he turned toward Will, who, until that moment, had been a silent observer in the shadows. That was until Connor gave him a nod—the signal.

At first Will hesitated, but the look on his comrade's face was enough to make him concede. "General Harrington told us to finish the job," he mumbled.

Instantly, the struggling man lying on the floor became very still.

"I'm not a murderer. Harrington can do his own dirty work. I got what I came for." Connor's quiet and eerie reply was the last thing Tobias Whitmore would hear before the candle was blown out and the door closed, leaving him bound, gagged, and well-convinced that he had been betrayed.

Back on the streets, Connor spotted a group of young boys kicking a ball of twine back and forth in the dirt. Seeing a face he recognized, he called out to one of the older lads, a curly, red-headed youngster with a face full of freckles. "Hey boy, come hither."

The cluster of youths all stopped as the one in question pointed a finger at his chest "Who, me?"

"Aye, you. Get over here." When Connor waved the boy over, he left his friends and the game as the lad reluctantly followed orders. Finally coming over to stand in front of him, Connor looked down at the tussle-haired boy. "You're Wallace Macintosh's boy, right? What's yer name lad?"

"Liam."

"Liam, I have a business proposition for ye," Connor said as he flipped a coin between his fingers. Being the child of a poor working man, Connor knew that the single pound was more money than the boy had ever seen, much less held. "Ye interested?"

With wide eyes the youth nodded his head as he watched the coin flip over and over in the air before landing back into Connor's hand. "Ye ken where Faulkner's Forge is, aye?"

"Aye, sir."

"Ye ken who Rob McClaren is?" Upon receiving confirmation, Connor continued. "Take this bag directly to McClaren, then come back here and I'll give ye this coin. But if McClaren ain't there, dinnae give it to anyone else, just bring the bag back here. Understood?"

Liam nodded and reached for the bag, but Connor stopped him with a hand on the boy's chest. "And, ye're gonna give him this message. Tell him that his package is waitin' for him behind the slaughterhouse. Ye got that?" When Liam nodded again, Connor made the boy repeat his instructions to ensure there was no misunderstanding. He then grabbed young Liam by his shirt, startling the youngster. Connor didn't curb the furious soldier behind his eyes as he glared into the face of the freckled youth, and gave the boy a menacing look before handing him the bag. "And if that bag dinnae make into McClaren's hands, just remember, I ken where ye live," he hissed, "Now go. I'll be waitin' right here for ye." Will and Connor watched the lad running as fast as his legs would carry him in the direction of the forge.

"So, ye're into intimidating children now, aye?" Will remarked, with a disapproving shake of his head.

"A little intimidation never hurt anyone," Connor replied with a satisfied grin. Crossing his arms, he leaned back against the post and waited for the boy to complete his task.

Rob McClaren took the bag after the breathless boy had relayed Connor's message. As he looked inside and glanced at the contents, a slow smile crossed his face.

"Do you have a message you'd like to send back?" Liam asked. The enthusiasm he felt in anticipation of collecting the reward for his task was palatable.

"Aye. Tell him I owe him, whatever he wants," Rob answered in a hushed tone as he slipped the bag under his work station and scooted it out of sight with his boot.

The boy smiled and held out his hand, but the stoic blacksmith only frowned at the lad. "Get out here, ye little beggar," he said, pushing the young messenger away.

Upon relaying Rob's message and collecting his coin, young Liam ran off with a smile as wide as his face would allow.

"Did ye hear that? Whatever I want," Connor said with a satisfied grin. "I think we've seen enough of this side of town, Will. Let's go see a man about a wedding ring."

William Buchanan slapped his friend on the back. "That's the first intelligent thing I've heard ye say all morning."

chapter 21

GRANT OR MACPHERSON, I DON'T CARE

"Are you sure about this? I hate to say it, but you look absolutely ridiculous."

Isaboe ignored Margaret's comment as she stood in the middle of the living room, wrapped in a green, blue, and red plaid kilt that was much too big for her. She had wrapped it around her waist twice, but even with three pins to hold it in place, it hung almost to her ankles. The matching tartan shawl over her shoulders seemed to drown her in fabric, and it too hung all the way to the floor. With her fair skin and her hair hanging loose, she looked like a young child dressed in her father's clothing.

"Desperate situations require desperate measures, Margaret. Now, please, go ask Connor and Will to come inside."

The look on Isaboe's face told Margaret there was no point in trying to talk her out of it, and to Margaret's credit, she didn't. She did, however, glance at Isaboe's mother for help, but Rosalyn, who was sitting quietly with Kaitlyn on her lap, only shrugged. "I've learned my daughter has quite the stubborn streak," she said before turning her reprimanding eyes on Isaboe. "Once this girl has made up her mind, it's hard to convince her otherwise, even if it would be in her best interest to do so."

Pointedly ignoring her mother's snide remark, Isaboe sighed. "Please, Margaret, just go find them."

Shaking her head, Margaret turned and walked out onto the porch, where Connor and Will were casually enjoying their mugs of mead. Minutes later, she reentered the house, accompanied by the two men.

When they saw Isaboe, both men came to an abrupt halt. "What the bloody hell are ye wearing?" Connor growled as he put his mug down on the table a little harder than necessary. "Is that a MacPherson plaid? Where did ye get it?"

Isaboe swallowed hard when she saw his disapproval. Mustering all the courage she could, she stood tall and straight. "Connor, I have something to say."

"Ye can start with tellin' me where ye got this," he grumbled as he reached out toward the tartan. But Isaboe quickly stepped back. "Ye've heard of the law of Proscription, aye? Ye must ken this is illegal. Where did ye get it?" he demanded, glaring at her with his hands on his hips.

The look on his face momentarily made Isaboe question what she was doing, but it was too late to turn back now. She had dragged Margaret to the bad side of town, down a dark staircase, and spent too much money for the tartan and kilt, all to make a point. To not follow through on her plan now would be a waste of money and courage, regardless of how foolish it may have been.

"That's not important right now, Connor. Will you please just shut up and let me have my say?" Though every nerve was charged, Isaboe found her resolve as she stepped forward. Standing close enough to touch him, she lifted her chin and looked up into his angry blue eyes.

"Connor, I see the fire that burns inside you, I do. You can't stop being a rebel, and you feel like you don't fit in here. You try to hide it to spare my feelings, but I know how this conflict tears at you. You doubt whether we're right for each other, if you're the right man for me."

"Not now, Isaboe," he interrupted. "This is not the right time for this conversation."

"This is the perfect time! We're surrounded by the people who love us the most, who only want the best for us, together. I'm wearing this ridiculous outfit so that you'll understand how I really feel. If you won't make me a Grant, maybe you'll make me a MacPherson." Isaboe said as she clasped her hands into his, locking fingers as she stepped closer.

"Just six months ago, when I almost lost my life, I realized what's really important to me. Everything around us—this house, this city, this lifestyle—yes, at one time these things did define me, but not anymore. I don't care where we live, what you do, or what name you go by. As long as we're together, that's all that matters. Since Margaret and Will have brought us this wonderful news about Anna and Benjamin, we can leave here now if you want. We can go to America. I'll follow you wherever you go. My home is where you are." Seeing the softness in his eyes and around his mouth, she felt a swelling in her chest knowing she was finally getting through to him. "You are my other half, Connor Grant. I just want to be yours. Will you please marry me?"

With a thin-lipped smile, he shook his head before cupping her face in his hands. Hovering above her, his eyes smiled down into hers. "I've been a jackass, a dunderhead, and a bloody fool," he whispered.

"Yes, you've been all those things, but I want you anyway," she whispered back, just before Connor kissed her.

Stepping back, he slipped a hand into his pocket and pulled out a small wooden box with a hinged lid. She stared wide-eyed at what he held in his hand and was able to guess what it was—a ring box. As she looked back up into his smiling eyes, he muttered, "Ye're not the only one who did a little shopping today."

Isaboe felt her heart leap, and she felt the smile that filled her face all the way down to her toes.

Placing an arm around her shoulder and with a cocky smile on his face, Connor turned to look at the attendants who were silently observing the moment. "Well Buchanans, it looks like ye've arrived just in time for a wedding."

A few weeks earlier over a cup of tea, their neighbor, Abby Graham, had warned Isaboe that purchasing the MacPherson colors off the black market was a terrible idea, but when Margaret showed up, Isaboe had found the courage she needed. However, she didn't come out completely unscathed. Not only had her little stunt not elicited the reaction she was looking for, she had received a stern lecture to boot. Shortly after she changed out of the colorful kilt and tartan, Connor cornered her in the kitchen, and she could tell by the look on his face that it wasn't going to be a pleasant chat about wedding plans.

"What the hell were ye thinking, and who told ye where to find those colors? Do ye not ken how dangerous it was to be on that side of town by yerself, doing something so foolish?"

"I didn't go by myself. I took Margaret with me."

"Oh, so ye dragged Margaret along, putting both of ye in danger." His eyes icy and furious, he paused and placed his hands on his hips. "Have ye forgotten that yer face is still on a wanted poster? The Brits have spies everywhere."

"Will said that they weren't investigating anymore."

"That's what he *thinks*, but we dinnae ken for sure. Ye made a thoughtless decision, Isaboe, and yer reckless stunt could've put us all at risk."

Isaboe took the scolding without flinching and spoke not a word in her defense. She knew she had it coming, how rash she had been, but it had all been worth it. The result outweighed his temporary anger, and she had endured it with a smile on her lips.

"Ye're not taking this seriously, *Breagha*." As much as he was determined to get his point across, Isaboe was being much too understanding, and too happy for him to continue being angry with her. Instead, he pulled her into an embrace and looked down at her radiant face.

"Promise me ye'll never do something as foolish as that again. I'm the one who does the stupid things in this family, not you."

Isaboe chuckled. "Alright, I promise to let you do all the stupid things from now on," she said as her face lit up. "Connor, we're getting married!"

She watched as a confident grin crossed his face. "Aye, we are. And I couldna be more happy."

"Do you mean that?" Isaboe felt her heart leap. *Happy* wasn't a word Connor used very often.

But then he cupped her face gently in his hands, and for long moment just stared in her eyes without speaking. "Isaboe, I love ye so much," he finally said. "When I look at you, even the most beautiful, bright summer's day is dimmed by the light and beauty that radiates off yer face. I promise to love and take care of ye and Kaitlyn for the rest of my life."

This time, she felt her heart do a summersault, and squeezed her arms around his waist a little tighter. "You'd better save some of those poetic words for your vows, soldier," she said with a smile she felt all the way to her toes.

When they kissed, it was tender and full of love, and Isaboe wanted to stay there in his arms forever. But there were guests in their home, and the sound of voices drew them out of their embrace.

"I'll put some food out," Isaboe said as she started to turn, but Connor stopped her.

"First, go bring me that tartan and kilt so I can show ye how it's worn properly."

And when the afternoon of their nuptials finally arrived, he also wore it proudly at their wedding. The only outsiders that saw him in his plaids were Abby and Foster Graham and a couple of well-paid fiddlers. With the ceremony held inside the house, where only the few attendees could see him, Connor looked splendid in his family's colors. Standing next to his beaming bride in her lovely wedding dress, they made quite a striking impression.

As they exchanged wedding vows, promises, and with a ring slipped on her finger, Connor and Isaboe formally committed their lives to one another at long last. Sharing their happiness with family and friends, it wasn't long before music and dancing followed the ceremony, filling their home with joy and merriment.

With a fixed smile on her face, Rosalyn stood at the door of her bedroom as she watched the celebration. On the floor of their shared room, baby Kaitlyn sat next to her on a blanket.

Held in her grandmother's arms, she had been an entertaining part of the wedding ceremony, but with two fiddlers and six adults dancing around in their living room, not to mention the amount of mead and wine being consumed, the best place for the child was out of the way. The day had been warm, and with all the bodies creating more heat in the small townhouse, Rosalyn had opened the bedroom window to allow a cool breeze to waft through.

Kaitlyn began playing with a set of wooden blocks, each block cleverly carved with a letter of the alphabet on two sides and a number on the other two sides. At only six months old, the blocks were still a never-ending source of entertainment for the precocious little girl. They were easy for her little fingers to hold, made a wonderful noise when she knocked them together, and the rounded corners were comforting on her swollen gums, often finding their way to her mouth, where they became covered with baby drool.

But today, Kaitlyn was not sucking on the wooden blocks. Instead, she studied them carefully, turning each one over in her pudgy little hands before placing them down one-by-one in a row.

Glancing away from the scene in the front room, Rosalyn noticed her granddaughter's curious interest and the precise layout of the blocks. Stepping away from the door, she looked down as Kaitlyn placed the last block in the row, and she silently gasped at what she saw. Spelled out on the blanket in front of her was the word: HELP.

Suspicious that her six-month-old granddaughter had just by chance put blocks together that spelled out a word of warning, Rosalyn squatted down next to Kaitlyn, looking questioningly at the babe, who only gazed up at her grandmother with a child's innocence. "Help?" she muttered. "Help who?" Rosalyn heard the anxiety in her words.

In the next moment, the child grabbed a block and turned it over in her hands before placing it on the blanket. Rosalyn watched with concern as she repeated the gesture until two letters lay alongside the first word—A and N.

Kaitlyn appeared to be looking over her options, and then she picked up a third block with the letter V on it, placing it next to the others, but upside down. Now Rosalyn immediately recognized a clear warning that read *HELP ANA.*

"Who's here with you?" Realizing that they were not alone, Rosalyn stood and looked around the room, but saw and felt nothing.

But baby Kaitlyn did see someone. She clapped her hands, smiled, and gazed pointedly, making eye contact with a being only she could see.

"Show yourself!" Rosalyn demanded, but nothing changed. Walking over to the door, she shut it quietly before returning to stand over her granddaughter. Closing her eyes for a moment, she prepared herself, drawing energy and strength from within. After mumbling a few words under her breath, she opened her eyes and raised her hands. Instantly, sparks shot out from her fingertips, bathing everything in the room in golden light, including the tiny fey she was looking for.

Standing in front of Kaitlyn was a small, green-skinned creature, only a few inches tall with transparent wings. The Underling's long face was wide at the top and narrow at the bottom. It had the eyes of a cat, set above a small nose and a thin-lipped mouth. Long wisps of green hair covered its tiny head, swirling and moving as if each strand was alive. A slender torso supported arms that were long and willowy, and it stood on feet with curled up toes like the slippers of a court jester.

Realizing it could now be seen, the Underling looked up and smiled. But rather than giving Rosalyn a sense of ease, the deceptive grin on the strange creature's face sent shivers along her skin. Sensing an eerie presence, Rosalyn bent down and picked up her granddaughter just before the Underling abruptly sprung up off the floor. Flying around the room with the speed of a hummingbird, the fey was a blur of green light before it shot out the open window. Rosalyn held tight to her granddaughter as they shared a silent moment of wonderment, but her thoughts were deeply tainted with concern. She jumped when she heard the door open.

Music and the sound of laughter flowed into the bedroom with Isaboe leading the way. Upon seeing her mother, the baby immediately started to whine and reached for her.

"Why are you two in here alone?" A smiling, breathless Isaboe walked into the room and took Kaitlyn from her mother's arms. "You should be out there with us, enjoying the celebration."

Rosalyn inconspicuously tipped the blocks over with her foot. "There's not a lot of room out there, so we're just trying to stay out of the way." She hoped that in her exuberance, Isaboe wouldn't notice the concern that was laced into her forced smile.

"Well, I'm going to feed my baby now, so go enjoy," Isaboe said as she took a seat in the rocking chair.

The faerie's presence had left a lingering feeling of foreboding, and Rosalyn stepped toward the window, starting to push it closed when her daughter stopped her. "Please leave it open. I'm really warm and the breeze feels good." If Isaboe had been looking, she would have noticed the flash of anxiety on her mother's face, but her focus was on the baby at her breast.

Smiling and humming, only contentment showed in Isaboe's countenance as she gently rocked her child. It was her wedding day.

Rosalyn would not allow anything to diminish her daughter's joy, not today. Reluctantly, she left the window open, knowing the warning could wait, but for how long? And how would she tell Isaboe? But more importantly, who was it from? The unknown only created more questions as Rosalyn walked out of the room, taking one more glance over her shoulder before closing the door behind her.

Though she joined the party, pretending that everything was fine, Rosalyn could not shake the impending feeling of dread.

In the fight against evil, warriors must never let their guard down, for the enemy never rests. When life seems most content, that is when we need to remember:

It is always calm before the storm.

chapter 22

whatever happened to "and they lived happily ever after?"

Summer in Kirkwall meant long days and short nights, and the wedding party went on long past sunset, which meant the sun rose much too early the next morning.

Isaboe rolled over and snuggled up to Connor's back, spooning her body against his and wrapping her arms around his waist. Along with Connor's natural musky smell, there was the sweet hint of mead. They had all overindulged, but it had been worth it.

Leaning back, she ran her hand gently across the faded scars that covered his back—a tally of all they had been through, together and apart. Men and magic had tried to destroy them, but against incredible odds, Isaboe and Connor had survived. Enduring months of agonizing separation, they had managed to escape death, dealt evenly with a sadistic British officer, and evaded the grasp of an evil Fey Queen. The simple fact that they were still together, after everything life had thrown at them, was nothing short of a miracle.

Glancing at the band on her left hand, Isaboe's thoughts went in a different direction. They were married now, and a satisfied grin crossed her face as she admired the ring on her finger, but where had Connor gotten the money? *He didn't ask me for it, and I know he doesn't make enough at the forge to buy a ring like this.* Concluding that he had borrowed the money from Will, she would have preferred a less expensive ring, and to not be indebted to their friends, but it was a thing of beauty. Holding up her hand, she turned it to catch the sunlight dancing off the delicate and ornately-etched silver band.

"Why are ye awake, *Breagha?* Ye should be sleeping," Connor mumbled as he rolled onto his back, his eyes still closed.

"I'm too happy to sleep, husband," she said with a smile as she laid her head on his chest.

Connor wrapped his arm around his bride and pulled her closer. Kissing Isaboe on the forehead, he held her for a moment before propping up on an elbow and leaning over her. "Well, since we're both awake, Mrs. Grant..." he said with a coy smile.

"Hmm, Mrs. Grant. I like the sound of that." She returned his smile just before kissing him. As he ran his fingers gently up her thigh to her hip, her skin tingled under his touch, and Isaboe moaned against his lips. It was, she thought, as she lost herself to the pleasure, satisfying to contemplate the words *consummate my marriage.* It was the perfect start to a new day and a new life together.

Later that morning, while Isaboe was feeding her baby before putting her down for a nap, Rosalyn cornered Connor in the kitchen and took the opportunity to tell him what had happened with Kaitlyn the day before.

"What'd ye think it means? Who sent the message?" Concern quickly replaced Connor's early feeling of contentment.

"Those are my questions as well. I don't know who sent it. I haven't been able to make a connection with any of my sources, and I'm afraid there is a foul presence at play. At first, the creature that was in the room with us was not visible to me, but Kaitlyn saw it. Someone is blocking me and making a direct connection with your daughter. I fear she's being used to manipulate us. I'm just unclear about what to do now. Do we take this warning seriously?" Rosalyn's voice was laced with anxiety. "More importantly, how do I tell Isaboe?"

"Tell me what?" Isaboe had slipped into the kitchen with Margaret at her side and was now eyeing both Connor and Rosalyn questioningly. Glancing between them, she took a few tentative steps forward. "How do you tell me what?"

While Rosalyn repeated the details of the eerie event, Connor watched anxiously as fear rose to Isaboe's face. "We have to warn her." Panic rimmed her words. "We must go to Anna and warn her! Now!"

"Warn her about what?" Connor asked. "We have nothing to go on. Even if we did, what would ye say? That her wee, six-month-old sister had spelled out a warning with baby blocks?" Connor knew that Isaboe wanted to protect Anna, but acting without thinking it through completely would be a mistake. Isaboe had made a rash decision in the past when she believed that those she loved were in danger, and Connor seriously questioned her thinking.

"Isaboe," Margaret added compassionately, "Connor's right. And besides, when William and I met with Jared and Anna, we let them continue to believe that you had died twenty years ago. How would you explain where you've been, or...or why you're seeking her out now?"

"I don't know yet. I just know that I have to warn her!"

"We dinnae even ken if this is a legitimate threat, Isaboe!" Connor said, placing his hands on his hips defiantly.

"What's going on?" Will said, somewhat guarded as he stepped into the kitchen and into a heated conversation.

Connor glanced in Will's direction before continuing. "Think about it, Isaboe. Will and Margaret show up with this news, so we now know where Anna is, and then this warning comes? It's just too damn convenient, and I dinnae trust it. It smells like a trap."

Taking a step forward, Isaboe looked up at Connor. "You don't know that. The amulet was a gift from Queen Brighid, and it was her scouts who were hovering over Kaitlyn's bed only months ago," she said frantically. Connor could see the fright building on his wife's face as she turned toward Rosalyn and continued. "Isn't that what you said? That they were Brighid's scouts?"

When Rosalyn only nodded, Isaboe continued her impassioned speech. "Isn't it possible that Margaret received the vision because she was the one who had the amulet? Since Brighid is Kaitlyn's fey guardian, don't you think it could be her trying to warn us?"

"I'd like to think so, but... I'm not sure," Rosalyn said, with an uncertain glance to where Kaitlyn lay sleeping on her blanket.

"Well I just can't ignore it. Sure or not, we must check on Anna. And we cannot ignore the fact that mid-summer's eve is quickly approaching. What if there's a portal somewhere near Edinburgh? Do I need to remind you both it was on a mid-summer's eve that I slipped through a portal and lost twenty years of *my life?*"

As Connor watched the panic bubbling up in his new bride, he hated the conviction that there would be no good outcome to this.

"And what if Connor's right, and this is a trap?" Rosalyn asked.

"If Lorien is behind this, going to Anna might be exactly what she wants us to do." Connor added.

"But if we don't go and, God forbid, something happens to Anna, or her baby, then what?" Isaboe snapped back. "You heard what Queen Brighid said the day Kaitlyn was born: *'Twice robbed. Will she go for a third?'* Anna is my daughter and," spinning to face Rosalyn, "*your* grand-daughter. She has to have faerie blood running through her veins, too. If there is any way to prevent Anna from going through the hell I went through, then yes! That is exactly what we are going to do."

The fear in her face was hard to watch, and Connor certainly didn't want Isaboe's older daughter to be hurt any more than she did. Even though he'd never met Anna, she was now his daughter by marriage, but despite all of Isaboe's intense justifications for going, he was still uncertain.

"But what if it's Kaitlyn that Lorien's after, and not Anna?" Margaret asked, with concern showing in her wide eyes.

"And if it is a trap, we may be puttin' our daughter's life at risk. Have ye thought about that?" Connor held Isaboe's frightened gaze, trying to make her see all sides of a bad situation.

"What about Anna's life?" Isaboe almost screamed. "At least Kaitlyn will be protected. She has all of us. Who does Anna have? No one's pro-tecting her! What if we don't go and she ends up suffering the same fate I did? If I could have prevented it, but didn't, how do I live with myself? How do any of us live with ourselves?" Isaboe glanced frantically between them for an answer, but none came.

She then turned and looked directly into Rosalyn's eyes. "If you had known what was going to happen to me before it did, wouldn't you have tried to warn me? Wouldn't you have sought me out, done whatever you could to prevent me from being taken? Wouldn't you?"

Connor watched intensely as Rosalyn stared back into her daughter's eyes. Swallowing hard, she answered. "Yes. I would have." Her reply came quietly, and Connor momentarily saw pain darkening her eyes.

He knew that none of them would let that happen again, and in knowing that, he also knew what they would now have to do. "If this is a trap, we go in with our eyes wide open," he proclaimed solemnly.

When Isaboe turned back to Connor, he sensed a small measure of relief as the tension in her shoulders eased. "Yes, of course. But Connor...." She stepped forward and clutched the fabric of his shirt, "we must do whatever we can to protect Anna and her family, please."

He knew he would. He would protect them all, as was his role, regardless of the arcane and the unexplainable challenges they were up against.

CHAPTER 23

A MESSAGE FROM A BLACK CAT

The following week was a blur of activity as they prepared to leave Kirkwall. Bringing only what they could carry on horseback or fit in the buckboard, they placed most of their recently purchased home furnishings up for sale. Only days before their ship was to sail for the mainland, Isaboe stopped by at Abby's home to ask if she and Foster would take care of what hadn't yet been sold.

"And please, keep any money from the sale for your troubles," Isaboe said with a forced smile as she stood on Abby's porch brushing the hair from her weary face.

"I have no intention of keeping the profits," Abby objected. "I'll make sure to give anything we make to the church and let the minister do what he thinks best." She gave Isaboe a pained expression before speaking again. "I don't understand the rush, Isaboe. Why do you have to leave Kirkwall so suddenly?"

Looking into her friend's eyes, Isaboe didn't want to lie, but knew she couldn't be completely honest either.

"A family emergency."

"Oh, I hope it's nothing too serious. Which member of your family is it?"

Uh, it's my…my sister," Isaboe said. She hated lying but couldn't tell Abby the truth. Besides, from what Margaret had said, Anna *looked* like she could be Isaboe's sister, so the lie was as white as she could make it.

"Is she ill?

"Well…" Isaboe paused, struggling for something to say.

"Oh, please forgive me for being nosy," Abby said apologetically. "You

don't need to tell me. It's just that I hate to see you go." Isaboe saw the
sadness in Abby's eyes as she continued. "We've only known each other
a short while, but I've truly treasured our time together. You've become a
good friend, Isaboe, and I don't know if I'll ever see you again."

Seeing the emotion in Abby's face caught Isaboe off-guard, and she
felt her own emotions brewing. She really didn't want to leave either. This
little town had become her home. For the first time since returning from
Euphoria, she had felt whole again in this place, and would have preferred
to stay put. But she managed to force a smile as she clasped Abby's hand.
"Believe me, Abby, I'd like nothing more than to stay here with you in
Kirkwall. I too have treasured our friendship, and I'll miss you terribly."
She swallowed hard. "But I have to go."

Finishing up his last day and making a bit more coin before leaving
for the mainland, Connor took a moment to reflect on his time spent at
the forge. It was hard, dirty work, and his lead man was a domineering
jackass. He had made very little money at it, but the job had given him the
opportunity to provide something for his family. It also created the avenue
to meet a group of fellow covert rebels. Though he'd only helped indirectly
with the brewing underground rebellion, and therefore felt justified that
he had kept his oath to Isaboe, it had been Connor's efforts from the
outside that had protected the cause and helped it to grow.

"I dinnae ken how ye did it, but Whitmore is singin' like a canary,"
Rob McClaren said in a hushed voice. "We've got more information from
him in the last week than we've gotten in the last year." Rob couldn't
hide his enthusiasm as he and Connor walked from the forge and onto
the street.

"So, yer rat's singing now, aye? Looks like a little intimidation and
deception can change a rodent after all," Connor said with a smug smile
before holding out his hand.

Rob clasped it, returning Connor's hearty handshake. "If ye ever find
yer way back up here, there'll always be an open door at my home for ye
and yers, Brother. And it goes without saying, if there's anything that I

can do for ye, all ye need to do is ask. I've got connections throughout Great Britain. I'm sure ye can sniff em out."

Despite the harsh efficiency with which they traveled, it took two long weeks to make the journey back to Edinburgh. Laden down by five adults, a baby, and their entire lives packed into overflowing saddlebags, Rosalyn's buckboard, and a buggy Will had brought from his hostel, the party was shrouded in foreboding.

No one had any real idea what they would do when they reached Edinburgh, but Isaboe's deep-rooted protectiveness kept them moving steadily forward, knowing they had no choice but to face what was directly before them. But when the afternoon finally came and they stood outside Anna and Jared's home, they had yet to develop a plausible explanation for their arrival, other than the truth, which would not be easy to tell. Isaboe sat uneasily in the buggy, wondering if there was any way to introduce herself to Anna without her daughter thinking they had all gone mad.

"Let William and me go in first, alone," Margaret offered when she saw the fear on Isaboe's face. "Maybe I can soften the blow a bit." Looking at her friend, she knew how many emotions were battling for dominance—it would be the first time Isaboe would see her daughter as a grown woman. Her last memory of Anna was as a two-year old child. What sort of pleasantries could there be in this unexpected reunion?

"It's lovely to see you again, truly, but why this unexpected visit? You said you have something to share with me." Anna was kind yet cautious as she took a seat across from Margaret and Will in her front room.

Margaret stared at her for a moment, trying to find the right words, but none came to mind. "Is Jared home?"

"No. He's at work. Why?"

Though she would have preferred that Anna's husband be available to provide support, Margaret found her resolve and plowed forward. "What do you remember about your mother's disappearance?" She was not surprised by the look that crossed Anna's face.

"Nothing. I was only a small child. I don't even remember her. What do you mean '*disappearance*'? My mother died." Curiosity and confusion warred for control on Anna's face.

Margaret paused and looked at Will for help, but he only shrugged. There would be no assistance from that quarter. Taking a deep breath, she turned back to face Anna. "Well, there's no other way to say this, so, here it goes; your mother didn't die. She's still very much alive."

Anna abruptly stood with a look of disbelief showing on her face. "What? Both of my parents died when I was a wee child. I know that. Why would you tell me this?"

"Because it's true."

"I don't believe you. If it was true, why didn't you tell me that the first time you were here?"

"I had my reasons then, but things have changed."

"If my mother was alive, why would Ben and I be led to believe otherwise? If she didn't die and is still alive, then where has she been all these years?"

"Well, that part's a wee bit hard to explain, but it's the very reason that we're here—all of us."

"What do you mean '*all of us*'? Are you trying to tell me that my mother is alive, and is here in Edinburgh?" Anna's tone was laced with suspicion, but before Margaret could reply, the sound of an infant's cry became a priority. After scrutinizing them for only a moment, Anna turned and left the room to attend to her child.

When Anna disappeared, Margaret rubbed her hands across her face. "This is a lot harder than I thought it would be," she confessed. The weight of the message she had to deliver was draining, physically and emotionally.

"Maybe now's a good time to bring in Isaboe," Will suggested.

Margaret had been with Isaboe during every agonizing step of her journey, and when she heard a scream echo from the nursery, she had a sinking feeling that the nightmare wasn't over.

As the sound of Anna's scream reached their ears, Isaboe and Rosalyn rushed in behind Connor through the front door. With Kaitlyn in her arms, Isaboe saw Margaret and Will running toward the back of the house as they followed the sound of Anna's screams. Within seconds, they had filled the small nursery to capacity.

Holding a baby blanket in her hand, Anna frantically searched the room. "I can't find my baby! Gabriel is missing!" Anna's desperate words matched the wild terror in her eyes, but she went silent as she took account of the strangers filling her home. It was a long, uncomfortable moment before she finally found her voice. "Who are you people? Where is my son? *What's happening here?*" Anna shouted as fear and anger rimmed her words.

Margaret put her arm around Anna's shoulder before turning to look at Will. "Do you remember where Jared works?"

"Uh…a merchant's office, but I dinnae remember the name."

"It's Archibald's Merchant and Bank on Brickford Street," Anna said, her voice shaking.

"Will you go fetch him?" Margaret asked. "We need him here, now."

As Will ran off to do his wife's bidding, likely pleased to be away from the madness, Connor walked over to the open window of the nursery and glanced outside. "Was this window open before?" he asked, looking directly at Anna.

She paused a moment before responding. "No, it wasn't. Where's my baby? Who are you people?" Anna's voice and body shook as she looked over the congregation of faces. When her eyes landed on Isaboe, she gave her a double take before looking questioningly at Margaret. "What's happening here, Margaret? Where is Gabriel?"

Isaboe saw the fear and confusion written on Anna's face, and it seemed all too familiar. It reminded her of how she'd felt when Margaret found her after returning from Euphoria, though now it seemed a lifetime ago. She glanced at Margaret, who was still standing at Anna's side and offering comfort. Seeing the same look on her friend's face, she knew they had just shared the same horrible realization.

But before anyone could provide any answers, a sleek, black cat leapt onto the ledge of the open window, sauntered across the sill, and jumped down to the nursery floor.

"Is this yer cat?" Connor asked suspiciously.

Anna shook her head, "I've never seen it before."

Turning once, twice, then three times in the center of the room, the black cat began to spin until it became a blur, a black vortex, growing in height and size. With all eyes watching on in disbelief, the cat metamorphosed into another creature, another *being*, like an exaggerated mockery of a woman.

Now standing in the middle of the room was a sleek, slender figure encased in tight black leather, showing every curve and line of her body. Her face was stark white against the darkness of her attire. Lips painted black stood out underneath equally dark and menacing cat-like eyes, and her ears retained their feline shape, even the pointed tips. Slicked back against her skull like an oiled cap, not a strand out of place, her hair was the color of night. Turning slowly, she took in the shocked looks on each face in the room.

Adorned with sharp, talon-like nails, the black tips at the ends of her feet clicked along the wood floor as she sauntered across the room before coming to a stop in front of Connor. Running one lethal looking talon teasingly down the front of his shirt, a vile and alluring smile slowly grew across her face. "Hello, Connor," she said playfully. "You're looking fine." She moved in closer and took a long sniff next to his ear, unnervingly close to his neck. "And you smell yummy, just like I remember," the beautiful seductress murmured as she inched closer. Lifting her face up toward his, she whispered, "We did have fun, didn't we?"

Connor didn't flinch, nor did he meet his wife's questioning look. Instead, Isaboe saw his angry glare burning into the fey creature, his mouth drawn into a thin, tight line. "Where's the child?" he growled between gritted teeth.

"What? No pleasantries? No *it's good to see you too, Lilabeth?* I thought we were closer than that," the muse giggled. "You know you desired me, you *lusted* for me."

But before Lilabeth could say anything else, Connor shoved her to the wall and pressed his forearm against her chest, the tip of his knife just brushing her throat. "And now I want ye dead!" he spat. "What have ye done with the child?"

Seeming honestly surprised at being caught off guard, the fey quickly recovered and vanished from beneath his grip, only to reappear in the middle of the room. Touching the spot on her neck where the knife had pierced her skin, she looked at the drops of blood on her fingertips and hissed. From Isaboe's view, the fey's blood looked more the color of black than it did red, but that seemed appropriate for the being who stood before them.

With her cat-like eyes narrowed to slits, Lilabeth glared in Connor's direction before she turned and looked directly at Isaboe, who was still holding tightly to her baby. "So, this is Lorien's heir," she said, taking a few steps forward, but Lilabeth's progress was halted when both Rosalyn and Connor stepped protectively in front of Isaboe and Kaitlyn, blocking the creature's path. Turning around, the dark muse chuckled at them before floating back to the center of the room, her nails clicking on the floor. "I have a message from Lorien."

"No surprise Lorien would send her pet viper to do her dirty work," Connor growled. Lilabeth spun around and faced the three of them as Margaret and Anna stood by, speechless and clinging to each other as they watched the dark woman's every move.

"The problem with you mortals is that you have limited perception. You think this child is yours, the product of her parents' copulation. But what you don't understand is that she is more than just mortal. Not only does she have fey blood in her veins, it is Lorien's blood, *royal* blood." Looking defiantly at Isaboe, the muse paused. "And she will take her place as next in line to be the Queen of Euphoria."

As Isaboe shuddered, she felt her anger brewing, along with her fear.

"So, you see," Lilabeth continued, facing Isaboe directly, "the child was born specifically to be a queen. She will be royalty, honored above all. Your gifted daughter has been bestowed with very powerful magic, making her special, one of a kind you might say." Lilabeth's demeanor suddenly changed, and her whole body seemed tense for battle. Her black eyes darkened, becoming even more menacing than before as she turned in a circle, addressing the room. "This is Lorien's demand. You have two of your mortal weeks until mid-summer's eve to hand over Kaitlyn," she said, before shifting to face Anna directly, "or the boy child will die a most terrible death."

Isaboe watched helplessly as the color drained from Anna's face and her knees buckled, but Margaret caught her and held her up.

"Until then, the boy will not be harmed," Lilabeth continued. "He will be well cared for. But know this: mortals are not welcomed in the land of Euphoria, even those brought in for entertainment are eventually discarded," she sneered. As her eyes fell back to Connor, curiosity crossed her face. "Present company excluded, my mysterious hero. We still haven't figured out how you slipped in and out of Euphoria undetected."

"That's because yer royal highness isn't as great as she thinks she is," Connor snarled before Lilabeth turned away from his glare.

"The infant male is worthless to us. If you want to see him again, be south of Edinburgh at the Standing Stones of Glochmoor in two weeks on the night of the full moon. If you give us Kaitlyn, you can have the boy back—healthy, happy, and whole. If not, his death will not be the last. Lorien will have possession of *her* child, whatever it takes." Looking smug and confident as she slowly turned, Lilabeth didn't notice when Isaboe passed Kaitlyn into Rosalyn's arms.

That was until she barged past Connor, charging at the fey. "You can tell the Queen of Euphoria she will *never get my child!*" Isaboe screamed at Lilabeth, who was once again caught off guard, taking quick steps backward. "I will fight her until I'm dead before I let that happen. *You tell her that!*" Somehow, Isaboe's tone sounded even more threatening than Lilabeth's, and her voice was laced with vengeance.

The startled muse again vanished, only to reappear back on the windowsill. Crouched down like a cat ready to leap, she gave the room of wide-eyed faces one more look, her dark eyes black as ink. "You only have the one night—mid-summer's eve on the full moon. Give us Kaitlyn and she will live a life of royalty, raised as Lorien's daughter, and you will get the boy back. But if you don't, the child will be sacrificed. It's not a hard choice to make," Lilabeth sneered before she leapt off the ledge through the open window and disappeared.

CHAPTER 24

CONFESSIONS

When she turned to look at Anna, Isaboe found her gripping Margaret's arm with white-knuckled hands. Approaching her daughter cautiously, she felt only guilt and remorse when she saw the penetrating fear in the girl's eyes. Though a stranger, Anna was her daughter, and Isaboe could see hints of the child she had once been. She couldn't help but see herself in this beautiful young woman, masked by the terror that was clearly written across her face.

"Who are you?" Anna finally asked, her voice quivering with fear. But before Isaboe could respond, Jared rushed into the room, his face flushed from the run home. Seeing his panic-stricken wife, he immediately went to her side. Now joined by a face she trusted, Anna allowed herself to break down, sobbing into his arms.

"What's going on here?" Jared snapped, glaring around at the strangers in his child's nursery. "Who are you? Where's my son?"

Finally finding her voice, Isaboe mumbled, "Anna, Jared, I…I'm so sorry. I didn't mean for this to happen. I just thought…"

"Where is our son?" Jared roared, jolting Isaboe into silence.

Glancing at Margaret for help, Isaboe felt paralyzed by anguish, and it must have shown on her face.

Fortunately, Margaret didn't miss it. "Jared, Anna," she said, gesturing toward the door, "please, come with Will and me, and I'll try to answer your questions."

After her friends had escorted a crying Anna and a furious Jared out of the room, Connor fell in behind, but he only made it out of the nursery. Stepping up next to him, Isaboe grabbed Connor by his arm, making him stop, though he wouldn't make eye contact with her. Trying to compose herself as best she could, Isaboe watched as Connor stood in the hallway with a blank stare, looking down at his feet with his arms folded against his chest. "Do you want to explain what that was all about, or shall I just use my imagination?" she hissed.

Lifting his gaze to meet hers, Connor saw the accusation in her eyes and found himself chewing on the inside of his mouth before he was finally able to speak. "It's not what ye think."

As the anxious voices of Jared and Anna in the front room grew louder, Isaboe knew she had more important matters to address, but she also knew that if she allowed this suspicion to fester, nothing else would be accomplished. "Were you intimate with that fey creature?"

"No."

"She certainly made it sound like you were. Don't lie to me, Connor. Did you have sex with her?

"No!" he said again, but this time with more force. Avoiding her angry stare, the distraught new husband struggled to find the right words. "But I almost did," he finally confessed.

Isaboe felt her ire rising, as well as the heat on her face. "We'll finish this conversation later," she snapped. "Right now, I have to help my daughter, a daughter who thought I was dead, and probably wishes I had stayed that way. Somehow, I have to face her now and figure out what to say and what to do." Isaboe's voice wavered as she lowered her eyes. "But what I could say right now that would make anything better is beyond me."

"Isaboe, nothing happened with Lilabeth. I swear," Connor said defensively, placing his hand on her arm.

Jerking away from his touch, Isaboe shot him an angry scowl. "If that's true, why am I just now learning of this? Why didn't you tell me about your encounter with that vicious fey before?"

"I had my reasons, and they're not what ye think."

"I don't know what to think right now. But whatever *stupid* thing you did will have to wait." Taking a step closer, Isaboe paused, observing that Connor looked less like a warrior at the moment and more like a scolded school-boy. "But we will address this in detail, and you better have a *damn* good explanation!" Isaboe spat before spinning away.

Hearing the onslaught of panic-filled questions coming from Anna and her husband, Isaboe paused and swallowed hard before stepping into the front room. To Margaret and Will's credit, they were doing their best to answer, but as soon as Isaboe entered, everyone went quiet and all eyes turned on her.

Locking gazes with her daughter—a woman who looked even more like herself than she had expected—Isaboe crossed the room and took a seat opposite Anna. After taking a long, deep breath, she spoke. "I'm your mother, Anna. I didn't die twenty years ago. I was taken to another realm, another world, and I lost everything. My life and everyone in it were stolen from me, including you and Benjamin, and your father." Seeing the confusion and doubt in her daughter's face, Isaboe paused, and at that moment, she fervently wished she'd done as Connor suggested and stayed away. But it was too late to wish for a different outcome, so she struggled to speak the words she had to say.

"When we came here today, I thought it was to prevent the same thing from happening to you, and I certainly didn't expect that I would bring my curse down on you as well. I am so sorry." Isaboe's remorse was a living presence that filled the room. Between her immense regret and her anger with Connor, what little satisfaction she had found in facing Lilabeth in the nursery had been sapped away.

When Connor entered the sitting room and stepped up behind her chair, Isaboe didn't even turn to look at him, but she did glance at Rosalyn, who was standing off to the side holding Kaitlyn.

"Where is Gabriel?" Anna asked, staring at Isaboe. "How could he have been taken by that horrible cat-woman?" Anna's intensity oozed out. "I want to know where he is. *Where is my baby?*" she screamed.

Standing behind her, Jared placed his hand on his wife's shoulder and stared at Isaboe. "What has happened to our son?" His eyes wild and confused, he turned toward Margaret and Will. "What the hell is going on here? And who are these people?" he shouted.

"Isaboe is who she says she is, Jared," Will answered, "Anna's mother."

"Bullshit!" That's not possible. Even if Anna's mother was still alive, she would be much older than you," he growled in Isaboe's direction.

"Yes, under normal circumstances," Margaret added, "but something strange and terrifying happened to Isaboe, and that is why she is younger than she should be. But you must believe us; this is Anna's mother."

Still sitting, Isaboe looked up at the frightened young couple, who were both staring at her with eyes full of doubt and suspicion. "I don't care who in the hell you are," Jared snarled as he stepped toward Isaboe, his eyes flashing with fury. "I want to know where my son is!" he shouted in her face.

Sinking back in her chair, Isaboe felt her anxiety spike as Connor stepped around and put himself between her and her enraged son-in-law.

"If ye can step back and calm yerself down, we'll try to give ye the answers ye're looking for. I ken ye're upset and confused, but ye dinnae get to speak to my wife like that." Connor's voice was low and controlled, but Jared didn't miss the threat. Finally stepping back, he stood by Anna, never taking his gaze from Connor's, and Isaboe was frightened by the fury she saw shadowing Jared's eyes.

"Jared, Anna," Margaret said, drawing the young couple's attention as Connor stepped back. "Just as Isaboe told you, she was taken twenty years ago to another world, but for some reason, she didn't age. We came here today because there was concern that the same thing might happen to Anna."

"Why would you think that?" Anna asked, with curious fear resonating on her face.

"Because," Isaboe stood, "you are my daughter and you carry the same blood I do, the same blood as your grandmother." Isaboe glanced over her shoulder at Rosalyn, who was standing off to the side, still holding Kaitlyn.

Anna was near hysteria. She looked over and studied the older woman for a brief moment before returning her focus on Isaboe. "Why does that matter? How does this explain what happened to Gabriel? What do you mean—another world?"

"Anna, I know this is hard to accept, but what I'm telling you is the truth. I swear." Isaboe spoke softly, hoping to connect with her daughter. Her story seemed impossible, but she needed to somehow convince Anna of its authenticity. "There is another world that exists on a different plane, in a different time, and, though I know it sounds insane to say this, I've been there. I was taken there twenty years ago and just returned last summer. If it hadn't been for Margaret, I would surely be dead. We have spent the last year searching for you and Benjamin across the whole of Scotland." Isaboe glanced in her friend's direction. In a flash of acknowledgement, all that Margaret had been through for her sake raced through her mind, and she was touched with a renewed sense of gratitude. Giving Margaret a weak smile, she turned her attention back to Anna.

"Rosalyn, your grandmother, has special abilities, abilities that were bestowed upon her by her father. You see, her father was a...a fey."

"A what?" Anna asked, incredulously.

"A being from the world of the Underlings, a faerie."

"A faerie!?" Jared scoffed. "What kind of cruel joke is this?"

"It's not a joke, though I wish it were."

"What does any of this have to do with my little boy?" Anna asked.

"We had reason to believe that you were going to be taken too, so we came here hoping to prevent that from happening. But I had no idea that the Fey Queen would do something like this and steal your baby!"

"That cat-woman said that if we wanted to see our son alive again, you have to hand over this child." She gestured toward Kaitlyn. "But why? Who is this queen, and why did she steal my baby?" Anna's questions were laced with anxiety. "Why does she want your child?"

Stepping forward, Rosalyn handed Kaitlyn to Connor. "Because, unfortunately you are family, my dear." The sorceress began pulling up the sleeve of her right arm, and then nodded at her daughter to do the same. "Just as Isaboe said, you have fey-blood running through your veins, too."

Standing side-by-side with their right forearms exposed, Isaboe and Rosalyn displayed their matching marks. When Anna saw the starburst on the inside of each woman's elbow, she too lifted her right sleeve to reveal her matching mark. "So, you are my mother," Anna mumbled before looking at Rosalyn, "and my grandmother. But that doesn't explain where Gabriel is."

"The Queen of Euphoria from the realm of the Underlings took your child, and as you already know she is holding him for ransom to get what she wants." Isaboe turned and took Kaitlyn from Connor. "Your sister."

"My *sister?*" Anna stared at Kaitlyn with wide eyes. "What makes this child so special that this…this queen from another world would threaten my son's life?"

"Just as I was," Rosalyn answered, "Kaitlyn was conceived in the Fey Queen's realm, and therefore, we are both gifted with special abilities, or cursed, if you wish. Because your sister will be able to perform incredible magic and achieve amazing things, Lorien, the Queen of Euphoria, wants to control Kaitlyn and raise her for own demented purposes."

"Until now, we've been able to prevent that," Isaboe added. "But not without great sacrifice. There is not one among us whose life has not been drastically altered by the lengths this queen will go to achieve her goal. People I care about have been seriously injured—or killed."

"This is horse shit!" Jared bellowed. "This made-up story about faeries is nothing but a ruse! We want answers, and we want them *now!*"

"Jared, I saw her," Anna said, trying to calm her husband. "She was in Gabriel's room. At first she was a cat, but then she turned into a woman. I saw it with my own eyes," she whimpered as the tears began to flow. "That thing said Gabriel will be put to death if they don't get what they want!" Anna's tears choked back her words.

"I don't believe any of this!" Jared shouted, stepping away from Anna to address the strangers in his home. "My son is missing! Someone in this room better start explaining what really happened!" His furious gaze jumped from one face to another. "Or I'm going to the authorities to have you all arrested." Stepping forward, Jared's glare bore into Connor's. "And let them sort out." Jared's tone was threatening, fed by his fear.

"The best thing for ye to do right now is stay calm and let us figure this out," Connor replied, but his voice dipped low and his tone was intimidating. With Isaboe's face still on a wanted poster for the murder of a British officer, the last thing they needed was attention from the authorities.

"Figure out what?" Jared shouted in Connor's face. "Where's my son? And don't give me that bullshit *faerie* story again!"

"Jared," Anna said, stepping up to her husband and pushing him aside. "Please, don't. We can't go to the authorities. How could I possibly explain what I saw?"

Giving the people in his front room one more angry yet curious look,

Jared escorted Anna into the kitchen, but the home was too small for their conversation to be private, and they all listened uncomfortably as the young couple continued their heated debate on what to do. After a moment of silence, the frightened and angry parents stepped back into the front room.

Jared looked desperately at the empathetic faces acknowledging their pain and grief. The anger and denial that was etched into his features began to melt away, and was replaced with an anguish that mirrored his wife's. "So, what do we do?" he muttered. "How do we get our son back?"

Isaboe could see that her daughter was barely able to hold herself together. There was a moment of silence as she looked around the room to seek the wisdom of her companions, but she saw only the same uncertainty on each face, leaving her with a horrible sense of dread. As Isaboe struggled for something to say, Rosalyn finally spoke up, "We go get Gabriel."

"What do you mean?" Shocked at her mother's words, Isaboe looked at Rosalyn, as they all did.

"And how do we do that?" Connor asked.

"I am a feymora. I have the capability to create a portal and cross over into realm of the Underlings."

"And you know how to do that?" Isaboe asked her mother with renewed hope.

"No. But I know someone who does—Demetrick."

"Well, in case ye haven't been paying attention, Demetrick is dead," Connor grumbled. "So, unless he was such a great wizard that he can bring himself back to life, how can he help us?"

Shooting Connor a reprimanding glare, it was obvious Rosalyn didn't care for his comment. "Demetrick may not be with us physically, but his wisdom and knowledge will never be lost." Her body language and tone were laced with irritation, but she softened as she turned toward Isaboe. "I have all of his manuals, his ledgers, everything he knew and discovered about the realm of the Underlings. He told me that if I ever needed to cross over, it was all recorded in his books. I've never had the desire to examine them before, but I think the time has come."

As Rosalyn paused, Isaboe saw a slew of emotions cross her mother's face. Whatever the outcome would be, she knew the huge weight of responsibility that Rosalyn had just placed on her own shoulders. "So, I suggest we take this group up to my home in Lochmund Hills, and hopefully we can decipher the wizard's knowledge on how to create a portal."

While Jared and Anna quickly threw traveling bags together, Margaret took Will to the market to replenish their supplies, and Isaboe took the opportunity to interrogate Connor in greater detail about Lilabeth. Knowing that her mother had an intimidating manner, she asked Rosalyn to join them. Though this was a private matter between husband and wife, Isaboe knew that Connor would be less likely to dodge her questions or sweet-talk his way around her with Rosalyn present.

Cornering him in the kitchen, Isaboe stood with her arms crossed and stared at Connor with a lethal gaze. "Well?" she said, waiting for an answer.

"What do ye want me to say?"

"I want to know exactly what happened. When? Where?" Isaboe watched Connor shoot a quick, uncomfortable glance at Rosalyn, who was standing off to the side with Kaitlyn in her arms. She saw the subtle disgust in Rosalyn's eyes, though her mother said nothing.

Connor let out a long sigh. "It was right after I left Rosalyn's home, on my way back here to Edinburgh, to be with ye and Margaret. I stopped to water my horse at a small creek, and she was there. But she didna look anything like what ye saw today. Then, she was just a wee girl, a young waif in a slip of a dress, injured, bleeding, and running for her life. What was I supposed to do? Let her die out there?"

"So, you *almost* had sex with a young homeless girl? Please tell me you don't think this sounds any better."

After running his hands through his hair in frustration, Connor started again. "I agreed to take her into the city so she could catch a coach to Lollyhock, to her auntie's house. I thought I was helping out a stranded, scared lass. But in the middle of the night, she changed. Something magical happened, and Isaboe, she turned into...*you*."

"What do you mean she turned into me?"

"*Breagha*, ye ken how much I wanted ye before I left," Connor's voice was hushed. "I got caught up in her spell, and it was you with me under the stars. I was in a daze that night, and when Lorien dangled the right carrot, I bit. No, I *nibbled*, I didna bite."

"So, she took on my image, and that's when you were *almost* intimate with her?" Isaboe placed her hands on her hips. "I know your sexual appetite, Connor, and that woman was beautiful, whether she looked like me or not. Yet, you expect me to believe you didn't give into temptation, despite the illusion of her faerie spell?" As much as Isaboe wanted to believe him, she was having a hard time accepting Connor's story, and it didn't help that he had never mentioned this to her before.

Glaring at Connor with a piercing stare, Rosalyn took a step forward. "Did I not warn you to be wary of Lorien's deceptions?" the sorceress said, dark and threatening. "It was the last thing I said that morning before you took your leave. I knew she would use any means necessary to delay you, but I hadn't considered that she would use man's greatest weakness." Her disappointment in Connor was clear, but Rosalyn softened when she turned toward Isaboe. "But he is telling you the truth. If he'd had relations with Lilabeth, he wouldn't be here with us now."

"How do you know that?"

"The day Kaitlyn was born, you told us that it was a fey named Lilabeth who drug you up the hill attempting to pull you into the circle of stones. I did some investigating and discovered just who this Lilabeth is, and how she's connected to Lorien. It turns out they grew up together in Euphoria, almost like sisters. Lilabeth is not only a shape-shifter who can take on the likeness of anyone or any living thing, she is also a dark muse."

"What's a dark muse?"

Before answering her daughter, Rosalyn returned her disapproving gaze on Connor. "When a mortal man couples with a dark muse, he loses his mind, and no mortal woman will ever satisfy him. He becomes a drooling fool trying to find that which he can never again attain—the intense ecstasy of faerie glamour. As questionable as it is, his mind still seems to be intact," she said, giving her son-in-law another chastising glare.

"Ye could've provided that information a bit earlier and saved me the tongue-lashing." Connor said, snarling at Rosalyn.

"Why did you keep this from me?" Isaboe addressed her husband. "If you're really being honest, why haven't you told me this before?"

"I was hoping I'd never have to," he answered, dropping his gaze to the floor. When Connor looked back at his wife, his eyes were filled with regret. "It was my fault. I fell into her trap like a blind fool, and I didna make it back in time. I was supposed to save ye from her. I have no idea how much time I lost, but it was enough for Lorien to finish sinking her claws into ye. I wasn't there to spare ye from all those dark months alone with that filthy fey bitch. I felt ashamed that I failed you, and I couldn't forgive myself. I didna ken how to tell ye."

As Isaboe listened to his explanation she softened, knowing how easy it was to be swept up in the glamour and deception of faerie magic. "Connor, if anyone knows how manipulative Lorien can be, and how easy it is to get caught up in her illusions, it's me. I broke a promise to you and left my best friend in a sick bed—not sure if she would live or die—because of the lies she told me. She was so convincing that I almost took my life, and the life of our child." Taking a step closer, Isaboe placed her hands on his chest, looking up into his guilt-ridden eyes. "But that didn't happen because you came after me. You saved me, and our daughter. There is nothing for you to feel remorse about, Connor." She paused for a moment and studied his face. "What I really want to know is, if she looked like me, as much as you must have wanted to, what stopped you from taking her?"

"Her eyes," he answered without pause. "She may have looked like ye in every other aspect, but even in the dark, her eyes were a dead giveaway. No one has eyes like yers, *Breagha*." Connor took her face in his hands and looked deeply into her soft green eyes, speckled with flecks of gold. "Ye're the only woman I want to be with. I only wanted to spare ye this. That's why I didna tell ye."

As Isaboe felt her anxiety slipping away, confident that he was telling the truth, she gave him a soft smile. "A brave warrior once told me, '*Always ken who the enemy is, and trust your comrades; for if you don't have both, the union is doomed to fail.*' Do you remember telling me that? I do trust you,

Connor, and I want you to trust me enough to always be honest with me. I'm strong enough to hear the truth. I'm stronger than you think I am."

He chuckled. "Aye, I ken that. When ye had Lilabeth dancing backward, I've never been more proud o' ye," he said with a glint in his eyes and a grin on his lips. "I love ye, Isaboe Grant, and I promise I'll never keep anything from ye again," he whispered, just as his mouth found hers.

Isaboe wrapped her arms around his waist and sank into his kiss. However short, she allowed herself this brief moment and was able to forget about everything else, including her mother.

"Excuse me," Rosalyn interrupted, "but I've lived with the two of you long enough to know how this argument usually ends, and now is not the time."

Feeling the blush on her face at Rosalyn's comment, Isaboe replied, "We've just always preferred to finish such discussions in our room privately."

"Hmm, but discussion is not what I normally heard coming from your room. You forget, Isaboe—the walls were thin."

"What?" Isaboe suddenly felt overexposed.

"She's right, *Breagha*. Ye're not very quiet," Connor added with a sheepish smile.

Suddenly feeling embarrassed, Isaboe didn't know how to respond to either of them. After giving Connor a fierce scowl, she turned to face Rosalyn. "Do you really think you can do this? Not that I doubt your abilities, but, can you really create a portal into the world of the Underlings? Will we really be able to get Gabriel back?"

"Well, there's no way to know for sure unless we try, right? Besides, I don't see that we have any other options." Placing Kaitlyn back into Isaboe's arms, Rosalyn gave her daughter a weak smile. "Let's go find a way to get Gabriel back."

CHAPTER 25

DUSTY MANUALS
AND OLD MEMORIES

Before leaving Edinburgh, Will had offered his small buggy to Jared and Anna for transporting themselves and their luggage. After making sure that Margaret was tucked safely on the buckboard with Rosalyn, Isaboe, and Kaitlyn, he joined Connor in riding horseback up into Lochmund Hills. But the slow moving party didn't get far before darkness overtook their progress, and they spent the night camped out under the stars.

The following morning they woke to find the land covered by fog, completely blocking the warmth of the sun. Staying to a course she knew well, Rosalyn had the group up the side of the mountain by late morning. The fog had cleared off just as Rosalyn's amazing home came into view—a cave dug deep into the mountain.

After settling in and putting on a pot of tea, Rosalyn led Connor and Will into one of the smaller passages off her main living area, instructing them to haul out three trunks, one of which contained the wizard's manuals and artifacts. Sitting on the deck overlooking the great canyon that provided a panoramic view, Connor, Isaboe, and Margaret began going through the trunks, searching for the promised information.

"I'll go take care of the horses," Will said as he stood at the opening of the cave, looking as if he needed something to do.

Shortly after arriving, Jared and Anna had gone for a walk to explore the area. As much as Isaboe desperately longed for a deeper relationship with her daughter, the anguish of losing Gabriel kept Anna distant and aloof. Isaboe knew she had to wait patiently until she was ready, if she ever would be.

"I've made some chamomile tea," Rosalyn said, stepping onto the deck and holding a tray, "and I added a bit of mint for extra flavor. Help yourselves." Placing the tray on the table, Rosalyn took a seat and began joining in the search, rummaging through one of the trunks.

Isaboe and Margaret sat in front of another trunk, lifting Rosalyn's treasures from their protected resting places. Setting aside some silver dishes, serving ware, and an elegantly crafted clay vase, all protected by a heap of linens, they discovered cloaks, dresses, and other garments at the bottom of the trunk. Lifting out one elegantly embroidered gown in deep-blue silk, Isaboe openly admired it, quietly wondering when her mother had found use for such an outfit. It hardly seemed her style. As she gently passed the dress to Margaret, something else caught her eye. Reaching down into the chest, Isaboe lifted out a burlap bag. Wrapped inside was a small, round, white box embossed with raised gold ivy along all the sides and across the lid. When she turned it over in her hands, she noticed it was slightly blackened on the bottom and instantly recalled the story her mother had shared months earlier over a campfire—the story of how Isaboe had come to be. Looking up, she caught Rosalyn's attention.

"This is the box, isn't it? The one my father gave you."

Rosalyn was rummaging through another trunk but glanced up at her daughter and at what she held in her hands. Her face showed no emotion, but her long pause of silence said plenty. "I don't know why I've kept that all these years. Maybe because I knew I'd never go to Paris, and that scarf was the closest I'd ever get."

Isaboe regarded her mother, silently wondering if there might have been another reason she had held onto it. "May I?"

Rosalyn only nodded.

Removing the lid, Isaboe lifted out the beautiful blue scarf. Along with the silken fabric, a slight scent wafted up out of the box, and Isaboe tried to identity the smell before it vanished. It was a mix of faded cologne, wood smoke, and Rosalyn's memories, all of which had been protected by the beautiful vessel and were waiting to be released at this moment. Though she had long wanted to learn more about her absent father, Isaboe knew how much it had hurt her mother to share the story of her conception. Concerned that further questioning might only push Rosalyn away, she opted not to take the risk. After being raised by an unloving woman, Isaboe finally had what she'd always been denied—a mother's love. She would not threaten that relationship for the sake of needlessly prying questions about the man who had broken Rosalyn's heart.

"What's this?"

Isaboe's thoughts were interrupted by Connor as he pulled out a large bundle from the chest he was sitting in front of. Untying the binds, he let the heavy fabric drop to expose a pile of books. The neatly stacked manuals were strapped together by a heavy braid of tightly woven leather.

Rosalyn stood and walked over to Connor, looking at what he held in his lap. "Put that on the table please."

After Connor did as instructed, Isaboe shoved the scarf back into the box and returned it to its resting place. Joining the others at the table, they examined the braid that bound the manuals. Whoever had placed the binding around the stack of books had intended to keep them securely closed, and there was no clear sign of how to release it. Stepping closer, Rosalyn mumbled a few incoherent words and then passed her hand over the bundle of books. Instantly the braid snapped open. "These are Demetrick's manuals," the sorceress said. "Everything we need to know should be in here."

Rocking Kaitlyn in her arms, Isaboe stood next to the cot in the small alcove tucked in the back of Rosalyn's expansive home. With the lamp turned down low, the soft light in the cave was soothing, and she quietly hummed, attempting to lull her child to sleep. But young Kaitlyn was restless and fought the much-needed nap. With all her focus on her baby, Isaboe didn't notice Anna standing at the doorway, silently observing.

"Isaboe? Can I talk to you for a moment?"

Turning in the dim light to look at Anna, Isaboe saw that she could have easily been looking at her own reflection. After spending months imagining a reunion with her daughter, she had never pictured it like this. Her fantasy was always happy, blissful, with shared tears of joy. But re-entering her daughter's life had only brought pain to Anna and her husband, so Isaboe held back her first instinct to ask how Anna was doing. She already knew.

"Of course, please, come in. I was trying to put Kaitlyn down for a nap, but she doesn't seem too interested in the idea right now."

"How's it going on the research? Has Rosalyn found the manuals?" Anna asked tentatively as she entered the small room.

"Yes. Rosalyn and Connor are pouring over the books right now. It's just a matter of time before she finds what she's looking for," Isaboe said with a reassuring smile, giving up on putting Kaitlyn down for a nap. As she turned up the lamp, Anna only nodded, but Isaboe could see the anguish in her face, and the panic that hovered just below her composure. "How did Jared manage to get the time off from work?"

"He fabricated a story that Gabriel…" Anna swallowed hard, fighting back the tears. "…that Gabriel was very ill, and that we'd heard of a healer from Inverness who could deal with his affliction. He told his employer that he would need at least two weeks. I just hope he'll still have a job to go back to."

"Jared is a good man, Anna. I'm sure his employer sees that too." Isaboe offered a soft smile, but Anna's expression remained stoic, and as she stared at her mother, an uncomfortable silence filled the small room.

"Margaret told us everything," Anna finally confessed, "All that you went through after you came back sounds like a horrible nightmare. I can't imagine what it must have been like for you."

Isaboe hesitated before responding. "It was a horrible nightmare. I still find myself wondering if I will eventually wake up, but I've learned to accept it. Losing you, your brother, and your father in the blink of an eye almost killed me. I wanted to die those first few weeks, and if it hadn't been for Margaret, I most likely would have."

"So, you really have no memory of where you were all that time?" Anna asked skeptically.

"I occasionally have flashes, but, no, no real memories. Rosalyn explained that the reason I don't recall my time there is because I passed through a veil of faerie glamour on the way out, kind of like a magic curtain. It washed away my memories."

"It all seems so hard to believe. Just the fact that you're my…my mother, and that you were gone all those years to another world..." Anna dropped her tear-filled eyes to the floor. "And now my son's been taken there."

Isaboe heard the anguish in her daughter's voice and wished there was something she could say to offer hope, but at the moment, she had nothing to give. "I'm so glad that Margaret's here," Isaboe finally said. "She's been a great friend and an amazing source of support. When you were a baby, she couldn't spend enough time with you. You were her favorite playmate."

"Yes, Margaret has been very kind," Anna said, sniffing back the tears. "I can tell how much she loves you, and how protective she is of you and Kaitlyn." When Anna glanced at the squirmy child in Isaboe's arms, the look on her face changed. "What makes this baby so special? My son's life is at stake because of her. Why does this Fey Queen want her so badly?"

Feeling an intense stab of guilt, Isaboe knew that Kaitlyn was the direct cause of Anna's baby being abducted, but she could not regret protecting her child. Anna was speaking from a level of anguish that Isaboe knew all too well, and she also knew that no logic could mitigate the pain of losing a child.

"Your sister is a feymora, a human child born with very special abilities. Your grandmother and I don't yet understand exactly what those powers will be, but I have seen firsthand what Rosalyn is capable of. We suspect Kaitlyn will be even more gifted. That is why the Queen of Euphoria wants possession of her, to raise Kaitlyn as her own, and she has no good intentions for your sister's talents."

Isaboe thought about how her six-month-old child had laid out a warning in baby blocks, encouraging them to make the trip, all in an attempt to save Anna. Realizing now that Connor was right—that it had been a trap after all—she saw how they'd all been used in Lorien's twisted game of power, and she feared deeply for the future of her family. Isaboe watched as Anna attempted to digest all this new information about fey magic, but she could see that knowing of Kaitlyn's abilities gave her older daughter no comfort.

Offering a distraction from their thoughts, the baby whined and pulled at her mother's bodice. "I just fed you," Isaboe said with a hint of frustration. She knew that her milk was starting to dry up, but Kaitlyn had not gotten enough to fill her little belly. "Sorry, wee one. That's all I have to give you right now."

Glancing up, she caught Anna's body reacting to seeing the baby's desire to nurse. When she cupped her breasts and pulled her hands back, her dress was wet. Watching the reaction of both daughters, Isaboe knew how to help Anna's affliction as well as Kaitlyn's hunger, but she couldn't bring herself to ask. Fortunately, she didn't have to.

"Do you think Kaitlyn would let me nurse her? I have all this milk and no baby to feed."

Hearing the sorrow in Anna's words, Isaboe swallowed hard before answering. "We can try." As she started to hand Kaitlyn over to her sister, Isaboe stopped when she noticed a tear running down Anna's cheek. The two women—a mother and daughter who looked more like sisters—stood looking at each other, and for a few silent moments they shared the unspoken understanding of each other's pain.

As Anna wiped the tears from her face, she broke the silence. "Can I ask you another question? And please, Isaboe, tell me the truth. Do you really think Rosalyn can bring Gabriel back?"

Isaboe paused and wondered to herself if Rosalyn could really pull this off, but she needed to offer some reassurance. "If it can be done, Rosalyn is the one to do it. Your grandmother is gifted, so much so that I would be dead if she weren't here with us." Isaboe placed a hand on Anna's arm. It was the first time she had attempted physical touch, and it gave her some comfort that her daughter didn't pull away. "Anna, I promise we will do everything in our power to bring your son back," she said with a silent prayer that it would not be a promise made in vain, but one she would actually be able to keep.

chapter 26

passages

The following morning's weather was quite dramatic as the clouds rolled in, propelled by a vicious wind that cut through the canyon and across the treeless, peat-covered ridge, forcing the team to continue their research inside the protection of the cave. They settled around the long, stone slab that Rosalyn used for dining. It gave easy access to the open kitchen, and the high windows, strategically carved through the cave walls, provided a surprising amount of natural light.

Even though she lived alone, Rosalyn's home was quite spacious. Years of carving and blasting into the rock had created a unique and comfortable dwelling, but not without the help of her strange companions, Leo the giant and Turock the dwarf. They too lived on top of the ridge, and though Rosalyn knew where Leo's sleeping cave was located, only a stone's throw away from her own, she had no idea where Turock laid his head at night. But the three outcasts had made a deep connection, in their own ways, having been rejected by a harsh and judgmental world, they had found solace living together in the protection of the hills. The physical assistance her unusual friends provided had allowed Rosalyn to live comfortably in this isolated place, and their company was an important side benefit in warding off loneliness. These two strange souls had become her closest friends, living free from persecution under the protection of a sorceress.

Over the years, small rooms had been dug into the rock wall along the breezeway that flowed through the open cavern, providing resting and storage areas away from the main room. Leo and Turock had provided the skill and strength to carve the cave into a livable abode, and Rosalyn had provided all the trappings of civilization. Their combined passion had made it a home.

It was in one of the storage coves that Rosalyn was approached by Isaboe later that afternoon, and the look on her daughter's face spoke of anxious concern.

"How do we know for sure that Gabriel is actually in the realm of the Underlings?" Isaboe asked. "He could have been taken from his bed and hidden somewhere here, in our world. Just because Lilabeth said he was taken to Euphoria doesn't make it true. Don't forget that she's a liar and a murderer who killed my sister. We don't really know for sure that Gabriel has even left this world."

As Isaboe stared at her, waiting for an answer, Rosalyn could see the fear in her eyes. "Do you think we would be going through all of this if I hadn't already considered that possibility?" Rosalyn watched the expression on her daughter's face sink. "No, I did not forget what Lilabeth is, or the damage that she and Lorien are capable of. I made a connection with my own sources in their realm, and it's been confirmed. Gabriel is in Euphoria. I know that is not what you wanted to hear, but it is what we have to face."

As the afternoon lengthened, Will and Margaret worked in the kitchen to prepare the evening meal while Anna and Kaitlyn napped. Jared offered to help peruse Demetrick's manuals, and Rosalyn directed him toward anything that mentioned *passage, gateway, or transport*. As a former college student, and now an employee of a prominent merchant bank in Edinburgh, he was not only skilled at reading the wizard's often incomprehensible handwriting, but this also let him do something useful in an attempt to save his son.

After hours of reviewing, carefully flipping through yellowed, fragile parchment, and squinting at hand-written, cramped pages of text, they still had not discovered the way to follow Gabriel into Euphoria. As Demetrick's former student, only Rosalyn seemed to understand what she was reading, and she commented to Isaboe that there were many passages she would like to reexamine in more detail when they weren't facing an emergency.

But it was Jared who found the first possibility, concentrating intensely as he followed the wording on a page with his finger. "I think I might have something here." Getting everyone's attention, he continued reading aloud. "...to create the space and time deviation...projection of matter between dimensions ...celestial mechanics and the placement of elements must be in accordance with the quadrature of the moon in relationship to the position of the catalyst...velocity of mass from one point in time to another, and there are some charts and formulas here as well," he said, before turning the page.

Stepping up behind him and looking over his shoulder, Rosalyn picked up the book. Across the top of the page were written the words: *Viae et Viatores*. Rosalyn had retained enough Latin to recognize: *Ways and Wayfarers*. They had found what they were looking for, she knew that much, but the Latin was dense and theoretical. She could even see places where it looked as if the wizard had created new words to denote his studies. The charts and formulas were even more foreign as she tried to interpret the wizard's genius mind and intricate instructions.

Placing the book back on the table, she flipped through the pages, shaking her head. "I don't know what any of this means!" she cried out in frustration. "It might as well *all* be written in Latin, and you know how I feel about *Latin*!" Rosalyn spit out her last word while giving the book another scathing look.

"Aye, ye killed a nun over it," Connor said nonchalantly, standing at the other end of the table as he munched on a handful of nuts.

When Rosalyn shot him a deathly glare, his self-assurance instantly melted. Knowing that Connor had regretted the words the moment he had spoken them, she watched him turn a bit green as he stopped chewing and swallowed hard.

Jared looked up, scrutinizing Rosalyn. "You killed a nun? Because of Latin?"

"Thank you, Connor!" Rosalyn snapped.

"*What is wrong with you?*" Rosalyn heard her daughter hiss. "When will you learn to keep your thoughts to yourself?"

"Sorry," Connor managed to choke out an apology before Isaboe elbowed him between the ribs.

As Rosalyn paced back and forth, she met Isaboe's apologetic eyes to share a silent moment of commiseration. She was already frustrated, and now Jared was waiting for an answer.

"It was an accident, Jared," Isaboe spoke up in her mother's defense. "Rosalyn was raised in a convent where the nuns mistreated her. She was young and surrounded by magic, but she didn't understand it or know how to use it." She dropped her gaze to the open books lying on the table. "That's really all you need to know."

"A pat answer—that seems to be this group's response to everything," Jared said with quiet anger as his gaze jumped suspiciously from one face to another. After a long uncomfortable silence, he glanced back down at the open book. "These look like scientific formulas, perhaps even complex physics."

"Knowing that might be a start," Rosalyn said with a calm voice, attempting to defuse the residual feelings of mistrust. "But it puts us no closer to being able to read it, let alone understand it."

"No. But maybe we can find someone who can. The University of Edinburgh has a very sophisticated science department," Jared offered.

"Aye. The lad makes a good point. Universities are full of brainy, young minds. Let's go recruit one," Connor agreed.

"And how do you propose we do that?" Margaret asked, holding a paring knife as she stood behind the cooking table, which was covered by the pile of potatoes she and Will had peeled. "Are you just going to walk into a science class and ask if anyone can interpret that book?"

"Unless you have another suggestion, why not?" Jared asked.

"Gabriel needs us," said Isaboe. "So, unless anyone else has a better idea, let's do as Jared suggests," she said before turning toward him. "And you ought to go. You'll fit in best on the university campus."

"Well, there's no time like the present," Jared announced as he stood. "The sooner we can decipher this, the closer we are to getting my son back."

"I'm going as well," Rosalyn added. "We'll need supplies and food to feed this group for a few more days."

"Why don't we all go then?" asked Isaboe. "No one wants to sit here and wait."

"And I'd enjoy a stroll about the city," Will added. "How 'bout you, Maggie?"

Rosalyn watched as Margaret looked about the room, and when her gaze fell on Jared, she could almost read Margaret's thoughts. *And if Anna doesn't wish to make the trek back down into Edinburgh, who will stay here with her?*

Removed from the group, Anna had avoided interacting with anyone except Jared, and her absence was now noted. Rosalyn had observed that her granddaughter had been spending most of her time alone with her newly discovered, younger sister. Despite Kaitlyn's direct link to Gabriel's kidnapping, she seemed to find some comfort in nursing Kaitlyn. In fact, without any formal arrangement, Anna had taken over that duty. It was obvious that Kaitlyn's ongoing demands for nourishment had lessened the void created by Gabriel's absence. But Rosalyn silently wondered how Isaboe felt about being replaced. Though she knew her daughter would never let on, it had to bother her on some level.

"I think I'll stay," Margaret finally answered. "We have a baby that needs to be cared for and clothes that need washing. Maybe I can convince Anna to give me a hand."

The following morning, Margaret was digging around in the storage alcove. "Why would one woman have so many crocks?" she muttered to herself as she set aside another stoneware pot, frustrated at not being able to find what she was looking for by the light of one small lantern.

The Edinburgh traveling party had left in the wee hours of the morning, and Margaret had approached Rosalyn as she was preparing to leave. Since she was staying back with Anna and Kaitlyn, Margaret needed to do something other than laundry to keep occupied. She wasn't good at being idle.

"Yes, you can take inventory of what preserved meats I have left," Rosalyn had suggested. "It's been a few months, and I don't recall what might be left of the salted pork or the brined beef. Leaving home last fall, I wasn't able to restock my winter's supply, so you may not find much, if anything at all. If not, please ask Leo to fetch us some fresh venison, or maybe butcher a lamb. Either works. We just need enough to feed this group for a few days." Rosalyn turned to leave but stopped to look back at Margaret. "And don't let him offer up my hens in place of hunting down fresh meat. We need all the eggs those chickens can provide right now."

As Margaret looked into one more empty clay pot, it was becoming obvious that Leo would have to procure a fresh kill, as she hadn't yet found any meat in the food storage cave behind the sleeping quarters. She did, however, find a crock of flour and one of lard. All she needed was a few eggs and she could at least bake some bread. Continuing her search she found a crock that contained dead animal parts—including pigs' and rabbits' feet, large talons that appeared to have come from very large birds, the heads of rats and other small vermin, and what looked to be the tail of a skunk. Closing that one, she picked up a crock that contained some strange powder. When Margaret sniffed it, she instantly sneezed, just before the room began to spin. It took her a while to shake off the residual effects, but after her head cleared, she proceeded with her investigation, uncovering a number of stoneware vessels filled with dried herbs, odd-smelling liquids, and one with some sort of rotting matter that could no longer be identified. Grimacing at the smell, she quickly slapped down the lid before more of its putrid odor could escape. Continuing her search, she found a large crock filled with oats, and other containers of dried grains and flowers, but no meats.

"What are you doing, Margaret?"

Startled by the voice behind her, Margaret jolted upright. "Anna! Oh, my Good Lord, child!" she said, clasping her hands to her chest and taking a deep, relieving breath.

"Sorry," Anna offered. "I didn't mean to startle you." Stepping forward into the storage alcove, Anna glanced around in the dim light of the lone lantern. "Has everyone else left?"

"Yes, they all left about an hour ago."

"It's so quiet with everyone gone," Anna almost whispered, as if the silence was a sacred thing. "Kaitlyn's still sleeping."

"Aye, those men don't know how to talk softly," Margaret said, turning back around to peruse the array of stoneware vessels, pots and baskets, wondering if she had checked them all.

"Jared didn't even say good-bye."

Hearing the ache in Anna's words, Margaret stopped her investigation to give the young woman her attention. "He probably just didn't want to wake you."

"Or he just didn't want to talk to me. He's been really distant ever since we've arrived here. It's like he doesn't know what to say to me, so he's not saying anything."

"Jared's just been staying busy. He misses your son and is desperately trying to find a way to bring him home."

"Don't you think I want that?" Anna sounded almost offended.

"I only meant…"

"Don't you think if I *knew* how to bring Gabriel back, I would? I would do anything, but I don't understand what's happened to him. I'm still trying to wrap my brain around the idea that my son could have actually been taken to another world!" Anna paused, and her agitation melted into a look of hard suspicion. "If you want to know what I think, the fact that Rosalyn dabbles in sorcery makes this all sound like witchcraft and black magic, and my son just happened to get caught up in the middle of it. At least that makes more sense than believing in this crazy story about some land called Euphoria where *faeries* live," Anna scoffed.

"Oh, does it?" Margaret chided. "Well, you may have the black magic part right, but you've got the rest of it wrong. Both Rosalyn and Isaboe have fey blood in their veins, just like you, child." Margaret saw the doubt in Anna's eyes and softened. "I understand all of this is hard to grasp, but you've been told the truth, Anna, and we're doing everything possible to bring your child back. No one feels worse about this than your mother."

"*She's not my mother!*" Anna shouted. "My mother was Helena Reddington, the *only* mother I've ever known. She was the one who held me when I was a child, crying in the middle of the night from bad dreams. Helena was the one who took care of me when I fell out of the apple tree and broke my arm, when I had my first broken heart, and it was she who was there on my wedding day." Anna's memories quickly faded, and her face hardened. "And it's probably a good thing she didn't live long enough to see this. No, Margaret, Isaboe may have given birth to me, but she's *not* my mother," she said coldly.

"She most certainly is, and I'll not let you deny her that!" Margaret snapped back, quickly coming to Isaboe's defense. "Anna, I know you're hurting, and yes, Isaboe wasn't there for your childhood, but none of that was her fault. She wasn't there because those moments were stolen from her. There was nothing she loved more than you and your brother, and it almost killed her when she discovered what she had lost."

"But why come looking for me now, after all these years? I thought she was long dead, and I was fine with that. I can't even tell you the last time I had even thought about her. I didn't ask for her to come back into my life and bring her curse down on me. I didn't ask for any of this!"

"And you think Isaboe did? When she returned a year ago, in her mind, you were still her two-year-old baby girl. She only wanted you back, just like you want Gabriel back." Margaret took a step forward and felt her protectiveness building for both women. "I'm gonna let all that bitterness slide on by, my love, because I know how you feel right now. But I will ask this of you: take all that pain and fear you're feeling, thinking that you may never see Gabriel again, and then multiply it by three. That's how Isaboe—*your mother*—felt when she found out she'd lost her husband and both her children. Please try to have a little empathy, my dear. You're not the only one who's lost skin in this battle."

Turning away, Anna went quiet, and when Margaret heard her sniffles, she worried that her words may have come out too strong. "I didn't mean to be insensitive, Anna, but you've come late into this game. After what I've seen, and what we've all been up against, I guess I've built up a bit of hard skin." She gave Anna a comforting smile before picking up the lantern and heading for the opening. "Come along. I'm not finding what I'm looking for here."

"So, what were you looking for?" Anna asked, and Margaret was pleased to hear her voice sounded less heavy.

"Well, I was searching for some meat Rosalyn thought she might have put up, but I didn't find anything edible." Looking back at her, Margaret knew keeping Anna occupied and her fragile mind off of her worries was the best course of action. "Let's go see if we can at least gather up a basketful of eggs for breakfast. And it appears I'll have to ask Leo to hunt down some fresh meat."

"Who's Leo?"

"That's what we're gonna find out," Margaret said as they exited the cramped storage area. "Rosalyn said there's a bell outside her front door. Apparently, all I need to do is ring it and Leo will show up." Stopping halfway through the main cave, Margaret turned. "She also mentioned that he's kind of a big fellow, so we're not to be frightened by his size, whatever that means."

Anna only shrugged. "Well, like you said, I guess we're going to find out."

CHAPTER 27

NOBLEMEN AND SCHOLARS

The traveling party arrived in Edinburgh by mid-afternoon and split up. Rosalyn and Isaboe left to gather the supplies needed to make Rosalyn's home livable for such a large group, while Connor, Will, and Jared rode off in the direction of the university, hoping to recruit the mind of a scholar intelligent enough to interpret a wizard's words.

In the aftermath of their hurried exit from Kirkwall, it had been a number of days since Isaboe and her mother were alone together. For weeks they had been nearly inseparable, but their easy camaraderie now felt overshadowed by the weight of their mission. Isaboe's mind was filled with misgivings, and she knew Rosalyn must have them as well.

Months earlier, when she'd walked the streets of Edinburgh, Isaboe had been lost in a fog of sorrow, bewitched by Lorien into believing that she had nothing to live for. Those memories felt like a heavy chain around her neck, and the remnants of those links still lingered, invisible scars that ached deep beneath her skin. Though she had finally managed to free herself from the Fey Queen's control, the memory of that time rekindled a familiar, oppressive feeling that triggered Isaboe's deepest fears. Having denounced the queen's controlling grasp—thanks entirely to Queen Brighid, Kaitlyn's fey guardian—she knew that Lorien could no longer communicate directly with her, but she had never doubted that the deceitful queen would return. And, unfortunately, she had been correct. However, this time Isaboe was not alone and not nearly so vulnerable. She had found a new resolve to continue the fight, surrounded by people who loved her.

"Let's stop here," Rosalyn said, turning down a side street lined with vendors. Falling into step together, the ladies strolled through the outdoor market, where they could hear idle chit-chat about the quality of the merchandise as prospective buyers bartered with vendors on the prices of their wares. This somehow calmed Isaboe's anxiety, and they made quick work of their chores—picking up supplies, food, and other necessary items. After ducking into a small apothecary, Isaboe saw the surprise on the store clerk's face when Rosalyn asked for some very potent herbs and ointments. But Rosalyn's presence gave off an authoritative air, and few ever questioned her when she donned her matronly role. Rosalyn's demeanor demanded a certain fearful respect, and when the clerk looked at Isaboe with a questioning expression, she gave him only a charming smile. Though Rosalyn's order was filled without a negative comment, they did not leave without a suspicious glare.

Back on the boardwalk, carrying enough supplies to feed their small army, the two women bustled through the streets toward the edge of town where their buckboard and horses awaited them. As they approached their destination, they came across a group of people gathered in front of a theater. Having to push their way through the crowd, they stopped just short of tripping over a large sign placed in front of the building, and Isaboe stepped back to read it:

FOR A LIMITED ENGAGEMENT –THIS WEEK ONLY
Monday, Wednesday, and Friday Evenings at 5:30
Come hear the projected economic forecast
For the next decade in the Kingdom of Great Britain
As presented by His Lordship,
Marcus Vanderburgh, The Baron of York
Public admission by ticket only
See concierge for private audiences only by appointment

Feeling her breath catch in her throat when she read the Baron's name, Isaboe immediately tried to shield it from her mother, but the damage had already been done. Oblivious to the crowds pushing by, she watched Rosalyn's lips twitching as a dark look flashed in her eyes. Isaboe couldn't tell if it was anger or panic, but to take the edge off this upsetting revelation, she attempted to lighten the mood "Oh, look Mother, Father's in town!"

Trying to defuse her mother's reaction, she injected as much playful sarcasm into her words as she could, but Rosalyn didn't find it humorous. Shooting Isaboe a look that said so, the sorceress turned and began firmly pushing her way through the crowd. "It'd be nice to at least get a look at him," Isaboe said, falling in behind. "You have to be just a little curious, right? It would be nice to see him in person and maybe even talk to him." Having only recently discovered that her father was, in fact, the Baron of York, but having never laid eyes on him, it seemed too good an opportunity to miss.

Before Rosalyn could protest, another board advertising the Baron's visit caught her eye, and she stopped to examine the detailed sketch of Marcus Vanderburgh hanging in the theater window. Standing in front of a large, marbled-stone fireplace, he was dressed in a nobleman's finest attire. Without the crowd to rush them, Rosalyn carefully studied the drawing. As Isaboe watched her mother's face, it looked as if she were trying to see the young man she had once known, though it was a lifetime ago. Isaboe thought she saw something pass across Rosalyn's eyes that resembled the hurt of a vulnerable young girl, but it was gone too quickly to be sure.

"As you know, my amazing mother, time can change people, both inside and out."

Rosalyn turned to look at Isaboe with a sober expression, but the earnestness in her daughter's comment had softened her, though only for a moment. "I sincerely doubt there has been any improvement to his morals," she said firmly. "No, Isaboe, I don't want to see him again. And I dare say you will be happier with just that picture of your father, rather than the man in truth." Gesturing toward the image, she snarled fiercely, "I wouldn't have paid money to hear that man talk when he was young and handsome, so I certainly won't do it now. We have more important matters to attend to than listening to a baron's lies."

With that said Rosalyn spun on her heels and began swiftly walking toward their horses. Realizing that this was now a closed subject and that it was unlikely she would be meeting her father, Isaboe had to quicken her steps just to keep up with her mother's new pace.

Connor and Will hadn't had access to the kind of education offered at the University of Edinburgh, and the high, sweeping walkways and intimidating buildings were entirely new to them. Fortunately, Jared felt right at home, and the two former warriors were happy to follow his lead down the enormous hallways. The elaborate stone buildings encompassing the University of Edinburgh were daunting enough, but finding the right person was turning out to be more challenging than they'd first hoped. The three men had agreed it would be best to avoid professors and educators who would ask too many questions. But after presenting the piece of parchment, on which they had scribbled some of Demetrick's formulas, to more than a few young men, they had received only confused looks.

As they passed by the large, open doors of a library, the men glanced in, wondering if there may be a genius mind hiding inside, just waiting to be found. Jared caught the attention of three young men exiting the library and called them over. Showing the parchment and expecting the same unsatisfying results, he instead received an encouraging reply.

One of the young men, a curly-haired youth, sporting a face of freckles, was the one to provide the first solid lead. "If anyone knows how to decipher this, it would be Hammy." The other two nodded, confirming the opinion of their fellow student.

"Where can we find this Hammy fellow?" Connor asked.

After they were pointed toward the back of the library, Connor and Will followed Jared as they made their way across the spacious room. But their heavy footsteps echoed on the polished floor, drawing baffled looks from the students, as well as a disapproving glare from the librarian.

Finally reaching their destination, they stood in front of a table where a young man sat alone, completely engrossed in a book. He hadn't noticed their approach until Connor made his presence known. "Are ye Hammy?"

The rather stout youth, whose dark brown hair was combed back and neatly tied, removed his reading glasses before he glared defiantly at the men hovering above him. "The name is Hamish," he corrected in a sour tone. "And who wants to know?"

Jared placed the piece of parchment on the table and asked, "Does this make any sense to you? Can you decipher this formula?"

As he slid the parchment closer, Hamish shot a look of suspicion at each man towering over him before glancing down. Taking his time, he read and re-read the scratched-out formulas and Latin instructions, scrutinizing the words and diagrams that Rosalyn had transcribed for them to show an expert. When the young student's eyes shot back up, they were full of questions. "Are you trying to… travel through time?" he almost whispered. "Where did you get this?" Wide-eyed and round faced, Hamish closely examined the three men looking down at him.

"So, you can interpret this? Do you know how to decipher this formula?" Jared asked.

"I don't see why not," Hamish replied as if he had been insulted. "But I won't, not until you tell me where you got this. Who wrote this?" he asked, turning the page over as if he would find its secrets on the other side.

"That's not important right now," Connor snatched the parchment from the young man's hand. "If ye can make sense of how this works, we can get ye more. If ye can interpret this, we've a very important task for ye, and ye'll be doing somethin' that's never been done before—somethin' that's fucking amazing. Plus, ye'll be saving a child's life. Are ye interested?" The intensity in Connor's face and his hushed tone spoke of the importance of their mission.

"I've never skipped a class, or even taken a sick day," young Hamish Francis Cambridge the Third said, his eyes wide with excitement as he stood. "But I've never seen anything like this! It appears to bridge the gap between magic and physics in a way that the greatest minds of our generation haven't yet uncovered! Of course I'm interested."

"*Shhh!*" Alerted by the chastising sound and glare from the librarian, the three men, along with an eager young scholar, took that as their signal to leave.

By late-afternoon, the traveling party had reassembled, along with their newly recruited scholar.

"Hello, Hamish," Isaboe said with a smile and a handshake. "I'm Mrs. Grant, and I'm very pleased to meet you. We're so thrilled that you've agreed to help us."

Surprise flashed through Hamish's eyes, and after introducing himself politely, he turned a skeptical look toward Connor. "This is *your* wife?"

"Why'd ye say it like that?" Connor replied, somewhat defensively. The student only shrugged and quickly swallowed his tongue before turning and walking briskly toward the others. Apparently, he hadn't missed Connor's intimidating glare.

"Connor, don't be rude." Isaboe scowled.

"What? I dinnae do anything."

"You know what I mean. Just, don't be *you*," she said sternly, before joining Rosalyn and Hamish already on the buckboard.

With people and supplies all boarded, the traveling party was ready for the trip home. Riding on horseback, Connor, Will, and Jared led the small army out of town while Rosalyn drove the buckboard toward Lochmund Hills. Young Hamish had asked just enough of the right questions for Rosalyn and Isaboe to fill in all the necessary blanks by the time they made camp. That night they slept under a star-filled sky, kissed by a waxing half-moon that would be full in just over a week. A plan had been laid out, the tools acquired, and now all they had to do was to accomplish the impossible. But time was not on their side.

CHAPTER 28

IMPOSSIBILITIES

By the time the travelers returned to the hills, Hamish completely understood his role in the upcoming event, and he was fidgety with the anticipation of getting started. "Though I'm a student of physics and science, I am certain we are not alone in this world," he babbled in his excitement. "This is what I've dreamt about, the stuff that keeps me awake at night, wondering if it could be real. The idea that a parallel universe exists with creatures that the intellectuals believe only to be figments of our imaginations, or made-up characters from our childhood is grand enough, but to move between our worlds would be a thrilling and astounding achievement. I can hardly wait to get started!"

"Well, just hold on to that enthusiasm, young man," Rosalyn said. "You don't know what we're up against yet."

After arriving at Rosalyn's home, Hamish immediately went to work, spending the next few hours perusing Demetrick's manuals and books, trying to absorb every detail, while writing notes in his cramped, scholar's hand.

Watching him from a distance, Isaboe heard the young scholar occasionally making small noises of pleasure, sounding a bit like a giddy girl on her first dance. Mumbling affirmations as he read, it became increasingly clear that his young mind ran along the same lines as the author. He was so excited it almost seemed that they had handed him the key to the universe.

Leaving their newest recruit to decipher Demetrick's notes, the rest of the group peeled away to relax for the first time in days. Happy to put her skills to use, Margaret had taken to the kitchen. She immediately joined

Rosalyn in putting up the recently purchased supplies and discussing meal ideas for the next several days while Will and Jared gathered firewood for the stove.

Traveling for the last two days and being away from Kaitlyn for the first time since her birth had been challenging, but Isaboe knew she was well cared for, and that had made the separation much easier. Now, back from their excursion, she took the time to be alone with her baby. Taking a walk outside the cave, she found a perfect spot to lay out a blanket and then settled down with Kaitlyn. A warm breeze blew up from the canyon floor, tossing Isaboe's hair and stirring to life the dried flora that covered the top of the ridge. Turning her face toward the invisible force, and behind closed eyes, she breathed in its essence, wishing that the wind could blow her troubles away.

Isaboe's thoughts were interrupted by the sound of boots crunching over rocks. Looking up, she saw Connor walking in her direction and felt herself smile.

The late afternoon rays bathed the air with a golden glow, throwing shadows into the canyon as the sun dipped toward the horizon. Summer's lengthening days created beautiful, rose-colored skies, and when Connor took a seat next to her, Isaboe attempted to etch the fleeting beauty of the moment into her mind. The simple act of taking in the glory of a sunset with the people she loved was often an overlooked gift, and one she had not been able to appreciate in a very long time.

After getting comfortable next to her, Connor gently brushed Isaboe's hair from her face and let his hand slip down to rest on the middle of her back. "How are ye holding up? I ken this hasn't been easy for ye," he said, and Isaboe saw the concern on her husband's face.

"I'm fine, just a little tired," she replied with a forced smile. "You know, Connor, up until now I wasn't sure that creating a portal was really possible. But after seeing Hamish so enthusiastic, I'm starting to believe that this might actually happen."

"Well, that is the goal, aye? Create a portal to retrieve the boy." Dropping his hand, Connor leaned back. "I too've had my doubts. But if Hammy can actually figure this out, I guess it *is* possible. You and I have both passed through and returned. It can be done."

"Aye, we passed through and returned, but not without losing an enormous amount of time. What good does it do to bring back an infant child if the parents are too old to care for him? What if so much time slips by that they've passed on? If Rosalyn and Hamish can actually create this portal, there's no guarantee that time won't be lost. You and I can certainly verify that."

Up until then, Isaboe had kept her questions silent, but they were up against so many unknowns that no guarantees or promises could be made. When Connor didn't even bother to offer up a few hollow reassurances, that only confirmed her doubts.

Seeing the concern showing in his eyes, Isaboe realized the weight of the responsibility that Connor must be feeling, and she knew he would do whatever he could to save Anna's child. But this was an area in which he had no experience, and there was no way to predict the outcome.

"We've seen the impossible happen, Isaboe," he said, breaking the silence. "We've made it through the worst, and we're still alive to talk about it. With Rosalyn's powers, Demetrick's knowledge, and hopefully, Hammy's intelligence, there's a real chance that we'll manage this too. So, let's wait on the worry and see how it all unfolds, aye?"

Though she appreciated Connor's optimism, Isaboe knew it would take more than a few positive words to save Gabriel and bring everyone back whole and sane. Everything would have to go perfectly. Dropping her gaze, she let it fall on her child's innocent little face. Seeming completely naïve to the fact that she was the center of controversy, Kaitlyn sat contently next to her parents. She was able to find joy in the simplicity of existence, with every day being a new experience.

Isaboe watched as Kaitlyn became completely absorbed and captivated by the sound emitted when two small rocks clanged together in her tiny hands. But even the baby's soft noises of delight offered only a momentary distraction from her worries and concerns.

"You were right. This was a trap," Isaboe finally said, looking up at Connor. "I thought I needed to warn Anna, to save her, but all I did was bring her heartache by endangering the life of her child," she whispered as the tears stung her eyes. "The Fey Queen wanted to prove that she still has control." Swallowing hard, she felt her face harden as she heard the loathing in her voice and felt it in her gut. *"I hate her!* How many more people in my life must suffer to satisfy this vile, self-serving fey's desire for control? I hate her for what she's done to all of us. Why *my* family? Will we never be free of her? Connor, do you actually think we can get Gabriel back?" No longer able to hold her tears at bay, Isaboe let them run freely as she looked desperately into his eyes for any hope to cling to.

Connor leaned forward and placed a hand on her shoulder, his sky-blue eyes turning serious as he met her gaze. "Isaboe, I need ye to be strong. Ye found the strength to stand up to her once before. I need ye to be strong again. We havta stay positive; that's the only thing we can do. Not saving this precious boy ain't an option. We need to see him home and safe, just as we wish it." After wiping the tears from her eyes, he continued. "Before goin' into battle, I'd spend time alone and see the conflict already over in my mind's eye. I'd always be standin' on a hill, covered in the enemy's blood, holdin' my battle-axe high and screamin' a victory cry, often with Will at my side. Even though we were scared to death going in, seein' the outcome is what got us through the fight."

Lifting Isaboe's chin, he looked into her eyes. "So take all that hatred and use it to feed the fighter that I ken ye have inside ye. Dinnae give in to Lorien's threats, cause we're gonna turn them against her and call her bluff. Ye're not alone in this fight anymore, *Breagha*. Wasn't it you who reminded me that we must trust our comrades?"

Sniffing back the tears and wiping away the ones she couldn't stop, Isaboe gave him a forced smile. She wasn't alone in her fight anymore. The small army they had banded together was fiercely determined in its mission, and Connor would always have her back. Knowing that gave her a brief moment of confidence as she tried to shove aside her residual doubts.

They were jolted out of their moment when Kaitlyn's rhythmic clanging was suddenly replaced by a soft thump. One of the rocks had missed its intended target and struck her thumb instead. The child instantly broke out into pitiful wailing, but before either of her parents could offer consolation, Kaitlyn threw the offending rock as hard as she could with intense anger written on her tiny face. As the rock flew out of her hand, sparks shot from the baby's pudgy fingertips, and the energy she released was matched by her angry cry.

Completely startled, Isaboe looked at Connor and saw the same surprised look on his face. "It looks like yer daughter has a temper," he said with a mischievous grin.

"*Our* daughter has unfortunately inherited the MacPherson temper," Isaboe said playfully as she lifted her crying child onto her lap, kissing Kaitlyn's injured thumb. "I've seen that same tantrum on someone else before."

Connor gave an acknowledging smirk at her comment. "Well, I'll make sure to never make her angry then. Faerie magic *and* a MacPherson temper—that canna be a good mix."

Though Connor was pretending to be serious, Isaboe broke into a chuckle, and for a moment her heart felt a little less heavy. She would never take these precious moments for granted again.

"Ye know, it's been a while since we've been together," he whispered, as his hand slipped around her waist. "I need to be alone with ye, *Breagha*, to feel yer body against mine. A little distraction would do us both a bit of good, aye?"

Isaboe saw the need in his eyes and the hunger on his mouth. He was right, and the distraction would be welcome, even needed, right now. When Connor made love to her, when their souls entwined in their passion for one another, only then did she feel completely safe and free from the threats swirling in her mind. When they were together, it felt like they could take on the world.

As usual, Connor sported multiple days of stubble across his rugged jaw. She ran a hand teasingly down the side of his rough, prickly cheek, knowing that her skin would pay the price for their intimacy, but it would be worth it. "It's just about time to put Kaitlyn down for the evening. I'll grab another blanket and meet you back here. We can go for a walk," she said with smile, before leaning in to kiss him.

Meaning for it to be just a quick peck, she leaned away, but was caught off-guard when Connor drew her back in. "I love you," he said tenderly, holding a hand softly against her cheek as he stared into her eyes. "Sorry I haven't told ye that lately. We've been a little busy."

Isaboe felt her lips curling up. "Yeah, a wee bit. But you just wait here, and when I get back, you can show me just how much you do love me, my Scottish warrior." Leaning in, this time she kissed him slowly and passionately, teasing him with her mouth hard against his. When she finally drew back, she saw the unmistakable longing in his eyes, the desire on his alluring mouth, and felt a familiar tingle shooting down the center of her body. Oh yes, she needed him too.

"Hold that thought. I'll be right back," she said with a coy smile as she stood, holding Kaitlyn in her arms. Regardless of what their future might bring, tonight would be a good night.

chapter 29

The Ring of Odin

Midsummer's long days meant very short nights, and the following morning dawned much too early. Awakened by the sound of her crying granddaughter, Rosalyn made her way to the kitchen still groggy and wiping sleep from her eyes. After stirring up the coals and bringing the fire back to life, she threw a few small logs into the belly of the woodstove. Quickly filling a teapot, she placed it on the stovetop before turning to see Hamish asleep on one of the large, overstuffed cushions not far from the table where he had left Demetrick's books scattered and open.

Walking over to where the boy lay, she noticed that he still held one book in his hands, open and face-down on his chest, which rose and fell quite rhythmically as he snored loudly. His spectacles had slipped haphazardly down his nose, and his hair was mussed, having slipped out of its binding.

Anna and Isaboe had both risen with Kaitlyn's cries. Margaret and the men folk weren't far behind. One by one, they made their way out to the privy, and then back for that first cup of morning tea.

Isaboe took a seat across from where Hamish still slept, completely unaware of the activity around him. As she sipped on her tea and watched him snore, her mother stood behind the slumbering scholar. "The poor boy must be exhausted from being up all night," she whispered.

Looking down at the multiple candle stubs she had provided him the night before, Rosalyn saw only piles of melted wax on the table. "Should we wake him? Find out if he's discovered anything yet?" she whispered in return.

"What are ye looking at?" Connor's deep, sleepy voice came over Isaboe's shoulder.

"Good morning," Isaboe replied. "Hamish is still sleeping, and we were just discussing if we should wake him or not. It appears he was up all night studying the journals."

Leaning forward with his forearms braced on the back of the sofa, Connor's eyes seemed abnormally cheery for the early hour. He glanced up and shared a mischievous look with Rosalyn before addressing his wife. "So, ye think it might be rude if we were to wake him?"

"Aye, I think it would," she replied. "Kaitlyn's been crying, and we've been talking none-too-quietly, yet he's not woke up. Obviously, the boy's exhausted."

Apparently unimpressed with his wife's reasoning, Connor picked up a small throw pillow lying next to her on the sofa.

"*Connor, no!*" Attempting to prevent her husband's foul play, Isaboe couldn't stop the pillow he had already launched at the sleeping scholar. Startled, Hamish's head slipped off the cushion and thumped down hard on the wooden frame. When the boy jolted upright, both the book and his spectacles tumbled to the floor.

"Morning Hammy," Connor said. "We're all waitin' to hear what ye've discovered."

Clearly disoriented, and with blinking, unfocused eyes, Hamish fumbled around until he retrieved his spectacles. Quickly brushing his hair down, the boy sat up straight before shooting Connor a glare as he rubbed the back of his head.

"What part of *don't be rude* didn't you understand?" Isaboe hissed, shooting a scowl in her husband's direction.

"He's awake now. Isn't that what ye wanted?"

"Seriously? Connor, sometimes you have no tact whatsoever," Isaboe spat. After giving Hamish a moment to gather himself from a rather brutal awakening, she caught his attention and offered a smile. "Good morning, Hamish. Sorry you were woken so abruptly," she said, giving Connor a sideways glare. "It looks like you've been hard at it all night."

"Aye, and good morning to you, Mrs. Grant," Hamish nodded, forcing a smile.

"Please, call me Isaboe."

"So, what have you discovered?" Rosalyn asked anxiously.

Hamish glanced over his shoulder at the woman behind him, then around the room to take in the rest of the faces that had gathered. He quickly ran his hands over his face before responding. "This man was an absolute genius! I haven't encountered equations and theories like this since the likes of Galileo!" The young scholar's enthusiasm lit up his face.

"That we already knew." Rosalyn was both amused and impatient. "Have you learned how to build the portal?"

Hamish stood up and took a few steps before turning to address them all. "I have good news and bad news."

"We'll take the good news first," Connor interjected.

Looking around the room with wide eyes, the young scholar paused before replying, "This can be done. A portal from our world into theirs can be opened, from anywhere on Earth so long as it is created in the quadrant preceding or following the full moon of the summer solstice. There is a seven-day period, with the equinox—or mid-summer's eve—at the center. This, according to Demetrick's notes, is when the two realms are most connected. He provided all the formulas and equation modifications that, depending on where the portal will be created, based on its latitude and longitude in correlation to the mass of encompassing elements, this can be done." The boy's enthusiasm bubbled out faster than his mouth could speak the words.

"Well, since I didn't understand most of what you just said, let's hear the bad news." Isaboe answered for the group, who all looked a bit puzzled.

Hamish walked back to the cushion and took a seat, looking only at Isaboe. "Some of the ingredients we need are incredibly rare, and there are others I've never even heard of."

"Like what?" Rosalyn asked as she walked around and stood next to her daughter, keeping her eyes on Hamish.

Hamish bent down and picked up the book that had fallen off his chest. "It mentions here that four primary items are required: two elements, sulfur and hydrargyrum, and something he refers to as 'the catalyst.' These two elements can be obtained fairly easily, but I have no idea what he used for a catalyst, as it's not ever identified in the book."

"I can provide the sulfur and the catalyst," Rosalyn answered. "What is the fourth item?"

"The last item required is the most concerning, as I have no idea if it even exists."

"Well, what is it?" Isaboe asked.

Hamish took a moment to study the eyes that were staring at him. "Demetrick wrote that once the portal is created, it must be contained in a magic ring—the magic Ring of Odin. It is within this ring that time will remain the same between the two worlds. I've read stories, mostly just fables about the Rings of Odin, but even if they do exist, what are the chances we can locate one in time? The first day of the quadrant preceding the full moon is in three days. We don't have much time, and we're up against nearly impossible odds."

Most of the eyes focused on Hamish were blank, but Rosalyn said, "Maybe not," as she turned to Connor. "Please bring me the ring that Demetrick gave you." She then quickly left the room, leaving the rest of them with their curiosity piqued.

"Hydrargyrum. Isn't that the Latin name for quicksilver?" Jared broke the silence.

"Aye. It is rare and can be expensive to obtain, but I know the geology department at the university will have it," Hamish replied.

Rosalyn scurried back into the room with an open book in her hands and placed it on the table. Seconds later, Connor returned with a small bag. He pulled it open and presented the ring in question. Holding the ring in her hand, Rosalyn leaned over the table and compared it to the page. A slow smile grew across her face. "I thought I recognized this ring when you first showed it to me." Rosalyn held it at arm's length as she studied its intricate design. "This is one of the Rings of Odin. There were only eight created by the great king, and each holds incredible power. Demetrick has provided everything we need." As she spoke the words, an eerie look of reverence crossed her face, never taking her eyes off the silver band.

"If we only have three days, do you think you can obtain that quicksilver from the university?" Jared asked Hamish. "Can you help us accomplish this?"

"Aye, if things go smoothly, that won't be a problem."

"Then it looks like we'll be making another trip back to Edinburgh this morning," Connor added.

"I'm going back with you," Jared said. He glanced quickly about the room, and with Anna having taken Kaitlyn back to the sleeping quarters to breastfeed, he gave Connor a desperate look. "I can't just sit and wait here. I have to do something, anything that will help get my son back."

Acknowledging the desperate father with a nod, Connor stepped over to stand next to Will and Margaret, who had been staying out of the way as they sipped their morning tea. "What about you Buchanan? Are ye and the missus up for another ride back to the city?"

Will glanced at Margaret, who had kept close to Anna, hoping to keep the poor girl from tearing herself apart over her lost boy. She shook her head. "If Jared's leaving, I think I'll stay here."

The rugged, former warrior looked back toward Connor. "Looks like I'll pass too, and take a walk around here to explore this place," he said before giving his friend a half-hearted smile. "Maggie tells me there's a giant that lives on this ridge—a big fellow by the name of…uh…"

"Leo," Connor provided the name. "Aye, I've met him before. Kinda quiet and gentle-like for a man of his size. But watch out for the short, slippery stump with a knife. That one's dangerous."

Seeing the confused expressions on her guest's faces, Rosalyn smirked. "Turock is a dwarf," she chuckled, "and he's not dangerous unless provoked—or if you're an unexpected guest."

"Well, just watch yer back out there, and I mean that literally. I still have a vivid memory of that hairy beast. Before I ken he was even there, he knocked me off my horse, pinned me to the ground, and pressed his blade against the back of my head."

"Are ye telling me that Mac the Fierce got taken down by a dwarf?" Will chuckled.

"He took me by surprise!" Connor almost shouted. "And he's not just a dwarf. He's built like a bloody bull! He's about as wide as he is tall, and twice as heavy. So watch yerselves."

Rosalyn chuckled at the near-fear in Connor's voice. "Obviously, Turock has made an impression on you."

"Aye, as well as an impression in the ground he pushed me into, sitting on my back like a bloody boulder."

"By the way yer carrying on about it, it looks like he bruised more than just yer back," Will chuckled.

Connor only glared at his friend's comment. "Just wait, Buchanan. Ye're gonna eat those words."

"Connor, may I talk to you alone for a moment?" Rosalyn interrupted.

As she turned from the group, he followed her to a secluded corner of the cave, where she produced a drawstring bag. She opened it and pulled out a black writing tablet and a piece of white chalk.

"What do ye want me to do with this?"

"Isaboe will be staying here to help me prepare, so it will only be you, Jared, and Hamish going into the city. There's not much time left, and we can't take the chance that things will simply fall into place. Since we've returned to my home, I'm no longer blocked, and my lines of communication have been restored. If something of concern happens, either on your end or mine, this will keep us in contact, should we need it. This tablet is imbued with esoteric properties. Just write on it with this chalk, and I'll see your message on my tablet." Though she understood Connor's hesitation about using any tool that was laced with magic, this was too important. He would just have to deal with it.

Taking the board and chalk, Connor placed them both back in the bag. "I hope I never have to use 'em."

"Watch out, Connor," Rosalyn said playfully as she looked across the room. "It appears you might have some competition." Connor looked over his shoulder to see Hamish and Isaboe working together chipping the melted candle wax off the table. Though Isaboe was simply being a polite host, engaging the young student in pleasant conversation while attending to their task, it was obvious that she was completely unaware of how fixated Hamish was on her. He smiled too much, agreed too easily, and was overly eager to offer any assistance. The boy actually looked smitten.

"Should I be worried?" Connor snickered.

"I don't think so. Isaboe's attracted to the strong, rebellious type, not the highly intelligent, so I'm sure you have nothing to worry about," Rosalyn jested, but her face remained serious.

Connor shot her a curious frown. "I'm not sure, but I think I've just been insulted."

Rosalyn only offered him a brief smile. "Let's have a quick breakfast. You'll want to be in the city by nightfall."

CHAPTER 30

ALWAYS THE REBEL

Even though their ride into Edinburgh took all day, arriving well after sundown, that didn't mean they were coming in under the cover of darkness. On the contrary, the city was alive and bright on this warm, summer evening. Residents mingled at corner cafes, entertained by traveling minstrels who roamed through the crowds trying to impress prospective patrons, while buggies attached to their clomping horses passed over cobblestone streets, all filling the air with the sounds of life.

Leaving their horses tethered on the street, the men decided it would be best to have Hamish sneak into the university alone to obtain the quicksilver. That seemed the fastest and most logical way, and it minimized the chance of having to explain themselves should they run into people who would ask uncomfortable questions.

Silently, they wound their way through the darkest parts of the campus until arriving at the science hall. The grand courtyard that encompassed the University of Edinburgh was partially lit with streetlamps that created glowing pools of light in the darkness and left shadowed alcoves. Connor and Jared waited in a dark corridor just outside the building that housed the laboratory. A couple of people passed by but gave them no notice, and Connor hoped it would remain that way. As they silently waited, staying out of sight, he pulled out a small bundle of jerky from inside his coat pocket and made a gesture to Jared. Having ridden hard into Edinburgh without eating, they were both in need of a good meal.

Jared, who paced nervously back and forth, declined Connor's offer and instead asked, "So what is it like, this…other world, the realm of the Underlings? You've been there, aye?"

Though it was dark and Connor couldn't see the expression on the young father's face, he heard the concern in Jared's voice. Despite his anxiety and his many demanding questions to Rosalyn and Isaboe, Jared had been relatively well-behaved on this journey, following directions and trusting Connor's judgment. And Connor had to admit that he wasn't sure he could have put his faith in a group of virtual strangers, as Jared and Anna had. But then, they really had no other choice.

"Aye, I've been there." Connor finally broke the silence. "But I dinnae remember much about it."

"You were there for twenty years. How can you not remember?"

"Aye, twenty years mortal time," Connor snapped back. "But when I returned, I had no memory of it. Something called the *veil of forgetfulness* blocks all recall. But Rosalyn broke through it, and the little I do remember, I canna share with ye." Silently replaying his memories of Euphoria, Conner saw Isaboe's face in his mind's eye and realized how closely their destinies were entwined.

"But do you remember what it looked like, this land of Euphoria?"

"Just like this. The realm somehow exists on this same soil, just in another dimension, in a different version of the world," Connor mumbled, finding it difficult to explain. Perhaps it was wholly unexplainable. He knew Jared wanted to know more about the place where his son was being held, but Connor could offer nothing else to ease the young man's worries.

"I got it," Hamish said as he appeared around the corner of the building, holding something under his coat.

"Then let's get out of here." Connor turned and led the group, sticking to the shadows and trying to remain inconspicuous as they made it back to the horses. Stashing the can of quicksilver in one of the saddlebags, they quickly mounted and rode back into the center of town.

"I dinnae ken about you fellas, but my throat's parched and my stomach's empty. What'd ye say we find a pub, fill our bellies and empty a few mugs?"

"Aye, I'm starving!" Hamish agreed enthusiastically.

"Not used to missing a few meals, aye?" Connor asked as he glanced at his new companion.

Hamish's affluence showed around his middle and in his round face, and though he scowled at Connor, the boy was far from intimidating. "All the men in my family are big-boned; our ancestors were Norseman."

"Aye, but ye could push yerself away from the table a time or two," Connor muttered under his breath.

Though Connor didn't intend for the young scholar to catch his cruelly sarcastic remark, Hamish did. "I would expect more from you than childish taunts, Connor, but your lack of intellect leaves no doubt that your type doesn't seem to understand common courtesy, or a gentleman's protocol. You need me in this operation. It would behoove you to remember that."

When they arrived at the pub, Connor dismounted, wondering what had burrowed under his companion's saddle. "Oh, lighten up Hammy. I'm only...."

"And for the last time, the name is *Hamish!*" he shouted. "But apparently, that too is another area in which you lack intelligence—the ability to remember a person's proper name." The boy's superior attitude oozed out in his rant and demeanor. "I seriously do not understand what a fine woman like Isaboe sees in a boorish brute like you," he mumbled as he dismounted. But when Hamish landed, he had to take a quick step back from Connor's threatening visage.

Knowing the fierce intensity of the look in his eyes as he stared down at Hamish, Connor felt a sense of accomplishment at seeing the fear on his face. As he leaned in closer, the young scholar's eyes widened and he pressed himself back against his horse, but he could not evade the threatening glare of the Scottish rebel.

"Ye're right, we need ye in this operation, so I won't kill ye—yet." Connor's voice remained calm, yet lethal. "I dinnae care if ye insult my intelligence, but ye dinnae disrespect me or my wife. I ken ye're sweet on the missus, and ye think ye're better than me. That's cute. But the next time ye show me disrespect, or feel comfortable enough to refer to my wife by *any* other name than Mrs. Grant, my boot will be so far up yer arse that ye won't be able to shit for a month." Connor paused, letting that sink in. "I think someone as highly intelligent as yerself—*Hamish Francis Cambridge, the Third*—should be able to understand my meaning, aye?"

Hamish stood frozen and could only nod. His eyes were wide, and his spectacles were barely hanging onto the end of his nose.

"A nod is as good as a wink to a blind horse, so let me ask ye again—do we have an understandin'?" This time, Connor stood nose-to-nose with his nervous companion, making him squirm.

"Yes." Hamish choked out his answer.

"Yes, what?" Connor toyed with him for a bit longer as Jared stood by quietly watching.

"Yes, *sir*, Mr. Grant," Hamish finally said under duress.

Stepping back from the terrified young man, Connor's expression brightened like the sun coming out from behind a cloud. He smiled as he pushed Hamish's glasses back up the bridge of his nose and slapped him on the back. Connor placed an arm around the boy's shoulder, jolting him into movement. "Well, now that's settled, let's go see if we can still get some grub this late at night. Look at this kid, Jared! He looks starved, melting away in front of our eyes."

Watching his young companion's lips twitch into an uncomfortable smile, Connor knew he had made his point, though he doubted that this would be the last confrontation they would have.

As the three men entered the pub, the smell of cigar smoke and whiskey wafted out along with the sound of murmuring voices and clinking mugs. A group of men stood at the long bar, which ran the length of the small tavern from wall to wall. Most of the tables were occupied, with the exception of one that sat directly behind the line-up of patrons at the bar, but there was only one chair. Grabbing two empty stools, the three men took the vacant table.

"I wonder if we can get anything to eat here," Hamish asked, looking around. "I don't see anyone with food, only drinks."

As if knowing the new arrivals were hungry, a barmaid, looking tired and wearing a dirty apron, suddenly appeared at their table. "What can I get for ye, gents?"

"What do you have to eat?" the young scholar asked.

"Got some Shepherds' Pie left, if that interests ye."

"Aye, bring us all some, and a round of ale, too," Connor said.

"Uh...I don't have much money on me," Hamish said as the barmaid walked off.

"It's alright," Jared said. "I'm sure that between us all, we've got this covered."

"Well, empty yer pockets," Connor said to Hamish. "Let's see what ye got. Come on, son, empty yer pockets."

A well-dressed man who had been standing behind them at the bar suddenly turned around and took an interest in Connor, staring at him curiously. When he felt the stranger's eyes on him, Connor looked over his shoulder and shot him a scowl. "What?"

After a moment of just studying Connor's face, the man finally spoke. "I know you. You were in Kirkwall about a month ago, weren't you?" He was deadly serious, even angry.

Fuck! Connor's memory abruptly settled into place, and he recognized the stranger but fought to keep the realization off his face. "No," Connor mumbled, not breaking eye contact with the man while attempting to keep the expression on his face neutral. But inside he was preparing for a fight.

"Hmm," the stranger said, unimpressed with his reply. Taking a step closer, the man now hovered next to Connor, still studying him. "What about the name Tobias Whitmore? Does that mean anything to you?" Connor only shook his head. "How about General Harrington? No, wait, what about Rob McClaren? Do those names mean anything to you?"

Connor quickly denied knowing these men, and in a quick sideways glance he saw the wide-eyed look of confusion on the faces of his companions.

"Though I didn't see the thief's face," the accuser continued, "just before I was bound and gagged, I did hear his voice when he demanded that I *empty my pockets*, and his voice sounded very much like yours."

"I told ye, I wasn't in Kirkwall," Connor growled, but he had no idea how to get out of this—short of killing the man. As he glanced across the table at the two men he'd come in with, wondering what his next move would be, Hamish provided one for him.

"Excuse me, sir, if I may interrupt," the young scholar said. "Though nothing would please me more than to have a good reason to boot my worthless, free-loading cousin out of my mother's home, in good conscience I must speak up on his behalf. You see, Garwin here has been sponging off my mother's good heart for far too long. Three months ago, he showed up at our house one afternoon and said he was passing through, just needed a place to stay for a few days, he said, but the moocher hasn't moved on yet. So, unfortunately, I can vouch that he was here in Edinburgh a month ago, sleeping off a drunk, no doubt, and this is just a case of mistaken identity."

"Yeah, ye must be mistakin' me for someone else," Connor added, turning away.

Scrutinizing them both, the man seemed to be considering Hamish's reply. "Why should I believe you?" he finally asked.

Jared suddenly stood. "Excuse me, are you Tobias Whitmore?" he asked. "The man who owns the newspaper empire in northern Scotland?"

Studying him, the businessman nodded. "Do I know you?"

"I'm Jared McKnight. I work for Archibald Merchant and Bank on Brickford Street, here in Edinburgh. I believe we handled a business transaction for you in the purchase of a cargo ship a few months back." Jared held out his hand, and the businessman took it in greeting.

"Oh, yes, your establishment has been assisting me for a number of years, in one business matter or another." Jared's introduction seemed to lend legitimacy, and the accuser appeared less guarded.

"This young man is Hamish, my good friend," Jared said, placing a hand on Hamish's shoulder, "and a highly-educated honor student in the science and physics departments at the University. He's been complaining to me for months about his bum-of-a-cousin who has overstayed his welcome, taking advantage of his mother's goodwill. So you see, Mr. Whitmore, this really is just that—a case of mistaken identity."

The newspaper mogul seemed to be considering Jared's story before he finally conceded. "Well, you may be correct." He then turned his glare on Connor. "But there is a man in Kirkwall with your build and your voice who is up to no good. If you do go to there, I'd watch your back if I were you."

Connor nodded, not willing to look directly at Whitmore. "Thanks, I'll keep that in mind."

The barmaid returned with food and drinks, causing Whitmore to step back. After one more lingering glance at Connor, he turned back to his drink, which was still sitting on the bar. Connor watched from the corner of his eye as Whitmore picked up his mug and moved down the row of patrons lined up at the bar, either standing or holding themselves up, depending on their various degrees of intoxication. Coming to a stop, the businessman struck up a conversation with another man before Connor finally let out the breath he'd been holding. "Thanks guys," he muttered.

"What the hell was that about?" Jared whispered.

"I'll tell ye later. Just eat and act natural."

"What did you do, Connor?" Hamish asked, though not as quietly as Jared. In the next moment he was startled by a sharp slap on his back and a chuckle from the warrior, as if Hamish had said something humorous.

"Aye, that's what I'm talking 'bout," Connor said, still chuckling. "Act natural and dinnae ask any fucking questions," he said with a forced smile.

Connor only glared at Hamish before stabbing his fork into the Shepherd's Pie and stuffing a bite into his mouth. He watched as the young scholar swallowed hard before picking up his own fork and following suit. "I'm not sure I can eat now."

The cacophony of voices, scooting chairs, and clinking mugs in the small pub drowned out the awkward silence of the three men as they ate and downed their mugs of ale wordlessly, shooting each other an occasional, uncomfortable glance.

Finally finished, Connor and Jared paid the barmaid and then casually walked toward the front door. When Connor glanced back over his shoulder, he saw Whitmore watching him carefully as they walked out.

CHAPTER 31

BUT YOU CAN'T TAKE
THE WARRIOR OUT OF
THE SCOTSMAN

Out in the cool night air, Connor walked briskly toward the horses, while his companions struggled to keep up with his longer stride until he finally felt comfortable enough to slow his pace. "Thanks lads. Ye saved my arse back there, or, at least, ye saved Whitmore's. Really didna want to have that scene. Let's get out of this city."

"Oh no!" Jared said, as both he and Hamish stepped in front of Connor, cutting off his path. "You don't get off that easy," he snapped.

"Yeah, I just lied back there for you, *Garwin*. That businessman said he was robbed," Hamish proclaimed. "Why would you do that?"

Connor looked at them for a long uncomfortable moment. Both men had just lied to protect his identity. He at least owed them an explanation. "Because, that businessman is a rat traitor, and he had information that would've proved harmful to a lot o' good men if he'd gotten to General Harrington on the mainland. I prevented that."

"What information? Who are these good men you refer to?" Jared asked.

"Fellow rebels. Whitmore approached them, saying he would lend his connections and money to the rebellion, but he was a mole. He dinnae ken they were onto him, and someone had to stop him from boardin' that ship."

"Fellow *rebels?* The *Rebellion?*" Hamish said, not bothering to hide the surprise in his voice. "Just who are you?"

"You can't seriously be talking about a rebellion?" Jared added. "Overthrowing the British Empire? Who's crazy enough to lead that attempt?"

"That doesna matter and it doesna concern ye. The less ye ken, the better. I appreciate what ye fellas did, but please, do me one more favor—dinnae mention any of this to Isaboe."

"What?" Hamish said, and Connor didn't miss the arrogance on his shocked face. "Isaboe doesn't know who you really are, does she?" He paused and his face grew hard. "You don't deserve her."

"Probably not, and the last thing I'd ever want to do is hurt her. But I made an oath to her that I'd not get involved, and if she finds out…"

"You broke an oath to your wife?" Hamish exclaimed. "You owe it to Isaboe to tell her the truth. She needs to know who she's really married to."

Connor felt his anger rising at the boy's accusatory tone, but he reminded himself of what Hamish had just done for him, so he swallowed his first instinct to pinch off the righteous student's windpipe. "We weren't married at the time, and I dinnae owe ye an explanation," he hissed.

Taking a step back from Connor's glare, Hamish lifted his chin in defiance. "If you don't tell Isaboe, I will."

This nice-guy shit ain't working, Connor thought, taking a step toward the wide-eyed student and grabbing him by the scruff of his shirt. "Look, Hamish, I appreciate what ye did for me back there, so I won't kick yer arse, but ye're crossing the line. This is between me and Isaboe—a man and his wife." He paused and shot Jared a side-ways glance. "Ye're married, Jared. Back me up."

"I can't, Connor. Hamish is right."

"What?" Releasing Hamish with a shove, Connor jerked around as the boy stumbled back a few steps before regaining his balance. "If I tell Isaboe, she'll kill me!" Connor whined, the wind stolen from his sails.

"Maybe you should have thought about that before you broke a promise to her. And what you did was no small thing, Connor. She deserves to know the truth."

"It was one job, just the one time! That doesna mean I joined the rebellion. If I hadn't stopped that bloody traitor, a lot of Scotsmen across this country would've been arrested and murdered. I did it to save lives," Connor snarled.

"But what if Hamish and I hadn't been in there with you? What if it had been Isaboe with you when Whitmore started making those accusations? Think about that, Connor. If it should ever happen again, wouldn't it be better if she knew about it in advance, instead of being taken by surprise?"

"It won't happen again."

"You don't know that, and Hamish is right. You have to tell Isaboe."

Connor bit his lip, trying to keep from lashing out at his companions, because their words were speaking directly to his conscience. He had convinced himself that doing this one little job didn't really make him involved with the rebellion. He'd only gone to one meeting, and he didn't really know the rest of the men, other than Rob McClaren. But that one job had made a huge difference for the cause, and now it had followed him to the mainland. So, how innocent was he really? A part of his conscience tried to justify that he had kept his promise to Isaboe and stayed out of the rebellion, but he knew he hadn't. As angry and hurt as he knew she would be, Jared and Hamish were right; he owed her the truth. *"Fuck!"* he finally spat. "Fine, I'll tell her," he said, stomping toward his horse.

"Well," Hamish said, "all this excitement has exhausted me. I don't know what you fellows are going to do for the evening, but I have a bed waiting for me at the residence hall. So I'll bid you good night." He then turned to walk off.

"We could go back to my home," Jared suggested, "as long as our neighbors don't see us. Anna and I told them we'd be gone for a few weeks, and I don't want to have to answer any questions."

"Come on Ham…" Connor stopped the offending name from slipping past his lips. "Hamish, how often do ye get a chance to sleep out under the stars?"

Stopping and turning back around, Hamish replied. "Give me one good reason why I should give up my perfectly comfortable bed to sleep on the ground?"

"Because it will put hair on yer balls, make a man out of ye," Connor teased.

"Come on Hamish," Jared added. "We should probably stay together so we can head out first thing in the morning."

But before Hamish could either accept or refuse this less-than-attractive offer, a commotion drew their attention across the street. Four British soldiers were dragging a man still in his bed clothes out of his home while his wife screamed behind them, begging for his release.

"Leave him be!" the woman screamed. "You can't beat a man and drag him out of his bed in the middle of the night! We paid our taxes this month. Let him go!"

"That tax payment was for last month. You're in arrears and have been for the last three months!" one of the soldiers retorted.

"We've no more money left to give!" the man pleaded. "The King has left us nothing to live on. How's a man supposed to feed his family if we have to give all our profits to the Crown?" The beaten man's plea was ignored as he was pushed down onto the street and placed in irons.

"Make haste, woman, and pack up your belongings," shouted one soldier. "Your man's going to jail and your home and business are now property of the Crown!" He turned his back, not noticing the boy running out from behind his mother.

"Let my papa go!" the youngster shouted. Running up behind one of the red uniforms, he pulled the soldier's pistol from its holster and held it up, pointing at the men who were threatening to drag his father away in chains.

"Watch out! The boy has a weapon!" shouted a soldier. The fourth man in uniform spun around and fired his musket.

"NO!" the father cried, but it was too late.

The flash of light, the explosion, and the following scream happened so fast that it took the onlookers a moment to realize what had happened. But in the next second, as the boy lay bleeding in his wailing mother's arms, it quickly became apparent.

Driven forward by instinct and rage, before Jared or Hamish could stop him, Connor ran across the street and swung a fist into the offending soldier's face, dropping the man where he stood. Connor was on top of the damn Brit as soon as he hit the ground.

Pulling back, he let loose with both fists. Blood flew as the soldier took blow after blow to his face, unable to defend himself. Though brutal and damaging, the attack was short-lived when the butt-end of a rifle slammed into Connor's head, sending him tumbling to the ground. As the

British officers jerked Connor to his feet and shackled his hands behind his back, another solider tried to help his beaten comrade, whose face was so covered in blood that he could barely see.

When Connor cleared his head and glanced across the street, he saw Hamish and Jared still standing in the same spot with looks of horror plastered across their faces. But before he could call out to them, one of the soldiers rammed the butt-end of a rifle into his belly, expelling his breath and doubling him over.

The soldiers yanked Connor upright, and with a red uniform on each arm, led him toward the center of the city. Taking a quick look over his shoulder, he shouted, "In my saddlebag—write Rosalyn a note with the chalk!" But he was again jabbed in the ribs and jerked forward, just before disappearing around the corner and out of sight of his companions.

Rosalyn bolted upright in bed, trying to identify the noise that had awakened her from a sound sleep. After a few moments of silence, she convinced herself that it was nothing and laid back down. But just as she started to slip away into slumber, she heard it again, and this time, she knew exactly what it was.

Donning her night robe and lighting the candle beside her bed, Rosalyn made her way to the dressing table where she had placed her writing tablet. Rubbing the sleep from her eyes, she read the words written across the black surface:

HELLO ROSALYN.

Directly below that greeting, one by one the letters began to materialize. As each letter appeared, it was accompanied by the familiar sound of chalk scraping across a blackboard. Feeling her heartbeat quicken, Rosalyn placed the candle on the dresser. She knew Connor wouldn't be trying to contact her this way unless something was wrong. With bated breath, she watched the following words appear:

ARE YOU THERE?

Grabbing a cloth, she rubbed the writing off her board. Picking up her piece of white chalk she quickly wrote a response:

Connor, what's wrong?

Anxiously she waited, but she didn't have to wait long. Almost imme-diately a response began to appear under her question:

IT'S HAMISH AND JARED HERE. CONNOR HAS BEEN ARRESTED.

"What? Damn it, Connor, we don't have time for this," she grumbled. Quietly, she made her way to Isaboe's sleeping cove, trying not to disturb the rest of the home. After returning to Rosalyn's room, the two women stood at the dresser. Isaboe gasped when she read what was written on the tablet. "Why? What happened?" she asked looking desperately at her mother.

"I don't know yet," was all Rosalyn had time to say before once again the letters screeched their appearance on the black surface:

WHAT SHALL WE DO?

Wiping the words away, Rosalyn wrote again: *Where are you? Are you both alright? Did you get the quicksilver? Where's Connor now?*

Isaboe paced circles on the floor of the small room and then stopped to address her mother. "What could have happened?" she whispered. "They hadn't been in the city that long. What could he have done in such a short amount of time to be arrested?" Isaboe paused, her face full of worry. "What do we do now?"

But before Rosalyn could answer, her words disappeared from the tablet, and were slowly replaced.

STILL IN THE CITY. WE ARE FINE. YES, WE HAVE IT. ASSUMING HE IS IN JAIL.

"Ask them what happened to Connor. Why was he arrested? Is he alright?"

Isaboe's frantic questions weren't helping, and Rosalyn turned to her daughter. "The reason he's in jail is not important right now. What we need to focus on is how to get him out." As her thoughts jumped from one option to another, she returned to the tablet. Erasing their response, she preceded to write out directions.

Isaboe and I are coming to Edinburgh. We'll take care of Connor.
Return now with the quicksilver.

Rosalyn looked at her daughter "Do you recall which trunk that white box was in, the one with the scarf from Paris?" When Isaboe nodded, she said, "Good. Go retrieve it. You wanted to meet your father, aye? I think it's time we paid the Baron a visit."

chapter 32

who wields more power—a baron or a scorned feymora?

Rosalyn and Isaboe were on the road by sunup. Taking the buckboard was slower than horseback, but for Isaboe the thought of riding on the back of a horse all day was wholly unappealing. Rosalyn's body didn't recover as quickly as it once had, and she, too, was grateful for the gentler ride.

Keeping the line of communication open with Jared and Hamish, they met late that afternoon at a prearranged rendezvous point outside the city. During a light meal of cold meats and red wine, the two men shared the events that had led up to Connor's arrest. Before leaving town, they had stopped by the jail to inform the prisoner that the women were coming.

"Isaboe, Connor doesn't want you at the jail," Jared said.

"Why not?"

"When we asked the same thing, he told us to look at the wanted posters on the wall as we left the station. Just when I thought this family's story couldn't get any stranger, I see a poster with your face on it, wanted in connection for the murder of a *British Officer?*"

"Oh, that," Isaboe's curiosity melted away, and she diverted her eyes.

"Did you kill a ...?"

"I didn't kill anyone!" she snapped before Hamish could finish his question.

"Let me guess; it's a long story." Jared's jab was met with an unimpressed glare from Isaboe and a disapproving scowl from Rosalyn.

"Oh, and Isaboe," the science student added, "Connor has something to tell you."

"Hamish!" Jared scolded, giving his companion a chastising glare.

"What? What *else* did Connor do?" Isaboe asked, but both men went quiet.

"You must return to the cave," Rosalyn said firmly as she lifted herself back onto the buckboard and then looked down at Hamish and Jared. "Have Will seek out Leo to ask him for the sulfur, then prepare everything that's needed. When we return with Connor, we won't have much time."

After Isaboe joined her on the bench, Rosalyn slapped the reins of her team, startling the horses into action, and they were back on the road into Edinburgh.

People dressed in all manner of attire funneled out of the theater and into the night air. The most affluent were garbed in fine linen, bows, and wigs, and they stood out from the common rabble, but they had all come for the same reason—to see and hear the Baron.

Rosalyn and Isaboe waited for the crowd to vacate the building before entering. When the two women entered the atrium, they found the concierge ushering the last of the stragglers to the door. Addressing him, Rosalyn requested an audience with Baron Vanderburgh, but was quickly cut off.

"I'm sorry, but his Lordship has retired for the evening, and he will not be taking any further private appointments," the man said, turning his back to them. But he didn't get far.

"Sir." Rosalyn quickly stepped in front of him. "This is a matter of extreme urgency." Digging into her pocket, she pulled out a small piece of parchment. Before leaving home, she had retrieved the card from the white box Marcus had given her years ago, and now offered it to the concierge. "Please give this to his Lordship. I'm sure he'll be willing to see us tonight."

"What is this?" he asked suspiciously.

"It's a note meant only for the Baron's eyes. Now, please, we need to see him. Tonight." Rosalyn knew the power of her gaze as she stared down the poor fellow who had the misfortune to be standing between her and her goal. He studied both women for a moment before he finally reconsidered their request.

"I'll check to see if he is available to receive you. However, I cannot guarantee an audience at such a late hour." The man was obviously annoyed at being challenged, but he nodded before quickly turning and walking away.

Watching as the concierge disappeared into a room adjacent to the stage, they looked around as they waited. The theater was empty, except for one man, the lamplighter who slowly walked around the room putting out the wall sconces with a long, bell-shaped snuffer. As each lantern was doused, it threw the large room deeper into darkness.

"What are you going to say to him?"

Rosalyn heard the anxiety in Isaboe's voice, and it matched the uncertainty that had taken up residency in her own chest. More than a few moments passed before she finally replied. "I truly don't know yet."

A light from the side door announced the man's return, and he made his way back to where the two women stood. "Please, follow me," he said, as his countenance oozed with controlled irritation.

Walking through the stage entrance, they followed the concierge down a narrow, poorly lit hallway. He stopped in front of an ordinary door and opened it, then stood back and motioned them in. Once inside, Isaboe and Rosalyn found themselves in a warm, well-lit sitting room. A cozy fire burned in the stone fireplace, and its ambience cast a comforting glow.

"His Lordship will be with you shortly" the man offered with a forced smile before walking out and closing the door.

The small room was filled with rich décor; overstuffed red sofas with matching pillows lined two walls, and a well-stocked bar took up residence in the corner between them. Elegant crystal containers, filled presumably with expensive wines and spirits, were displayed on a cart that was designed more for show than practicality. An ornate silver tray held equally fine goblets, waiting to be filled. The fire and candles shed a soft light, along with a lantern that hung over a wooden desk in the opposite corner. A long, feathered quill, an ink bottle, writing papers, and sealing wax sat on the desktop next to a lit candle.

After carefully examining their surroundings, Rosalyn took a seat on one of the elegant sofas, but immediately stood back up when the door opened again.

When Marcus Vanderburgh walked in, Rosalyn suddenly felt the room was too constrictive, too small to contain his egocentricity. If Rosalyn's memories of him were drenched in his arrogance, it was nothing compared to the reality that stood before them. His narcissism and self-importance seemed to fill the room, along with the smell of his cologne.

The Baron's face looked freshly washed, and his speckled brown hair, mostly gray at the temples, was neatly combed and tied. An elegant black and red silk robe hung loosely over his white, ruffled shirt and embroidered vest, which sat above his linen knickers and black leather boots. Though hidden behind a veneer of age and responsibility, Rosalyn could still see the young man who had stolen her heart so many years ago.

Looking first at Rosalyn, then at Isaboe, he shut the door behind him before giving them both a charming smile. "Good evening, ladies. I hope I haven't kept you waiting long. I was on my way out when the concierge handed me this." Holding the card in his hand, Marcus took the few steps forward to stand in front of Rosalyn, and she instinctively curtsied.

"Don't," he said, reaching out to rest his fingers on her arm.

Locking gazes, Rosalyn realized that his eyes and smile hadn't been changed by time, and she was equally surprised to feel her heartbeat quicken with a rush of memories and feelings that she'd thought were long dead and buried. It may have been a lifetime ago, but her heart had not forgotten her first love. For a moment, she was fourteen all over again.

"Thank you for receiving us at this late hour, Your Lordship."

He chuckled softly, making him look even more like the Marcus she remembered.

"Rosalyn. How many years has it been? Close to forty, I daresay. Yet you are as beautiful as the day we met," he said charmingly before taking her hand. Kissing the back of it, his eyes met hers. Releasing her hand, he turned and looked at Isaboe. "And this enchanting lady is…?"

"Isaboe Grant, Your Lordship." Following her mother's lead, Isaboe also offered a curtsy as she studied her father's face.

"Good evening," he said as he gently grasped Isaboe's extended hand and offered a pleasing smile. "So, what can I do for you lovely ladies at such a late hour?" he asked as he sauntered over to the bar and poured himself a drink. Lifting an empty goblet in their direction he gestured, but both declined the offer. "The concierge tells me this was a matter of extreme urgency. What is it you need from me that couldn't wait till the morrow?" Though he remained cordial and polite, it was obvious he wasn't used to having his schedule dictated by others, and Rosalyn could hear irritation lacing his words as he passed in front of her. "Please, sit."

Both women held their place. "Thank you, but we prefer to stand," Rosalyn said.

"Suit yourself." Baron Vanderburgh leaned back against the solid wooden desk, swirling the dark liquid in his goblet as he regarded his guests. Lifting her chin, Rosalyn took the opportunity to make her case and took a step in his direction.

"Your Lordship, we apologize for the late hour, but our need *is* an emergency. You see, Isaboe's husband has been arrested and sits in jail. I'm here to ask a personal favor—that you intervene on his behalf and have him released. Immediately."

The Baron was plainly shocked at the request. "What did your husband do?" he asked, looking at Isaboe.

"He attacked a British soldier, but only after the soldier had shot an innocent child, Your Lordship."

"Attacking a soldier of the Crown is no small offense, but he should be able to plead his case before the magistrate within a week, two at the most. Why bother me with this?"

"Because, we don't have a week," Rosalyn said as she took another step forward. "We don't even have one day to let him sit in jail. I'm asking you, please, have him released tonight."

"And why should I?"

Somehow, his tone and demeanor managed to stir up a young girl's fear, but Rosalyn was worldly now, more than the boy in her memories could ever imagine. Standing tall, she swallowed hard and looked him in the eyes. "Because you owe me." Hearing the seriousness in her words, she knew she had nothing to back up her claim, but she was no longer that young girl in the dark barn forty years ago, and she certainly didn't hold the same innocent adoration for him.

Surprise crossed the Baron's face. "Don't be ridiculous. I owe you nothing," he said smugly.

Rosalyn felt the blood rising to her face, but she held her poise. "I know that I was nothing to you, just some foolish shepherd girl with whom you could alleviate your boredom. I was just another pretty face you had your way with, only to leave me standing on a hillside watching your carriage take you away. You had no care for consequences then, and I imagine nothing has changed now." Anger rising in her words, the sorceress knew she had given herself away and had made herself vulnerable, yet she stood her ground.

Marcus, however, was not convinced, and a weak smile pulled up one corner of his mouth. "First of all, *my dear*, you were hardly just another pretty face. I often thought about you after that summer, and I am truly sorry if I hurt you in any way." His attempt at compassion was short lived. Placing his drink on the desk, he stepped away to walk behind her. "But if I owed a favor to every young maiden that I…*deflowered*, or every young girl whose heart I broke, then you'd have to stand in line. And I dare say it would be a very long line."

Swallowing hard, Rosalyn struggled to keep her composure, but his arrogant attitude was testing her control. Taking one step closer, she tried a different approach. "Marcus, when you rode out that morning, you didn't leave just a broken-hearted girl on that hilltop. Not only did you take my innocence, you left me with a child in my belly. My life went into a downward spiral after you left, and I hated you for a very long time." Her words sliced the air with the same cutting look she carried in her eyes.

As the cocky Baron stared at her with a cold gaze, she felt a burst of the same hatred she'd felt decades ago.

"A child?" he finally said, raising his eyebrows. "Hmm. Don't you think it's a little late to be throwing out the dependent waif card? That was forty years ago, my dear. Even if I did seed your child, it is no longer relevant, nor any reason to be obligated to you now."

"Oh, but I think you are. You may have no compassion for the damage you've left in your wake, but we all had lives, lives that you used and then tossed aside like dirty laundry. It was a game for you, Marcus. Your triumphs over young, naïve girls were no more than notches on your belt."

Though she tried to keep it contained, the angry young girl came out in her words, fueled by pain she had thought was long overcome. But she refused to stay there.

Noticing that her argument seemed to have had no effect, Rosalyn quickly composed herself. Turning away from his arrogant smile, she walked over to Isaboe and placed an arm around her shoulder. "*This* is your daughter. We are here to ask you to release her husband. For once in your life, Marcus, do the right thing."

At first he only stared at them both with a straight face, but soon began to chuckle. "You honestly expect me to believe any of this? There is no way this girl is mine, she is decades too young. Seriously, Rosalyn, if it was your intention to gain something from me, couldn't you have at least found someone more age appropriate?" he scoffed.

"This is not a game, Marcus!" Rosalyn snapped back. "For the same reason that I could not tell you why I was so isolated at that monastery, I cannot explain why *your daughter* looks younger than she should." She stepped forward, standing directly in front of him. "But I tell you the truth. Isaboe is our daughter, and there's nothing you have that I want, so don't flaunt your nobility at me, because I don't give a damn!"

"Ah, there's that fire-spitting lass I once knew," he said with a brilliant smile.

"Don't toy with me, Marcus. I'm not that scared, naïve girl that you used your charming smile on all those years ago. And believe me, I wouldn't be here if this wasn't urgent. You were the last person I ever wanted to see again."

"You still hate me, after all these years?" he asked, and his mirth seemed to disappear.

"Oh no, Marcus, I stopped hating you a long time ago. You aren't worth it," she spat. Turning her back to him, she took a few steps, then stopped and spun around. "No, I don't hate you. I *pity* you. You've always lived in a sheltered world and have no idea what real life is like. What do you know about sacrifice, commitment, or living life in the trenches? Do you have any idea how many nameless children you've fathered?" As she paused, a cruel smile crossed her face. "Of course not, nor would you give a damn."

An awkward silence fell between them as he held her gaze with a cold stare. "There have been very few people in my life who can get away with speaking to me as you just did," he said firmly before his look softened. "But then, my title never meant anything to you, did it?"

"Why bother asking a question to which you already know the answer?" She watched his face twitch slightly, just enough to give his arrogance a kick in the ribs, but it was quickly replaced with a forced smile.

"Now that we both know where we stand, I'll overlook your disrespect, this time. But I will not be intimidated by you. So I'm afraid your ploy to release your son-in-law won't work with me, and the hour is late, so if you don't mind…"

However, Marcus made a mistake. While attempting to show Rosalyn out, he reached for her arm, but she was already charged with emotion. At the touch of his hand, the power she had kept contained was released, and he jumped back at the sparks that shot from her hands. He was equally startled by the flash of illumination that engulfed the room. The flames of every candle, every lantern, even the fire in the stone fireplace, roared to life, growing in size and intensity as they matched the fervor on Rosalyn's face.

Then, just as quickly as it started, the flames dwindled back down. The shock on the startled Baron's face told Rosalyn that her display had the effect she was looking for. Never taking his gaze from Rosalyn, he walked over to Isaboe and leaned in her direction. "I forgot that about your mother," he said cautiously, before finally looking at Isaboe. "Do you also have her…special talents?" he asked in a hushed tone.

"No. And I certainly try not to make her angry," Isaboe offered a sardonic smile.

"Good advice," he said, turning his eyes back on Rosalyn as she stood menacingly before him. After a moment, he readdressed Isaboe. "What is your husband's name?"

"Connor Grant."

"I don't suppose you can tell me why it's so urgent that he be released tonight?"

"If I told you, you wouldn't believe me."

Muttering something under his breath, the Baron shot a furrowed glare at Rosalyn before returning his attention back to Isaboe.

"What about your appearance? If you are in fact my daughter, can you at least explain why you look so young for a woman who must be close to forty?"

Isaboe only offered a smile. "I'm afraid I can't explain that either. But my mother is correct; this is urgent. Please, Your Lordship, please help us."

"Why should I? You want me to release your husband tonight, a man who has committed a crime against the Crown, yet you offer me no explanation. If you can't tell me what is so urgent, or anything else about this unusual reunion we're having, I don't see why I should involve myself."

"Then do it for all the girls you left holding their shredded hearts in their hands and your children in their bellies as you rode away." Rosalyn finally broke her silence as she stepped forward to stand in front of him. "Do it because it's the right thing to do, Marcus. I know you must have a heart in there somewhere. You'd be surprised how good it feels to do something for someone else, something that's not completely *self-serving*."

He stared at her long enough to make her feel uncomfortable, and Rosalyn shifted her stance, but her gaze never left his. "If you had contacted me, I could have made your life easier," he finally said.

"Why? You could have cared less about me or your child. There wasn't anything I wanted from you," she answered coldly.

"Did you ever make it to Paris?"

"What do you think?" His question caught her off guard, and Rosalyn's answer was curt.

"Do you still have the scarf? I believe it was blue. The same color of the sky on the first day I saw you. You were standing on that hilltop, the wind in your hair, a staff in your hand, and surrounded by your little herd of sheep."

Rosalyn wasn't sure how long she had been staring into his eyes, but she couldn't seem to pull her gaze away. He remembered. Why? *Damn him!* It was easier to hate him when she thought he had forgotten her.

"As I already mentioned, Rosalyn, I didn't forget you." He let his eyes roam over her until a sly smile stole across his face. "The years have been very kind to you, Rosalyn. You still carry the beauty of your youth." When he reached out to touch her, she leaned back.

"So, how is the Baroness? I hear she's lovely." Rosalyn's guarded eyes bore into his soul, and her words were a slap of reality.

Acknowledging that he had overstepped his bounds, he nodded, but only offered an apologetic smile. "I'm leaving in the morning, going back to York," he said as he walked to the desk and retrieved his drink. Swallowing it in one gulp, he placed the goblet back on the desk before turning to address Isaboe. "As long as your story checks out, I'll see to your husband's release tonight."

"Thank you, Your Lordship," Isaboe said as she approached him. "It was a pleasure to have finally met you, and we appreciate your generous assistance." She held out her hand, offering him a gracious smile.

"The pleasure was all mine, my dear."

Rosalyn thought his reply sounded sincere, but she already had her hand on the doorknob. She couldn't make her escape fast enough, nor look at him another moment. Though a lifetime had passed, and she no longer was that scared, intimidated young girl, her heart pounded in her chest so loudly she was sure he could hear it. How was it that after all this time he could still have this effect on her? It was irrational, immature, and completely senseless, yet she couldn't deny it. For all the years she had spent hating him, Rosalyn had to acknowledge that, under all that anger, she still cared for him. It felt weak and pathetic, and it completely infuriated her.

The Baron turned toward Rosalyn, apparently choosing to ignore her obvious disdain. "In case I don't see you again before I leave the city, it was good to see you, Rosalyn. Maybe our paths will cross again someday."

She stood staring at the wall, not wanting to look at him, but finally glanced in his direction. "I doubt it," she paused to soften her tone. "But we do appreciate that you took the time to see us tonight, Your Lordship. Thank you for your help." She gave him the respect of his title, but that was all. Opening the door, she quickly left the room before it closed in on them.

With Isaboe in tow, she rushed back out into the night air, hoping it would cool the heat she felt radiating off her face. Once outside, she stopped to take a few deep breaths, attempting to calm her racing heart and regain her composure.

"Are you alright?" Isaboe asked when she finally caught up to her mother.

"Yes. I'm fine," Rosalyn said, rubbing her hands over her face.

"I'm proud of you, Mother." Rosalyn turned, and even in the dark she could see the compassion on her daughter's face. "I know that wasn't easy for you, but you did well. You stood up to him with grace and dignity. You made me proud tonight, Mother."

As Rosalyn embraced her daughter in a tight hug, Isaboe was caught off guard, but she returned her squeeze with equal passion. Drawing back, Rosalyn could hardly believe that this woman was Marcus's daughter—*her* daughter.

"Well, at least he gave me you, so I can't hate him entirely. Now, let's see what power the Baron of York actually holds."

chapter 33

not without me

The last time Connor had been inside a British prison cell he didn't even have a cot to lie on. For two hellish weeks he had been alone in his tiny cell, starving, tortured, and near-death.

That was until Demetrick had arranged his mysterious release. In his current situation, it didn't take long for that remembered pain to be rekindled.

As the former warrior lay in the dark with his hands folded behind his head, he stared at the ceiling, seeing nothing. But in Connor's mind's eye he could clearly see Isaboe, as well as the look that must have been on her face when she learned the news of his arrest. But it was Rosalyn's frame of mind that he was most concerned about. *"We don't have much time, so everything must go as planned from here on out,"* she had warned him before they left. So, what did he do? He had gone completely out of control and gotten himself arrested. That certainly wasn't part of the plan.

So far, this simple trip to acquire the quicksilver had gone disastrously. In hindsight, they were stealing from the university, and getting arrested was always a risk, but it would have gone much worse with Whitmore at the pub had it not been for Hamish and Jared. They were so focused on creating a portal to another world it seemed ironic to Connor that something as unexpected as a tussle with the damn Brits could threaten the entire operation. Connor realized his actions were rash, that he had put everything in jeopardy, and that he should have acted more responsibly, but, unfortunately, thinking things through before acting was not his strongest attribute.

The sound of a key turning in a lock drew Connor's attention. Glancing at the thin beam of light shining through the crack in the door that separated the holding area from the jail office, he could hear a conversation between two men on the other side but couldn't make out the words. Then the door was pushed opened.

Prepared to face whatever shit the Brits had decided to throw at him, Connor stood up as a well-dressed gentleman strolled in and passed under the light of the lone lantern in the holding cell. Some kind of nobility, he guessed, but that hardly explained why the man was here. The jail block was no place for his sort. While Connor took measure of the stranger, the nobleman seemed to be doing the same, but beyond that, he struck Connor as just another arrogant British asshole.

"Do you know what the punishment is for attacking a soldier of the Crown?" the man asked without preamble as he paced in front of the cell bars, repeatedly slapping his gloves into his palm. After receiving no reply from the prisoner, he continued. "It's five years hard labor at a stone quarry."

"And what's the punishment for shooting an innocent child?" Connor demanded.

"That was an unfortunate accident. The soldiers were only doing their job, and you shouldn't have interfered."

Connor scoffed. "And how is the bloody redcoat who pulled the trigger?"

"I understand he's in pretty bad shape; a broken cheek bone, broken nose, and missing a few teeth, but he'll recover, and that's fortunate for you.

"And the boy?"

"Sadly, the boy didn't survive."

"Yet, I'm looking at five years of hard labor. There's some justice for ye." Connor watched the nobleman as he stopped pacing and stared hard at him. "Who are you?" the prisoner finally asked, glaring at the man on the other side of the bars.

"Someone who can help you," he replied.

"Well, unless ye can unlock this door and let me out of here tonight, there's nothing ye can help me with," Connor snarled before he dropped down onto the cot, stretched out, and prepared for a long detainment.

"It appears that fortune has smiled on you this night, young man, for that is exactly why I'm here. Your mother-in-law can be very persuasive."

Immediately jolting upright, he realized to whom he was speaking. "Ye're the Baron of York." Connor had seen the theater billboards, too.

Marcus Vanderburgh nodded, clasping his hands as he resumed his pacing. "As I made my way here from the theater tonight, I had created an image of what the man who had married a fine young woman like Isaboe would look like." The Baron stopped to look closely at Connor. "I dare say, my son—you're not it."

"Aye, says you and everyone else."

"I don't suppose you can shed any light on those two, could you?" When he stepped up to the cell door, Connor could see the curious expression on the Baron's face. But the prisoner didn't offer up an answer, and that didn't seem to surprise Vanderburgh, although he did look a bit disappointed. After another long, awkward moment with the Baron scrutinizing him, Connor watched with surprise as Marcus Vanderburgh inserted the key into the lock and stepped aside, swinging the cell door open.

Standing, Connor stared at his way out, and then at the man who was giving him his freedom. "Why?" he muttered.

The Baron's face twisted with irony, "It was recently impressed upon me that in the past I may have been an egotistical bastard. This seemed a good way to begin making reparations." Vanderburgh paused and smiled, as if recalling something. "They wait for you, so go, before I change my mind."

Connor didn't need to be told twice. Grabbing his coat off the cot, he quickly walked out the open cell, never taking his eyes off his benefactor. When he stood freely outside the bars, he stopped to face the nobleman. "Thanks," he uttered, then nodded before turning to make his exit.

"Mr. Grant," the Baron called out as Connor was about to leave the holding area. "Whatever it is that you're up to, can you take care of them?" He paused, glancing intently at the just released prisoner. "Not that I have any rights, but it would be good to know that..." He paused again, checking his words. "That those two ladies will be well cared for. Are you the man who can do that?"

Connor was surprised to see genuine concern written on the Baron's features. "As long as I'm alive, I'll do my best. I promise ye that," he replied with a nod, then slipped out the door and through the jail office, back onto the street where his wife and mother-in-law waited.

Once reunited and back on the road, the three late night travelers made camp not far from Edinburgh. After they had started a fire and finished eating the meal Margaret had prepared that morning, Isaboe addressed her husband alone, asking him what Hamish meant when he said that Connor had something to tell her. When he reluctantly shared the story about being confronted by Whitmore in the bar, the conversation suddenly turned cold, and the rigid look that crossed his wife's face had him groveling like a delinquent child. "I'm sorry, Isaboe. Please, just let me explain," Connor pleaded, but her heated anger only grew more intense, and without saying a word, she turned her back to him and stomped off. Crawling into the buckboard with Rosalyn, she left Connor alone in the dark and contemplating how to make this right.

Arriving back at the cave the following evening, Connor dismounted as the buckboard, with Rosalyn and Isaboe, pulled up behind him. Immediately, he walked over to where Jared stood watching Hamish, who was immersed in studying a small, shiny object in one hand with a lantern in the other. Multiple candles and oil lamps had been strategically placed around the perimeter, and Connor presumed that this was where they planned to build the portal. Noticing his arrival, Jared shook his head with wonder and smiled as Conner walked his way. "I don't know how she did it, but I'm impressed. We didn't expect to see you again for a long while," he said, shaking Connor's hand.

"Nor did I," Connor muttered as he returned the handshake.

"So, did she use some magic words on the jailor, or will the British Army be riding up at any moment to retrieve their escaped prisoner?"

"Aye, she used some magic words, alright, but not with the jailor. 'Twas the Baron of York who gave me my walking papers."

The startled look on Jared's face revealed his surprise. "Baron Vanderburgh? How did she convince the Baron of York to arrange your release?"

Softening his voice, Connor leaned closer. "Turns out his Lordship is Isaboe's father, but Rosalyn doesn't like to discuss it, so dinnae mention it to her."

"If Isaboe's father is the Baron, that makes Anna the Baron's grand-daughter," Jared said as his eyes lit up.

"Aye, *and* nay. There's no claim to the family name, or anything like that. So dinnae get any ideas thinkin' that ye married into nobility, cause ye didn't," Connor said as he glanced across the open area. Standing on the opposite side of the clearing, Hamish was staring at the shiny object in his hand. "What's going on here?" he asked, nodding toward the scholar.

"He's charting the alignment of the stars, or something like that. He's holding a compass and has been walking around in circles over there for a while now. Occasionally he'll look up and move a step or two, but to be honest, I have no idea what he's doing."

Glancing over his shoulder, Connor saw Isaboe coming his way, and her expression was stern. "Are ye ready to turn in, my love?" he asked, overly sweet, but Isaboe didn't respond—she didn't even look at him—just walked past Connor to where Hamish stood.

"I take it you told her," Jared whispered.

Connor only nodded, his mouth pulled into a thin line of disapproval as he watched Isaboe and Hamish. But when he saw her plant a kiss on the side of the scholar's face, Connor's expression turned lethal. "What the fuck?" he growled.

Walking back over to them, Isaboe didn't even look at Connor. "Jared, I want to thank you as well for what you did for my *stupid, foolish* hus-band," she spat, shooting Connor a deadly glare before softening her expression as she addressed Jared, "Though I'm not sure that lying for his sake was worth it, I do appreciate what you did." Feeling a bit out of place, Jared only nodded. "Connor, we're turning in," Isaboe said firmly. Taking a few steps away and then stopping, she looked back over her shoulder.

"Are you coming?" she asked sharply.

"I'm right behind ye, *Breagha*."

Isaboe didn't move, only glared at him. "I'll be right there, love of my life," he said again, forcing a smile. His words of affection did not crack her angry mask, and she stared at him for a long, uncomfortable moment before finally turning away and walking toward the cave.

"Looks like you're going to be paying for that mistake for a while."

Connor didn't respond to Jared's observation as he watched Isaboe disappear into Rosalyn's home, but as soon as she was out of sight, he stomped in Hamish's direction. "I hope ye're happy," he snarled at the scholar as he circled by him.

"Not particularly, but I am surprised to see you." Hamish's words stopped Connor, causing him to glance back at the young man. "I figured that was the last we'd see of you after you charged across the road and mauled that soldier like a crazed bear."

"Yeah, ye'd like that, wouldn't ye?" Connor said, stepping back toward the young scholar.

"What you did to that man was brutal."

"Brutal? I'll tell ye what's brutal." Connor's tone turned hostile as he glared at Hamish. "That boy died! He was an innocent child trying to protect his family, and that goddamn bloody Redcoat killed him! That *fucking* bastard deserved worse than he got."

"Come on, fellas," Jared said, trying to diffuse the tension in the air. "Let it go. We've got more important things to focus on, like the location of this portal." He turned toward Hamish. "Have you figured it out yet?"

Taking a side-step, Hamish distanced himself from both men before responding. "I would feel more certain if I could see the celestial landmarks," he said, looking up with deep concern showing in his eyes. Both of his companions could hear the frustration in his words. "But now that the clouds have moved in and are covering most of the sky, I can't identify the exact location where this portal needs to be placed. None of this will work if I can't see the bloody stars," Hamish grumbled.

"Well, there's always tomorrow night," Jared said, as he patted Hamish on the back. "It's been a long couple of days, and we could all use a good night's sleep."

"I couldn't agree more," Rosalyn said, suddenly appearing beside the men. "Is this where you're planning to create the portal?"

"Oh, hello, Rosalyn," Hamish replied. "Aye, I believe this is the best location, but with the clouds obscuring the sky, I'm unable to get the correct coordinates."

"Well, we're all exhausted," she said, covering a yawn. "Let's start again tomorrow. Maybe the spirits will be with us and the sky will be clear." Giving them both a nod and a smile, she turned toward the cave.

"I'll go with you," Jared said, stepping in line with Rosalyn. "We should *all* turn in," he said over his shoulder, glancing at the two men who were now left alone.

"Sounds like a good idea." Connor started toward the cave, but then stopped and stepped back, letting his glare burn into the young scholar just enough to make him squirm. "Just so ye ken the situation very clearly—that's the first and last kiss ye'll ever get from my wife's lips. If I dinnae owe ye, I'd kick the shit out of ye right now."

Hamish leaned back from the intensity of Connor's words, and for a few moments was speechless, but that didn't last long. Clearing his throat and tucking his compass into his pocket, he pushed his spectacles back up his nose and turned toward the cave. "Well, I think I'll turn in now, too. I've heard quite enough. Good evening, *Mr. Grant*," he said with more emphasis than necessary.

"See ye on the morrow, *Francis*."

Connor knew he and Hamish rubbed each other the wrong way, and neither did a very good job at trying to hide it. But the arrogant little bastard had spoken up for him at the bar when he didn't have to. And even Connor had to admit that as bad as the picture Hamish had painted of him, it was quick thinking on the boy's part to prevent a potentially deadly scene. Running his hands through his hair, Connor felt his own exhaustion deep in his bones, and he begrudgingly walked toward the cave to go find Isaboe. Though he was sure his wife wanted nothing to do with him at the moment, and there was most likely a tongue-lashing coming, he had to at least try to seek her forgiveness.

Standing at the opening of the small room, which was not much bigger than a storage cove, Isaboe quietly observed the peaceful scene. Inside the cozy enclosure, lit only by a single candle, she watched Anna and Kaitlyn sleeping together on a large cushion, spooned in a loving embrace. The contented look on the baby's face was matched by that of the woman whose arms were wrapped around her.

Isaboe recognized Connor's heavy footsteps a moment before he rested a hand on her shoulder. She glanced at him and then focused back on the faces of her daughters, so comfortable and safe in each other's arms. It was beautiful, and yet in its own way, heart-wrenching.

She looked up at Connor. "We need to talk," she whispered as she grabbed his hand, leading him back outside the cave so as not to disturb the sleepers. Out in the night air and under the cover of darkness, Isaboe stopped short and turned to address him. "What the hell is wrong with you?!" she hissed.

Startled by her abrupt halt and furious words, Connor stumbled to a stop. When his eyes met hers, he took half a step back.

"It was bad enough when I found out you'd been arrested. I was scared to death you'd be taken away and I'd never see you again!" Isaboe heard the fear in her voice as it hovered right beneath her anger. "But then I find out that you helped the rebellion, *after promising me you wouldn't*; part of me wishes we could have left your *sorry ass in jail!*"

"Isaboe, I already said I was sorry. It was only the one time, and I did it to save the lives of some real patriots. I'm sorry I didna tell ye before, and I promise I'll never keep anything from ye again."

"That's what you said last time."

When he reached for her, Isaboe drew back. "When will you start putting me and Kaitlyn first?" she asked coldly. "When will you finally realize that this rebellion could destroy you? Destroy us! If you'd been arrested as a known rebel, rather than just a hothead who butted in when he shouldn't have, we couldn't have gotten you out. If Whitmore had you arrested, then what?"

"That wouldna've happened. If he turned me in, he'd be ratting himself out."

"So instead, you find another way to get yourself arrested."

"Isaboe, again, I'm sorry I dinnae tell ye about Whitmore before. I'm sorry that ye're frightened, but when that soldier fired the shot and the boy went down, it all happened so fast. I just reacted. I didnae think…"

"That's right, *you didn't think.*" She cut him off and took a step forward. "You could have been locked up for months, even years, and then what about me? What about Kaitlyn and Gabriel? *What about us?* Damn you, Connor!" she said, shoving both hands into his chest, forcing him to stumble back. "You need to put our needs first before you just react! Your actions jeopardized this entire mission. I swear, your obsession for revenge against the English will be the death of you—of all of us!"

"Isaboe, an innocent boy was shot and killed. Would ye really expect me to stand by and do nothing?"

"Yes. That's exactly what I would expect you to do. What happened was tragic and horrible. I understand that, but it didn't involve you." Isaboe took a step closer, looking up into his dark eyes, trying to make him understand. "By jumping to that boy's defense, you brought unnecessary attention to all of us, and worse than that—I could have lost you!" She grabbed a fistful of his jacket in both hands and locked gazes with him. "Connor, I need you. I need you here, with me."

As he wrapped his arms around her, Isaboe threw hers around his waist and buried her face against his chest. More than a few moments passed as they just held each other, but eventually she pulled back and looked up at him again. Even in the dark, she could see his head tilted to one side as he looked at her curiously. "What's on yer mind, Isaboe?"

"Connor," she started, but paused to calm her shaky voice. Swallowing hard, she continued, "It looks like Rosalyn and Hamish are going to create this portal. The first of the seven nights is tomorrow, and I know you. I know you won't let Rosalyn go alone."

As she held his gaze, he didn't reply right away, only looked into her searching eyes. But she already knew the answer. "I havta go with her. Ye ken that."

Isaboe pulled out of his embrace and took a few steps back before turning around. "But we don't know for sure that the portal will remain open, or that it won't lose time. If you and Rosalyn go, and you can't get back, I would never see you again in this lifetime." Isaboe heard the fear in her words, felt it pulsing in her blood.

"Isaboe, there are no other options. We havta believe it will work, and that the portal *will* hold time still."

She knew Connor was trying to be reassuring, but the truth was no one knew for sure. It was all speculation and theory from an old wizard's notes. "Belief isn't enough. There are no guarantees that this will work. Even if Rosalyn and Hamish can create the portal, and you can cross over, what if you can't get back? What if time doesn't remain still? What if you do come back and fifty years have passed? What then?" Each word brought Isaboe's panic closer to the surface.

"What would ye have me do?" Connor asked. "I canna let Rosalyn go into a foreign realm alone with no idea what she'll be up against. And I ken ye dinnae want that either. We dinnae have another choice. I havta go with her."

"Then I'm going too."

"Like bloody hell ye are!" he growled. "Yer place is here, with our daughter," he pointed toward the cave to punctuate his point.

"And your place is with me! You promised you'd never leave me. You told me that you'd take care of us. If you go with Rosalyn and don't come back, what about me? How am I supposed to go on without you?"

"And what of our daughter? What if the worst does happen and I dinnae come back? Kaitlyn needs you here."

Isaboe's eyes grew wider when she realized he had his own doubts. "You're not sure either. You don't have any more faith than I do. And that's the very reason I have to go with you!"

"Isaboe, ye're tired, and ye're not thinking straight. We'll discuss this more on the morrow." He reached for her, but she pulled away.

"No. My thoughts are very clear. I know exactly what I'm thinking." She held her ground defiantly, even as her hands shook. "Yesterday, I thought I had lost you, and how I felt about that was very clear. If you leave me and don't come back, I might as well be dead to our daughter. I know how selfish this sounds, Connor, but I will not live a life without you." As much as she willed them not to come, Isaboe felt the tears choking her words. "Or what if you do come back and we're all gone? Connor, I won't let you go through the hell I went through."

The distraught husband sighed and ran his hands through his hair before looking at her again, struggling for the right words. "And what of Kaitlyn? Have ye given her any thought? Ye could very well be denying her a life with her mother, just like Anna. Is that what ye want?"

His words were harsh, and they hurt, but she knew he was only reminding her of the very real risk they were taking. Isaboe felt her lips quivering, but she lifted her chin to face him. "At least Kaitlyn and Anna would have each other. You saw them tonight. Since my milk has dried up, Anna has all but replaced me. If I don't come back, Kaitlyn will have a family that loves her and will protect her. But if you go without me, and you don't come back, what will I have, Connor, besides a broken heart and an adult daughter who blames me for the loss of her son? I would shrivel up and die a slow death; I promise I would," she paused to wipe away the tears that felt cool against the heat of her face. "I've experienced living through that agony once before. I refuse to be put in that position again."

Seeing that he could find no words to convince her otherwise, instead of arguing, Connor pulled her into his embrace and held her tightly as she wrapped her arms around him and buried her face in his chest, letting the tears flow. When she felt his hand on her chin, Isaboe let him lift her face, and he gently wiped away her tears before he kissed her. Wrapping her arms around his neck, she returned the kiss with equal passion.

After Connor finally pulled away and looked down at her, he brushed back Isaboe's hair and held her face in his hands, softly gazing into her teary eyes. "You are the most goddamn, stubborn woman I have ever met...and I wouldna want ye any other way." Giving her a crooked smile, he put his arm around her shoulders and turned them back toward the cave. "Let's hope Rosalyn and Hamish ken what they're doin' and can get us *all* back without losing time."

The last candle around the perimeter had finally burned out, and the only remaining light came from the entrance to the cave. With her arm still around his waist and his around her shoulder, they followed the dim light back. After washing off the dirt from the road, they found a cubby hole with a cushion and a blanket to crawl into.

As exhausted as she was, when he reached for her, kissing her gently, she didn't deny him. As her tears continued to flow, the young couple quietly made love. Their bodies wrapped around each other, they moved in perfect harmony, though both continued to struggle with a complex knot of emotions. They never spoke a word, but both knew what the other was feeling. When words failed them, they found another way to connect. Surrounded by so much uncertainty, it intensified her need for intimacy, and she never wanted to leave the safety of his arms again.

chapter 34

what choice do i have?

The days preceding the summer equinox were extremely long, and the morning sun pushed back the twilight almost as fast as it fell. The sun's rays pierced over the top of the ridge, shooting spears of golden light across the horizon, tinting everything in a glorious shade of yellow. A thin layer of fog hovered over the canyon, moving, drifting, and trying to hold onto the last droplets of water before they evaporated and disappeared.

Rosalyn woke to the smell of breakfast and the sound of voices in her kitchen. Wrapping a throw over her nightclothes, she shuffled from her cove while rubbing the sleep from her eyes and found Will and Margaret busy preparing the morning meal.

"Top o' the morning to ye!" Will was far too happy for the hour, and Rosalyn only nodded at his greeting. Grabbing a cup from the cupboard, she took the kettle off the stove and poured herself a generous serving of hot coffee.

"You got in quite late last night," Margaret said, wiping her hands on a towel. "To be honest, we didn't expect to see you back so soon, and with Conner. How did you pull that off?"

"Someone owed me a favor, and I called it in," she replied, taking her first sip of coffee.

"It must've been someone with a lot of clout," Will added, as he looked on with interest and waited for Rosalyn to fill in the blanks.

But Rosalyn only offered a nod and took another sip of coffee before placing her cup down on the counter. "Thank you for taking care of things here. I really appreciate that the two of you have stayed and helped out

so much," she said, giving them both a smile. "Now, if you'll excuse me."
She turned to go outside.

"Oh, Rosalyn." As Will caught her attention, she stopped and looked
back at him. "There's quite a large rock outside the door, so be careful. It
wasn't there before we turned in last night, and I almost tripped over it
this morning on my way out to the privy."

Rosalyn eyed him for a moment before hurrying to investigate.
Stepping out into the misty morning air, she shivered slightly before
coming to a stop. Squinting into sunlight, she examined the very large
boulder that sat on her stoop. It was nearly three feet around, a foot high,
and looked like it weighed as much as an ox. The surface was chiseled
and polished into a smooth, perfect, flat circle, ridged with a small edge
around the circumference. She knew immediately what it was, and a slow
smile grew across her face. No one had to tell her who had chiseled the
incredible piece of stone, or who had left it on her doorstep. But how
Turock could know that they needed just such a portal base was something Rosalyn couldn't fathom.

The dwarf was a solitary being who did his best to avoid contact. How
he always seemed to know when he was needed was something Rosalyn
had yet to figure out. She always assumed that the squatty little man had
more powers than just being able to split rocks, and now he had apparently created something quite amazing out of a stone slab.

"Oh, it's here!" Hamish announced as he walked up behind Rosalyn,
also squinting in the brightness of the early morning sun. He bent down
to examine the smooth surface of the large boulder, running his hand
across the coolness of the stone.

"Did you order this from Turock?" she asked, incredulously.

"Well, not directly, but ultimately, yes." Hamish hesitated as he stood
up straight and looked at her. "After meeting Leo yesterday, I figured a
man his size shouldn't have a problem finding us the right rock base. I
hope I've not overstepped. I mean, you did tell me to prepare, right?"

Surprising the young scholar, Rosalyn reached out with both hands
and pulled his head forward, planting a kiss in the middle of his greasy
forehead and giving him her best smile. "Yes, of course!" she said, taking
a deep, satisfied breath of fresh morning air. "You know, Hamish, I'm

beginning to think we can do this. As long as the sky stays clear tonight, we could manage it this evening." Hearing those words cross her lips suddenly made this whole undertaking very real, and the look of satisfaction immediately melted off her face. She hadn't given herself much time to think about it. Feeling her heartbeat quicken, she turned to look at Hamish. "Are you ready?"

"I will be by nightfall," he answered with confidence.

Though this is what they had all worked so hard to accomplish, knowing that the time lurked ever so close brought on a new anxiety in the pit of Rosalyn's stomach. Suddenly, the smell of breakfast drifting from the kitchen that had earlier made her stomach growl, now had it rolling. But she swallowed hard and forced fortitude into her demeanor. "Good. Then let's be about it. Now, if you'll excuse me," she said abruptly before turning to walk in the direction of the privy.

By the time Isaboe and Connor lumbered out of their sleeping cove, what remained of breakfast sat cold on the dining table. The sound of voices drew their attention outside where they found Will and Jared wrestling with a large boulder that sat not far from the front entrance.

Isaboe shook her head at the scene and went off to take care of her morning business, leaving Connor to investigate on his own.

"Where are ye moving that stone? And why?" Connor asked, absently scratching his backside as he approached the two men.

As they stood up to catch their breath, Will gave Connor a nod, wiping the sweat from his brow before responding. "We're takin' it over there, where our young scholar is walkin' in circles."

Looking where Will had pointed, Connor saw Hamish pacing off a section of ground before he stopped, turned, and began pacing in another direction, occasionally scribbling notes on a writing tablet.

"Apparently that's where the portal will be," Jared added, "and it will rest on this base. We just have to get it from here to there."

"How did it get here in the first place?" Connor asked.

"Hamish said a base of this size and dimensions was needed. Since

Rosalyn had told us that Turock is a master stonemason, we put in a request for it, through Leo—the big guy," Will answered. "But the bloody thing is heavy as sin! I still haven't figured out how one little dwarf could manage it by himself."

"Have ye not seen him yet?" Connor asked wide-eyed. "He ain't no little dwarf!"

"And he didn't move it by himself," Rosalyn added, walking up behind the men. "I'm sure Leo helped him."

"Well, then maybe ye can ask Leo to help us again," Will moaned. "I'm 'bout to break my back," he complained, pressing his hands into the base of his spine.

As if he knew his assistance was needed, the slow, lumbering giant arrived at the scene, carrying a barrel on his massive shoulder.

"What's he carryin'?" Connor asked.

"Water," Rosalyn answered. "Every few days he collects fresh water from an underground spring that bubbles up in a cave that's not far from here. The spring provides water when the rains do not."

When Leo lowered the heavy barrel to the ground, it sent a rumble through the Earth that they could feel vibrating through their feet.

"I brought water, Mistress," Leo boomed. The sheer size of the giant dwarfed all that stared up at him in awe.

"Thank you, Leo." Rosalyn approached the huge man with an expansive smile on her face. Her head didn't reach past his belt as she looked up at him. Reaching for his enormous hand, she held it in both of hers. His rough-looking hand was as big as a turkey and large enough to squash her in one swipe, but he patiently allowed her to examine it with tender and gentle movements. "It looks like your injury is healing nicely. Are you still using the poultice I gave you?"

"Yes, Mistress, every day." This time his voice came softer, less amplified, as if being so close to Rosalyn somehow humbled him.

"I assume you had something to do with the delivery of this stone. It needs to be moved. Can you please take care of that for us?"

Lumbering over to where Will and Jared had managed to push the stone, not far from where it had started, Leo bent over the huge bolder. Reaching his massive arms around the enormous rock, he hugged it tightly and lifted with his knees. Slowly, the immense block of stone rose up off the ground as Leo stood upright and looked over his shoulder "Where do you want it?" he asked the three men, who were staring at him in awe.

When Jared pointed toward Hamish, who was also completely astonished by the giant's display of strength, Leo slowly made his way, one large, booming footstep at a time to the appointed location. Once there, he placed it down carefully, moving it into position as directed by Hamish.

"I could use a giant like that at my hostel," Will jested. "He's a handy fellow to have around."

With most of the morning's activity taking place outside, Isaboe cornered Rosalyn when she came back into the kitchen. "Mother, I need to talk to you."

"What is it?"

Isaboe stared at her mother, searching for the right words. "You know that Connor's going with you."

"Yes, we've already discussed it. Are you alright with that?"

"I am," she said, "because I'm going too."

"What are you talking about?" Rosalyn was shocked at her daughter's statement.

"Connor and I have already discussed it. It's done and decided. Where Connor goes, I go. So, if you don't want your granddaughter to live without her parents, you and Hamish have to make sure that we come back."

Having seen that determination on her daughter's face before, Rosalyn knew that an argument was futile. "Well then, you had better hope and pray that the Goddess sees favor on our mission, and just maybe we'll accomplish the impossible."

After washing up and changing clothes, Isaboe found Margaret, Anna, and Kaitlyn in the garden gathering vegetables. Anna carried the baby on her hip with one arm while holding a small basket in the other, as she somberly followed Margaret through the rows of green, red and gold.

Knowing that today could be the last day she would have with them,

Isaboe wanted to spend it with both of her daughters, if only for a few hours. Keeping a safe emotional distance, Anna had remained cool, but Isaboe still had to try.

Kaitlyn saw her mother approaching before the women did, and her small, muted whine, accompanied by the outreaching of her pudgy little arms, announcing Isaboe's arrival.

"Good morning!" she said cheerfully, taking the baby from Anna's arms. Turning slightly, she hugged and kissed Kaitlyn as the baby happily hugged her back. "Hello, my little wee one. Mommy has missed you," she said before looking at her older daughter. "Hello, Anna," she said lightly, giving her best smile, but Isaboe saw only hurt lingering in her daughter's eyes and regretted that she hadn't tried harder to respect Anna's current emotional state.

Turning her back, Anna didn't say a word and then walked to the end of the row.

"Good morning, my dear friend," Margaret said, attempting to offset Anna's cold reception.

Doing her best not to let Anna's mood deter her, Isaboe forced a smile. "Good morning, Margaret. Can I help?"

"Well, Anna and I were just gathering a few vegetables for dinner tonight, but we have almost everything we need, except for some berries," Margaret replied as she lifted a smaller basket into her hand. "How about it, Anna? Shall we fill a pail of raspberries for dessert?"

"No, I have clothes to wash." Without looking at either of them, Anna handed her basket of vegetables to Margaret and hurried from the garden.

"Anna, wait!" Isaboe called out. "Please. It'd be nice to spend a little time together before I leave."

Stopping, Anna turned and walked back up to Isaboe, but the look on her face was anything but pleasant. "Nice? You want *nice*? What would be *nice* is to have my baby back! I was perfectly happy until you showed up, Isaboe. I grew up fine without you, and I don't need you now. Why did you have to come back to your life *and ruin mine?* I really wish you would've stayed dead and left me alone!" Anna screamed as tears spilled down her cheeks. Turning quickly, she fled toward the cave.

Isaboe was speechless as she looked over at Margaret, who was immediately at her side "She didn't mean it, Isaboe. Anna's just scared. She doesn't know what she's saying."

"She hates me, and I don't blame her. She's absolutely right. I should have stayed out of her life."

"She doesn't hate you," Margaret said as she led Isaboe and Kaitlyn to a small bench. "Each day that passes and we get closer to, well, you know, the more despondent she becomes. She reminds me of how you were just a year ago, but I've been trying to keep her positive."

"But she is right, Margaret. None of this would have happened if I had stayed away. The Fey Queen lured me here, and if I had listened to all of you, Anna would still have her baby. I have to make this right. I have to go to Euphoria and bring Gabriel back." Isaboe heard the desperation in her words.

"What do you mean, *you* have to go? I thought Rosalyn was crossing over to retrieve the child."

"Connor and I are both going with her."

Now it was Margaret who was speechless. She stared at Isaboe as if she couldn't believe what she had just heard. "You're going into the realm of the Underlings, *voluntarily?* What if the portal doesn't work, Isaboe? What about Kaitlyn? Are you willing to take the chance that you may never see her again? Are you willing to go through that *all over again?*"

Isaboe looked down at her baby and stroked the soft down on her head. She felt the tears burning at her nose and welling in her eyes. "What choice do I have? Connor won't let Rosalyn go alone, and I won't let him leave me." Turning to look squarely at Margaret, she choked out her words, trying to make her friend understand. "You're right; I am taking a chance. But if the portal doesn't work, at least Kaitlyn will have a family that will love and protect her. But if Connor goes without me, and they can't get back, I may never see him again in this lifetime. You may not understand or agree with my reasoning, Margaret, but I would rather live in a strange foreign land with him than a lifetime in this world without him, and with a daughter who hates me." No longer able to hold them back, the tears spilled down her cheeks as she hugged her younger daughter tightly in her arms, rocking her gently. Apparently sensing her mother's distress, Kaitlyn, too, began to cry. "I just wish we didn't have to do this, but…" Isaboe's tears prevented her from finishing.

"None of this is your fault, Isaboe," Margaret said as she placed a comforting arm over her friend's shoulder. "We all fell into Lorien's plot. None of us saw this coming, and you can't blame yourself. But if you need to do this, then go, and God forbid, if you don't come back, you're right; Kaitlyn will be loved and protected. And I promise she will know how beautiful her mother is, inside and out."

With her tears now turning into sobs, Isaboe could no longer speak. Wrapping her arms around both mother and baby, Margaret rocked with them until there were no more tears left to cry.

CHAPTER 35

PLEASE DON'T FORGET ME

The rest of the day was spent in preparation for the evening's event. Rosalyn and Hamish spent hours together reviewing Demetrick's manuals, walking around the portal base and discussing procedure. But for Rosalyn, it was her time spent with Leo later in the afternoon that solidified the real possibility that she may not return.

Instructing the enormous man on how to maintain and prepare the garden for future plantings, Rosalyn also provided ointments, oils, and elixirs for the treatment of any ailment or malady, just in case.

After Leo had received all his instructions, patiently waiting until she was finished, he finally asked, "Are you never coming back, Mistress?"

Rosalyn looked up at the man's concerned expression and saw the worry in his eyes. With a face as large as his, it was hard to miss. She had left the hills many times before but had always promised to return. However, this adventure could end up being a one-way trip. She had to be prepared for that.

"I hope to be back, Leo. I just don't know how long I'll be gone this time," she said honestly. "I may be leaving as early as tonight. These people are our guests for as long as they choose to stay. I can count on you to make sure their needs are attended to, aye?"

"Yes Mistress. You can count on me."

Isaboe spent the late morning with Margaret and Kaitlyn. They walked through the garden, then out to the top of the ridge, where they strolled along the canyon cliff until they found a perch from which they could watch the shifting sunlight over the Highlands. The view was spectacular, and on any other day Isaboe would've found the scene to be breathtaking. But today, with such a heavy heart, and in the face of so much uncertainty, she barely noticed. During these last few hours, she had eyes only for her daughter and her best friend, and she spoke of anything that popped into her head, except her looming departure.

"One day Mother had taken my sisters shopping, and of course I wasn't invited, so Father took me to a parade that day. It was a special treat, having father all to myself." Isaboe paused from her nostalgic reflection. "Be sure to tell Kaitlyn about her grandfather, Henry Cameron. Tell her that he was a good man, and though everyone said he was a very shrewd businessman, he always put his family first. Father was always kind to me, and I never understood his relationship with Marta. I have absolutely no recollection of ever seeing any affection pass between them." Isaboe paused to reflect on those times before Henry had died, when she was only twelve, and before Marta had sent her away to an all-girls school in Glasgow. It had been a very long time since she had thought much about her adopted parents, though her spare thoughts had often caught a whisper of warmth from Henry Cameron's spirit.

Isaboe stared at her daughter sitting on her lap and playing with her stuffed doll, knowing that the innocent child had no idea her own parents' departure was imminent and that she would soon be separated from her mother, a separation that could last a lifetime.

"Please, Margaret," Isaboe turned her tear-filled eyes to her friend, "tell her what a brave soldier her father was. And maybe someday you can tell her all that we went through to make sure she was born into this world." She paused again, choking back the tears. "And every new thing she does, from taking her first step to her first love, and all the life that happens in between, please let her know how proud I am of her."

"I'm sure I won't have to." Once again, Margaret was the positive one, always looking for hope to hold onto.

Through her tear-blurred vision, Isaboe saw the worry in her friend's face hovering just below the surface of her optimism. In an attempt to take both their minds off the inevitable, Isaboe kept talking, despite the anxiety bubbling up in her stomach. "I grew up in Edinburgh with three sisters, but I'm not sure she'll care to know about them. I went to Larbaness Boarding School in Glasgow from the time I was twelve until I married Nathan at sixteen."

"Why are you telling me this, Isaboe? I already know these things about you."

"Aye, you do, but Kaitlyn doesn't. I just want you to remember, so you can tell her when the time is right." Isaboe glanced down at her child. "I know she won't remember me, but you can tell her about me, and maybe keep the memory of me alive for her." She paused, sniffling back tears.

"Of course, I would, but you'll be back, so that won't be necessary," Margaret said with certainty, trying desperately to insert optimism into her words. "But what about Marta? What do you want Kaitlyn to know about her grandmother?"

Isaboe looked at her friend for a long moment before she finally answered. "Marta is probably burning in hell, so there is nothing she needs to know about that unloving woman. Kaitlyn has only one grandmother, Rosalyn." Isaboe stopped abruptly and was hit with a new sorrow. "But you know what my greatest regret is?" Margaret shook her head. "That I didn't get to see Benjamin. I was so hoping that I would see him again in this lifetime."

"Your life isn't over yet, Isaboe—quit talking like you're gonna die!" Margaret's words were sharp, but Isaboe knew that her tone was only a cover for her own fears.

"But I don't know if I'm coming back. Please, Margaret, tell all my children how much they were loved. Tell Kaitlyn that her mother loved her so very, very much, and how it broke my heart to leave her." Not being able to hold them back, the tears rolled down Isaboe's cheeks as her friend silently consoled her.

"Oh, I almost forgot," Margaret drew back and dug into the pocket of her skirt. "I think you should have this." She pulled the blue amulet from her pocket and watched it swing from its green cord as she presented it to Isaboe.

Queen Brighid—Kaitlyn's fey guardian—had appeared to Isaboe disguised as an old crone not long after she had first returned from Euphoria, before she realized that she was carrying the gifted child. When the old crone gave her the amulet, she said it held powers of communication—communication with beings from the other world. Isaboe had long suspected that it held more powers not yet revealed, but she wasn't sure she wanted to know what they were. "No, I want you to keep it," she said, pushing Margaret's hand away.

"Queen Brighid gave this to you, not me. Besides, it kinda makes my skin crawl. I really don't want it, so you're just gonna have to take it." Margaret took hold of Isaboe's hand and placed the amulet firmly in her palm. "Who knows? You may need it where you're going."

Isaboe nodded, slipping the amulet around her neck and under her bodice, feeling the coolness of the stone against her chest.

"Maggie, are we gonna have lunch today?" Will shouted from the entrance to the cave.

Margaret sighed heavily and rolled her eyes. "Yes, William. I'll be right there!" she shouted over her shoulder before returning her attention to Isaboe. "I guess I better go feed this bunch before it gets ugly." After patting her friend on the knee, she managed a forced smile before taking her leave.

As Isaboe watched Margaret walk away, she suddenly felt a spark, then a warm glow where the amulet touched her skin. Instantly, the image of the crone took shape before her eyes, wrinkled and grey, reaching out with one boney arm. *"Now you are the vessel."* The voice was faint, and as the words floated away on the breeze, the crone's grasping fingers turned to dust before Isaboe's eyes, and then vanished. Her arm followed, and then her thin, wispy hair; but it was the crone's amazing eyes that stayed the longest, unreadable and watching Isaboe closely until they, too, were taken by the wind. The vision lasted only for a few seconds, just long enough to send a shiver down her spine. But what unnerved her more was that Kaitlyn seemed to sense it too. The baby jolted in Isaboe's lap and then glanced up at her. Reaching out with a pudgy little hand, she gently patted the stone that lay beneath her mother's dress, as Isaboe and her gifted child exchanged a fearful look.

Too restless while he waited for nightfall, Connor went for a ride, dragging Will with him. The two men traveled side-by-side along the ridge at a slow, steady pace, going nowhere in particular. The sun was making its descent toward the horizon as the moon climbed faintly on the opposite side of the rose-colored sky. Only a few wispy clouds swept lazily across the distant mountains—it would be a clear night for stargazing.

They rode in silence with the beauty of the canyon and the surrounding Highlands as a backdrop, but Connor wasn't seeing any of the panoramic view. Lost in his thoughts, he brought his horse to a stop and stared across the divide. But when he felt his friend's heavy gaze, he turned to look at him.

"What's on yer mind, Mac?"

"I feel like I'm goin' into battle, Will. Got that same twitchy feelin' in my gut. I just dinnae ken who I'll be fighting," he answered honestly.

"I still canna believe that ye're doin' this, Mac. 'Tis bloody crazy, it is."

"Aye, I ken its crazy, but what choice do we have? That fucking faerie bitch took one of our own, and we've gotta go and get him back."

"And if you dinnae come back?"

"I ken the risks, Will, but if I pull back on this mission because of what we dinnae know, and Anna never gets her bairn back, Isaboe would never forgive me, and I could never forgive myself. I cannae live with that. We gotta try," Connor said, almost in a whisper as he pulled on the reins and turned his horse toward Will. "Anna's losin' her grip, and though Jared's been holdin' it together fairly well, it's easy to see the stress on his face too. We've got seven nights to get back before the portal closes. But in three nights, the moon will be full. Regardless of what happens, I'm asking ye, Buchanan—dinnae let them take my daughter to the ring of stones. I'm worried that in Anna's current state of mind, she might do something rash, thinking that she can still bargain for her son's life. I need ye to take charge over my daughter, Will."

"Ye dinnae even have to ask that, Mac. Yer family is my family. Maggie and I'll watch over Kaitlyn. Ye can count on us."

The evening meal brought everyone back into the cave and around the table. Connor thought the quiet, solemn group felt a bit like the gathering of the Lord's last supper. A noticeable silence hovered over the table with only the sound of utensils scraping against plates, and Anna's absence only added to the uncomfortable tension. Jared offered only a simple explanation for his wife's absence—she would not be joining them. But it seemed that no one had an appetite this evening, and much of the meal that Margaret had prepared still lay on their plates. The only ones who really seemed interested in eating were Will and Hamish, and those two very seldom missed a meal.

"If you'll excuse me, I think I'll check on Anna," Jared said, breaking the heavy silence as he pushed away from the table. He was soon followed by Rosalyn, who said that she still needed to prepare a few things, and she grabbed Hamish on the way out, pulling him from his plate.

As Connor leaned back, he silently observed the people left at the table. They were, as Will had recently pointed out, his family. Margaret and Will had been through the highs and lows right alongside them. He now was relying on these good friends more than ever to protect his daughter until they returned. But now, the question was—would they return? Could they accomplish the impossible, recover the boy, and actually make it back? There was only one way to find out.

Pushing his chair back, Connor grabbed his mug and stood. "A toast to ye, Buchanan, and to yer Missus. It appears that fate has once more brought us together to face the crossroads." He turned his gaze to Margaret, offering her a warm smile. "Ye've been our rock, Margaret, solid and steady. Ye've held both Isaboe and me up more than once and now ye're doing it for Anna and Kaitlyn. Ye ken how much we love ye, aye?"

Reaching out to clutch Isaboe's hand, Margaret only smiled as Connor continued.

"Will, you and I have saved each other's arses more than a few times, and I'll be forever indebted to ye for Isaboe's life. But now I leave in yer care my most treasured possession, my amazing daughter." As Connor looked at the faces staring back at him, he saw acknowledgment and respect. No more words were needed.

Standing, William Buchanan picked up his own mug and followed suit, pushing out his barrel chest as he held up his own drink. "Well then, may ye get in and out of hell before the devil kens that ye're there!"

"Amen to that, Brother!" Connor said, clinking mugs with his comrade, fellow Scottish rebel, and truest friend.

chapter 36

CROSSING OVER INTO THE UNKNOWN

Twilight cast an eerie glow over the ritual space as light from the candles around the perimeter danced shadows across the assembled faces.

Hamish poured the sulfur powder onto the portal base, along the inside ridge of the stone's perimeter, making a perfect circle of yellow. He then picked up the container of quicksilver and removed the lid. As he poured a ribbon of the liquid metal onto the center of the base, it separated into little beads and rolled about the surface, stopping only when they came in contact with the yellow powder.

Now it was Rosalyn's turn. She walked over to stand next to the base and held her hand above it. Beginning slowly, she spun her hand in a clockwise circle above the surface, and the small beads of silver began to spin as well. As the speed of her hand increased, so did the liquid metal until it became a blur of spinning silver, flattening out and filling in the center of the base. In a flash of light, both Rosalyn and the spinning metal stopped as a wispy vapor drifted upward from the stone. Instead of small, individual beads of quicksilver, the metal had frozen into a solid reflective sheet. Just off-center, the reflection of the moon appeared on its surface with perfect clarity. It was a mirror image of the night sky, and each and every star was visible.

"Now we just have to wait until the moon is in the center, and the rest of the celestial landmarks should align," Hamish added in a hushed tone.

Will and Margaret stood to the side, watching with rapt attention. Next to them, Connor, Isaboe, and Kaitlyn did the same. Nobody said a word. Cloaked for travel, both Rosalyn and Isaboe had a bag on the ground, ready to go. Connor had retrieved every weapon he owned, plus some that Rosalyn had stashed away, carrying them in a bag slung across his shoulder, with his sword hung visible at his side. He, too, was cloaked and looked ready for war.

Out of the corner of her eye, Isaboe saw Jared and Anna silently making their way to the circle, but they kept to themselves off to one side. She saw Anna look in her direction and desperately wanted to speak to her. But when the somber girl cast her eyes down, Isaboe knew she would not be welcome. Anyway, what could she possibly say that would make a difference?

After a few moments of heavy silence, Hamish finally made the announcement they were waiting for. "It's time. The moon is now at center and the stars are in proper alignment." He looked at Rosalyn. "I believe this is where you come in."

Rosalyn took a deep breath and strode up to the base. This time, as she held both hands over the surface, a new charge of power appeared from her person. Closing her eyes, she tilted her head back and began to mumble unintelligibly. Between her outstretched hands, a small ball of energy began to blossom. The sorceress manipulated the vessel of light until it grew to the size of a small melon. Then she cast the orb down onto the surface of the base, and it erupted in a blinding flash of light.

Unprepared for its intensity, Isaboe shielded her eyes from the brilliant light, and it took a moment for her sight to recover. But when it did, what she now saw on the surface of the base held her—held all of them—speechless.

The reflection of the night sky was now a twisting, ever-morphing ocean of images and flashes of light, moving across the base as if caught in a wave. Just as a picture would start to solidify, the fluid movement transformed into an abstract of swirling colors and broken forms.

Again reciting words that meant something only to her, Rosalyn bent over the base and then lifted her arms skyward. At the same time, the fluid, moving energy of light and darkness lifted as well, swirling atop the base. Still in constant motion, a cylinder of pure, ever-changing power hovered above the platform, an abstract visual of engaging life into another world—another realm.

Stepping back, Rosalyn dropped her arms and took a moment to gaze upon her creation. Bending down, she picked up a rock and threw it into the whirling mass that swirled above the portal base. The rock disappeared into the ceaseless movement as if it were swallowed by the sea.

"I'd say we have created a portal," Hamish stated with an air of confidence.

Rosalyn turned toward him. "The ring," she said with an outstretched palm.

Hamish dug into his pocket and pulled out The Ring of Odin, placing it in Rosalyn's hand. She took a few tentative steps forward, then stopped and looked down at the ring.

Just then, Isaboe noticed that her mother's hands were shaking. During the few months she had been reunited with Rosalyn, fear was an emotion she'd never seen on her mother's face. But now it was clearly visible, and Isaboe felt her own anxiety bubbling up in her stomach.

She watched intently as Rosalyn swallowed her fear and slipped the ring onto her index finger before continuing forward. Lifting her hand, she was only inches from the rotating cylinder of energy, swirling and throwing off a wind created by its own force. Rosalyn closed her eyes and pushed her hand into the whirling disorder of broken images. The moment her hand entered the pulsating force, it immediately condensed into a tight vortex and then disappeared into the ring.

As everything fell instantly still, Rosalyn pulled her hand back. Once again, the night sky was reflected in the mirror of the portal base, and the space around them was dark and quiet, as if the amazing hadn't just happened.

"Now can you put it back?" Hamish asked.

Again, Rosalyn raised her hand over the surface of the portal base, and just as quickly, it reappeared from the ring the same way it had vanished. Standing back, she shared a wide-eyed look with Hamish before turning to address the congregation.

"For the next seven days, every night while the moon is in this alignment, the portal can be reopened here, on this spot, as long as it is contained in this ring."

"And can ye open it from the other side as well?" Connor asked.

"We won't know until we've crossed over," Rosalyn replied. "But with what we've all just witnessed, I feel confident that won't be a problem."

"Rosalyn, wait," Isaboe interrupted. "What about the veil of forgetfulness? Won't we forget everything after we cross back over?" On her first experience, when she was unwillingly transported into the realm of the Underlings, all memory of her time there had been stripped away, and she had no recall of the other realm.

"If we cross back through the portal held in this ring, we won't lose any of our memories. This moment in time will be locked into the portal, so we should lose neither time nor memory."

"But what if we dinnae make it back within the next seven nights?" Connor asked standing behind Isaboe and sharing his wife's concern.

Rosalyn turned to Hamish before responding. "If we don't make it back this week, then you must bring them all back here for next summer's equinox, and the one after that, and you must keep doing so until we *do* come back. Since the portal is contained in the ring, you won't need to do anything but wait."

Hamish nodded. "By my calculations, you have approximately five minutes and twenty-nine seconds before the moon shifts and the portal closes tonight. If you're going, you should be about it."

Isaboe hugged Kaitlyn and kissed her on the cheek before handing the baby to Margaret. "Don't forget to tell her, Margaret." Isaboe's voice shook with tears.

"I won't. Just, *please*, come back," Margaret pleaded.

Hugging her friend deeply, Isaboe could only nod. As she wiped the unshed tears from her eyes, she glanced quickly in Anna's direction, but made no move to approach her.

Connor walked over to Will and shook his hand with the fierceness of friends who had faced death together. "Hopefully this won't be our last farewell, friend."

Will returned the handshake heartily. "Haste ye back, my brother. Just try not to get yerself killed, aye?"

Turning to look at Rosalyn and Isaboe standing side-by-side in front of the portal, Connor walked over and took his wife's hand. "No time like the present, aye? Let's see what's on the other side." Giving a nod to the faces that were staring in awe and amazement, Connor turned to face the whirling cylinder of energy.

"Wait!" Anna's shout broke the focus, and they all turned to see the young woman briskly walking toward them. She stopped in front of her mother and locked gazes with the woman who looked more like her sister. "Isaboe, I'm sorry for what I said to you. Please, come back." Anna said, choking on her own tears.

Isaboe gave Anna a soft smile. "It's alright, Anna. You don't owe me any apologies. When we get back with Gabriel, I'd be grateful if we can start over."

But Anna could only nod as she stepped back into the arms of her husband and buried her face in Jared's chest.

At the same moment, Kaitlyn let out a whimper of her own, and for the first time Isaboe heard her baby utter "*momma*." It felt like a gut-punch, and she fought the urge to turn back around and swoop up her child into her arms. Instead, she closed her eyes tightly as she struggled to hold back the tears.

"The clock is ticking people. It's now or never." Hamish's reminder broke the moment.

Preparing to face the unknown, Isaboe was able to wipe away the tears that slipped down her cheeks, but she could do nothing about the pain in her chest.

"It's not too late for ye to change yer mind, *Breagha*," Connor said quietly. "No one would blame ye if ye decided to stay."

Isaboe slipped her hand into his and looked up. Even through her tears she could see the compassion and the commitment in his eyes.

"No. I'm ready."

Giving her a tender smile, Connor squeezed her hand, then reached out and grabbed Rosalyn's hand with the other.

When she took one more look over her shoulder, Isaboe saw the depth of anxiety in the faces watching them about to step over into the un-known, a feeling that reflected her own. As she turned back to the base and took a step forward, a rush of air from the spinning whirlwind of energy tossed her hair and clothing, sending a shiver down her spine.

Isaboe felt Connor squeeze her hand a little tighter, and she looked up at him as the light from the portal danced in his blue eyes. In that moment, she saw a flood of emotions cross his face. "I love you," he murmured. "I wanted to make sure to tell ye that—just in case."

"I love you too," she said, forcing a nervous grin as she tried to appear ready, but her insides were quivering. How could anyone really prepare for what they were about to do?

"Ready?" he asked, turning toward Rosalyn. She gave him a nod.

Stepping up to the swirling vortex of energy, they crossed over together into the blended fields of light and whipping wind. With a flash of luminance, their bodies were immediately enveloped into the pulsating vortex as they passed through and disappeared into the unknown.

In the next instant, they were gone, and in the following second, the portal vanished as well. What remained on the base was a perfect reflection of the night sky, as if the portal had never been there at all. Though the experience itself had lasted only a few moments, it felt like an eternity as Margaret stared at the block of stone, waiting to see if something else would happen.

Hamish had begun his count backward in the last minute before the moon shifted and the portal could not be opened again this night. After he uttered the word *one*, the stillness that fell around them was heavy and laden with grave uncertainty.

Margaret watched as Hamish looked anxiously at Jared and Anna, then at her and Will, but nothing was said. Apparently, there was nothing left to say. It was done, and there was nothing they could do now but wait. But for how long? Would the brave traveling party return tomorrow night, or the night after, or not at all? Would she have to raise Kaitlyn and be forced to keep Isaboe's memory alive through the stories she would share with her 'adopted' child? When she promised Isaboe she would do just that, she had prayed she wouldn't have to, but after watching Isaboe disappear into an abyss of pulsating energy and broken images, she had serious doubts.

"Momma," Kaitlyn whimpered again as Margaret gave her a soft hug before turning toward her husband. "I think we should turn in."

Will nodded solemnly before putting his arm around his wife's shoulders. Following the lights that illuminated from the cave, the four adults, a science prodigy, and a small gifted child made their way back into the home of the sorceress, where they would wait to see what the morrow would bring.

A barred owl screeched overhead in the dark, black sky as Will reached back and closed the door on a night that none would forget.

Enjoy this bonus excerpt from book four:

OF LACE AND LIONS

chapter one

an unwelcomed arrival

Rocketing forward recklessly, moving at unfathomable speeds through a tunnel pulsating with magic energy, Connor Grant struggled with a plethora of broken thoughts that raced through his mind. '*What the hell are we doing!?*' was just one of them. The only thing he knew for sure was that he still held onto his two astral traveling companions; his wife, Isaboe, and her mother, Rosalyn. Squeezing both of their hands, the three realm-travelers were caught in a vortex of magic that had been created to transport them into another world: the realm of the Underlings.

But Connor had no control in this phantasmagoric projection that he had volunteered for, and as he tried to focus on the swirling forms, the whirling images, and flashing lights that zipped by him, he fought the urge to vomit. The continuous roar in his ears only escalated the pressure growing in his head, and Connor felt his heartbeat pounding in his bones. As the visions sped past him, he squeezed his eyes shut, letting the freefall take him. With his eyes closed he could have been floating, or even flying, and as odd as that thought was, Connor was very cognizant of his separation from the Earth.

Though the portal held no measure of time or distance, as fast as their journey started it was over. On legs that felt weak and wobbly, the realm voyagers took their first steps onto foreign soil.

"Are ye alright?" Connor asked, first looking at his wife, then her mother. After receiving confirmation with only head nods, he glanced back at the spinning column of energy they had just stepped out of, and was grateful that they all appeared to have come through the astral projection whole and in once piece. Though his own legs still felt weak, he sensed that the women were struggling to stand on their own—their balance effected from their slingshot-journey—and he supported them both, giving them a moment to regain their equilibrium.

Now assured that they had all survived the catapult through space, his new concern was; *where are we?* It appeared they had entered into the world of the Underlings into a gray haze, and as Connor squinted through the thick fog, all he could see was a barren and desolate landscape. Ash and dust particles floated around them, and the air smelled hot, like a scorched mist burning its way down their throats.

"Do you think there's a fire nearby?" Isaboe asked between coughs.

"It dinnae really smell like smoke," Connor said, still trying to see anything through the haze. "But the air here's too thick. We've gotta get out of this." Clutching tighter to their still-linked hands, Connor took the lead.

"Wait!" Rosalyn pulled free and stepped back toward the portal they had just passed through. Inserting her hand into the whirling vortex, the spiral of energy condensed into a slender thread before it disappeared into the ring she wore on her hand. "We'll need this to get back home," she said before falling into step.

Connor could only see a few paces in front of them, and rocks, tumbleweeds, and gaping holes in the earth seemed to appear out of nowhere, forcing their path to curve erratically. When he occasionally looked up, he saw small patches of sunlight break through the bank of haze and found it odd. They had left their world under the cover of darkness only moments before, but now sunlight cast down between the thick, hazy layers. A sure indication of how time moved differently here. Connor couldn't help but wonder what other oddities they would discover before this adventure was over.

"Of all the introductions into this world," Rosalyn mumbled through her cloak, "our first encounter feels a bit like we've landed in hell!" she coughed. "I hope that's not a bad omen."

Connor heard the hint of humor in his mother-in-law's voice, though he knew it was just a disguise to cover her fear. No one had known what to expect when they decided to make this journey, or where they would enter when they crossed over. But they hadn't had a choice, and it was

Rosalyn that had made the journey possible, because she wasn't merely Isaboe's mother. Some called her a sorceress, others called her a witch, but she was neither. She was a Feymora, the First Feymora, and was born with fey blood pulsing through her veins. The blood of the fey not only helped Isaboe's mother hold on to her youthful attributes longer, looking years younger than a woman entering her sixth decade of life, it also gave her unique abilities—the gift of faerie magic.

It was this magical gift that allowed them to make the journey into the unknown and foreign land, but not without assistance from Hamish; the brilliant, yet sometimes challenging, science prodigy. Combining their talents, they had created something deemed impossible: a portal into another world—the world of the fey.

aCKNOWLEDGEMENTS

Writing a story is a solitary endeavor, but creating a book so you can share your story with the world requires a team. Fortunately, the universe provided a very creative group of talented people to help me bring this incredible tale to life. A huge thanks goes out to my fabulous editors, Sara Kraft and John Thompson, as well as my very talented book designer, Erik Jacobson. Each one of these like-minded souls has brought color and artistry into this project, helping to push me out of my comfort zones, while being there to offer support during the challenging times. Knowing how close this story has been to my heart for the last twenty years, these incredibly talented individuals have shared my determination to release the magic of this amazing adventure that I now share with the world. Thank you, Sara, John, and Erik. You are the best!

A very big thank you goes out to my ARC readers and my proofreaders. What you do for me is priceless. I also want to thank my family for their continued support and for being my greatest fan base. Stepping out of your own way and allowing your talent to be examined by the world is not always an easy thing to do. So, thanks to everyone who gave me encouragement to hang in there, to keep going and follow my dream. I want you to know that I have placed each of one your supportive words into the foundation I now stand on.

Lastly, I want to express gratitude to all the fantasy writers who have blazed the trail before me, and who have inspired so many authors like myself to follow their own storytelling passion. It's the storyteller who keeps magic and wonderment alive in the hearts of those who chose to believe.

ABOUT THE AUTHOR

As far back as I can remember, I've been enchanted by the magic of the fey and fascinated by anything Scottish. My love for literary fantasy and storytelling began at an early age, and I knew I was destined to share this incredible tale with the world someday. I just hadn't expected "someday" to take so long. But as life will do, it threw some obstacles in my path as an author.

Being a career-oriented woman, I've owned and operated two successful businesses, raised two wonderful sons, and have managed to stay happily married to my best friend for over forty years. But my desire to share this story—a story that has been twenty years in the making—has always remained my golden ring.

CPSIA information can be obtained
at www.ICGtesting.com
Printed in the USA
LVHW112142140422
716272LV00018B/119